Y0-BGE-404

Tempered by Fate

Book 2

of
The Battle Axe Ranch Series

By
JMC North

Copyright © 2020 by JMC North. All Rights Reserved.

This is a work of fiction. Names, characters, places, and incidents either are the product of the author's imagination or are used fictitiously, and any resemblance to actual person, living or dead, businesses, companies, events, or locales is entirely coincidental.

No part of this book may be used or reproduced, scanned, or printed or electronic form without permission, except in the case of brief quotations embodied in critical articles or reviews.

Copyright © 2019 by R. T. Artwork "Viking Axe." All Rights Reserved

Dedication

This book and its series are dedicated
to my father who instilled the thirst for knowledge,
to my family for their inspiration and support,
to my friends and colleagues for their encouragement,
to my many students, and
to those who love to read.

Chapter 1

Bad Memories

The month of April brought the orange and pink predawn behind the steep pinnacles of the mountain's white snow-filled peaks. Spring filled the fresh mountain air, turning the grey cold winter days to warmer bright days. The new green leaves and grass were sprouting everywhere.

Near the small western town of Riverside, the Battle Axe Ranch stood at the edge of the rugged forested land with a broad valley stretched out before it. The Fletchers—a family of tall, wide-framed men-- had purchased the ranch from Hans and Ingrid Severson in March. The two Fletcher brothers, Clyde and Fred, were preparing to feed the herd before the rest of the family had awakened.

Years ago, during a Wyoming winter blizzard, the two brothers had been left orphans in their teenage years. Both parents had been killed instantly in a head-on car accident returning home from a shopping trip. Working together ever since then, the two brothers had finally fulfilled their dream of owning their own ranch. In the past weeks, the Fletchers were busy with getting their lives back to focusing on the ranch.

After loading the hay wagon and hitching the draft horse Jack, Clyde, in his mid-forties with dark brown hair flecked with grey and a scruffy beard, started toward the pasture. His mind worked on making a list of the things that needed to get done for the day. He kept his thoughts away from the haunting memories of the recent days. Only at night did those dreadful memories come roaring back to him—her death, the wake, the funeral, the loneliness.

Last night, alone and asleep in his dark bedroom, Clyde had dreamed those horrible memories of his wife's death. Those memories had thrown him into a dreadful dream. The nightmare had been so real with images of her death-staring eyes, his failure to help her, his need of her love, and the bloody sight of his sons fighting. Seeing her familiar face, she hovered beside him. Waking up in a cold sweat, he had called out for her-- *Beth*. Sitting up in bed, he gazed into his dark bedroom. But she wasn't there. He swore that he could still feel her presence in the bedroom. Lying back down, he thought of his wife, her unexpected suicide, and the horrible funeral that followed.

Shaking away those dream-like images, he knew her belongings were still here in their bedroom. Her thin cotton dresses, two skirts, and three blouses still hung in their closet; her dresser drawers were still filled with her nightgowns, her scarves, her sweaters, and her blue jeans. In the bottom of their closet, her worn out black and white saddle shoes, a pair of faded tan tennis shoes, a pair of brown heels, and an old pair of scuffed up cowboy boots (which her dad had given her). Tonight in the dark bedroom, her items on top of the mirrored dressing table stood as dark sentinels of her life. On the dresser sat her hairbrush and comb, two lotion bottles, a little blue cobalt bottle of *Evening in Paris* with a matching blue bottle of talcum powder, a box of tissues, and a small carved wooden jewelry box. In that jewelry box, Clyde had slipped their golden wedding rings in there. Her faded yellow robe still hung on the back of their bedroom door.

For years on her parents' ranch, the Diamond V, her whole early life had centered around their ranch. Wearing those cowboy boots, she had worked alongside her father. One time with her small hands, she even helped with a breeched foal and another time, fed an orphaned calf in the barn. As a young teenager, she had ridden her horse every day through the long-grass and around the sagebrush of the prairies near their ranch. And during those years, she developed her debilitating headaches. The doctor couldn't find anything wrong and prescribed the barbiturates for the headaches. He suggested that too much sun may be the cause. She stopped riding and her headaches didn't come on as often. Her family and friends started thinking of her as being sickly as she looked so pale. Since she had stayed inside more, her cowboy boots had sat at the back of her closet.

5

As a young man, Clyde had fallen deeply in love with her. After losing his parents, she had given him the needed love and comfort of a home and of a family. Now, she was gone. His brother Fred had been at him to pack up her belongings and to clear them out of the closet and the dresser. Knowing that his brother was right, he couldn't bring himself to touch her clothes without shuttering. Maybe, Fred, or someone, would box up her belongings when he wasn't around. However, this became at the bottom of his list of things that needed to be done-- more important work on the ranch kept him focused.

In his nightmare, he dreamed of her suicide that tragic day he couldn't forget. In the evening hours, he hadn't been able to shake his sadness, guilt, and pain of losing her. Her sudden death had left his heart in shambles. The dream of the Battle Axe Ranch had been nearly shattered with her death. The whole family stood in shock. But his brother Fred and his three sons-- Chet, twenty-one years old, Matt, nineteen, and Tom, seventeen-- had moved on. Every day it got easier for them. Hope still resided in their hearts for their dream of running their own ranch, the Battle Axe Ranch.

A few weeks after the funeral in Scottsville, the youngest son Tom had returned to the ranch. He'd been staying with his Vanover grandparents (the in-laws) until he finished his junior year at the Scottsville High School. With the death of his mother, Clyde and Fred talked to the principal to arrange for Tom to finish early to come home. For him to complete his junior year early, his teachers had assigned a couple of reports and had set up two final tests for him. He had worked hard and completed the requirements in a week and a half following the funeral.

Before Tom left, Grandpa Paul had loaded up three old saddles with blankets and bridles that had been stored in the back of his tack shed. He had told Tom that he knew that his Uncle Fred would be able to repair them. Knowing that his son-in-law wanted to take people fishing and hunting, Grandpa Paul had realized he could use those extra saddles. For years, those old saddles had been collecting dust in his tack shed. He had told Tom not to say anything to Grandma Nancy about them. Along with those old saddles, Tom had loaded his single bed, his small dresser, his own saddle with a blanket and a bridle. By the time he pulled out of their ranch, the old pickup bed had been covered with a big tarp. The pickup sat nearly down on its axles. With his Grandpa Paul's old '50 red pickup, he was ready to head out on the long drive to his family's ranch.

All the Vanovers were there to see him off, telling him to drive safely. Grandma and Aunt Josey had packed him a lunch sack. His two cousins, Harry and Lydia, would miss him. This last year Harry had started to help his dad Ray and Grandpa with the ranch work. He worked sometimes with Tom and grew to know him. He respected his tall cousin whose friendliness and cheerfulness dominated his personality. Lydia would miss his playful teasing, but she wouldn't miss him pulling her two braids. As Tom drove away from the Diamond V, he waved 'goodbye' to them all.

Riding in the cab with him, his Australian healer Blue kept Tom company on the long, lonely trip. He eagerly looked forward to settling in at their family's new ranch. With light brown hair and blue eyes, he favored his mom's side of the family. Like all the men in the families (except for Matt), he loved ranching. From an early age, he eagerly did his chores, including milking their cow Sunny, to mucking out the manure in the stable, and to helping with haying on his Grandpa Paul's Diamond V. Now, he could work on their own mountain ranch, the Battle Axe Ranch.

After arriving at the ranch, he moved upstairs into one of the bedrooms. He unpacked his saddle, and the three old ones for his uncle to repair. In no time at all, he fell into being with his family at the ranch and getting reacquainted with his horse Brute. Since he had arrived home, he had worked alongside his Uncle Fred and his brothers, feeding, protecting their herd, and cleaning the stalls, pens, and corrals.

Starting early in the morning, the Fletchers worked together doing the needed ranch work. Tom's horse Brute, a grey stallion, had been one of the best horses they had. Each of his brothers also had good ranching horses; Chet had a red sorrel named Rusty and Matt had a big black stallion named Diablo. The new hired ranch hand Dave Knox rode a brown stallion named Bullet. The family had a favorite saying--'ranching was in their blood.'

Thinking about the ranch, Clyde's hope stirred at the thought of branding those new forty calves in a few weeks. Those calves were their future.

Today, the young and older heifers would be driven into a different pasture with their bull Twister. Since they wanted to increase the size of the herd, they needed Twister to earn his keep since coming here in the middle of March. When they moved here, they had purchased Twister from Clyde's father-in-law Paul Vanover who raised his special breed of bulls on the Diamond V Ranch.

Above and around the Battle Axe Ranch, the danger rested with the predators that roamed in the wild forested mountains. A pack of six timber wolves or more had remained in the area for a while and had killed three of their steers. The pack finally moved on frightened away with their trap lines. Setting up several trap lines, Hans Severson and the Fletchers had trapped a large red female timber wolf. Prior to that, Matt had shot and killed a black male timber wolf while riding early one morning above the ranch. The last timber wolf trapped had been a young pup. The men, then, decided to pull the trap lines up to be stored until next year.

However, other predators made the Fletchers still watchful for tracks or signs of grizzlies, bears, or coyotes. The grizzlies would be coming out of hibernation up in the high country. And from the national park, pesky black bears were brought over and dumped on their side of the mountain range. All the ranchers were on alert, protecting their herds from these constant predators, especially during calving season.

Holding the reins on Jack, Clyde's hands gripped the leather so tight his fingers felt the strain. Jack reacted to the tightened reins, stretching his neck, and shaking his head. He snorted loudly as finally Clyde came out of his thoughts and eased up on the reins. "Sorry, ol' boy. My mind's on other things," he spoke under his breath. His brother Fred, in his mid-forties, clean shaven with greying temples, rode up behind him on his chestnut horse Captain. Recently, his Australian healer Bandit had taken to riding out to the herd on the hay wagon. With his tongue hanging out, the dog jumped up on the wagon and sat beside Clyde after catching up. Clyde freed his right hand, caressed, and stroked Bandit's head and ears. Today would be a long, hard-working day as most days were.

****

More than a month ago, on a dark stormy night at the end of March, the tragic events left the Fletchers horrified and filled with grief. The events of that day and night still haunted the family, especially Clyde. Driving out to their ranch a month ago, the Sheriff Tom Lindon had arrived and told them of the wrecked red Corvette near Grady's Hill. After hearing about the wreck and the death of a young man, Beth went into hysterical sobbing and crying for her son. That red sports car had been their son Matt's car.

"Oh, no, no. Not my baby Matt," she screamed as Clyde caught her as her knees weakened and she collapsed. He caught her in his strong arms and took her into their bedroom down the hall. Sobs racked her body as she cried out for her son. He laid her on the bed, trying to comfort her. Knowing that she needed her pills, he went to her dresser to get them while Fred went to get a glass of water. He had given her four pills, thinking those would settle her down. Recalling that stormy night, he still couldn't understand how his wife managed to wake up later and take the rest of the barbiturates and sleeping pills in the two bottles. In the past, giving her the pills would put her to sleep for several hours, at least that's what he thought that night. With her adrenalin running high, she must have been so stirred up that the pills hadn't settled her down. The mystery of that night would haunt him forever.

Leaving her resting in their bedroom at the ranch, he and Fred had driven into town to the sheriff's office to identify the body. After viewing the bloody dead body, they both knew instantly it wasn't Matt but his friend Ronnie McClure who had died in the wreck. At twenty-one, Ronnie had reddish brown hair and on his torn pocket, Fred had found the white blood-caked words 'McClure's Garage.' No one had noticed the torn pocket with the name on it, the sheriff felt terrible that he had brought the Fletchers in to identify the body of this young man who wasn't Matt as they had all assumed.

Earlier that day before the accident, Matt had dropped off his red sports car for Ronnie to work on at his dad's garage. After working on the car, he had taken that much-adored red Corvette for a test drive when a highway patrol officer spotted him speeding. Without his wallet and driver's license, Ronnie had panicked and thought that he could outrun the patrol car. The fast chase ended up on the dangerous curve at the top of Grady's Hill when the Red Devil's back tires lost their grip, spinning out of control throwing Ronnie to his death and landing overturned in the deep rocky canyon below.

After clearing up the misidentification of the body, Clyde and Fred thankfully thought everything would be all right. They both breathed a sigh of relief that Matt had not been the victim of the accident. When the truth eventually came to light, the officials, the town folks, and the families involved were all stunned. This mistaken identification had shaken the folks of Riverside because one of theirs--a much-loved young man-- had been killed. The McClure's--- Bobby and his wife Doris with two sons and a daughter--- were longtime residents operating their gas station, garage, and renting a couple of small houses. Entertaining the locals with country songs, Ronnie, their youngest son, had played his guitar and sang with his deep, strong voice at the bars on Saturday nights for years. The town folk were going to miss him. He was well-loved by all who knew him.

After leaving the sheriff's office, Clyde and Fred had stopped at a local bar, the Pole Cat, for a couple of drinks before going back to the ranch. Talking with the folks in the bar, the two brothers had heard the story of how the 'old

10

man' Carter had called the highway patrol about the young guys drag racing their cars on the highway near his ranch. Over the years, he had threatened to call the authorities if they didn't quit racing. On either side of the highway, his pastures were filled with his cattle. Besides that, at the turn out with all the ranchers' mailboxes, the crowd would leave their trash of empty beer and soda cans lying around. He'd have to clean up the turn out each time they had a drag race. The town gossip didn't stop there; they heard that Bert's daughter Eveline had turned up pregnant. She had fainted in the doctor's office after hearing of the wreck. Eveline and Matt had been dating for a week before the accident. They had been seeing each other and Matt had taken her for a ride in his Red Devil. Everyone in town had seen them drive down main street the day before the accident.

Hearing that Matt's girlfriend came up pregnant, Clyde angrily drove back to the ranch to confront his son. Without thinking logically, his dad's mind leaped into a rage that he had never felt before. After a blustering accusation at the ranch, Matt explained that it couldn't have been him. He explained that he had just met Eveline a week before at a wedding reception held at the Dark Horse Tavern. After accusing his son Matt and realizing his mistake, Clyde felt terrible. He thought that it was the biggest blunder that he had made that day. But it wasn't. When he went to tell his wife that Matt was alive, he found her dead. How could she have awakened and taken those two bottles of pills? He would forever feel the guilt.

There were other mistakes made that stormy night. Prior to their dad and uncle returning to the ranch from town, Chet and Matt had a strained argument in the ranch kitchen about informing their mother about who was killed in the accident. Matt had insisted on telling his mother that he had not been driving his Red Devil. That he was alive and well. Chet had talked him out of telling her since in the past years, their drug induced mother would go into hysterics in times of trouble. Only their dad could handle her, quieting her fears, her worries, or her sobbing. They waited until their dad returned from town to tell her. Since that night, a silent tension of anger resided in the two brothers' hearts about their argument. That unspoken resentment had grown and grown after her death.

However, sensing that something was wrong that terrible night, the dog Bandit tried to alert Fred and Clyde. Whining, the dog kept nudging them trying to get their attention. He would go back and forth from the bedroom door to the kitchen. Finally, he gave up and laid down in the hall by the bedroom door. The men were oblivious to the dire situation playing out in the bedroom as Beth had earlier swallowed two bottles of her pills to end her life. By the time he went into their bedroom to tell his wife that Matt had not been killed, she had taken all those pills and had died.

Clyde would never forget the devastation that he felt walking into their darkened bedroom. He saw his wife asleep on the bed, looking peaceful. She always had a little snore when she slept, so he had stopped and listened. But the silent room gave him an eerie feeling. The deadly silence had frightened him. Panicking, he had realized that she wasn't breathing. Lightning flashed as he saw the two empty bottles and a broken drinking glass lying on the floor next to the bed. Bending over and picking up the empty bottles and some of the broken glass, he grasped at the reality of the situation. A voice deep inside him rose and in horror, and he shouted, "Noooooo Beth!" Dropping the empty pill bottles and the broken glass, he stumbled out of the room to the find his brother. Hearing his brother shout, Fred came running down the hall. Clyde's eyes were filled with horror as he stared at his brother and struggled to breathe. Fred grabbed him and held him up as his knees weakened and threatened to send him to the floor. He clung to his brother.

"What's wrong, Clyde?" shouted Fred, holding his brother up.

"It's Beth. Oh, God, Fred. It's Beth." The world blurred around him, as tears filled his eyes. Stumbling on into the kitchen, Clyde sat down at the long table. Holding his head in his hands, he gasped and wept. Stunned, his sons Chet and Matt looked at him in disbelief. They too ran down the hallway, just as Fred turned on the light in the bedroom. There, lying on the bed, they saw their mom with her opened eyes lifted in a death stare at the ceiling. The two sons gasped at seeing her with that vacant stare. "Oh, mom!" one cried out; the other hollered, "Maaaaa!" Glued to the floor, the two young brothers were frightened and shocked at the sight that they both saw.

Turning to his nephews, Fred wrapped his arms around them and pushed them out of the room, telling them to call for the doctor and to take care of their dad. Walking over to the bed, he saw the shards of broken glass and one empty pill bottle on the floor beside the bed. Bending down, he picked up the bottle and saw that the other one had rolled under the bed a little. He reached for the second pill bottle as his hand moved against a shard of glass. Cussing he felt the sting of the broken glass cutting into his hand. He put the two empty bottles on the bedside table. He pulled the small shard of glass out as blood dripped out of the cut. Reaching into his back pocket, he pulled out his handkerchief, wrapped his hand, and stopped the bleeding.

Moving closer to the bed, Fred sadly looked down at his frail sister-in-law. He took a deep breath and shook his head. *What have you done, Beth?* He pressed his fingers to the side of her neck-- for a possible pulse. Nothing. He slowly closed her two eyes with his fingers. With a top blanket, he covered her body and head. Bending down, he picked up the rest of the broken glass from the floor. Sadly, he sighed, knowing this would be the hardest death they would all have to face. When their parents were killed during a Wyoming blizzard, he and Clyde had had a hard time moving forward. But this death would be far worse for the whole family—his brother and three nephews. He left the bedroom, turning off the light and closing the door.

Shaking and barely able to dial the phone number, Chet had made the call to Dr. Carter who had driven out immediately to the ranch. Fortunately, the doctor had been in town at his small local office that day. For years, the doctor had driven to Riverside once a week. His main practice resided in Winston, two hours away. When he arrived at the ranch house, Fred took him down the hall to the bedroom. The doctor checked Beth for a pulse and listened to a possible heartbeat through his stethoscope. Nothing. As the doctor looked at the empty bottles of barbiturates and sleeping pills, he noticed the recent refill date of ninety pills for each prescription. Shaking his head, he saw a deadly mixture of drugs that she had taken. After asking how long she had taken the pills, the doctor realized that she probably had been addicted to them.

He had noticed that two small pills were lying in the bed under one of her arms. Picking them up, he slipped those two back into one of the bottles. Obviously, she missed those two. Little did he know that those two pills were the sleeping pills that Clyde thought she had taken earlier. In the sobbing and the hysterics, Clyde had given her four pills—two barbiturates and two sleeping pills. As he handed her the pills, her hand shook as she sobbed. Giving her a glass of water, the two sleeping pills slipped from her palm as she took only the two barbiturates. In the confusion of the moment, Clyde nor Beth didn't realize that the two pills had fallen from her palm onto the bed. No one would ever know. The mystery of how she had awakened would forever be unknown, lost in time.

Concerned about his brother and nephews, Fred looked at the doctor and asked if there would be an autopsy or an inquest. The doctor indicated that he didn't know, but first, he would send her body to the hospital in Winston for tests. After determining the cause of death, a certificate would be mailed to them. Fred asked if it was possible that her suicide be kept quiet. The doctor said he would be discreet and not say anything. But he cautioned Fred and told him that her suicide could someday come out.

As the evening drew on, together the doctor and the widow Anna Severson, who had driven out to the ranch to be with the family, took over calling for the hearse and making the arrangements for the body. After notifying the Vanovers, the in-laws, they wanted her to be buried in Scottsville. In his grief-stricken state, Clyde had been in so

14

much shock that he couldn't even consider the details about where his wife should be buried. He stood frozen in time, not believing that she had taken her own life. Fred had stepped in and had given the okay for her funeral to be held in Scottsville, her hometown, at the request of the Vanovers. The whole affair that day and night had been a deadly, comedy of errors, one after another.

Chapter 2

Death

On that stormy Tuesday night, Beth Fletcher had awakened in their darkened bedroom after her husband had left the ranch. After hearing that her son had wrecked his red sports car, she had collapsed and had taken her pills. Resting in her bedroom, her swollen eyes popped open soon after they had left. For a time, she had laid there in shock, devastated by the thought of her son Matt's death. Her mind had reeled and spun around and around. More tears had spilled out of her eyes, down her temples, and on to the pillow as she had turned on her side. Drawing her legs up, she had curled up into a fetal position. Looking over at the bedside table, she had seen the two pill bottles and a glass of water. Again, her mind had spun out of control. *No. no. no. She couldn't go on living her miserable life. She could end this all tonight.*

Many incidents in her life had built up to this night. Recalling her twenty-one years of marriage, their love had been strong at the beginning. When Clyde, a good-looking tall man, married her, he had nothing. But she didn't care, for she had fallen in love. They had met at a local dance in the summer after she had graduated from high school; she was seventeen and he was twenty-two. They had dated all that summer. Falling in love, they had married that autumn and moved onto her family's Diamond V Ranch. Living in utter bliss, they had loved each other passionately. Together they had built a joyful family with their three sons until their happy life turned tragic.

With her first miscarriage, life for the Fletchers had changed. A week after she had lost the first boy, her episodes of hysterics started. One afternoon, their sons had returned home from school with their mother sobbing in her bedroom. Concerned, her sons had tried to talk and quiet her down, but she screamed at them to leave her alone. In her bedroom, she had thrown her hairbrush at her son Chet, frightening him away. He had not known what to do, but

16

being the oldest, he finally had called the mining company where his dad worked. Since his dad had worked underground, it took them a while to find him and tell him about his wife. By the time he had returned home, her sobbing cries had reached to a wild high pitch.

After getting the call down in the mine, Clyde had quickly returned home. Ever since the miscarriage, he had been worried about his wife. His sons were sitting at the kitchen table, waiting for their dad. Nodding to them, he had hurried down the hall and into their bedroom, closing the door. He had called out to Beth. With his tall, solid muscular body, he had gathered her into his strong arms and held her tight. Sobbing, she had pounded his chest, slapped, and cursed him. But he had remained steady and held her, taking the pounding and the slapping. He had hated seeing her like this, but he had loved her and wanted to support her. Finally, the hysterics had run its course.

Calming down, she had looked into his troubled brown eyes with her sad blue eyes. Sobbing, she had thought herself a failure not to be able to carry a baby. She had cried out, "Oh, my baby, my baby. Oh, Clyde. I lost my baby." He had held her tight against his pounding heart, feeling his own pain of losing a baby.

Clyde had comforted her and said he loved her. He had told her to think of their three sons who still needed her. Finally, leaning into him, she had lifted her head and kissed him on the lips. Kissing her back, his heart had pounded. With her recent miscarriage, he had whispered, "We can't, Beth." She had kissed him on his neck, "I know, but stay with me." He knew that his wife needed to feel loved. He had understood his wife's fragile state of emotionalism.

Picking her up tenderly into his strong arms and walking over to the bed, he had placed her gently down on the bed. Slipping in beside her, he carefully had caressed her. Clyde had hugged, kissed, and consoled her. Feeling his gentle rough hands on her body and his loving kisses, she finally had relaxed and fell into a deep sleep. He had waited for a while, holding her close to his warm body. Quietly rising,

17

he had covered her with their faded red quilt and left, closing the bedroom door.

Talking to his sons in their small kitchen, he had explained her miscarriage, her depression, and the hysterics their mother had experienced. He had felt they needed to know. For the young boys, this information had come as a surprise since most adults would have left those subjects ignored. But Clyde had needed his sons to be aware of their mother's condition since he had worked away from the ranch in the mine. Sometimes he would work different shifts and be gone at night. Chet and Matt had realized their mom's situation, but Tom was not quite old enough to fully comprehend. However, he did know that his mom was sad and crying.

And a year later, with another miscarriage, she again had gone into sobbing hysterics until another call to the mine. This time, the older boys had realized this situation sooner and made the call for their dad. Her inability to carry a baby had distressed her even more. Her sobbing and hysterics had been worse with her second loss of another baby boy. With the heavy loss of blood, she had to spend a night in the hospital. Her husband had done his best to reassure her, telling her to think of him and of their three sons who needed and loved her. She did love her three sons more than anything in life. With Clyde's strong compassion, she had come through that episode. Only afterwards, she had seemed more fragile and even more dependent on her pills.

Within those two years, she had slipped into a world of depression. After her miscarriages, she had changed. Mentally, she had collapsed into hysterics several times. Her pills—the barbiturates and the sleeping pills—had become more important to her as she had struggled to keep going. Before as a young girl, she had taken the pills only when her headaches had overcome her. But now, they had become her way of living, day by day.

During her medical examination following the last miscarriage, the doctor had informed his wife that with her weakened physical condition that she should not get pregnant again. That's when she had turned from her husband and never let him make love to her again. She had to protect herself from another pregnancy. Something inside of her had broken and his love meant nothing to her anymore.

Frustrated, Clyde had turned to the bottle of whiskey, trying to drown out the hurt and rejection. In his drunken state, he had slept on the couch. But he couldn't continue being rejected like that. He would occasionally go to town, coming home before dawn. He had tried to lie and be careful, but he wasn't good at deception. He had hated himself for doing so. Eventually, she had found out about his nights in town with other women. She knew that she had pushed him away. Everyone had known of his indiscretions.

That had put more distance between them until they became just companions. They had kept up the appearance for the boys of sleeping in the same bedroom. She had let him comfort her, but that was as far as she would let him go. He had told her that he would use protection, but she wouldn't hear of it. She had told him that her sexual life was over. Her anger of losing the babies had landed on him.

Several times after her miscarriages, Clyde had feared for her health and the drugs which were making matters worse. He had tried to get his wife to go to another doctor about those headaches and about her medications. To him, the barbiturates only had made her life worse. But she would take them more and more. Sometimes, she would take them three or four times a day. Once, he even had hidden them from her, hoping she would get off them. That hadn't work because her mother Nancy just had replaced the lost pills with a call to her doctor. He was at the mercy of the mother-in-law with her meddling ways. Then, Beth began hiding her pills, afraid that he would keep her from taking them. He didn't want this constant battle about the pills with her. He finally had given up, knowing he couldn't do anything to stop her addiction or her rejection. Eventually, he had closed his heart to her and went to work, had focused on raising his sons, and had saved his wages to own their own ranch—his dream.

Then, against her urgent wishes, Clyde had purchased a ranch-- the Battle Axe Ranch. That major decision to buy and move to their own ranch had brought on the final events. To Beth, it was the worst mistake. This purchase would move them away from her family roots at the Diamond V Ranch. She had argued with her husband for more than a month against the move. The Vanover family had a tight grip on their daughter, mentally and physically. For many reasons, Beth could not live without them, continually needing and depending on them. Her mother Nancy had been by her side when her three sons were born and had taken care of them as babies. In addition during Beth's bad headache spells, her mother would step in, had cleaned their small ranch house, and had cooked their meals. Many days after the miscarriages, Beth could not function. His wife had depended on her mother's help without much thought.

After Clyde had told them he had purchased the ranch and had left to sign the papers, she had taken her pills and had closed her bedroom door for a week, collapsing on her bed. He didn't know that her mother and her sister-in-law Josey had packed and sorted their belongings for their move. As she had done for years at the ranch, she let her mother step in for her.

Adding to this unwanted move, a new ranch had brought new responsibilities for this thin, frail woman addicted to her pills. She had feared that she wouldn't be able to do what Clyde expected her to do—to maintain the ranch house. Plus, she didn't have the will nor the desire to start over. She had told him that she couldn't face starting over somewhere so far away from her parents. All these thoughts, worries, and pleading had sapped Beth's mental and physical strength. Besides, her arguments had fallen on deaf ears. Her husband had his dream of owning a ranch, for he and his brother had been chasing that dream their whole life.

Fearful of the new obligations, she had a bad premonition about the Battle Axe Ranch. At the ranch, a year before, the Severson's only twenty-four-year-old son

Caden had been mauled to death by a grizzly. With the death of their son, the family had succumbed to grief and had sold the ranch to the Fletchers. It had become a fearful premonition, for she believed in dead spirits. Before leaving the ranch, the Severson's children had scattered little notes throughout the ranch house, telling their dead father that they had moved into town. When Beth had discovered and read all the little notes tucked in the windowsills, she had imagined that the dead spirit was being called forth by the children. In her imagination, she had become terrified of the ghostly spirit of the dead father. Later, finding another yellow stained note written a year before stuffed in attic window finalized this eerie dreadful curse that she had sensed from the beginning. She believed the ranch held a curse. She superstitiously had feared for the lives of her family.

That Tuesday, thinking that her precious Matthew had been killed, she felt that the curse had been fulfilled. Now, two sons had been killed who lived here at this ranch—first, Caden, and now, Matt. Losing her middle son hit her harder than her miscarriages. Matt had been different from her other two sons, Chet and Tom, who were tough like their dad. Having a unique kindness and sensitivity, he had looked at life differently than the other men in their family. He had loved the horses, had loved his guitar and music, and had loved getting away from the ranch. She knew that he had sought to escape the ranch work that Clyde had demanded of him. She had just discovered that he had inherited her debilitating headaches. Giving him a few of her pills, she had hoped that she could help him through those headaches. Unbeknown to her though, Matt had not been killed. But in her mental and physical state, Beth had been drained of hope with all those incidents over those many years. She felt that the world had defeated her, crushing her will to live. She simply didn't want to go on living without her dear son.

Adding to her fear of a curse and the death of her son, Beth's imagination had ran crazy with the thoughts that they lived at this cursed mountain ranch surrounded by the wild and rugged forested lands filled with treacherous grizzlies, wolves, and other wild animals. The men had spoken of their trappings and had told the stories about those vicious wild animals. Hearing the story of her son Matt killing a timber wolf a week earlier had added to her wild imaginations about living here. She had feared for the lives of her sons as they rode into those rugged mountains.

A few days earlier on another stormy night, standing by their bedroom window, she had seen shadows racing through the timber near their log ranch house. As the lightning flashed, she had glanced at the shape of a huge dark timber wolf followed by many dark shapes racing through the forest behind their ranch house. Thundered cracked above as she had held her mouth closed with her hands to keep from screaming. Clyde had been taking a shower, so she waited, shaken at what she had seen. After he returned to their bedroom, she left to take her shower. She did not tell him of the dark shadows, for he would simply tell her that it was her imagination running away with her. He would tell that her that those were silly, wild ideas. But her imagination did not create these dark creatures running through the forest behind their house. Terrified, she kept silent about seeing them.

Thus the culmination of all these— her mind had taken her down into a gradual death spiral, taking her beyond reality into a world of illusionary fear and imagination day after day, night after night. Everything had tipped her over into this suicide. Tonight, she sat up and reached for both bottles sitting on the table next to her bed. Opening one bottle at a time, she had downed the pills with the glass of water. Trying to put the bottles and the glass back on the table, they had slipped from her shaking hands and fell crashing to the floor. The glass had broken, and the bottles had rolled around. She had stretched out on the bed and had waited for the pills to take her away from this cruel world. Finally, taking her last breath, she had entered the dark world of the dead spirits.

Chapter 3

The Wake

Following Beth's traumatic suicidal death, her wake and funeral had become an ugly, nasty affair. Since she had been raised on the Diamond V Ranch, the Vanovers (the in-laws) demanded that she be buried in Scottsville, not in Riverside. Filled with grief and sorrow, Clyde couldn't bring himself to fight the strong arms of Beth's parents—Paul and Nancy. Trying to help, his brother Fred felt that it didn't matter where his sister-in-law was buried. She was dead. When she had been alive, her parents had dominated her life beyond Clyde's reach anyway. Over the years, Fred had witnessed the decline of their marriage and his brother struggled against her family, living on the Diamond V Ranch.

Not only burying her in Scottsville troubled them, but also the callous religious practices left both families aghast. The church and the religious views of suicide made her burial more complicated. With the unforgiving act of suicide, the staunch minister refused to hold the funeral in the church. The minister said they could have a graveside ceremony with a prayer. They were denied the comfort of a church service with the congregation, the church choir singing hymns, and solemn minister's prayers. Along with that, Paul and Nancy decided to forego burying her in the town cemetery. The final arrangements put Beth's funeral and burial at the Diamond V Ranch.

Decades before, the Vanovers' ancestors had been buried there on their ranch's small family plot which occupied the top of a small hill with a tall, wind bent pine tree and an old weeping willow. The old trees stood outside of a run-down grey wooden fence that surrounded their ancestors' headstones and graves. In the back of their family cemetery, their great grandparents' headstone read: *In Loving Memory, William and Alice Vanover.* In the hallowed ground lay their young children's grave—three small headstones. Their names—Eliza, Rose, and

23

William—were forever etched in the terrible memory of their tragic deaths. Typhoid took Eliza and William; Rose died of scarlet fever several years later. Only their son Henry survived. Then, their grandparents' headstone read: *Dearly Loved, Never Forgotten, Henry and Cora Vanover*. Immigrating to America from Holland, the Vanovers were Dutch. Their ancestors' culture had continued here in Scottsville with their tight-lipped, stoic mannerisms, and their closed doors.

Arriving at Scottsville on Friday, the day before the funeral, the Fletchers—Clyde, Fred, Chet, and Matt—were staying at the Stagecoach Motel, a cheap, but comfortable motel. The men had left the Battle Axe Ranch an hour before dawn to be here in Scottsville for the afternoon wake. Their long drive had been a silent one—all of them still trying to grasp the reality of Beth's death. They felt odd returning to Scottsville under these circumstances. Noticing that the Fletchers were back, the town's folk had heard about Beth's death and planned funeral at the Diamond V. Even Chet and Matt's friends had heard about her death.

That day before the funeral, the Vanovers had made arrangements for a customary wake—a candle vigil held in their living room at the main ranch house. The furniture had been pushed back against the walls with the coffin situated at the far end of the room. Chairs were arranged on either side of it for the two families to sit as friends and neighbors called to give their condolences. The two curtains of the big picture window had been half-drawn closed, making the room darker. A wreath of white flowers adorned the top of the pine box coffin. Three candles burned beside three framed photographs on an end table near the coffin. One large picture showed a beautiful young Beth with flowing brown hair and a wide happy smile. Another one showed an older Beth with her three sons, towering around her. Her hair had thinned, and her small body looked frail in that photograph. She still had a happy smile on her face. A third photograph showed a young Clyde and Beth at their small wedding, holding hands with his arm around her. His tall

24

figure shadowed out her small, delicate frame. They both had the giddy smiles of a newly married couple.

The three young Fletcher brothers were not sure how to conduct themselves in this seemingly awkward situation of a wake. They felt uncomfortable sitting next to the pine coffin which held their mom's body. The three of them were filled with sadness and grief so that they quietly sat with their eyes cast down. As the social gathering proceeded, Clyde and Fred knew many who had come to the wake, talking quietly to their ranching friends.

As the two families sat separated by the casket, a silent tension fell upon them. For over two hours, people had streamed in with their mumbled words, their hugs, their nods, and their shuffling feet. Several of their friends had brought flowers, so on Beth's coffin lay a beautiful bed of blue, yellow, red, and white flowers adorning the wooden box. The living room smelled heavy with the sweet scent of the flowers, the burning of the wax candles, and a hint of pine from the coffin.

The oldest, Chet, had kept his sad emotions of grief tapped down. As people came and went, two of his friends—Ben Ramsey and Adam Prattler-- showed up. Surprised to see his old friends, Chet talk with them. Just married a year, Ben introduced him to his wife Nellie, a pretty, short dark brown-haired woman. The men all had gone to high school together nearly four years ago. Giving their condolences, they asked if Chet wanted to get together that night. He nodded, anything to detract from the sorrow. They made arrangements to meet at the Dry Creek Bar downtown later that night, their old meeting spot.

In contrast, Matt couldn't deal with his grief and kept tearing up occasionally. Sitting on his chair, he didn't look or talk to the people who moved in and out of the room. Occasionally, he'd lean over resting his elbows on his knees and putting his right hand on his forehead, rubbing it, and covering his eyes. Heavy with guilt, Matt couldn't forget that night that his mom died. As soon as he had gotten back to the ranch from riding his black stallion Diablo up to Stewart's Lake, he had wanted to see his mom and tell her that he hadn't been the one that wrecked his car. But Chet had argued against waking her. That one single moment would have changed everything: his mom would still be alive. His insides shuttered to think what a difference their lives would be today if he had insisted more strongly. He damned himself repeatedly. He felt like such a coward for not standing up against his brother's opposition.

The youngest, Tom, just kept shaking his head as if he couldn't get his mind around the fact that his mom laid dead in that pine coffin. She had just left Scottsville not more than four days ago. Still finishing his junior year in high school, he had been staying with his grandparents at the Diamond V Ranch. He hadn't heard all the details of how his mom had died, so he sat totally in the dark. Knowing that his brothers, his dad, or his uncle would eventually tell him, his jaw ticked as he kept quiet while people shuffled in and out, giving them their sympathy. *What had happened? How did she die?*

Finally, the wake was near its end. Ever since he'd been here at the wake, Clyde had been tight lipped and grinding his teeth. His brother Fred knew that something bothered him, for he had a permanent frown on his face since they had arrived at the Diamond V Ranch. He seemed to be simmering just below the surface.

Glaring at his father-in-law Paul, Clyde growled finally through his teeth, "She should o' have had a better casket." Shaking his head, he couldn't believe that his wife rested in a plain pine box.

"What?" answered Paul, surprised at what Clyde had said. The Fletchers hadn't been here to make the funeral arrangements, so the in-laws—the Vanovers-- had made all the arrangements for their daughter.

"My wife deserved a better casket," he growled louder. He had been upset since he saw his wife's plain pine box coffin. To say it was a casket was a stretch. The plain wooden coffin was a square rough wooden box with no adornments—except for the blue, yellow, red, and white flowers on top. The rough-looking coffin had not been sanded nor stained, smelling of fresh pine.

Fred tried to 'shush' him without much luck. Whispering, "Let it go, Clyde...What the hell are you sayin'?"

The Fletcher boys looked at their dad with their bewildered eyes. *What did he say?* The pine box coffin looked fine to them, not realizing what was their dad's objection. This was their first experience with death—a wake or a funeral. Their loving mom was dead and lying in that coffin. They were emotionally devastated.

"It is a nice coffin, lined with white satin inside," Paul insisted as he glared back at his son-in-law. He and his wife Nancy saw no need to spend money on an expensive highly polished casket. A pine unfinished casket was cheaper and just as nice as one of the large, costly caskets that the funeral director suggested. Beth's brother Ray asked for an interior of a white satin bedding and a pillow be added to the pine box. They had all agreed that Beth deserved a comfortable resting place.

"That *pine box* is not *good* enough for *my wife*... She deserved better," Clyde harshly responded.

No one said anything for a moment as the stuffy room closed in around them, making it hard to breathe. They glanced around at each other, waiting for the tension to lessen. But it didn't.

"I don't know what she ever saw in you," Ray spoke up with bitterness in his voice. His sister had been a kind, gentle, and once, a beautiful woman. Marrying a brute like Clyde had defied all sensible reasons for him. He thought she had deserved better. His mom and dad had let them move onto the ranch after they were married. Ray had been irritated with Clyde, a man with no money and no family. He thought they should have paid rent all those years. But he knew that his sister relied on his parents to help her with her nauseating headaches and depression since she had been a young teenager. He stood back and kept his opinion to himself for the sake of his dear sister. Later in their marriage, he felt that Clyde had destroyed their marriage with his drinking and later, going to town and spending nights with other women. Rumors followed him every time

27

he left Beth and went into town. Everyone knew about their marital problems.

"What did you say? I lov'd her. You're an asshole," replied Clyde to Ray, who had been glaring at him.

"You killed her movin' to that god-forsaken ranch," Nancy finally pointed out. She had to have her say in this matter about her daughter's suicide. She blamed Clyde.

Standing up, Ray's wife Josey started to leave the living room. Looking at her husband, she quietly said, "I should check on Harry and Lydia." Their children were upstairs in their bedrooms, away from the funeral wake. She didn't like being here with these bitter comments going on between the two families. Remaining neutral, Josey felt she had walked a narrow line between these two families for years. She wanted to protect her children from all of this. Her mother-in-law even insisted that her grandchildren should view their Aunt Beth in the pine coffin before they buried her. Josey couldn't stop it. Unfortunately, she found out that she had little control over her mother-in-law's strong hand at their ranch life here.

Concerned about her other grandkids who were still young—twelve and ten, Nancy whispered, "How are they doin'?" When the two children had viewed their aunt, little Lydia had cried and cried. Harry had looked sadly at his feet. They both had grown to love their Aunt Beth who lived in the old house by the faded red barn. She always had cookies and milk for them when they came over to that little house.

"They're really upset about Aunt Beth. You know how she loved the children," replied Josey. She couldn't stand looking at the Fletchers any more today. Living beside them all those years, she knew of the miscarriages and the marital problems. She stood back and felt sad to see Beth become so addicted. Facing the reality of Beth's death had left her cold towards Clyde, and the words he just had spoken to her family just added to her bad opinion of him. However, she had come from a different background where such hateful words would never be spoken. Grudges against family members were unknown to her. Living here with her in-laws, she felt herself in a precarious position, never sure of how to speak or act.

Beth's parents just looked at each other, slightly shaking their heads. Their tolerance had run thin because they too blamed Clyde for pushing their daughter to the brink of this suicide. Learning of their daughter's death just three days ago, they were doing their best in making the funeral arrangements. Besides, Paul and his wife were holding on to their family's tradition; all their ancestors had been buried in pine coffins. Their family had been fond of the old pioneer saying, 'bury me in an ol' pine box.' In addition, joining their family's ancestors in their cemetery plot on the hill, their daughter would be honored here more than in the local cemetery. At least, she would be among their family ancestors.

Clyde couldn't stand being civil any longer. "You're a damn bunch of cheap son o' bitches!" he growled at the Vanovers. Standing up, he stomped out of the living room.

After leaving the house, Clyde stood on the porch flexing his hands on the porch's handrail. With his head down, he took several long breaths, trying to calm his pounding heart. Dealing with his wife's death had been hard enough without seeing the Vanovers make a mockery of his dead wife, putting her in a pine box. He had just another day of this—the funeral would be held the next morning—Saturday. After her death three days ago, Fred had made the decision to bury her here in Scottsville. Clyde wished he had said 'no' now. They would at least have had a decent casket and she would have been buried near the Fletcher family in Riverside, nearer to their Battle Axe Ranch.

Quickly following him out of the main ranch house, Fred stood beside him on the porch. Putting his hand on Clyde's shoulder, he squeezed it. Looking at him, he said quietly, "Keep it together, brother. It doesn't matter. Beth wouldn't 've cared. She was a simple person."

His brother shook his head, and replied, "I know, but it doesn't seem right. Did you hear what Beth's brother and mother said in there? They accused *me* when they had given her those pills for years. We've got to get Tom out of here."

"What in the hell are you talkin' about, Clyde?" he asked. This comment surprised him.

"Nancy never liked me, and from the start, she had meddled in our lives. She pulled Beth and me apart. She's responsible for takin' away the peace and happiness we had. Knowing my mother-in-law, she'll get her claws into Tom next. I don't want Tom livin' here any longer than he must. He's got to come home to the ranch."

Confused, Fred asked, "What are you goin' to do? He can't just leave school."

"After the funeral tomorrow, we're goin' to call the principal about gettin' Tom out of school. With his mother's death, the school ought to understand that he needs to come home. Somethin' can be worked out, I'm sure."

"But you better come back in an' apologize."

"Never. I meant what I said, Fred. They should be apologizin' to me… Go get the boys. We're headin' back to the motel."

Shaking his head, Fred turned and went back in the ranch house to smooth over his brother's words. Clyde never did have a sense of good manners. Of course, neither did the Vanovers. This funeral had brought out the nastiness in both families.

****

After sitting for two long hours during the wake, Clyde needed some time alone. Stepping off the porch, he walked over to their pickup. Getting in, he sat thinking. They needed to get back to the Battle Axe Ranch. While he, Fred, and his sons were here for the funeral, his hired hand Dave Knox along with the previous owner Hans Severson were feeding the herd and taking care of the ranch for a couple of days. Surprising him, Hans had called as soon as he had heard about his wife's death. Clyde felt gratitude toward the Seversons. After moving to the Battle Axe and meeting the ranchers from there, Hans had said, 'When trouble comes,

30

we're here to help each other.' He meant that with not just words but also with action. Anna Severson, his widowed daughter-in-law, had also been there the night they found Beth dead in her bed. She had driven out from town to help where she could. She helped Chet and the doctor make the phone calls and the arrangements.

Coming back to this run-down ranch for her funeral had brought back all the bitterness he had felt living here. *Penny pinchers—that's what they were.* Paul and Nancy had plenty of money, but they never spent it—saving every little penny they could, like misers do. *They never painted a damn building.* As a young man, he had been surprised that they had let them live at the ranch without paying rent. For twenty years, his family—all five of them—had lived in that small two-bedroom grey clapboard house next to the faded red barn and corrals.

As Clyde continued to recall his married life, the Vanovers had nearly choked the dreams out of him and Fred. But they had resisted and found a way out. Finally, after ten years of working on the Diamond V and getting nowhere, Clyde had made the decision to hire on at a nearby coal mine, making much more money than he did ranching. For ten years, he had worked underground and had saved enough to put a down payment on their own ranch. Along with his sons, his brother Fred had continued to work on the Diamond V Ranch. He had run the rodeo circuits for those ten years, saving his money. Gaining a reputation at the rodeos, the cowboys had nicknamed him 'Lucky.' When his sons were old enough, he had put them to work doing odd jobs with the ranchers around the area, saving half their wages towards their ranch. The whole family had worked on the dream of owning their own ranch. That dream had been fulfilled.

A couple of weeks ago after signing the papers at the bank, the Battle Axe Ranch was theirs. Clyde had hoped that Beth would like their new ranch and that they could rekindle their love for each without the in-law's influence. He had hoped that they could start over. But it was not to be. Even though her dad and brother had helped them move that one weekend, Beth had not wanted to move, saying she couldn't live without her family. And now in death, they had controlled her funeral and resting place. He had been defeated. Clyde sat anxiously waiting for his brother so that they could leave and head back to town. He needed a couple of drinks to get through the next twenty-four hours.

Meanwhile, back in the living room at the ranch, Fred and his three nephews were ready to leave. Their grandparents were telling their grandsons about the decision to have a pine coffin, about the funeral tomorrow, and other small details as the young Fletchers just listened and nodded.

Grandpa Paul was still upset about their dad's comment about the pine coffin, but Grandma Nancy tried to smooth over the confrontation for the boys, "Your dad just doesn't understand why we arranged all this. It's a family tradition... Fred, try to talk to him, please. We had no choice in the church service, so we moved the funeral here for it to be just a family affair under the terrible circumstances." Even though her words sounded reasonable, Fred knew they wanted to control everything they could. There had never been any negotiations with the Vanovers.

Fred replied, "Yeah, I'll tell him. Listen, he's waitin' in the pickup. If it's all right with you, we'll head into town." Looking over to his nephews, he said, "Let's go. Tom, come and stay with us."

He could sense that Grandma Nancy was about to protest, but Grandpa Paul jumped in, "We're glad you made it here for the wake. Knowin' that long drive here, you must have left awfully early to be here. We'll see you tomorrow morning at nine o'clock for the funeral."

The young brothers eagerly left the living room and headed out of the main ranch house. They felt the need for some fresh air after being in that stuffy dark room with the candles, the flowers, and their mom's coffin sitting there. They were ready to get out of there.

As they stood on the porch, Matt's anger had finally come to the surface about the night that their mom died.

32

Looking at Chet, he said, "If you had let me tell mom that I wasn't drivin' the Red Devil, she'd still be alive." Sitting at the wake, his fury had been building ever since his mom died on Tuesday night. His mind and heart wouldn't let go of this feeling of guilt. He had to get it out in the open; he could have changed the outcome and he had failed his mom.

Chet just glared at his brother's angry, deep brown eyes, "Don't you dare bring this up. We did what we thought best... I'm not goin' there, Matt. You're talkin' crazy. ...Settle down." He turned and walked down the steps of the porch.

"Stop, Chet. Because of you, she's dead," shouted Matt at his brother's back. His anger grew. Leaping off the porch, he tackled his brother from behind. They both rolled on the ground. Cursing, he was pounding his fists into his brother's back. Turning and pushing his brother off, Chet struggled as he got up, ready to fight.

"Damn it to hell, Matt... You've asked for it, now." With his right fist, he pulled back and slugged him in the midsection, followed by a left hook to the face. Matt doubled over, his head snapped back, and he staggered backward regaining his balance. Ready to fight with his fists flexing, he came at Chet, hitting him in the face with double punches: a right and a left with quick short jabs. Blows kept flying back and forth as the brothers fought. They swung at each other, hitting their faces-- eyes, noses, and mouths. Seeing his sons fighting, Clyde jumped out of the pickup. Running, he grabbed Chet while Fred coming down from the porch grabbed Matt. They pulled the two brothers apart as the two cursed at each other. The fighting had drawn blood—lots of blood flowing down their faces.

"Matt! Chet! Stop this! Stop this, now!" shouted Clyde, holding his son back the best he could.

"What are you boys doin'? What's this all about?" added Fred, as Matt struggled to hit his brother again. His uncle held him tight, trying to calm him down.

Tom came off the porch asking, "What's wrong with you two? Why are you fightin'?" He couldn't understand why his brothers were fighting.

33

Seeing blood and his young sons fighting, Clyde shouted, "That's enough! Get a hold o' yourselves, do you hear me? We're headin' out. We're not settlin' this here. I want t' talk to you both when we get back to the motel."

Hearing the commotion, Paul and his son Ray came running out of the main ranch house and stood watching from the porch. Seeing the two brothers struggling and calling each other names, they shook their heads, disgusted with the two fighting. Another family fight. Turning, they went back into the main ranch house, closing the door to the argument.

Wiping their bloody faces with their shirt sleeves, the boys headed toward their pickups. Matt crawled in the cab with his uncle and dad while Chet and Tom got into his old white pickup. They drove back to town, leaving the Diamond V Ranch behind them. In Chet's pickup, Tom kept asking what was going on. His brother just shook his pounding head, trying to calm his beating heart. He was so angry that he couldn't talk; he just kept driving.

In the other pickup, Fred sat between father and son who were mad at each other. Matt kept insisting that Chet had caused his mom's death. Clyde hollered back that he didn't know what he was talking about and to be quiet. Finally, Matt stopped arguing with his dad and leaned his head against the back of his seat with his head throbbing. They sat with tension in the cab.

By the time they drove into town, the boys' tempers had cooled a little. Going into their adjoining motel rooms, Clyde asked them to sit down in their room. On the drive back to town, he had made a list of the things in his mind that he needed to talk about with his sons. When they parked near their rooms, Fred jumped out and walked over to the main office where a cola machine sat. He bought five cold bottles of cola and headed back to their rooms. As he stepped into their room, he handed the boys each a cold cola. Matt and Chet took the cold bottles and put them against their bruised faces. They thanked him, and they sat down except for their dad.

Pacing back and forth, Clyde began. "I can guess what you two were fightin' about. But listen to me. Your mom was in bad shape, worse than you boys ever knew. In the past years, you've seen her get her headaches, go into depression, and, sometimes, into hysterics. You also know about her miscarriages which she never fully recovered. As you all know, she was addicted to those barbiturates."

"A day or two before she died, she began havin' crazy, wild ideas about the Battle Axe Ranch. After we moved into the ranch house, she found some little notes that the Seversons' children had written to their dad and stuck in the windowsills and one in the attic window. She told me that she feared the ghostly spirit of the dead dad had cursed the ranch. She believed in the spiritual world which made her lose touch of reality. On top of that, she also got terrified when we told her the stories about the timber wolves and grizzlies in the mountains. After hearin' about the Red Devil wreckin', she mentally lost it, boys. No one is to blame. She's responsible for takin' all those pills. You aren't. Do you understand?"

He didn't stop for an answer, for he went on to apologize. "I'm sorry I lost it at the wake. I wanted a nice casket for your mom. But...if anyone's to blame, it's the Vanovers. They kept your mom dependin' on those pills for a long time. I tried to get her off those pills, but it wasn't to be. And that's my point. We can't control everythin' in our lives. Some things are beyond our reach."

He stopped for a moment, taking a couple of breaths while he choked off his grief. Clyde's voice got quiet as he sat down, "We've got to go on livin'. That's what a man does. Now, tomorrow, pay your respects to your dear mom without fightin' like ya' done today. She never would put up with your fightin'. Think of how she'd want you to act." Looking at each of his sons, Clyde took another few minutes to let his words sink into their heads. He finally said, "Put this argument to rest, boys."

Uncle Fred, taking the cue said, "Shake it off, you two. Apologize and get cleaned up. We need to get somethin' to eat."

At that moment, both the two brothers realized that there was nothing more to say. Both knew the depths of their family's honor and responsibility when it came to their mom's funeral. They needed to honor their mom and act accordingly. Even though they knew their dad was right, both found it hard to forget about that night she died. After fighting each other, they did feel better, getting out their anger and frustrations.

Chet looked at his brother, "Mom wouldn't want us fightin.' She'd be on our tails in a minute."

Nodding Matt extended his hand; Chet took it, drew him in for a shoulder hug, and said, "Sorry about your lip."

He nodded back at his brother, "Looks like I might've broken your nose."

Matt replied, "No, you just clipped it, but got my eye."

Looking up at both his brothers, Tom said, "I'd still like someone to tell me what this was all about." As they moved into the adjoining bedroom, Chet explained to Tom the events of that day and night: the misunderstandings, the trauma, the accusations, and the final suicide of their mom.

Going into their bathroom, Matt turned on the water faucet and washed his face, cleaning off the dried blood. Looking into the mirror, he noticed that he'd probably get a black eye and bruises from the hits he took. Taking a washcloth, he turned on the cold water. Putting the cold cloth on his eye, it relieved the pain. After his mom's death, Matt had become wary about taking his mom's pills that she had given him. Throwing them down the toilet, he certainly didn't want to get hooked on those barbiturates like she had. He still had his headaches, but he had doubled the aspirin dosage (four instead of two) which helped.

Right now, he wanted to call his good friend Bill Dickerson, who had wrecked his green coupe and was still recovering from his injuries. While he was in town, Matt wanted to see his friends—Johnny Horton, Rob Ritter, and Dan Langley—who lived and played music together in their Platte River Band. As he left the bathroom, he walked over to the telephone beside the bed and sat down. Picking up the receiver, he dialed Bill's phone number.

As he waited for someone to answer, Matt thought about last weekend when he, Ronnie McClure, and the band had played a gig for a church group's charity dance. With his deep singing voice, Ronnie had stepped in for Bill who was so busted up with a broken arm and broken ribs from his wreck that he couldn't play. After the gig, Ronnie had hooked up with Gail Gibson, a well-to-do cowgirl who had dated Bill. Spending the night with Gail at her parents' ranch, Ronnie had fallen in love. But with her living in Scottsville and Ronnie in Riverside, the match had been doomed from the start.

Thinking of Ronnie working on his Red Devil, Matt still couldn't believe that he had wrecked his car and had died at the scene. He knew that his friend couldn't wait to drive his red sports car, but why did he think he could outrun a highway patrol car. *And why did he wreck on Grady's Hill?* He knew of that dangerous curve because he had warned him and his brother about it when they moved there. Ronnie's funeral would be held the same day as his mom's—tomorrow, Saturday. He felt miserable since he would be missing Ronnie's funeral in Riverside.

Finally, he heard Bill's mom answer the phone. He asked to speak to Bill. Then, he heard Bill say, "Hi."

"Hi, Bill. This is Matt." Getting in touch with his friend always made him feel better.

"Great to hear your voice, Matt. I heard about your mom. I'm terribly sorry. I can't believe it. How are you doin'?" he asked.

"I'm fine. We're in town for tonight. I wondered if we could get together. That is, if you don't have anythin' goin' on."

"Yeah, let's go up to Lookout Point. I'll call the guys and gals. We'll pick up some beer. Denise and I will pick you up. Are you stayin' at the ranch?"

"No, we're staying at the Stagecoach, room numbers 10 and 11. Did you get a hold of Gail and tell her about Ronnie? His funeral is tomorrow in Riverside. I can't help it, but I'm goin' to miss his funeral."

"Yeah, I did call Gail. She was shocked, but she's okay. Ronnie was a good friend of mine, too. I still can't believe it…. What time will you be ready to go?" After making the arrangements to meet, they hung up. Matt wanted to get out with his friends tonight, maybe just to forget about his mom's funeral for a while.

As he finished his phone call to Bill, he turned to look at his two brothers who were talking about that night their mom had taken all her pills. Tom finally understood what his brothers were fighting over. Shaking his head, Tom said, "Wow. That must have been a tough day and night. But, you know, dad is right. Mom was in bad shape. That whole week before we moved, she never packed our stuff. She let Grandma Nancy and Aunt Josey do all the packing. Mom just took her pills and went into her bedroom, closing the door. Whenever I saw her, she was sad, and her eyes were red and puffy from crying. You both know she didn't want to move. She must have lost it when she heard that you were killed Matt."

"Right, but we should have told her the truth, despite her state of mind. I don't know if I'll ever forgive myself," said Matt, still feeling the hurt inside.

"Matt, don't you think I haven't felt guilty about that evenin'," agreed Chet, "but dad had said somethin' important. We can't control everythin' in our lives. I feel that we lost our mom long before she took all those pills." Silence fell on them for a moment as they recalled that she had changed so much in the last years. They recalled the past years of her miscarriages, her periods of depression, and her spells of hysterics. Their dad's explanation of her death helped them understand a little more.

Tom looked at Matt, "Are you headed out tonight with Bill and your friends?"

"Yeah. Do you want to come? We're goin' up to Lookout Point for some beer." Matt looked first at Tom and then at Chet.

"I might, just to get away," answered Tom. Like his brothers, he didn't want to be alone tonight. Going with Matt and his friends would relieve the tension he felt.

"Thanks, Matt, but I'm goin' to meet my friends Ben and Adam at the Dry Creek Bar. Let's finish cleanin' up and go eat," Chet added.

He went into the bathroom and splashed water on his face, cleaning off the dirt and blood. Looking into the mirror, he noticed that his cut lip and his bruised cheek and face which were starting to turn purple in spots. Shaking his head, they would look like a bunch of rough necks going to their mom's funeral. Turning off the faucet, he gently dried off his face and hands. Moving into the bedroom, he went over to his bag on the floor. Both brothers had taken off their torn, dirty bloody shirts. Both, then, slipped on clean shirts from their bags. Chet put on his sheep skin vest over his shirt. Opening the door to the adjoining room, the men left their motel rooms, stepping into their pickups, and driving down to a restaurant to eat dinner.

Going into a restaurant, the four men slipped into a brown booth with Uncle Fred grabbing a chair to sit at the end of the table. After ordering their meals, the waitress brought them five coffee mugs with a pot of coffee. Sitting and drinking their coffee, the men made small talk for a while.

Finally, Clyde spoke up, "After the funeral, I'd like to leave as soon as possible. We need to get back to the ranch."

"Clyde, we have to stay a while. They've planned a funeral dinner or luncheon or whatever--at the main ranch house for all of us," said Fred. His brother just stared at him, shaking his head. After this afternoon's wake, he had no interest in staying around for his in-laws to throw more stinging insults at him or his sons.

"Okay. Okay. We'll eat and then leave. By the way, Tom, let me ask you somethin'. When Grandpa Paul gave you his ol' red pickup, did he also give you the title?" asked Clyde.

"No, he didn't," answer Tom, surprised. A few days ago, Grandpa had given him the keys to his old red pickup. It reminded Tom when his uncle had given Matt the keys to the '59 red Corvette when he had graduated high school. Of course, their dad had called the car the 'Red Devil' since it had no use on the ranch. But now, Tom had been busy every day after school, working on that banged up old pickup, cleaning up the inside and checking over the engine. He didn't know much about engines, but he knew enough to check the oil, the radiator, and the battery. Obviously, his dad was right. He didn't own that old red pickup until he had the title.

"What should I do, Dad?"

"I'll talk to your Grandpa. Did he ask you to pay anythin' for it?"

"Yes, he wanted me to pay him, but we hadn't settled anythin'. Is somethin' wrong, Dad?"

"Damn it, son. He told your mom he was *givin'* it to you. I'll talk to him tomorrow. Have you given him anythin', Tom?"

"No. What money I had, I bought a few quarts of oil and a new battery for the pickup."

"Well, I'll have to iron this out tomorrow after the funeral. Does the pickup run okay?"

"Yes, for all I know." Tom seemed worried now. He should've called his dad and talked to him before agreeing to pay for the old pickup. Grandpa Paul seemed a little peculiar about the deal.

Seeing his son worried, Clyde said, "Listen, we'll get it settled. Don't worry. Another thing, Tom. We're goin' to call the principal of your high school tomorrow. I'm goin' to talk to him about you finishin' early at school. We need you at the ranch."

"Hey, I'll do whatever it takes to finish early," answered Tom. He would love to be with his family at their new ranch. Even though he loved his grandparents, he missed his family more.

Just then, the waitress brought out their meals. As they hungrily ate their meals, silence descended on the men. Finishing their meals, they ordered dessert. Uncle Fred ordered a piece of apple pie while the others ordered a chocolate sundae, their favorite. As they finished their dessert, they sipped another cup of coffee. Exhaustion was setting in after a long day of driving to Scottsville. Followed with the two-hour wake over at the Diamond V Ranch, the men felt the strain of a long day.

After paying for their meal, Clyde and Fred left the restaurant to go to have a few beers at the Raging Bull Bar before heading back to the motel. Chet drove Tom and Matt back to the motel to wait for their friends to pick them up. He then drove downtown to the Dry Creek Bar to meet up with his friends Ben and Adam.

Chapter 4

The Night Before

Parking their pickup at the Raging Bull Bar, Clyde and Fred got out and walked into the loud, smoke filled bar where many of their friends had hung out. Looking around, they walked over to the bar and sat down on two barstools at one end of the bar. The bartender came over and they ordered each a shot of whiskey and a draft beer.

Sitting there, Clyde turned to Fred and said, "Did you hear what Tom said about that red pickup of Paul's? He's makin' him pay. This whole deal smells of Nancy. She's behind this, I know."

Nodding his head, he added, "I bet if you just talked to Paul alone, he'd give Tom that old pickup. Listen, a couple of years ago, Ray slid off the highway on black ice and that pickup ended up in a ditch. They had to tow it to Vic's garage, and he replaced the radiator. It burns oil, too. Neither Paul nor Ray would put in a new battery, so they have had to jump start it for some time. Hell, Tom shouldn't have to pay for that ol' heap. Now, he's gone and bought a new battery. He's got his heart in it, for sure."

As the bartender poured them each shot, the two gulped down the dark amber liquid. He said, "I'm goin' to talk to Paul. I don't want any ties to those Vanovers."

The bartender brought over their two mugs of draft beer. The two sat drinking down the cold beer. For Clyde, tomorrow looked like it was stacking up to be a busy day in settling everything. He knew he needed to keep his cool or he'd blow up and not get anything done. The bitterness he had for the Vanovers had just built and built over the years. With his wife's death, everything seemed to come to a head.

Just then, a broad-shouldered man came up to the bar next to Clyde and looked at him. He said, "Is that you, Fletch? I haven't seen you since you quit the mine weeks ago."

Clyde looked at his mining buddy Randy Hawthorne, a younger man in his thirties, who stood next to him. "Yeah, it's me. Hey, you remember my brother Fred… How are you doin'?"

"Yeah. Hi, Fred. Gettin' by. Why don't you two come join us at our table over there? Gavin Wulff is with me tonight. We stopped in for a cold one after our day shift. Let me buy you both a beer."

Randy then motioned to the bartender and told him they needed a pitcher of beer over at their table. The men got off the barstools and walked back to the table. Everyone said 'hi.' After sitting down, the bartender brought a pitcher of beer. Randy slapped down some money for the beer. After filling up their mugs, Randy raised his mug and said, "Here's to the ol' days when we were together as a crew." Gavin said they missed Fletch. The men had always called him that, never using his first name 'Clyde.'

"What are you doin' in town? I thought you had moved and bought that ranch near Riverside." Randy looked at Clyde, who looked down, shaking his head.

Looking back up, he quietly told Randy and Gavin about his wife's death and that they were here for her funeral. He told him that they were burying her out at the Diamond V Ranch in the Vanovers' family plot.

Randy looked shocked and said, "Man, I'm sorry about your wife. We've been on a two-week vacation and were out of town. We didn't hear about your wife." Both miners were saddened by the news of his wife's death. They remembered his wife being younger than Clyde. They didn't know why she had died, but neither were going to ask him about it right now. Later, they'd find out through their wives who would most likely know all about it from the town gossip.

Wanting to change the subject, Clyde asked, "Who's runnin' the mine now?"

"Do you remember Herman Grittsfeld? He's in charge now," answered Gavin. As they drank, the men recalled the days they worked in that underground mine and the risks they took each shift they were there.

"Man, we used to get the tonnage out. We moved a lot of coal when you were runnin' the crew. It's not been the same

43

since Herman took over for you. Production is way down, nothin' like the records we had set before. We have a lot of new guys on the crew and Herman is takin' chances with them," said Randy.

Shaking his head, Gavin added, "Remember how you used to partner a new guy with an old hand. Herman doesn't do that. He partners two new guys and sets them out on their own…only a matter of time before that bastard will get one of them seriously hurt or killed."

"Hell, last week, Gavin caught two new guys headed into the return air drift with a cuttin' torch. They said Herman had told them to bring out some old rebar. There is enough methane in that return air drift to cause an explosion. If they had lit up that torch, they would have killed everybody in the mine. We both complained to the superintendent, but he blew it off because we had caught them," said Randy.

"Yeah, Herman pulled the same shit in the past when he was partnered with a new guy. Remember what happened about five years ago. That new kid was killed by that rock fall in number eight entry off the East main. He was in there scaling loose rock and was killed by what he had knocked down. It was his first day on the job and Herman had set him up and had wandered off, just left him there by himself," added Gavin, recalling the terrible aftermath of a fatality in their mine. All the miners had been deeply affected by that accident. It shouldn't have happened.

Recalling another serious incident, Randy said, "Fletch, I recalled he damn near got you killed over on the west side about eight years ago. He hooked a come-along to a prop when you weren't lookin'. He put a pull on it and tore out the damn timber and dropped the roof. As I recall, the slab scuffed the heels of your boots when it dropped. If you were standin' a couple of inches back, you would have been a dead man… Ha! As I recall it you beat the crap out of Herman and the superintendent acted like nothin' ever happened." Silence fell on the men as they sat drinking their beer. Fred looked over at his brother. His eyes were wide with surprise. Clyde just looked down, avoiding his brother's eyes.

Gavin added, "Well the superintendent is not payin' any attention, so all of us are lookin' out for the new guys. I think the new folks are gettin' the message that Herman is a careless bastard. Some of them have come and asked Randy and me about things Herman told them to do."

"I agree about Herman. Caution the guys to be wary. Look out for yourselves and the new guys. If I run across the superintendent, I'll talk to him—he used to listen to me. I hope he isn't coverin' his ass because of the low production," answered Clyde. The men sat drinking more of their beer, recalling the years they had worked together in the mine.

Changing the subject, Randy asked, "How is the ranch goin'?" The two told the men about their Battle Axe Ranch, the cattle they were raising, and the new calves that were born. They told them about the rugged mountain range around them and the deadly predators they had to guard the herd against. Since they were trying to get guests out at the ranch, Fred gave them their phone number in case they wanted to come fish or hunt. He told them about their three log cabins that they could stay in. As time seemed to slip by, the miners said they needed to leave, go home, eat, and get some sleep.

"It's good to see you guys. Thanks for the beer," said Clyde. They said 'goodbye,' shook hands with each other. As they walked out of the bar together, they separated and walked over to their vehicles. Clyde called out to them, "Be safe down there." Randy and Gavin both waved back. Getting into their pickup, the two brothers drove back to the Stagecoach Motel.

Parking in front of their rooms, they stepped out of their pickup and went into their room. Each took turns showering and getting ready for bed. Setting on his bed, Fred wanted to talk about what he heard at the bar from the miners.

"Clyde, you never told me about that minin' incident that nearly killed you," he said concerned. He thought his brother and him had no secrets. He had a sick feeling of

45

betrayal that his brother didn't trust to tell him about the near-death incident.

"Look. I just didn't...that was years ago. Forget it," he replied. He wanted to forget about that day and how he had lost his temper and beat up Herman, the bastard.

"But, why didn't you tell me?"

"I didn't want you...or anyone else...to worry. Hey, workin' underground has its risk, like any job. Look at yourself an' rodeoin'. You crawl onto those maniac broncs and ride them. One misstep and a hoof could crush your skull in a second. Don't talk to me about the risks," he replied. He worried that his brother would get seriously injured riding those broncs. As a miner, he took the risks in stride, and did what he could about it like most men did.

"Yeah, but I get a thrill out of ridin' those ragin' broncs, though," replied Fred. He did recall a couple of times that he thought he was a goner, but he wouldn't admit it to his brother.

"Enough...We need to get some rest." Both shook their heads. Relaxed, the alcohol had made them both sleepy. Silence descended on the two as they thought about the next day's event—the funeral. Exhausted after the long drive and the wake, they crawled under their bed covers and fell asleep.

****

After leaving the restaurant and dropping off his brothers at the motel, Chet drove his old white pickup to the Dry Creek Bar. Parking, he sat in the cab looking at the pickups and cars parked in the lot. He recognized a few of the vehicles; one of which was his old girlfriend, Lois Sterger— a little yellow 'bug' with a set of sparkling beads hanging from her rearview mirror. Shaking his head, he hoped he wouldn't have to talk to her. He didn't look forward to seeing her tonight. Finally, he stepped out of his pickup and headed into the Dry Creek Bar, his old drinking spot. Walking into the smoke-filled bar, he heard the jukebox playing a song by the Everly Brothers. The dance floor was filled with couples. The crowd seemed ecstatic tonight. Seeing his friends at a booth towards the back, he nodded at them and then, stopped at the bar. He ordered a shot of whiskey. First, he needed something to smooth out the edges he felt after the fight with his brother. As he downed his shot, his cut lip stung from the liquor. He, then, ordered a draft beer. Looking around, he saw his old girlfriend Lois sitting at the bar. She looked at him, even though he looked down, trying to avoid eye contact with her. She rose off her barstool and walked over to him, standing next him at the bar.

"Hi, stranger," she said to him, leaning into his side. The old familiarity swept through them. Both remembered how they were together.

"Hi, Lois," he looked over and nodded at her. Turning towards her, he noted that she looked the same—long, golden brown hair with light brown eyes, a small body with delicate hands. She had on an exposing red blouse with her cleavage showing and a mini skirt with black stockings and a pair of black high heels. She smiled at him with her sexy eyes. She noticed that he had been in a fight.

Lifting her hand to his bruised cheek, she touched it and said, "What wall did you run into?" A whiff of her strong perfume hit his nose. He took her hand into his rough bruised hand. He held it with his thumb stroking her soft delicate fingers. Glancing down at her soft hand, he looked up into her beautiful face remembering their six months of their tumultuous love affair---a living hell.

As a divorcee, she had been abused in her marriage which made it hard for her to trust any man. For a long time, she would flinch when he went to hold her or kiss her. And other times, he saw fear in her eyes even after a few months into their affair when he would assert his desire too strongly. He tried to be patient, but Chet could not deal with anyone who feared him. Finally, he broke off their relationship with her hating him and spouting curses. It had taken him months to get clear of his hurt feelings. Even now after two years, he still felt sad about their breakup.

Tonight, his heart beat hard as he kept his emotions in check.

"It's nothin'. How are you?" he replied, looking into her light brown eyes.

"Can't complain. I'm engaged. My fella is meetin' me here in a little while."

"Glad to hear. Hope you'll be happy." He genuinely hoped that she had found someone.

"Sorry to hear about your mom. Is her funeral tomorrow?" She knew his mom Beth and felt sad to hear that she had died. His mom had been kind to her.

"Yeah." He shook his head and brushed aside his grief, wanting to forget about it tonight.

Just then, a big heavy cowboy with a pockmarked face and beady, black eyes came up to Lois. He glared at Chet with his hands flexing into fists. As Chet let go of her hand, she turned to the cowboy and said, "Larry, this is Chet Fletcher. Chet meet my fiancé Larry Kradock." She snuggled up to the heavy man who looked first at him, and then, looked down at her. Grabbing her around her waist he pulled her into his big body, giving her a quick rough kiss on her lips. One of his hands went down her skirt and pinched her bottom. Lois gasped and laughed a little too loud.

Chet took his cue to leave. Picking up his draft beer, he excused himself. As he was turning to leave, Larry grabbed his arm and said, "Keep your hands off my gal. I've heard about you." He wanted to challenge him.

Looking at the heavy cowboy in the face, Chet said, "She's all yours, buddy. Take your hands off me." He jerked his arm out of the guy's firm grasp.

"Yeah, what are you goin' to do about it," he growled. Seeing the two men challenging each other, Lois stepped in between them and said, "Let it go, Larry...Don't start a fight... We were just talkin'."

In the back booth where Chet's friends sat, they noticed the two men facing off. Adam jumped up and walked up to them, "Hey, Chet. Come join us....Larry, it's nice to see you and Lois. Heard you two are gettin' hitched.

Congratulations!" He grabbed Larry's hand and shook it. With Adam and Lois interrupting, he grudgingly backed down. Filled with jealousy, Larry had been ready for a fight.

Chet took a deep breath and walked back with Adam to the red booth towards the back. Shaking his head, he knew that Lois was into another abusive relationship with that big heavy cowboy who looked like he dominated her. Now, he felt relieved that he had broken off his affair with her.

Slipping into the booth, everyone said 'hi.' The black table had several empty beer mugs with an ashtray filled with cigarette butts. Chet's friends had always smoked; he couldn't bring himself to smoke like his friends. The tobacco bit his tongue and throat so bad that he'd have a sore tongue days after smoking with his friends. Since money was tight with him, he couldn't justify the cost of the habit. Years ago, he had sworn off cigarettes.

After ordering more draft beer, they talked among themselves, catching up on each other's lives. Both Adam and Ben had worked as ranch hands like Chet. Ben and Nellie talked about their lives together and their plans for their future. Adam talked about going on the rodeo circuit as soon as he could save enough money for the entry fees. Chet asked if he was still going with the same girlfriend Mary Younger. He said he was and that they were planning to get married sometime soon. They were making plans now. She was working tonight, so he was out on his own. Chet congratulated him as he thought of his two friends married and settled. As they sat and talked, a young good-looking woman walked back to their booth.

"Hi, everyone. Sorry, I'm late. The interview ran over," she said.

Chet looked up at her and stood up to give her his seat in the red booth next to Adam. He grabbed a chair from another table and swung it around as he sat at the end of the table. Sliding into the red booth, she shyly smiled and thanked him. As she took off her coat, he noticed that she had short blonde hair with big brown eyes that sparkled as she said 'thanks.' She had on a fancy blue silk blouse and a short-pleated skirt. Her slender legs with a pair of black

49

heels swung under the table as he glanced down at them. Feeling as if lightning had struck him, his heart skipped a beat as he smiled back at her. *Who is this pretty girl?*

Nellie asked her friend, "How did the interview go?"

Ben spoke up, "Sophia, this is our classmate Chet Fletcher. Chet, this is Sophia Schmitz, Nellie's friend."

Answering Nellie, Sophia shook her head, "Not good." Then, looking at Chet, she said, "Hi. I've heard Ben and Adam talk about you Fletchers. What brings you back to Scottsville?" She extended her hand to him and they shook. He had never met a girl who shook his hand before. A sudden thrill went through him as he felt her soft hand in his. He looked into her sparkling eyes. But her question made him stop.

Silence fell on the group. The grim reality hit Chet square in the face. Avoiding her question, he took a deep breath and looked down at his draft beer. He grabbed his mug and took a long swallow. Noticing the awkward moment, Adam spoke up and told Sophia about Chet mom's death and funeral. Looking with horror at him, she brought her hands to her mouth, and said, "Oh, oh, I'm so sorry, Chet."

Wanting to break up the uncomfortable moment, Ben waved his hand at the barmaid who walked back to their booth. "We need a few rounds of whiskey," he said. She left and came back with a bottle and five shot glasses.

Sophia said it again, "I'm sorry. I didn't know." She felt embarrassed but sadden by the news.

Trying to smooth over everything, Chet whispered to her, "It's okay." He knew he needed to drink a lot of whiskey tonight to forget about his mom's death. He still could not talk about it. Even after seeing the pine coffin today, he still hadn't faced the cold reality of her death.

To cheer everyone up, Ben poured each a shot. They raised them in a friendly salute and gulped the dark amber liquid down. Nellie called for another shot. They raised their shot glasses and gulped the whiskey down again. Adam then called for a third shot, saying that they should go rodeoing. This time though, Sophia turned her shot glass upside down to pass. She knew she couldn't drink too much tonight; she still needed to study for her exam tomorrow. Chet noticed that she had stopped drinking shots. After downing his shot, Chet said he needed another draft beer, so turning he waved to the barmaid. She came and they ordered a pitcher of draft beer. After she came back, they filled their empty mugs and sat around drinking. As friends, they made small talk as they drank and smoked.

While they talked, Chet grabbed the whiskey bottle and poured himself a fourth shot. His head was buzzing, but he felt relaxed as his thoughts of his mom were being slowly drowned out. When he reached out for the whiskey bottle the fifth time, Sophia grabbed his arm with one of her hands and with the other hand, flipped his shot glass upside down. She thought that he had had enough to drink. He looked at her and nodded. *Yes, I'm getting drunk. She was right. I'd better back off.* Looking at her hand, he took hers in his and held it. He noticed that she had long, slender fingers with pink nail polish on her fingernails. He squeezed her hand in his as she squeezed back. Another thrill went through him; she unmistakably attracted him. With his elbows on the table, he leaned over towards her. Chet couldn't believe her charm. His heart felt trapped by her sparkling eyes and smile.

"I know I'm drunk, but you're pretty," he winked at her. Shaking her head, she shyly smiled at him, surprised at his forwardness. Feeling uncomfortable, she never thought herself 'pretty,' but she had put on make-up and had dressed up for the interview. She looked better than her usual dull, intellectual self in her old red sweater and denim skirt.

Looking into his dark brown eyes, she saw that he was looking at her with fascination. As he held her hand, his large bruised hand was rough and calloused, but warm. Glancing at his handsome face, she noticed he had thick dark brown hair with a five o'clock shadow on his masculine jawline. He also had bruises on face with a cut lip. She wondered what had happened to him. Everyone in town talked about the tall, handsome Fletcher men. He certainly was easy on the eye. Her heart skipped a couple of

51

beats as she looked into his dark brown eyes. *No wonder everyone talks about them. This could get complicated.*

Recalling her reason for being here in Scottsville, she didn't want to get involved too deeply. Finishing her college degree in a couple of months, she would be graduating and headed for a career in teaching. Over the four years, she had dated but never got involved nor had any affairs. Knowing she still needed to study her notes tonight, she had arranged to take a make-up exam tomorrow at the high school. With her scheduled job interview, her professor had allowed her to miss today's exam at the college. Sending the exam to Scottsville High School, the principal agreed to proctor the make-up exam in the morning at eleven. She had to watch the time tonight. In addition, a guy in her life would only complicate her plans. However, she felt his desire pulling at her heart as she too felt a connection to this tall, good looking man who had just lost his mom.

As Chet and Sophia smiled at each other, their friends noticed that the two seemed to be attracted to each other. Ben and his wife Nellie decided to head home. Adam said he needed to get home and get some rest before going to work the next day. Sophia stood up and let Adam slide out of the booth. Chet said 'good-bye' to his old friends. The men hoped that they would see each other again at the rodeos. Adam said he would send Chet a wedding invitation.

Before she left, Nellie looked at Sophia and said, "I'll leave the door unlocked and a light on for you. The bedding will be on the couch. Okay?"

She replied, "Sure. Thanks for letting me stay with you and Ben. Bye, Nellie."

For a few minutes, the two sat together alone. Chet stood up from his chair and put it back to the table beside their booth. As he slid over next her in the booth, he felt her warm body next to his. He looked at Sophia and asked, "What do you want to do?"

"We could dance," she answered as she sipped her draft beer.

"Dance?" Just then a slow song by Elvis Presley was playing on the jukebox.

Grabbing his hand, she said, "I haven't been out dancing for a long time. Come on, let's dance." Wanting to get her into his arms, he stood up and took off his sheep-skin vest. He held her hand as she slid out of the red booth. He looked down at her slender legs swing out from under the black table. Together, they walked over to the little dance floor, crowded with other couples dancing. He placed his hand on her lower back as she moved into his warm strong arms. Everyone was bumping into each other, so Chet slowed his steps to a standstill and just swayed with her. She looked into his dark brown eyes as her tongue licked her dried lips. He looked into her sparkling brown eyes. He, then, glanced down further at those soft wet lips and thought how he'd like to kiss her. She noticed the glint in his eyes as she lowered and turned her head as her body felt herself stir with desire. He took a couple of steps and turned them in place. She liked the feel of his strong arms around her and his muscled chest against her cheek.

With his head buzzing, he leaned down and put his head against hers, smelling a fresh scent coming from her hair. As the song ended, they stayed together. A fast dance song rang out next on the jukebox. He whispered in her ear, "Let's go sit this one out. I'm too drunk to dance it." They turned and headed back to the red booth with his warm hand on her back. Feeling the blue silky blouse, she felt like velvet under his rough hand.

As they were walking back, a guy came over to her and said 'hi.' Knowing him, Sophia stopped and talked with him. As they chatted, Chet stepped back. Finally, she introduced him to Chet as Wes Worley. They shook hands and both said 'hi.' Wes asked her to dance. Looking at Chet, she said she'd be back. They turned and went back to the dance floor while he walked back to their red booth.

Slipping into the seat, Chet sat looking at the cluttered black table filled with empty beer mugs, the nearly empty bottle of whiskey, and the empty shot glasses. He felt alone and empty himself. The ash tray stood filled to the edges and smelled of old cigarette butts. The grief started to settle in again, so he turned and raised his empty mug at the barmaid, indicating that he needed a refill. After a while, she walked back with a full mug of draft beer, carrying a serving tray.

Looking at her, Chet asked, "What's your name?" He wanted to talk to someone.

"I'm Cindy. What's yours?"

"Chet. Do you like workin' here?" He couldn't understand why a woman would work at a bar.

"Yes. The pay is better than any day job," she answered. Looking at the handsome man, she smiled a big grin and said, "I've got to get back to work. Let me know if you or your date need another drink."

As she talked, she cleared the cluttered table of the empty mugs, the shot glasses, and the empty pitcher, setting them on the tray. She took the ash tray, emptying it into one of the mugs. With a wet rag she had tucked in her white apron string, she wiped the black table clean. Sophia's half-filled beer mug with her downturned shot glass, the whiskey bottle, and his mug of draft beer with his own downturned shot glass were left. She certainly earned her wages as a barmaid, getting everything together in one fell swoop.

"Thanks, but she isn't my date. We just met here tonight." He pulled out his wallet and handed her a tip. She reminded him of Betsy (Elizabeth) Crocket who he had met a week ago one night working as a barmaid at the Dark Horse Tavern in Riverside. They had spent that night in her apartment above the tavern, making love. He didn't know much about Betsy since she wouldn't talk about her family, saying her life was 'complicated.' He wanted to get back to Riverside to take her out and get to know her more. Tonight, Sophia had appeared, and his heart started to beat thinking of her.

"Thanks. You could have fooled me." She smiled, balancing the heavy filled tray as she walked away.

Chet sat sipping his draft beer, feeling the cool liquid quench his thirst. He probably should go, but he noticed that Sophia had left her purse and coat sitting in the red booth.

He'd have to stay until she came back. *Did they look like a couple?* Maybe. He did like Sophia. Her personality struck him so unusual that his curiosity had been stirred along with his desire to know more about her. He thought about taking her up to Lookout Point and getting her into his arms. He just didn't want to be alone tonight.

A couple of songs later, she and Wes walked back to Chet sitting in the red booth alone. Wes said 'good-bye' and left. Chet stood up, letting her slide into the booth. Her face was flushed pink as she reached for her beer mug. Smiling at her, he watched her drink, thinking that she looked sexy.

"Is he someone special?" he asked.

"Who? Wes? I've dated him a few times. No, he's just a friend." She wondered why he cared.

"Are you goin' with anyone?" He wanted to know what chances he had with her, if any.

"No. I'm too busy with college and studying," she answered. She didn't want to get involved with anyone right now.

"Would you want to go for a ride up to Lookout Point? My brothers and their friends are meetin' up there. They'll probably have a fire goin' with some beer." She thought about his proposal.

"Sure, but I'm too dressed up for a campfire. I have a change of clothes in my car. Let me get changed first. Then, we can go," she said. Standing up, he let her again slide out of the red booth, watching her slender legs move out. With her purse, she stood up, slipped on her dark coat, and left.

He sat with the bottle of whiskey and the mugs of beer left on the table. Taking the bottle, he turned his shot glass up and poured himself another shot. He gulped it down, chasing it with the draft beer. Taking a few more shots, he nearly finished off the whiskey. He, then, continued sipping his beer as he waited for her to return. Thinking of her, his attraction to her made his heart pound in his chest. With the booze, he felt good all over.

Out in the parking lot, Sophia opened her car's trunk with her overnight bag. Taking out a pair of jeans, her tennis shoes, and a pair of socks, she walked back into the

bar and went into the ladies' restroom. After changing out
of her heels, the skirt, a half-slip, and her nylons, she put on
her blue jeans, a pair of socks, and her white tennis shoes.
Looking at herself in the mirror, she primped herself,
powdering her nose and putting on some lipstick. Taking
out a comb, she fluffed up her short blonde hair. Shaking
her head, she didn't know what to think about this guy Chet.
He was like no one she had ever met. He had a broad
framed body with a raw strength that she liked. She
excitedly but nervously thought about being with him up at
Lookout Point. Soon, she walked back to him sitting alone
in the red booth, carrying her high heels, her nylons and slip
wrapped up in the pleated skirt.

"Let's go. I'll drive," she said, looking down at him.

"No, I can drive." He looked at her, surprised at her
assertiveness. But he knew he had had too much to drink to
drive anywhere safely.

"I'm sure you can, but you've had a little too much to
drink. I'd rather take my car," she responded. He shrugged
his shoulders and slurred out a "Sure." *She's right. My head
is buzzing.*

As he stood, he staggered a little, slipping on his sheep-
skin vest. Putting his arm around Sophia to steady himself,
she moved her arm around his waist as they walked out of
the bar. When they got to the parking lot, he said he needed
his jacket. They walked over to his old white pickup. He
opened his truck door and grabbed his jacket from behind
the seat. His jacket smelled like the ranch—the barnyard
and stable. Slipping it on, he closed the door as she stood
waiting.

Turning, he put his arms around her shoulders, and she
guided him to a red and white '56 Bel-Air. She took a few
minutes to put her clothes into the trunk while he got into
the car. Getting in, she started the engine, letting it idle
while she turned on the radio. She found the night radio
station out of Oklahoma which played the top hits all night.
A hit song by Bobby Vee played on the radio. Smiling at
her, Chet looked at her as she drove out of the parking lot,
heading towards Lookout Point. She asked for a few

directions. Even though she had been up there with Nellie and her friends, she had never driven there herself. In the past, she had been up there with a few dates.

"Tell me about yourself," Chet began. Sophia told him that she and her parents moved to Scottsville from a small town in Nebraska. Her father Art had his own small business as a plumber and her mother Wanda taught at the elementary school. They moved to Scottsville right after she graduated from high school. Following their move here that summer, she had started her first year at the college. She'd been studying to be a business teacher in high school and would graduate in May. Applying for a teaching position, she came to Scottsville for her first interview. But with her mother in the school district, the administration wouldn't hire her, even though they would be teaching at different schools. Scottsville had two elementary schools and one high school. Chet could tell she was upset about the interview. She told him they said she looked too young to be a high school teacher. *How outrageous!*

She asked about him. He told her about his family moving near Riverside to buy the Battle Axe Ranch. He described the beautiful mountain ranch with its pastures and the big log ranch house. He told her that they were just getting established, making repairs, and taking care of their herd. Telling her about their three small log cabins, he mentioned that he planned on taking hunters up in the fall into the mountains for deer, elk, or ramshorn sheep. He wanted to spend the summer scouting out for the game in those rugged mountains. He told her about his red sorrel Rusty and their other horses that they had. The danger of the timber wolves, the grizzlies, and the coyotes which preyed on their herd concerned his whole family. He spoke about their new calves and that they'd be branding them in May. Then, he clammed up after that since he couldn't bring himself to talk about his family and the recent tragedy.

Driving up to Lookout Point, they could see a big fire with a group of dark shadows standing around it with cars and pickups parked off to the side. Sophia parked her car and turned off the engine. Nervously, she took the keys out

57

of ignition and fiddled with them in her lap. Feeling shy, she kept her eyes down at her keys until he leaned over and took her keys from her hand and put them on the dash behind the steering wheel. She turned and looked at him. He pulled her into him, surrounding her with his strong arms. He leaned down, looked into her sparkling brown eyes, and down to her lips as she nervously licked them with her pink tongue. He wanted to kiss her, but she seemed out of his league, so educated. Her beauty mixed with her smartness intimidated him. *How could she like a simple cowboy like me?* But his buzzed-out head and his pounding heart took him closer to her lips, as he hovered over her soft wet lips. Smelling her sweet perfume, he sensed her nervousness.

"Relax," he whispered. His lips brushed hers just enough for him to feel the softness. As she gasped, she moved in to meet his lips. Lifting her arms around his neck, she kissed him back. That's what he had been waiting for—her to move into him. Doubting whether she liked him or not, he had waited. He felt her warm, soft body against his body as he kissed her passionately. His tongue teased her lips open as her soft mouth opened. She gasped as he kissed her. Finally, catching her breath, she looked into his dark brown eyes filled with desire. She found him hard to resist, but he was going too fast for her. She needed to slow down and get hold of her emotions.

Gently pushing on his chest with her hands as she backed away from him, she said, "Let's go warm up by the fire. I've heard so much about the Fletchers that I'd like to meet your brothers." He looked into her big brown eyes, wanting to stay and kiss her. But she was resisting his advances.

"Okay," he replied, a little disappointed and confused. He didn't know if she liked him or not. She seemed so collected and assertive.

Sophia opened her door and they slid out on the driver's side of the car. Walking past the parked cars, they moved together over to the warm red and yellow flames coming up from the pile of wood. Everyone turned and moved over to let them come nearer the fire. Two beer cans were passed over to them. Taking the cans, he opened one beer for her and handed it to her. After opening his can, he wrapped his arm around her, pulling her into his side to keep her near him.

He then introduced his brothers Matt and Tom. They both said 'hi.' They sat on an old log beside the fire, drinking their beer. Matt had his arm around a girl he introduced as Tammy O'Leary, who was a classmate of his. He also introduced Tammy's friends, Chelsea Paridy and Gail Gibson. They both said 'hi.' As old classmates, they had all met again the night when he and Ronnie came to Scottsville to play in the band at a gig for a church charity in Casper.

Still crippled up, Bill sat in a lounge chair with his date Denise Volmart sitting on a blanket on the ground next to him. With a soda can in his hand, Bill looked up at Sophia and said, "Hi, Sophia I thought I recognized your Bel-Air. I've serviced that car every summer when you were home from college." He hadn't forgotten about her. When she brought her car in, he had asked her out a couple times, but she begged him off saying she had to work or something. Her beauty attracted him, but somehow, he couldn't get her to go on a date with him over these past three years. He wondered how Chet had managed to get a date with her.

"Yes. It's my car, Bill. I heard about your wreck. How are you doing?" she asked.

"I'm miserable, but gettin' better." About two weeks ago, he had a freak accident in his green coupe that nearly killed him. The accident put him the hospital for a few days with broken ribs, a broken right arm, and a concussion. He was still taking his medication, so he had a can of soda instead of a beer. He couldn't play his guitar which made his life miserable. Even though he loved working on cars at his dad's gas station and garage, his music had been his life blood.

Bill went on to introduce his band members. "You remember Johnny, Rob, and Dan, don't you?" As young classmates, the four had formed a band called the Platte River Band, hoping to make a record someday. They had

59

played at gigs on weekends since they worked during the weekdays.

"Yes. Hi, again. Love your music. How's it going? " Sophia asked.

Johnny spoke up, shaking his head, "Not good. We've only had one gig when Ronnie and Matt came over from Riverside to play with us. It's been a bad time for us." Without Bill as lead guitar and singing, they couldn't play. In addition, mentioning Ronnie brought back the memory of his death three days ago.

"Damn it to hell, Johnny," said Matt angrily as he stood up and threw his empty can of beer into the campfire. He still couldn't talk about Ronnie's death. The little bit of liquid in the can hissed loudly in the can. Standing up next to him, Tammy put her arms around his waist, pulling him in for a comforting hug. Everybody stopped drinking. The bright fire, popping and crackling, kept roaring hot with sparks flying up into the night's dark sky. Thoughts of death sobered them up a little as they thought of Ronnie.

Looking around, Johnny said, "Sorry. I still can't believe it."

Feeling awkward, Chet said, "Hey, it's been tough dealin' with his death. It surprised us all. We thought Matt was drivin'." They had heard about the confusion that followed the deadly wreck, and they had heard about Mrs. Fletcher's death.

Just then, Bill raised his beer can and said, "Here's to Ronnie--the best country singer I've ever heard." They all drank a salute to him.

Continuing to drink, the group drank sips of the whiskey and the vodka pints which were being handed around as they saluted the dead. They couldn't get their heads around the tragic death of Ronnie after meeting him last weekend. Wrecking Matt's Red Devil came a surprise to them as they had watched him race his red sports car just two weeks ago. What really shocked them all was that both Bill and Matt's racing cars were totaled within a week of each other. *What a coincidence!*

The well-to-do cowgirl, Gail had her own warm memories of Ronnie as they made love that night after the gig at her parents' ranch. She still had his white t-shirt with his masculine smell on it. She would never wash it now. All his friends had precious memories of Ronnie as the group grew quiet around the roaring red-hot campfire. Not only was he an accomplished guitar player but also, he had a deep, strong voice that resonated throughout a room as he sang his favorite country songs.

Breaking the silence, Bill looked over at Matt, "Have you pulled that engine out of the Red Devil, yet?" He wanted to talk about something else besides death.

Surprised, he replied, "What do you mean, Bill?" He thought his Red Devil was worthless now.

"Hey, buddy. You may have lost the body of the Red Devil, but that engine, and even the transmission or the rear end might be salvaged. With repairs, you could drop it into another body and be drivin' it, depending on the damage."

"I didn't think that old wreck would be worth anythin'. A tow truck dropped it off on our ranch back behind the old barn. My dad has been after me to get rid of it. The Red Devil looks a mess."

"I'm tellin' you, buddy. Don't let her sit there too long. In fact, I might even drive over and help you. I can't do much with my arm in a cast and my ribs healing, but I can give you directions on what needs to be done to pull the engine. I'll keep an eye out for an old car—maybe somethin' for nothin'. My dad knows the guy at the salvage yard in town. Hell, I've been lookin' for new set of wheels, too. Even though my green coupe was totaled, I have salvaged the engine and the transmission. I plan on building another car for myself," added Bill. He loved working on cars as much as playing his guitar.

Matt seemed excited about the thought of fixing up another set of wheels for him to drive. Using the Red Devil's engine, the transmission, or the rear end had never crossed his mind. Again, Bill had been his anchor in life, giving him a way to deal with his unhappy situation at the ranch. The men talked more about their cars and their engines.

Tom spoke up, "Hey, Matt. I'll help you pull the engine out of the Red Devil. I also could use your help, Bill, on my old '50 pickup."

"Yeah, we can team up. I loved to help you out. I know it's early, but I better go. I'm still on my pills. I'll sure be glad when I can drink again. It's been great seein' you all. Denise, can you help me up?" asked Bill. Denise stood and leaned down to him, giving him a kiss on the lips. He grabbed her with his good left arm, pulling her into his lap. The lawn chair creaked at the extra weight.

Bill whispered to her, "Love you, Denise." He kissed her back. Standing up, she then helped him. Bill's many affairs with girls were well-known to all his friends. He'd love them and drop them when they got too serious. Even before Ronnie had met Gail and fell in love with her, Bill had had an affair with Gail. With his dating, he had left a long trail of broken hearts behind him.

As he stood up, one of the guys supported him as he hobbled to Denise's grey coupe. Someone else folded his lawn chair and put it in the back seat of the coupe. Turning, Bill looked at his friends, and said, "Stay," pointing to Matt and Tom. "Someone here can give you a ride back to the motel." His friends all nodded their heads 'yes' and 'don't worry' and 'bye.' After they had driven away, Johnny moved over to the old log where Matt, Tammy, and Tom sat.

"Say, Matt. I'd like you to think about playin' lead guitar. Even though Bill has his arm in a cast, he can still sing the lead. I know you don't play the melody, but you could still play the chords," said Johnny. All the band members wanted to find some gigs to play, but they needed a lead guitar. They needed him.

"You think that'll work, Johnny?" Shrugging his shoulders, "I suppose we could try it, but I don't have a car," answered Matt.

Tom spoke up, "Hey, Matt. I can give you a ride now that I have a pickup." Anxious to help, he hadn't heard his brother play recently. Besides, with the old red pickup, he found himself thinking of the freedom he would have driving it. In the past, he had always depended on his friends for rides. Having his own set of wheels made him feel more independent, making his heart jump at the thought.

"I've been makin' arrangements for a gig in Winston, near Riverside. What do you think?" Johnny continued to talk about how the Platte River Band desperately needed Matt. They talked and made plans to practice before the gig. In a few weeks, the event would be at Winston High School for a senior class dance. Matt seemed excited about playing his guitar again. Surrounded by the cold night air, the friends continued to talk around the hot campfire as it warmed them.

As Chet stood with his arms wrapped around Sophia, he leaned down and whispered in her ear, "Let's go back to your car." Together, they turned and walked to her cold car. Crawling into the front seat, he pulled her into him, looking into her sparkling brown eyes and down to her pink lips. He brushed her lips with his as she leaned closer to him. She felt his warm breath on her face as he looked at her.

Opening the front of her coat, one of his hands sought out her breast, squeezing it gently. Pulling up the soft blue silk blouse out of her jeans, he felt her warm soft smooth skin underneath. His calloused cold fingers moved along her little ribs on her side, to her slender waist, and to the small of her back. She caught her breath as she felt his rough hand on her. His other arm held her close to him. He kissed her neck, her soft throat, and back up to a spot below her ear. His soft five o'clock shadow on his face brushed against her skin. He felt her shiver as he moved against her.

As he passionately kissed and held her, her reluctance was soon forgotten. His hard-warm hands sent goosebumps up and down her warm body. Feeling the pleasure of his touch, she lost herself in his embrace. *How did I fall so easily for him?* She then wanted to feel his naked skin. Opening his jacket and then his vest, she moved her hands over his tight western shirt, feeling his muscled chest. Her

63

hands slid down to his waist and she pulled his shirt out, unbuttoning it and feeling his warm chest underneath his t-shirt. Pulling it up a little, her hands moved along the soft naked skin of his tight belly to his waist and around to his back. She gently dug her pink fingernails into his warm back as she kissed his neck. Her wet kisses continued along his neck. Feeling her mouth on him, her kisses stirred his desire for her. He pulled her into his lap; her legs naturally wrapped around him. She looked into his dark brown eyes as his hands roved over her warm body. Pulling her into another kiss, his hands felt her soft breasts against his chest. His mind emptied except his desire for her.

"Does your bruises... or... your cut lip... hurt?" she whispered in between her kisses. Slowly, her soft words hit him hard as he caught his breath as her words jerked him back to his mom's death. His desire suddenly went cold. Sensing that something changed, she moved back from him.

Grasping his masculine jaw with both her hands and looking into his dark brown eyes, she asked, "What's wrong? What did I say?" His eyes were filled with hurt. He closed them, wanting to shut out the hurt he felt. She moved her arms around his neck and hugged him tightly. "I'm sorry," she murmured into his neck. Something was wrong. *What did I say? What happened?*

"Let's stop. I'm sorry." He wrapped his arm around her warm slender body and held her tight against his chest. Under her coat, his hand came out from under her blouse, settling outside of the soft blue silk blouse. Breathing in her perfume, he relaxed with her against him.

"Is it those bruises? Are you hurting? Tell me, Chet. Please." Silence fell on the two as he continued to hold her, his heart beating hard against his chest. She spoke with such a sweet voice that he wanted to tell her.

He swallowed, trying to keep down his grief from surfacing. His mind spun as her questioning brown eyes looked up at him. Not wanting to be alone tonight, he had been attracted to this beautiful woman. But with the sorrow he'd been feeling for three days along with the suffocating grief at the wake today, his insides were in turmoil—the alcohol hadn't killed his sorrow. He had tried to close the door on those feelings of hurt, sorrow, and anger, but had failed. Now, Sophia had reminded him of his purple bruises and his cut lip-- the fight with his brother Matt.

"Please tell me, Chet," she whispered, resting her head on his wide-muscled chest.

Quietly, dropping his head and putting his cheek against her silky soft blonde hair, he began to tell her of that horrific day just three days ago. As she listened, his heart beat hard next to her ear and she felt his warm breath on her face as he breathed. His deep voice resounded in his chest against her ear as he spoke of each episode that day: hearing of Matt's death, finding out that his brother was alive, and discovering their mom dead in her bedroom. He didn't tell her of his mom's eerie vacant eyes staring at the ceiling. But he told of her today's wake, of his dad's outrage about the pine coffin, of the Vanovers' hurtful comments to his dad, and of his brother's accusations that ended with a fight. He told her all, opening his black grief-stricken soul to her. He took several deep breaths, clearing his mind. Silence fell on them as they sat, holding each other. He waited quietly for her to say something. She said slowly, "You're a strong man, Chet. You'll get through this." Her heart ached after hearing the grief and sorrow in his voice. She held him tighter to her--this strong man was hurting.

Looking down at her, he eyed her blonde silky hair, her pretty face with her concerned brown eyes, her small nose, and her wet lips. He leaned further in and kissed her gently on the lips. That kiss ignited his desire again. She seemed to understand him.

"I need you. Tell me yes," he mumbled, as he kissed her neck and throat. He wanted to hear her say 'yes,' but somehow, he knew she would say 'no.' She wasn't like anyone he had ever met before. His hands moved along her blue jeans to her small bottom, pulling her into him as he felt her against him. He pushed his hips against her, feeling her body.

Sophia gasped as she felt his desire. In a soft whisper next to his ear, she said, "I'm sorry. I like you, but I can't."

Breathing hard, he bowed his head as his hands stopped and moved to her waist.

He looked at her, "Why not? --just for tonight." His heart thundered in his chest; he wanted her.

"No, I'm sorry. This would be too complicated." She sat back quietly and waited. He took a few cleansing breaths. She spoke the truth; they had just met, and it would be just for tonight. They would both be going their separate ways tomorrow. His demand of her would be impossible and unreasonable.

Sighing, he whispered, "We better go." Their warm bodies moved apart. She slowly pulled his shirt together and buttoned it, closing his vest and jacket. She stopped for a moment and sniffed his jacket. The strong smell reminded her of a barnyard and horses. Glancing into his dark brown eyes, she tucked her blue silk blouse into her jeans, closing her coat around her. Watching her, he saw her beautiful face. He pulled her into him for another passionate kiss. Reluctantly, she moved away. His kiss nearly took her back into his arms again. *He is hard to resist.* She did like him— this rough, country, but lovable man. But lifting herself from his lap, she moved over to the driver seat. She reached for the car keys on the dashboard. He still sat near her, with his arm around her shoulders and his other hand on her thigh, gently squeezing and rubbing it. She had to keep her mind on starting the car.

Trying to distract him, she asked, "Do you want to ask your brothers if they want to ride with us to town?" She turned the key and started up the engine, letting it idle. She had to get a hold of her emotions. Realizing she wanted to leave, he nodded and slid over to his side of the car.

Chet opened the door and went over to the fire where his brothers and their friends were still partying. He asked his brothers if they wanted a ride; both refused, saying they wanted to stay a while longer. Nodding, he came back to the car and crawled in. Moving to her side, he put his arm around her shoulders. He told her that they were staying. Sophia smiled at him, backed the car up, and took off, leaving the roaring fire and their friends partying at Lookout

Point. They sat snuggled against each other all the way back to the Dry Creek Bar's parking lot where his old white pickup was parked. He gave her a 'goodbye' kiss as he held her for a moment. He crawled out of her car. Walking over to his old white pickup, he opened the door and stepped in. Starting the engine, he let it idle and warm up a little. He watched her car leave the parking lot.

****

As Sophia headed to Nellie and Ben's apartment, she thought of Chet, how she had been attracted to this tall, rugged man that she had just met. After parking her car, she took out her overnight bag and her college textbook with her notebook from the trunk. She needed to review those notes tonight, so that in the morning she could take the make-up exam at the high school. Opening the door of the apartment, she walked in, seeing Nellie sitting at their small kitchen table. She had a cup of hot tea that she was sipping. Seeing Sophia, she asked, "Do you want a cup of tea? The kettle is still hot."

Dropping her bag and the books, she walked into the small kitchenette. After taking down a cup from the cupboard and pouring the hot water into it, she opened the cannister of tea bags. Popping one teabag into her cup, she came over to the small table and sat down on one of the chairs.

Wanting to know how her interview went, Nellie asked, "Tell me about your interview."

"As I said, they wouldn't hire me because of my mom. Darn, I wanted to move back here to be near them. Now, I don't know."

"What did you and Chet do after we left? It looked like he was interested in you."

"Oh, well, first, we danced. I also met one of my old dates—you remember, Wes Worley. He asked me to dance. It was good to see him tonight. Afterwards, Chet suggested we go up to Lookout Point. He had had too much to drink so I drove my car. He is certainly a handsome guy."

"Do you like him?" asked Nellie. Her curiosity about her friend had kept her awake tonight.

"Yes, I do, but it's impossible. What do you know about him?" Nellie told her what she knew about the Fletcher family, about how Chet had gained a good reputation when he had worked the ranches, about how he had an affair with a divorced woman Lois Sterger about two years ago, and about how they had just bought the Battle Axe Ranch and had moved there. She also told her that he had rodeoed with Ben and Adam a couple of times. They two sat sipping their tea for a while.

"Ben and Adam always thought highly of Chet. He's a good, hard working man, Sophia."

"Yeah. How are you and Ben doing? Are you working?"

"Hey, you're changing the subject. Are you serious about him?"

Sophia just looked at her friend, smiled and shrugged her shoulders, "I don't know. He's nice. Now, how about you two?" Her heart was pounding in her chest and her lips remembered his gentle kisses. Her desire spun around inside her. She kept her eyes looking into her hot cup of tea, trying to focus on Nellie's words.

"We're doing great. I'm working part-time at Joe's Café downtown. Ben has been wrangling out at the Platte River Ranch. They raise horses along with their cattle. He is hoping to get on permanently there. If he does, we'll move out there. We want to start a family, but we are waiting until our lives are more settled… Listen, I'm going to bed. I hope you can sleep on that old couch."

"It'll be fine. I need to spend an hour studying. By the way, I'll be leaving after the make-up exam tomorrow. I need to get back. Thanks, again, for letting me stay with you. You've been a great friend. Good-nite. See you in the morning."

Getting up, Nellie took her empty cup to the sink, setting it down. Moving down the hall, she went into their bedroom, closing the door quietly. Sophia went over to get her textbook and notebook. Sitting at the small table, she began reviewing her notes as she continued to drink her tea.

After an hour, her eyes started to close, and she felt sleepy. She closed her notebook. Walking over to the couch, she made up her bed. Taking off her clothes and slipping into her blue pajamas, she crawled into the covers. Thinking of her night with Chet, she recalled his passionate kisses, his rough hands on her body, and his words of deep sorrow. Her heart raced on with the memory that he wanted her. She found it hard to resist his advances. Sophia needed to see him again. *When? The funeral-- before the exam. There should be time to do both.* Sighing into her pillow, she closed her eyes and fell into a deep sleep, as his unforgettable kisses scattered through her mind.

After Sophia left the parking, Chet drove to the motel. Getting into their motel room, he took off his jacket, his sheep skin vest, and sat down to take off his boots. As he pulled them off, he thought of Sophia and how he had opened up his grief-filled soul to her. Shaking his head-- *What a fool I am. She will never like a guy like me.* He'd never see her again. He took off his clothes and headed into the bathroom for a shower. Turning on the warm water, he stepped into the bathtub with the shower head flowing. The warm water flowed down his head to his back to his legs. Chills went down his body as the heat warmed him. Turning, he leaned against the tiles as the water hit his torso. Breathing in the hot air, he let the warm steam ease his throbbing headache. He had had too much to drink tonight. The heat and the water relaxed his sore body and mind. Scrubbing himself with the soap, he finished his shower, turning off the water. Grabbing a towel, he dried himself off. Then, walking into the other room, he laid down on the bed, pulling the covers over him. His eyes closed, knowing that his spinning head would be hurting in the morning. He again thought of Sophia—images of her sparkling eyes, her soft kisses, her pink fingernails in his back, and the feel of her blue silk blouse. Finally, sleep started to overtake him as he dozed off. Before he fell asleep, his final thoughts were of his mom and her funeral tomorrow.

Later that evening, Matt and Tom came back to the motel from Lookout Point. They had stayed around the fire until it had burned down to a cluster of dying embers and ash. Finally, Johnny and Rob gave the two brothers a ride into town to the motel. Knocking on their motel door, Chet grudgingly woke up and crawled out of his warm bed to open the door for his brothers. "Sorry," they mumbled as they came into the motel room. Both undressed and crawled into the other bed, falling asleep as soon as their heads hit the pillows. The room filled with the sound of snores coming from the three brothers.

Chapter 5

The Funeral

The next morning, the last day of March, the bright round red sun slowly rose above the vast open prairies coloring the sky with bright orange and reds. The cold night had left a thick frost on the fields, the roof tops of the town, the leafless trees, and the windows of vehicles. The wind started to stir the bare branches of the trees, swaying them as a breeze came alive across the wide opened prairies. On the horizon, dark storm clouds hovered, threatening to move into the otherwise bright clear sky.

Today, the Fletchers would be burying Beth—wife and mother—at the Diamond V Ranch. Rising early, Matt and Tom took quick showers. Then, they all dressed in their best, packed their belongings into their two pickups, and checked out of the motel. As they headed for the restaurant down the street for breakfast, the sky had turned from red to pink. The wind had picked up, swirling fine ground dust from the paved street into the air. A crumpled piece of white paper skipped along down the street and under some parked cars.

As they stepped into the restaurant, the wind howled through the glass door, gushing its coldness into the warm room. Finding an empty booth, Fred again grabbed an extra chair to sit at the end of the table. Ordering their breakfast from the menu, they sat waiting until the waitress brought them their coffee. Sipping their coffee, they talked about the long trip back to Riverside that faced them. The young brothers had hangovers from drinking. Knowing his nephews would have headaches this morning, Fred brought with him his bottle of aspirin. He handed them each two aspirins; the young men took them with their coffee. Laughing and kidding each other, they talked about their time with their friends. Bringing them their breakfasts, the waitress set down the tray that held their plates. She handed each of them their plates as she asked if they needed more coffee. Clyde nodded. They sat in silence and ate. Finishing,

71

they left the restaurant and headed out to the Diamond V Ranch.

As the Fletchers drove towards the ranch, their pickups kicked up dust from the dirt road as the wind kept a steady breeze. They saw a few cars and trucks parked near the main ranch house. Holding on to their hats and closing their coats and jackets against the wind, several people stood around, waiting for the funeral procession to begin. One of the Vanover's wagons held the pine coffin with the colorful flowers on top. Two matching beautiful roans were hitched to the wagon. The two horses with their grey bodies and black legs and mane matched the dismal mood of the funeral.

As the old minister drove up, the Vanovers from the main house came out of the door and down the steps of the porch. All dressed in black, they looked like a flock of blackbirds descending onto the wagon. Grandpa Paul helped Grandma Nancy step up onto the wagon. She sat on the seat as he stepped up next to her, grabbing the reins. The pine coffin had been pushed all the way up to the front, so there was room in the back for the family to ride. Grandpa waited as Ray helped the old minister to sit in the back of the wagon along with his two children, Harry and Lydia. Ray helped Josey to sit next to the old minister and then, he jumped up next to his wife. He told his dad they were ready. Grandpa released the brake and snapped the reins on the backs of the two grey roans, clicked his tongue, and hollered, "Yaaa."

As the big wagon moved toward the family plot across the far pasture, the wooden wheels kicked up dirt as the wind blew dust over those who followed. The Fletchers held back a little to let the wagon get ahead so they wouldn't be following to close with the dirt flying up in their faces and into their eyes. Others stayed behind the Fletchers, walking slowly towards the family plot. They moved across the pasture to the small hill with the old headstones and the grey run-down wooden fence around them. The strong breeze blew some of the blue, yellow, and red flowers off the pine coffin onto the ground. A few people stopped and picked up those bouquets of flowers. As they approached the family plot, a fresh pile of black dirt indicated a new grave that had been dug for Beth next to her relatives' headstones.

Pulling the roans to a stop, Grandpa stopped and set the brake as Grandma stepped off the wagon. Ray helped the old minister, the children, and Josey off the wagon. They stood aside as Ray jumped up onto the wagon to push the pine coffin nearer to the edge. Without any words, the five Fletchers came to help unload the pine coffin. They lifted the light pine coffin to their shoulders as they walked with it to the open grave. The many wreaths and bouquets of flowers had blown off the top of the pine coffin, leaving it bare. A few white and blue flowers lie in the bed of the wagon. Picking up the flowers from the wagon, a few people brought over the flowers that had blown off, arranging them again on the top of the pine coffin. After putting on a pair of wire-framed reading glasses, the old minister took out a little prayer book tucked in his front pocket of his long black coat. Standing at one end of the pine coffin, he waited while everyone else stood and waited for the prayers.

While he stood, the minister looked at the crowd and at the two families. He noted that two of the young Fletchers had bruised faces: one with a cut lip and another with a black eye. *What rough looking young men. Obviously, they've been fighting.* Clicking his tongue in disgust, he had known the two families for years. Most families in their church had their individual struggles, but these two families had caught everyone's attention with theirs. Everyone in town knew about the winter blizzard years ago that left the two teenage Fletcher brothers tragically orphaned. The two were known by all as hard workers struggling against the world to survive by themselves. The ranchers gave them jobs until they were older. Everyone also knew about the Vanover's poor sickly daughter. She had been unhealthy in her teens and then, she married. Raising a family of three boys, Beth had fallen on hard times. He felt sad for both families. This tragic death added to the bizarre lives these

73

people had lived. The town gossips would not be kind if they ever found out it was a suicide. As a minister, he wanted to protect them so he would keep his lips closed. The Vanovers were an important family in their town.

A grey jeep wagon was driving slowly across the pasture towards the little graveyard on the hill. More people were still walking across the pasture, so the old minister waited. The tense silence descended on the families and friends, as they bowed their heads and waited. The crowd also saw the bruised faces of the young Fletcher men. They wondered what had happened to make them come to blows. Their mother would not have put up with them fighting. She had always been kind, even though frail and sickly. Her curious death would long be remembered here in Scottsville.

The wind kept blowing as the old pine tree above creaked as the green branches swayed. A few pinecones dropped to the ground, knocked off by the strong wind. A pair of black ravens flew into the old pine tree, landing on one of the swaying branches. Curiously, they perched, rocking back and forth, viewing the crowd, the pine coffin, and the opened grave from above. Like two sentinels, one of the ravens 'cawed' several times. Next to the old pine tree, the old willow's hanging branches whipped around the big old trunk. The dried-out leaves at the base of the willow rolled and skipped on the ground toward the open grave. Some fell into the dark grave and some covered the fresh pile of black dirt.

As the grey jeep pulled up, Bill and Matt's other friends stepped out and moved towards the crowd around the grave. The others who were walking came up nearer to the open grave and merged with the crowd.

Chet felt someone come stand next to him. He turned and looked into those sparkling big brown eyes of Sophia Schmitz. Surprised, he kept his hands at his side, stepping closer to her. Finally, he took one of her hands and squeezed it as she looked up at him. He caught his breath as he felt his chest tightened. As she stood next to him, she felt his tense body. Her own heart soared as she felt glad to be here with him. Along with her came their other friends.

Tammy with Chelsea came and stood beside Matt and Tom. Johnny with Dan and Rob helped Bill walk slowly towards the crowd and stand behind the Fletcher family. Turning to look at them, Fred and Clyde noticed all of the young friends and nodded to them. The crowd around the open grave and pine coffin had grown.

The last time Clyde and Fred had stood by an open grave was years ago when they were teenagers. Their parents' funeral had been held in Scottsville with a small church service and a few prayers at the cemetery. Back then, the young boys stood by the two opened dark graves with dazed faces from the shock of their parents' sudden death. The dreadful blizzard that had killed them left mounds of drifted snow everywhere—at the cemetery, in the town, and on the highway. They had never returned to those two graves in the cemetery, not wanting to recall the devastation that made them orphans in one day. Today, they glanced at each other and sadly looked at the dark ground. Two brothers faced another tragic death in their lives. Clyde thought that his wife was so young—only thirty-eight. Fred felt the weight on his shoulders as he again would have to support his brother. This had been a sobering, unnecessary death.

Clearing his throat, the old minister opened his small prayer book and began to read. His dull quiet voice droned on and on. Occasionally, he would look up at the crowd, but his voice droned on. The wind took his voice and whipped it around, so the crowd heard only a few of the words—*God's mercies… our hour of grief… the soul of Beth… rejoice… thy blessings*. Ray and Josey's children were getting antsy and started to fidget. Little Lydia looked at her mom and said, "I'm cold." Bending down to her, she whispered, "Quiet."

The old minister finally closed his prayer book, indicating that the prayers were finished and said, "Amen." He took off his wire-framed glasses, putting them into a case and into his pocket. Everyone responded "Amen." With the wind swirling around, the crowd anxious to leave stood shuffling from one foot to another. Some holding on to their hats. Others huddled together against the howling wind.

Two ranch hands came up to Beth's pine coffin, slipping two ropes under each of the ends. Grandpa and Ray took one side with the ropes and the other guys held the other ropes on the other side, stretching the rope under the pine coffin to the other side of the grave. As Fred and Clyde watched them, they knew there should be a third rope in the middle to balance the weight of the coffin. But the men lifted the pine coffin and moved it over the six-foot opened grave. The two ranch hands standing on the pile of fresh dirt had trouble keeping their balance, as one shifted his rope from one hand to another. He used his free hand to keep from sliding into the grave. With a shift of balance, the pine coffin dropped off his rope and suddenly jerked the ropes from the men's hands. They were surprised. Slipping from the ropes, the pine coffin dropped into the grave with a loud, sick hollow thud. That hollow sound echoed up into the wind. The crowd grasped. The three brothers looked at each other, alarmed at seeing their mom's coffin disappear so quickly.

Hearing the loud thud, the shiny black ravens took flight into the sky. "Caw…Caw... Caw... Caw," they cried out in protest. Frightened by the sound, they shrieked and flapped their dark wings as they left the swaying pine tree branch. A long black feather floated down to the ground next to the old tree. Young Harry with big eyes saw it fall from the air. He waited anxiously to run get it, but his mother's hand kept him glued beside her.

Angrily, Clyde stepped forward and said, "Damn it! Can't you people do anythin' right?" Fred grabbed his brother's arm before he took another step towards Grandpa and Ray. Clyde's fists were balled up ready to swing.

"Let's go, Clyde," he whispered through his teeth. He too couldn't believe they dropped the pine coffin. They certainly hadn't planned this very well. A third rope could have steadied it.

Disgusted, the two turned and left the gravesite, pushing
their way through the crowd. Clyde had had enough.
Knowing he'd say something harsher, he had to get away.

The three young brothers looked at each other; nodding,
they too turned and left, following their uncle and dad. With
the girls beside them and their friends, they made their
made way across the pasture back to the main ranch house.
Meanwhile, at the gravesite, the crowd threw hands full of
dirt onto the pine coffin, giving a sad farewell to the small,
frail woman they knew.

Ray's son Harry seeing the big black shiny feather of the
raven float down to the ground patiently waited. As they
were getting ready to leave, he ran over to the old pine tree
and picked up the shiny black feather. Grandpa saw him
holding the black feather and asked, "What are you goin' to
do with that old feather, Harry? Throw it away."

"No, Grandpa. I'm going to put it in my old shoe box. I
don't have a raven's feather," replied Harry. Grandpa just
shook his head at his grandson. He had an assortment of
treasures in that old box as most boys his age had. Besides,
Harry would remember his Aunt Beth's funeral with this
black feather. He would miss his aunt. She was different
than most adults, quiet and kind, never said a harsh word to
him.

As they were leaving, a few friends hugged the
Vanovers as the old minister headed towards the wagon.
With Ray's help, the old minister and their family piled up
into the wagon. The two ranch hands were staying to shovel
the black dirt into the grave and cover up Beth's plain pine
coffin deep in the hole. The shovels of dirt hitting the pine
coffin made a sickening hollow sound.

With the snap of the reins, Grandpa released the brake
and turned the two roans around and headed back to the
main ranch house. Knowing they were headed back to the
corrals, the two roans eagerly pranced and stepped quickly
back across the pasture. The two snorted and neighed as
they arched their beautiful necks with their black manes
flowing behind them in the wind. The wagon and horses'
black hooves kicked up dirt as the wind continued to blow.

77

Grandpa had to hold the reins taunt to keep them from running. Moving quickly across the pasture, the wagon rolled up to the main ranch house as he pulled it to a stop. All the family descended from the wagon. Again like a flock of blackbirds, they stepped up to the porch and disappeared into the ranch house.

Grandpa slapped the reins on the roans as he guided them over to the faded red barn and corrals where he pulled them to a stop, setting the brake. Coming down from the wagon, he started to unhitch the team as one of the ranch hands came out of the barn, taking over for Grandpa. Leaving the chore to the ranch hand, Grandpa nodded at him and walked over to the main ranch house where the luncheon would be served.

As he walked, leaning into the wind, he thought about how they had handled the pine coffin. He realized he really hadn't planned out the details of putting the pine coffin into the grave. He felt bad that his daughter's funeral would be forever marred by the stupid mistake he had made. Paul shook off those thoughts; there were many things that hadn't gone right. His daughter's funeral had brought out all the bitterness between the two families. He would be glad when this day would end.

Looking around, he saw Clyde and Fred standing by their pickup. Walking up to them, he said, "Sorry…ah you know…about that. It was an honest mistake. I really am sorry." Both brothers nodded and kept their eyes on the ground. They didn't say anything as Clyde angrily kicked a small rock with his boot. With his hands flexing, he turned and leaned up against the bed of his pickup. With his arms resting on the side, his hands were clenched tightly together. He wanted to swing his fists. Simmering with anger, his words and his fists would only make the situation worse. He kept silent for a moment.

Looking up at Paul, Fred said, "We need to head back to Riverside. It's a long drive back, as you know."

Turning around, Clyde said, "Before we go, I want to ask about that ol' red pickup." One last issue needed to be settled before they left.

"Okay. What do you want to know?" Paul knew they needed to settle this today.

"Listen, Beth told me that you were goin' to give that pickup to Tom. Nothin' was said about him havin' to pay for it," he insisted, anxious to hear what Paul would say.

"Let's go into the house—to my office. We can't settle this out here. Come on in. Grab a bite to eat. Nancy will be upset if you don't come in," begged Grandpa. He didn't want them to leave just yet. Needing some time, he wanted to talk to Nancy again. Reluctantly, Clyde and Fred followed Grandpa. Another delay they didn't want.

As they came into the ranch house, Nancy met them, telling Grandpa that the old minister wanted to say grace before they ate. The crowd all stood around the living room with their bowed heads as he gave the blessing, ending with '*Amen.*' They formed a line and started serving themselves. The long table had been laden with lots of good food. Grandpa indicated that they should get in line, take a plate, and get some food. As they finished filling their plates, Grandpa nodded towards the hallway which led to his office. The men followed him and walked down the hallway into his office. Sitting down, they ate their baked ham, mashed potatoes and gravy, a fruit salad, and a piece of cake. Along with their food, they each had a glass of punch. Clyde asked if Grandpa had something stronger to drink. He got up and brought over a bottle of bourbon from a cupboard. Pouring a little into their punch, the men sipped their spiked drinks.

Finally, Clyde spoke up, "Now, let's get this settled. What about that ol' red pickup? You need to honor your word to Beth. So...what do you say?"

"I do want to give Tom the pickup. I've already given him the keys to it. Listen, Nancy's name is on the title, too. I need her to agree. But you know Nancy, she has it in her head that we can make some money."

Fred spoke up, "Paul, that ol' pickup is nearly twelve years old. It's a heap of junk. Here on the ranch, you have run it into the ground. Plus, I know that Ray wrecked it,

79

sliding it off the road into a ditch. Already, Tom has spent his money buyin' a new battery."

About this time, Nancy came into the office, checking to see if the men needed more food. Looking at all of them, she said, "What about Tom?... What are you discussin', Paul?"

"You know… I told Beth that I'd give that ol' pickup to Tom."

"Yeah, Paul, you didn't discuss it with me though. I don't want to just give it away."

Clyde, trying to keep his voice steady, said, "Nancy, you've gotten the worth out of that ol' pickup. Besides, Tom has worked here on this ranch since he was old enough to walk, doin' chores, takin' care of the horses, and any job you asked him to do. You've never paid him a red cent. I think you owe him that ol' pickup."

Looking at Nancy, Fred added, "If you don't give it to him, you know that your grandsons will resent you. They still think highly of you and Paul. Don't let this last bit of goodwill between our families be destroyed over an ol' pickup." He couldn't believe that Nancy was making such a big deal out of this. They had plenty of money, and they had just purchased a new pickup for the ranch last week.

Clyde spoke through his gritted teeth. "Enough talk. Nancy, make up your mind. We need to go before that snowstorm gets here."

Defeated, Nancy finally agreed. "Looks like you've all ganged up on me." The simple notion of giving something away didn't seem right to her. They worked hard for everything they had on this ranch. *Life just didn't hand you everything you wanted; you had to earn it*, that was her philosophy.

Satisfied, Paul went over to a closet and opened the door. An old black safe sat there. Squatting down, he turned the knob, clicking the combination. Pulling down the handle, the safe's black door opened. Inside, he pulled out a stack of papers tied together with a string. He thumbed through the stack and pulled out one of papers--the title of the '50 red pickup. Slipping the stack back into the safe, he closed the black door. Standing up, he came over to the desk. Unfolding the paper, he took out a pen, signed it, and handed the pen to Nancy who stared at her husband for a moment. She signed her name. As she shook her head, she slammed the pen down on the desk after signing. Typically, her display of disgust didn't surprise Clyde. He ignored her. Everyone in the room sighed a relief that the business of the pickup had been finalized.

Clyde slipped the title into his inside jacket pocket and said, "I'll have Tom sign it later. Nancy, have the boys come in to eat?" Nodding, she said that they and their friends had all come in and had eaten. Just before Clyde left the room, Paul quietly signaled for him to stay. The other two left the room.

With questioning eyes, he asked, "What, Paul?"

Making sure everyone had left, Paul said, "Here's Beth's weddin' ring. You should have it." He pulled out a handkerchief with the gold ring wrapped inside. He handed it to his son-in-law. Paul had snuck it away from Nancy who said she was going to sell it at the pawn shop. Just like that old red pickup, she wanted every penny she could get her hands on. It didn't set right with Paul, so he waited and took the ring from her jewelry box. He wouldn't tell Clyde about this. He'd really get upset if he told him that his mother-in-law wanted to pawn it. He'd deal with Nancy later when she found out. He'd be in 'hot water' for a while, but he wanted to do the right thing for his daughter's sake. She had loved Clyde, even though their life together hadn't turned out well. The world had handed them a cruel fate.

Seeing Beth's gold wedding ring took Clyde's breath away. He recalled her little gold ring with three little diamonds. It had been the biggest purchase he had made when he was a young man in love. He slipped the tiny gold band on his little finger next to his gold wedding band on his left hand. Paul squeezed his shoulder and said, "Let's go." Both felt the loss deeply. A husband who had lost his wife and a father who had lost his daughter. Putting away their thoughts, the two men walked together out of the office and down the hall. In the living room, there were only a few people left. The two brothers said their 'goodbyes' to the Vanovers and left the ranch house.

****

While walking back from the grave across the pasture, Chet and Sophia held hands and talked. In the daylight, her short blonde hair shined. The wind whipped her golden hair around her head. She looked beautiful. She wanted to rush back to town, so she anxiously walked fast with her white tennis shoes. He chuckled to himself as he easily kept up with her short, fast steps with his long strides. She seemed determined and focused. He had never seen a girl like this. Standing then by her car, she pulled out her keys from her pocket. She nervously dropped her keys but bent down and picked them up before he had a chance to help her.

Moving close to her, Chet said, "I'm glad you came." He didn't know what else to say. He felt everyone's eyes on them as he looked around.

"I wanted to. After last night, I felt I needed to be here. I'd like to stay, but I have to run. Sorry. Here's my address and phone number if you want to keep in touch," she said hurriedly. Sophia didn't know if he would call. She handed him a little torn off piece of paper from her notebook. He took it, looking at the address and the phone number.

"You want to me to call you? When?" he said, looking surprised. She nodded. He put the note into his breast pocket of his jacket.

"Yes. Call at night. I have a crazy schedule during the day." She turned to leave, but he stopped her with his arm, pulling her nearer to him.

"May I kiss you good-bye?" he asked, as he put his hands on her upper arms. Leaning down, he looked into her brown eyes. She needed to leave. Thinking he would give her a quick kiss, she lifted her head. As he leaned down and kissed her lips, his arms went around her as he pulled her into him. The kiss was a long kiss. Both of their hearts were beating hard. Pulling apart he whispered, "Goodbye, Sophia." Swallowing, she said, "Bye."

82

His kiss sent her head spinning. Looking around, she felt her face turn red from embarrassment. She nodded, opened her car door, and stepped in. Untying her white tennis shoes, she slipped on her black high heels. He looked down and saw her long, slender legs under the steering wheel. His chest tightened as he thought of her last night. Starting the car, she backed up and drove down the road away from Chet and the Diamond V Ranch.

As she drove away, he waved his hand. Seeing him in her rearview mirror, she raised her hand and waved back. He turned towards his brothers Matt and Tom who were talking with their friends, as they made smooching sounds, kidding Chet's kiss with Sophia. Shaking his head, he just ignored them and walked towards the main ranch house. They all headed in for something to eat. Walking up to the porch, they stepped up the stairs to the front door and disappeared into the house to eat before they headed back home to their Battle Axe Ranch.

****

As Matt walked up the porch stairs, he thought about the night before up at Lookout Point. He had paired off with Tammy together again. Being close friends, he held her close to him as they sat on the old tree log near the big fire. The two had kissed and held each other tight. He didn't want to be alone. After being at the wake that day, she sensed that he needed to be comforted. Matt had especially liked Tammy, a quiet, short blonde-haired girl who had gone to high school with him.

Last weekend, for the first time in about a year, they met up again when she and her friends came to hear the Platte River Band play a gig in Casper. He had given her a ride up to Lookout Point afterwards. On the drive up there, they had talked about their lives. She had an easy, calm way about her. That night, he had gotten drunk, trying to drown out his demons of that day.

That Saturday afternoon before the gig, Matt had lost his black mare Stormy whom he had loved. He had taken care of her for eleven months, trying to keep her away from the mean, black gelding Thunder who had bullied her out in the pasture. Thunder picked on his little mare by pushing, bumping, and biting her. He harassed her until one day Matt had seen her stumble and fall with Thunder kicking her while she was down. Furious, he took her out of the pasture and put her in the corral near the stable.

After the mare delivered a tiny foal, his Grandpa had to shoot Stormy. She had hemorrhaged inside and couldn't be saved. He had been devastated and distraught. The tiny orphan, a creamy white filly, became his family's responsibility. He named her Moonbeam since that night had a bright moon shining down on the ranch. After the veterinarian had come and had given them a supply of a special milk formula, they fed the little filly milk every two hours, trying to keep her alive. Prior to Stormy's foal, the Fletchers had made the trade with Hans Severson—the little foal for the black stallion Diablo. Hans wanted the foal for his granddaughter Heidi as a birthday present. Diablo, a big black stallion with white stockings and a white mark on his forehead, became Matt's horse.

The death of Stormy hit him hard, so he was drinking away the hurt that night. As they made out in his Red Devil, he had gotten too fresh with Tammy. She told him she was very religious, and he had backed off and apologized. Matt liked her even though she kept him at arm's length when they made out. She had a calming effect on him. She liked him and felt her emotions stir for him.

Now, today, Matt had to emotionally deal with his mom's funeral. Along with Tammy, his friends decided to come to be with him. As they came across the pasture to the gravesite, he had been stunned at their unannounced presence. Today, shocked at the event that took place at the grave site, his friends kept silent not wanting to bring up the ugly event of the pine coffin dropping into the grave. No one had ever been at a funeral when that had happened. That event would be the talk of his friends for some time.

After he and his friends had finished eating, they moved back outdoors to their parked cars. The wind still blew as the dark storm clouds continued to move closer. Bill again told Matt that he'd call him, and they would make plans for his wrecked Red Devil. The band encouraged him to consider taking over as the lead guitar. He felt comforted that his friends had come. Saying goodbye, Matt gave Tammy a hug and a kiss. They left as good friends. All his friends loaded up into their vehicles and took off with the dust kicking up behind them and the snowstorm moving towards Scottsville and the Diamond V Ranch.

Chapter 6

The Snowstorm

As the young Fletcher brothers braced against the wind, they moved over to their pickups. Their dad and uncle came out of the ranch house and walked over to them.

"Go say 'goodbye' to your grandparents. We need to go into town and call the principal before we leave town," said Clyde, looking at his sons.

"Dad, the principal is at the high school right now, giving a girl I met last night a make-up exam. If we drive there now, we can probably talk to him directly," said Chet. His dad looked at him surprised.

"Really? By the way, Tom, Grandpa's ol' pickup is yours now. I have the title here for you to sign," said Clyde. Relieved, he thanked his dad. The young brothers went into the ranch house, coming back out after a few minutes. They carried two small sacks. Chet handed one to his dad and told him Grandma had fixed them ham sandwiches for the trip. Even though she had been upset about the old pickup, she loved her grandsons more. She wanted to make sure they were taken care of on their long drive back to the Battle Axe Ranch. The men stepped up into their pickups and took off towards town and the high school. Tom drove the old red pickup, happy to have that issue settled. He had been worried about how he was going to pay Grandpa. He didn't know that Grandpa had told his mom that he was going to give him the pickup.

After stopping at the high school and making arrangements for Tom to meet with his teachers on Monday about finishing early, the men said 'goodbye' and thanked the principal for his help. Walking down the hall and looking into one of the classrooms near the principal's office, Chet saw Sophia with her head bent down, sitting at a desk. Deep into the exam, he saw her shiny, blonde hair and her pink fingernails holding a ballpoint pen as she wrote her answers. Sophia knew the material since she had wisely studied her notes. Too busy, she never looked up, never knowing that he stood outside in the hall gazing at her. Chet didn't want to interrupt her exam. He came back down the hall near to the principal's office.

Standing inside the door of the high school, Fred told Tom to do a good job with his assignments and that they needed him at the ranch. Clyde told him he'd call that night when they got back. After giving Tom shoulder hugs, they left the high school building and drove away. The cold wind still howled around their vehicles. Swirling fine dust flew into the air and loose dead leaves scudded across and down the roads. Reluctantly, Tom headed back to the Diamond V Ranch. The other Fletchers stopped and filled their gas tanks.

While Clyde was filling his tank at the Barb's Gas Stop n' Go, he looked over at one of the other men filling up. He noticed that it was the superintendent of the coal mine, Brian Echarte. Seeing each other, Brian walked over to him and said, "I heard about your wife. I'm so sorry."

He nodded his head, "Thanks. We're just headin' out before the storm hits here."

"Are you still ranching near Riverside?"

"Yeah, I am. Say, I talked to the guys last night and they are concerned about Grittsfeld. He's not takin' care of the young guys."

"Yeah, I got my eye on him. Well, it's nice seeing you, again. We sure miss you down there. Bye," said Brian. After Clyde said 'goodbye,' he turned and went back to his own pickup.

He finished filling up, grabbed his thermos behind his seat, and went into the station to pay for the gas. Inside the station, Barb, who ran the place, had a pot of coffee for the customers. He paid her for the gas and coffee. As she filled his thermos, she talked about the nasty snowstorm coming down from the north. Chet and Matt then came in to pay for their gas. She told the Fletchers that the roads would be bad with the storm. Leaving the station, the Fletchers went over to their pickups and crawled in, looking over at the horizon. With the dark clouds filling the skies, the heavy snowstorm came across the prairies in a fury. They drove out of

Scottsville with the long five to six-hour drive across the state of Wyoming ahead of them.

As the snow started coming down, Chet turned on his windshield wipers. Soon, the heavy snow piled up on the windshield so much that at times he couldn't see the highway. As he drove for a while, he felt the light back end of his pickup fishtail. Quickly, turning his steering wheel left then right until the pickup straightened out, he slowed down. He maneuvered his pickup to the far right of the highway; he could see the highway posts. This would be a longer drive than they had planned.

As he drove slowly, he wished he hadn't partied so much last night. Both young brothers had many thoughts about the last two days. Their mom's wake and funeral left a whirlwind of thoughts in their minds. They felt that they were abandoning their mom, leaving her buried at their grandparents' ranch. They remembered her as a loving mom. Only the last eight years were filled with bad memories of her hysterics and her addiction. Both brothers closed their minds to all their sorrow and grief as they drove on. They somehow had to move on, like their dad had said. As Chet drove, he and his brother focused on this storm which had blown into the area.

The full force of the snowstorm and wind made driving more and more difficult. Carefully, Chet slowed down even more, knowing that his dad and uncle were in front of him. The snow blinded them. They saw nothing but snow whirling around in front and behind them. The highway markings had disappeared—the center and the side stripes were gone. As he kept slowly driving, he watched for each delineator post to keep the vehicle on the highway. On top of them was a reflective strip that showed up when the headlights shown on them. Since it helped drivers in a blinding snowstorm or fog, many called them 'snow poles.' Suddenly, they came upon their dad's pickup, parked off the highway. After driving by him, Chet slowed to a stop in front of his dad's pickup. Looking back, they could see Fred brushing off the front windshield. Matt jumped out and trudged back through the blinding snow to their dad's pickup.

"What's wrong?" shouted Matt against the raging wind and snow, holding his jacket closed around him.

"The windshield wiper got stuck, so we had to stop to clear it. Tell Chet to keep goin'. We'll follow. We'll flash on our high beams if we need to stop again," replied his uncle. Getting back into the pickup, Fred waved him on. He would have to fix those wipers when he got home.

Pulling up his jacket's collar around his face against the wind and blinding snow, Matt plodded back to Chet's warm pickup and crawled in. Shaking off the snow, he told him about their stuck wiper and that their dad would follow them, flashing his high beams if he needed to stop again. He told Chet to focus on driving and he'd keep an eye on his dad's pickup behind them with his right-side rearview mirror. As Chet looked back ready to move back onto the highway, a few slow-moving cars passed them, blinding them further with the stirred-up snow. He waited for the blowing snow to clear, and then, drove back onto the highway again. Clyde's pickup followed behind him. They slowly continued to drive, from snow pole to snow pole.

With his left side mirror, Chet saw a big semi-truck coming up behind them. The truck driver pulled his big well-lit eighteen-wheeler into the left lane to pass both pickups. He was going fast and rolled past them quickly, blinding their vision as snow swirled around behind it. As he pulled past them, Chet slowed down, giving the semi-truck plenty of room to merge back into their lane. The many lights of the eighteen-wheeler gave off an eerie glow in the snowstorm. Soon after it had passed the pickups, their dad flashed on his high beams behind them, indicating he needed to stop again. Matt told his brother and he slowed to a stop as his dad pulled off the highway. Fred jumped out and cleared the packed snow from his windshield wipers. Then, waving to his nephews, he crawled back into the warm pickup.

Chet kept driving another hour from snow pole to snow pole. Soon, the blinding snow started to lighten up and he could see down the highway. As the two pickups drove farther away from Scottsville, the snowstorm lessened. Picking up speed, both pickups continued towards the Blue Ridge Canyon.

Looking over at his brother, Matt said, "Barb was right at the gas station. The roads are a damn mess. I hope the canyon won't be too bad."

"Yeah, me too. I'm goin' to pull off at the rest stop at the other end of the canyon. We'll need a break by then. We can eat those ham sandwiches that Grandma fixed for us," said Chet. Driving had been stressful, and he looked forward to a break. His stomach growled as he thought of the food. Relaxing a little after driving through the heavy snowstorm, he turned on the radio. The two listened to the music. Thinking about the time at Lookout Point, Chet looked at his brother and knew how close his friend Bill was to him.

"Your friend Bill looks as if he is comin' along fine after his wreck," he said.

"Yeah, he's been stuck in his house, healing up. Said he's been watchin' a lot of television. Last night, he went on and on about the world events—the missile crisis, the space program, the astronaut's space flight around the earth, and the new President," he answered.

During their conversation last night, Matt and his friends stood gazing up, thinking about the space challenges of going to the moon. The idea of space travel seemed impossible to most of them. Bill said he had been amazed that space was black, void of any bright sunshine like here on earth. Looking up, the group continued to gaze above at the twinkling star-covered night sky. That Friday night, the moon was just in the last quarter, a silver crescent fixed in the sky above the horizon.

"There's a lot goin' on in our country and the world. We need to get a television out at the ranch. I feel that we are cut off," commented Chet. The newspapers were filled with new and earth-shattering events happening around the nation and the world.

Matt agreed. He had felt so isolated at the Battle Axe Ranch. The outside world didn't touch them. Ranching had its own cycle, pulling in everyone who worked there into the constant phases of spring, summer, fall, and winter. The all-consuming ranch work filled up every day. *Nothing got in unless you, yourself, left.* That's what he had been trying to do with his red sports car, his music, and his friends. After being in Scottsville, he realized that Riverside was a much smaller town plus living at their mountain ranch further isolated them. He needed to get out of there sometime soon.

Thinking about their time up at Lookout Point, he wanted to know more about Chet's girl.

"I saw you with that new girl Sophia last night and today. What's her story?" asked Matt. His curiosity had been ignited when he saw them together.

"She's goin' to college. She's nice… different. It won't work out, though. You know how long-distance relationships are. Remember Daphne?" he said.

"Hell, yeah, I do. But do you like her better than the others?" asked Matt. His curiosity had kept him wondering today after the funeral. He had watched Chet give her a long kiss goodbye. In the past weeks, he also knew about his brother's attraction to the widow Anna and his long night with Betsy. Obviously, his brother had better luck with girls than he did.

"She gave me her number and address. I'll see. But this is none of your frekkin' business, Matt. Since you asked about Sophia, how about Eveline and her pregnancy. What about her?"

He saw Matt shake his head as he bowed his head, and said, "Damn it to hell, Chet. She seemed quiet and shy. I can't figure it out. I don't want to talk about it…. What a mess." He had been overwhelmed with his mom's death that he had forgotten about Eveline and her pregnancy—his last betrayal. Now, he wanted to forget about her, but he couldn't.

"I'm just sorry to see a young unwedded girl get pregnant. Life will be hard for her. By the way, you better

91

use protection. Just…a reminder," said Chet. He worried that his brother might not be careful.

"How about yourself?" quipped Matt back at him. He didn't like the accusation. Three days ago, he also didn't like it when his dad threw him up against the wall, asking him about Eveline's pregnancy. Of course, he hadn't known her that long. He had nothing to do with her pregnancy. *Hell, I never even got past first base with her. His dad was an asshole.*

"I'm always careful, buddy…just datin' around," he said as he thought of Anna, Betsy, and now, Sophia. Thinking of them, his mind became stirred up. Each of their situations were confusing. He'd better keep his mind on driving and getting back home safely.

"Looks, like I'll be datin' around, too," finished Matt. There were no more prospects for him right now. He'd have to throw that gum wrapper away that had Eveline's phone number on it. He'd been through a lot. First, he lost his long-time girlfriend, Daphne Neely from Scottsville this year. Going to college, she had really surprised him when she came home and gave him his class ring back before they moved. Daphne had been down at college dating and sleeping around. She had really changed.

After they had moved, Matt had met several high school girls (all cheerleaders) at a wedding reception at the Dark Horse Tavern. Ronnie had played his guitar and sang that night for the event. After the wedding reception, Ronnie, his friends, and the girls went up to Skyline to have a few beers, sitting around a warm fire. One of the girls, Suzie, slapped his face when he refused to let her give him a 'blow job.' Shocked, he didn't know what to think and didn't want anything to do with her after that. He had made an enemy with her.

One of the other cheerleaders, Eveline, had talked to him about Suzie. Smoothing over the incident, the two had talked and had ridden back into town, holding hands and kissing. For the first time since Daphne, he liked Eveline. She was a quiet, long curly black-haired girl with dark brown eyes whose parents owned Bert's Café in town. After getting his Red Devil, he had driven into town, met her parents and took her to the drug store for a soda. When he drove her home, they had kissed again. Later that week, he called her that night when everyone thought that he had been killed in the wreck of his Red Devil. That conversation ended with her telling him to forget about her. She said that she would be leaving to help her sick aunt in Colorado. Matt's dad came home later that night and accused him of getting her pregnant. Evidently, the gossip about her started in the doctor's office that day when she fainted. Of course, he hadn't known her that long, so her pregnancy hit him hard. He hadn't let himself think about it until Chet brought it up today.

Thinking back on all the conversations, he recalled that Ronnie had told him about Eveline. In January, the cheerleaders had gotten together with a few of Hadley High School's basketball players after a game one snowy night. Because of the heavy snowstorm, the coach and team stayed the night at a Riverside motel. The cheerleaders had gotten together with the boys at the motel. Since Eveline came home late that night, her parents had grounded her. When Matt met her, she couldn't go out on dates. Maybe, something happened that night. It didn't make sense.

Being shy and quiet, she didn't seem the kind who would sleep around. He'd like to talk to her and find out what had happened. She had been easy to talk to when they last met. He wondered how he could get in touch with her. Maybe, her parents would give him her phone number or even her address. He just needed to contact her, nothing else. So far this year, he'd had bad luck going out with girls. The ones he had dated had manipulated him. They had played him. Their betrayals left a cold feeling inside of him. His head started to throb.

As the two drove down the highway, they passed miles of snow-covered farmlands and pastures filled with livestock. They passed miles and miles of the snow-covered sagebrush. With the snow blowing, a small herd of antelope had bedded down in a gully away from the wind. This wet spring storm would be adding to the mountain peaks already heavy with the winter snowpack. The dark black storm clouds continued to follow them, rolling across the open prairies towards the canyons and mountains. Chet hoped that the snowstorm would stay on the eastern side of the state. Maybe the drive through the canyon and to the western side of the state would be clear. He could hope.

Behind them in Scottsville, the darkened clouds had brought the heavy snowstorm into the town, blanketing the roof tops, vehicles, and the people who had ventured out. At the Diamond V Ranch, Beth Fletcher's lonely grave with the freshly packed dirt sat among the ancient headstones surround by the grey old run-down wooden fence.

As scavengers, the two black ravens had returned to the swaying branches. Perched on a branch, they were ready to peck at the possible bugs, worms, or seeds dug up from the grave. They appeared as watchmen over the grave. The funeral flowers of white, red, blue, and yellow were arranged at the head of the dark mound. The two old trees swayed against the heavy snow that had descended and covered the little cemetery hill and everything on it.

****

As the two Fletcher pickups drove on towards the Riverside and through the Blue Ridge Canyon, the snowstorm had disappeared behind them, leaving only the wind blowing and clouds stirring above. The two brother Chet and Matt continue to drive around the sharp curves and through the dark stoned tunnels in the canyon. As they moved through the canyon, Matt recalled driving his Red Devil with Ronnie last weekend. His little sports car had hugged the road and had passed all the vehicles like they were standing still. Sadly, he thought of Ronnie and missing his funeral today in Riverside. Like his dad said, some things were beyond their control. His mind filled with thoughts of his mom's death and Ronnie's death the same day. Confused and upset, he took two deep breaths and looked ahead as they drove through the canyon.

Behind them, Clyde and Fred followed at a close distance. Both were quiet, thinking about the ranch and getting back to their daily lives. Glancing at his brother, Fred couldn't help but notice the small gold ring on his brother's little finger. Of course, he recognized it. Beth had worn it all her short life. *Who gave him the gold ring? Certainly not Nancy. Paul must have given it to him.* He felt miserable thinking of his brother and losing his wife. He hoped that Clyde could deal with her loss.

Finally, Clyde spoke up, "We have a lot of things to plan out at the ranch when we get home. It won't be the same without Beth." He sadly brushed away his grief; he needed to focus on the ranch.

Fred added, "Yeah. The boys will have to finish paintin' those pink colored bedrooms upstairs. I'm goin' to go up into the attic and bring down some of that furniture the Seversons left. Some need to be repaired, maybe even painted." He recalled that Chet and Beth had been painting those upstairs pink bedrooms that morning before she died. With her death, everything stood still at the ranch house, except feeding the herd and taking care of the horses and the one bull.

"What furniture?" Clyde asked. He recalled that his wife had gone up to the attic. He'd forgotten about the furniture that Hans said they left up there. He wasn't much in fiddling with the inside of the ranch house since his focus was outside --on the livestock.

"Well, there were two dressers, some room-sized floor rugs, old lamps, and some busted up chairs. Most will need some work. You know I'm good at fixin' things," Fred replied. Recalling that Beth had made some plans, he wanted to follow through. His nephews each had a bedroom now. He did look forward to finishing those dressers for them and repairing those chairs. The rugs were needed in the living room and maybe, the bedrooms. He'd figure where to put the lamps out later.

"As we come through Winston today, I want to stop at Bob's Feed Store. We need grain and dewormer for the horses and calves. Watch the market, Fred, see if we can sell a few steers after we fatten them up." He worried about the mortgage payments. That was one constant fear he had—missing a payment. He hadn't been keeping the books, so he didn't know where they sat in terms of the money.

"Sure. At the wake, I also spoke to John at the Bar W Ranch about gettin' a few older horses. You know that day we thought Matt was killed, he had ridden up to Stewart's Lake, checkin' it out for fishin'. He thought we could take fishermen up there this summer. Then, Chet said he wants to scout the high mountains for game and sheep. We're goin' to need some horses. John said he wanted to get rid of two and he knew that Shawn at the Muddy Creek Corrals wanted to sell two of his older horses. I did ask if they were healthy and in good shape. John asked what we wanted 'em for. When I told him for dudes, he said that they were healthy and that they'd do fine for just ridin'. What do you think, Clyde?"

"How much do they want for 'em?"

"Well, I traded for them—a steer for each of the two," Fred answered, hoping his brother would agree with the exchange.

"Ok. With that mortgage on our backs, we have to watch the cash. And those three small log cabins need to be used," Clyde said. Being so busy, he hadn't set up their ranch record book. He felt a little chill go down his back as he realized he didn't know exactly where they sat with the money. The last thing he wanted was to lose the ranch back to the bank.

"Good deal. When we get back, I'll give John a call. We can make plans from there."

As the two talked about the ranch some more, they saw Chet's pickup pull over at the rest stop at the end of the canyon. Parking behind him, the two brothers stepped out of the pickup. Clyde picked up the thermos while Fred grabbed the sack of sandwiches that Nancy had made them. Even though she had an ugly side to her, she was a good ranch woman.

The Fletchers sat down at one of the picnic tables, ate the ham sandwiches with a few cookies, and drank the coffee from the thermos. As they sat relaxing a few moments, Clyde told his sons he wanted to stop in Winston at Bob's Feed Store. They changed drivers for the last leg of their journey home, so Fred and Matt drove the rest of the way. The time grew late, but they managed to get to the feed store in Winston before it closed at six-thirty. The highway to Riverside seemed longer after their tedious day of driving. They all felt the ache in their backs and bones, driving across the state.

As they drove through the small mountain town of Riverside and towards their ranch, the Fletchers knew that they were returning to a house in disarray. They had just moved there; boxes were still sitting around, unpacked. They would still have to get fully moved in and settled. All of them knew they would have to make some major adjustments to their lives.

As the two pickups made the turn to their ranch, the sun had set long ago. The dark night had surrounded the ranch. Only a crescent moon hung in the dark sky with stars just starting to twinkle into the night sky. The bunk house next to the barn and corrals had a light on, shining out one of its windows. The ranch house stood dark except for the one porch light casting a light on the front door. Parking their pickups, the Fletchers headed into the ranch house. As Fred walked towards the bunk house, he said 'goodnight' to his brother and nephews.

Quietly, he opened the door to the bunk house as his dog Bandit barreled out. He squatted down to rough up, hug, and pet his good pal. "Hi, ol' buddy. Missed me?" Fred whispered to him. He stepped into the room and turned off the light. Walking over to his bunk bed, he sat down, pulled off his boots, and took off his clothes. Crawling under his covers, he laid down, closing his tired, burning eyes. He knew Dave was sleeping so he didn't say anything to him. For Fred, the exhaustion had taken its toll on his aging body while his brother was forty-three years old, he was pushing

97

forty-five. The years of rodeoing had made his back and knees stiffen up on a long drive like today.

Knowing that the owners would be coming home tonight, Dave Knox, their new ranch hand, had left a light on at the bunk house and on the porch. Earlier that day, he had attended Ronnie McClure's funeral in Riverside. The whole town had crowded into the small church as people also filled the front churchyard. All of the McClure's were there. Ronnie's older brother BJ (Bobby Jr.) his wife Sally and their two children (Roger and Pamela), and his sister Victoria (Torri) had driven home to attend the funeral. Dave had sat next to the McClure's throughout the church service and at the cemetery. Ronnie's mom Doris had clung to his arm and he supported her while she tried to keep her composure. It took both Bobby and him to help her walk to Ronnie's open grave at the cemetery. The solemn prayers didn't seem to soothe anyone's soul today.

His sad thoughts were of his friend Ronnie. They had become instant drinking buddies as well as good friends. Ronnie's parents had opened their home to him when his dad lost his ranch to the bank in Hadley. As a teen, he had come to Riverside to find work. They let him live with them while he finished school, working on week-ends and in the summer. He finally had saved enough to get himself a place. He would be forever indebted to them. Now, they would be devastated with their loss of their youngest son. Tonight, as Dave lay almost asleep on his bunk bed, he faintly heard the two Fletchers' pickups drive up the dirt road into the Battle Axe Ranch. He heard Fred come into the bunk house, undress, and crawl into his bed. He felt glad that the Fletchers had made it home safely.

Before falling asleep he thought of these last two days which had been busy for him and Hans. Together, they had fed the herd and had taken care of the horses in the stable. Hans had milked Sunny and had put the fresh milk in the fridge. He had checked on the bull Twister who had been pastured with the heifers. Hans had made sure that they were fed. Dave had to shoo away a cow moose from their haystack out behind their corral. The moose had wandered up from the willows by the creek to munch their hay.

That day, he had ridden on his brown stallion Bullet up into the timber above the ranch, getting more familiar with the area. Even though the early dawn was cold, he enjoyed riding through the lodge pole pines, looking for fresh tracks of predators. The cold air invigorated him as he breathed in the pine scent of the timber. The beautiful mountains and timber that surrounded this region kept him here. When living in Hadley, he loved that town and ranches there, too. After losing their ranch to the bank, he had bitter feelings about Hadley. But here, he had become acquainted with people he loved. He would miss Ronnie more than any other person he knew. He would like to settle down someday and maybe, get married if he could find the right girl. All the girls that he knew so far were immature. Recalling Ronnie's words when he fell in love with Gail, he wanted to find someone who didn't play around and tease. Finally, sleep came to him as he slowly drifted off.

****

After the long drive today, Chet and Matt walked into the ranch house. They both headed for their upstairs bedrooms. They were both tired and wanted to get to bed. The upstairs hallway still had the paint cans and the rollers with unpacked boxes in each of their bedrooms. They both said 'goodnight' to each other. They still left their bedroom doors opened, not able to sleep with their doors closed. After years of sleeping in one bedroom, the brothers still needed the connection with each other. While getting up or going to bed, they would speak to each other from the hall, the bathroom, or their bedrooms. With no thoughts to privacy, they never knew that someday that they would have to close those bedroom doors.

For Matt, he needed to take some aspirins for his throbbing headache. Going into the bathroom, he took four of them with a glass of water. He decided to take a hot shower to ease his aching head. Turning on the shower, the

99

room soon became filled with hot steam. After taking off his clothes, he stepped into the bathtub with the shower water spraying over him. He put his head right under the hot water. Breathing in the hot steam, the throbbing in his head started to ease. The water streamed down his body and eased his sore arms, legs, and back muscles. The long day of driving had been too much for him. Scrubbing himself with soap, he washed the events of the day off. His mind couldn't forget the horrendous events of the last two days— the wake and the funeral. *Would he ever be able to shake off those sad thoughts?* He had to focus on moving on, like his dad had said. For once, his dad had made sense to him. But he still needed to find some way to escape this ranching life that he had fought against since he was a teen. Turning off the shower, he stepped out and grabbed a towel and dried off. Picking up his clothes, he walked down the hall into his bedroom.

Crawling under the covers, he stretched out on his bed and closed his eyes. His guitar sat against the wall next to his bed. He needed to set some time aside to practice. His friends in the band wanted him to play the lead. He recalled that his wrecked Red Devil sat behind the barn. He'd get busy with that soon. His mind whirled with the possibilities.

His mom's death seemed unreal. Being more sensitive than the others in the family, he had felt her anguish and her sorrow. Year after year, he saw how her sad life had affected her. He wished that he had told her that he hadn't died, but he believed she was finally at peace. *Was he a heretic to think that she had found her own peace? God would strike him down if so.* His headache had eased enough for Matt to finally doze off and fall asleep.

In the other bedroom down the hall, Chet walked into his room. Taking off his clothes and crawling into his bed, he stretched out his sore body. After coming into the dark empty house, he recalled the last day that he had spent with his mom. They had painted the pink bedrooms light beige. Years before they moved here, there had been four Seversons' daughters who had these bedrooms—all now were married and had families. That day that they had painted the rooms, his mom had gotten one of her headaches from the paint fumes. She had gone downstairs to lie down. Around noon, he had fixed her a cup of tea and toast after he had finished painting the rooms that morning.

Tonight, he knew what it felt like to suffer the loss of a loved one. Living and working on the ranch, he had seen death up close with their livestock. But the heartache of losing his mom came tumbling down on him as he tried again to deal with his grief. He recalled last night with Sophia on Lookout Point. With her in his arms, she had comforted him when he opened his soul to her. At that moment when he felt vulnerable, she had told him he was a strong man. *Was he? Could he go on? Would he fall into the mire of grief like so many do? Like Anna had?* No, he wouldn't let grief take him down. His dad would want him to be strong. Sophia was right. His thoughts swirled about her as sleep took over his tired body and he finally dozed off.

Downstairs, Clyde walked into the kitchen and found the bottle of whiskey and a glass in the cupboard. He sat at the long table and poured himself a drink. As he sipped the dark amber liquid, he recalled these last few horrible days of the wake and the funeral. Finally, his eyes started to droop. Exhaustion started to take over him. After he stood up, he walked over and put the bottle of whiskey back into the cupboard. He walked down to their bedroom. Standing in the doorway to the dark bedroom, he knew he couldn't sleep in there tonight. He walked over to the mirrored dressing table, slipping his rings off, one by one. Opening Beth's little jewelry box, he placed their two wedding rings into the box. Looking at himself with his scruffy beard in the dresser's mirror, he glanced around the bedroom behind him. An eerie smell of death still hung in the air. Turning, he quickly took the faded red quilt from the end of their bed. Going into the living room, he eased himself down on the old couch. He pulled off his cowboy boots, but he was too tired to take off his clothes. Lying back, he closed his eyes as he covered himself with the quilt. *He realized that he was now a widower. His troubled marriage had finally ended.* For the second time in his life, he had faced death.

From the very start of their affair, he should have been wary of Beth and her beliefs and superstitions. In particular, he recalled one of the dates he had with Beth. The summer that they met, he had taken her to the carnival in Scottsville. After playing at a few game booths and eating some cotton candy, they had come to a fortune telling booth. She had become ecstatic about it, talking about how they could discover their fortunes.

With the name of Madame Julu written across the top, the eight-foot-tall dark wooden box had windows on three sides with a fake gypsy woman sitting in the booth with a tiny lamp in front to the right. The upper torso of the gypsy mannikin had a black veil over her long black hair, a red rose pinned above her ear, and a yellow satin blouse with several beaded necklaces.

After Beth had put her nickel in the slot, the gypsy eyes opened and rolled, her mouth opened and closed, and the lamp turned on. With her ringed fingers, the stiff gypsy hands had moved over a small glass orb in front of her. Faintly, violin gypsy music had emanated from the booth. After a few minutes, a piece of paper had come out of the slot below the window. Written on it told a person's fortune. The words were platitudes that would fit anyone's life: *love awaits, inner happiness, a charmed life,* and *an unexpected future.*

She had insisted that Clyde put a nickel into the slot to receive his fortune. He had laughed and played along, putting in his nickel. They had watched the gypsy move, had heard the music, and had picked up his fortune. These words were scribbled on his slip of paper: *charmed looks, strong views, life of joy,* and *surprising future.* She had read their fortunes out loud twice, connecting the words to their lives. With his heart filled of love, Clyde had barely listened to her words she spoke on and on. Her excitement had made him notice her beautiful, long brown hair and sparkling eyes, her lips he yearned to kiss, and her slender body he wanted to hold. He could care less about their fortunes.

102

He had considered the fortune telling worthless, as did others, and he had noticed that next to the booth sat a small trash can with all the torn-up fortunes of past customers. Amused, people had dropped in their nickels attracted by the gypsy's movements and the gypsy music. He had recognized that this fortune telling booth was simply another carnival game to make money—nickel after nickel. However, Beth had taken their fortunes seriously. Putting them in her small purse, she had kept them to contemplate and consider their meanings.

In their conversation about the fortunes, Clyde had found out that when Beth was younger, she and her girlfriends had played on the wooden board game called a Ouija board. It had become widespread among some. One popular magazine had portrayed a young couple playing the board on its cover. This uncanny game put two players opposite each other with their fingers on a heart-shaped piece that moved around the board after questions were asked. The board had the alphabet A to Z and the numbers one to zero written in the center and the words 'yes' and 'no' written in the corners. The word 'goodbye' was also written on the board. Asking questions, the heart-shaped piece would move around, giving the answers or spelling out the words. Most people had played it for fun, but some had believed that the board allowed dead spirits to speak to the living. There was a dark side to this board, for some had believed it to be real. Some felt it opened the 'gates of hell' and associated it with the devil.

When Beth had played the board with her girlfriends, she was one of those who thought that the board had opened the world of the dead spirits. For hours, she would talk about the kind of questions and answers that her and her friends had received from the other world. Clyde had listened to her speak anxiously about her past experiences with the board. She had said that she contacted the three dead children (Elisa, Rose, and William) from her family's ancestors. They told her that they were sad and lonely. She had treated the encounters as if they were real. Listening as she went on and on, Clyde would let her talk, thinking how

103

much he liked her. But she would get worked up. Then, he had to stop what he thought was nonsense. He would talk to her and quiet her fears, bringing her back into the real world. Even though he had tried to talk sense to her, she believed in all that weird spiritualism.

After marrying her, she would fall prey to her beliefs and delusions. She would be fine for a while, but then, with her headaches, she would get wild with ideas about the dead spirits. Over the years, those wild ideas never left her. And then when they had moved to their new ranch, the little children's notes had turned up stuffed in the windows; she had again become obsessed with the dead spirits. She had discovered those notes a couple of days before her suicide. *Along with the Matt's supposed death, did her wild beliefs cause her mind to snap?* He still could not understand fully why she took her life. They had so much to live for—their three sons and their new ranch. Clyde's mind whirled at all those dreadful memories of Beth's wild ideas.

He didn't believe in fortune telling or any mystery board, but he did believe in fate—a universal force outside of anyone's control. Even with a strong body and mind, he had incidents in his life where he had no control. At times in his life, a greater cosmic force had spun it out of control. He didn't like to admit it, but deep inside he knew that he had to be stronger and more committed.

He recalled as a young child, a classmate at school had a tarot deck of cards. Long ago, he had seen all the odd-looking figures and shapes as a girl flipped through the colorful cards, showing him the deck. He recalled noticing the card of Death, the thirteenth card, with a knight riding on a white horse. That's the one he remembered since he lived and worked on the ranches. The prancing white horse had a long beautiful mane and a body with strong hindquarters. Encased in grey armor, Death sat on the white horse with only the visor raised showing the skeletal face.

At the time, he discounted the belief in playing the cards to tell a person's future. However, that tarot card bearing Death meant something to him now. Fate had handed him that thirteenth card twice—once with his parents and now, with his wife. The great cosmic force had dealt him a hand that had put him to his knees. Tonight, the heartbreaking images of her death, the wake, and the funeral filled his mind, haunting him as he fell asleep.

Chapter 7

Old Friends

As usual, in the early dawn hours, their dad and uncle had fed the herd. As they returned, the young Fletchers were just getting up. After their mom had died, they had adjusted their lives at the Battle Axe Ranch. Clyde had ordered that the ranch work had to be done first before work on the ranch house. In order to get the housework settled, their dad had made his list of things 'to do.' He penciled it all down in a barely readable note, taped to the fridge. The list included the following: unpack boxes, paint, fix n' paint dressers, put down rugs, repair chairs, and fix lamps for rooms. To wash the dishes after a meal, the three boys had set up a rotation list, so each took his turn. Even Dave had added his name. After the funeral, most of their meals for a week were eaten in silence. That's when the reality would set in that Beth was missing. The kitchen had been her place on the ranch. But as the days and weeks past, the loss became less and less.

The brothers were told to do their own washing of their dirty clothes. In addition to the list of settling the house, there was another note taped to the fridge: plow, plant a garden. Following that was a list—potatoes, carrots, onions, cabbage, peas, and *what else?* Somebody had added radishes, cukes, and squash in wobbly handwritten letters. They needed to buy the seeds and get the vegetable garden planted this spring.

Chet and Matt had their own list to do upstairs: paint the pea-green bathroom that their mom hated and take down the pink ruffled curtains in their bedrooms. Matt had just wanted to throw some sheets over the windows, but Fred said 'no.' He came to their rescue when he brought down a few old faded curtains from the attic. He helped them wash, iron, and put them up in the bedrooms. Fred told them when they married and brought a woman into the house, then, she could change the curtains to her liking. He hinted about their possible marriage, but neither Chet nor Matt reacted to his suggestion. Their uncle had been looking forward to his own nephews or nieces. He felt that his nephews were both approaching that age where they had better find some girl to marry or they'd be like him with nobody.

Within a few weeks of coming home, the phone at the ranch rang one night. Clyde took the call. The caller was Matt's friend Bill. Clyde walked to the bottom of the stairs and hollered for his son to come down. As his son stood at the top of the stairs, he looked down at his dad.

Clyde said, "The phone call is for you. It's your friend Bill." Surprised, he quickly came down the stairs and headed to the phone in the living room.

"Hi, Bill. How are you?" said Matt, sitting down on the chair by the end table.

"Hi, ol' buddy. I'm fine. Have I got news for you! You better sit down for this," he replied.

"I am. What's up?" he asked, laughing to himself.

"Listen to this. My dad felt bad about Ronnie's death, so he phoned Bobby, you know McClure's dad. Anyhow, Bobby wants to sell Ronnie's '58 black Impala, the one he drove and raced. My dad asked around and found a guy who wants to buy the car. We're comin' to pick up the car."

"When are you comin'?" asked Matt. This was good news.

"Soon. Hey, and that's not all. We found an old '51 Chevy coupe for your Red Devil's engine. We were out at our salvage yard, and there it sat. The guy owed my dad some money, so we bartered for the ol' heap of junk. The frame is solid, Matt. It'll be lots of work. What do you think?"

"Hell, yeah. It sounds great to me. How much will it cost? " he asked. Bill told him they could settle later, but not to worry. He needed to make some arrangements, but maybe in a few days they would be driving over to Riverside. He explained that his dad wanted to help his friend Bobby out, so that they'd bring the old coupe with some of his tools to pull out that engine. Matt's mind filled with excitement as he thought of seeing Bill and of pulling the engine from his wrecked car. Finally he told Bill that he could stay in one of their small log cabins at the ranch. Bill said that would be fine since he thought that his dad would stay with his old friend Bobby. The two talked for a few more minutes, made further plans, and then said 'goodbye.'

After hearing him hang up, Clyde came into the living room and asked, "What's up, Matt?"

He filled him in and said that they were planning to pull the engine out of the Red Devil.

Nodding his head at his son, he said, "There's that the block and tackle in the utility shed... But don't forget your work here on the ranch. I depend on you to pull your weight... We're at a critical time here." He didn't like hearing about his son working on another car.

"What do you mean? Hell... I thought everythin' was goin' along fine. Tom's here and you've hired Dave," said Matt, worried.

"Matt, we have to make the mortgage payments to the bank. I may not be able to pay you boys full wages for a few months like I planned. My cash is gettin' low with nothin' comin' in at this time. I'm not sure where we stand today, since I haven't been able to set up the books," he said. He didn't like telling him about his situation, but they needed to be careful with their money.

"What about the books? Why didn't you say somethin' before now?"

"I'm tellin' you now, ain't I?... Don't be spendin' all your money on a car. It ain't worth it, son," answered Clyde. He ignored his dad's comment since he knew he had saved his money from the sale of the wolf pelt and the gig he had played. The fact that his dad said that his cash was low worried him.

"Do you need help with the books, dad?" asked Matt. This sounded serious.

"Oh, it's nothin'...Hell, I've just been too busy," he said, making light of the issue.

"I thought that Fred took care of the books," Matt replied. He wanted to know more about the record book.

"No, I've always done the bills. Fred keeps track of the markets, so we'll know what time is best to sell. Paying bills for our big ranch is different than our old place." This task was bigger than Clyde.

"Sounds like we need a family meetin' to help decide this," suggested Matt. He knew he didn't want any part of recording keeping for the ranch, but Chet or Tom could probably handle it.

"Damn it, maybe…at breakfast we can talk. Let me think on it. Okay, son?"

"It's late. We'll talk tomorrow. I'm headin' for bed. Good nite, dad," he said as he turned and left the living room, going upstairs to his bedroom. What he had just discussed with his dad greatly disturbed him. He couldn't imagine what would happen if they lost this ranch—the Battle Axe Ranch. Recalling Dave's family ranch in Hadley, he knew that families did lose their ranches to the banks. He had applied for a job at the lumber mill after talking with Dave who had worked at the mill. Without saying anything to anyone, he had taken a special license test. He hoped to drive a logging truck this summer. He was waiting to hear from them. Maybe, if he got that job, he could give his dad most of his wages, keeping enough to restore his car. His wages might help them out with the ranch.

As he walked down the hall, he noticed that both his brothers were asleep in their bedrooms, snoring. He went into his bedroom and took off his boots and clothes. With his head throbbing, he crawled into his bed, covering up. As he laid there, his mind filled with all the pressing issues: his wrecked car, Bill coming, the ranch, being short of cash, the mortgage payment, getting a job. All these had him awake deep into the night. His devastating headache kept getting worse.

Getting up, he went down to the bathroom to get some aspirin. As he stood in front on the mirror, he took the four aspirins with a glass of water. He swallowed the pills thinking of his mom's addiction and death. The images of her dead vacant eyes had haunted him ever since that night she had died. He put both of his hands on the sides of the bathroom sink, bowing his head as his heart flooded with sorrow and grief. Time stood still as he thought of his loving mom and the loss that he would forever feel at moments like this.

Shaking his head, he needed to forget that and focus on tonight with the good news that Bill was coming in a couple of days. Again, here was Bill, helping him out when he thought the world had handed him a bad deal. He had to fix a set of wheels for himself with the Red Devil's engine. He walked back to his bedroom, crawled under the covers, and closed his eyes. With his mind in turmoil, Matt finally fell asleep a few hours after midnight.

****

A few days later, one clear cold morning, Bill and his dad Vic drove the long miles from Scottsville to Riverside with a flatbed truck carrying a dull powder blue '51 Chevy coupe. After arriving in the small mountain town, Bill and his dad spent the night at his best friend Bobby McClure's house.

Years ago as young teenagers, Vic and Bobby were classmates in high school. With the same interests in cars, they had become instant friends. Both had dreams of running their own garages and after graduation, they each had gone to a mechanic school. They both had married their high school sweethearts—Vic married his Cathy and Bobby married his Doris. As years past, they had settled in different towns and started their own small businesses but had kept in touch. When they were first married, the two would get together for vacations and go fishing or hunting. As each of their businesses grew, they had found less and less time to get together. Hearing of his friend's son's death, Vic had wanted to help his old friend. After calling and talking to him, Vic found out that Bobby had wanted to sell his son's Impala. Vic had found a buyer in Scottsville. They were bringing an old '51 Chevy coupe for Bill's friend Matt. Bill and his dad had made the long trip with the big flatbed truck. They were able to take care of both of their close friends with this trip to Riverside.

110

After arriving at Bobby's house, Vic and his son had settled in for the night. Catching up with each other's lives, they stayed up late into the night as old friends do. Vic had brought a bottle of Scottish whiskey with him and the two had shared a few shots of the whiskey.

They spent some tough moments discussing Ronnie's death. Vic asked how they were handling it. Bobby admitted that his wife Doris had been devastated with their son's death, but with the support of their other son and daughter, she was accepting his death as time went by. His older son BJ, a man of twenty-four, had decided to move back to help his dad run the garage. They were making plans to move to Riverside soon. With his son and his family there, Doris would have the two grandchildren, Roger, five, and Pamela, three, to focus on. Their youngest daughter, Torri, a nineteen-year-old, had also come back to live with her parents after the funeral. With their daughter living here, Bobby knew that that would further ease his wife's grief over Ronnie's death.

Thinking of his son's death, Bobby said, "I just don't know what my son was thinkin'...tryin' to outrun that highway patrol officer. We've all been ticketed for speedin'. Then, wreckin' it on Grady's Hill where everyone knows that curve is dangerous. I just don't understand why." He still hadn't figured out why his son tried to outrun the officer. His death still hung deep in his soul.

"Most likely, he wasn't thinkin'. Just reactin'. He must have panicked," replied Vic, trying to comfort his friend's sorrow.

Over the years of driving their own cars, they both had their own close brushes with the law. Both knew that cars could be dangerous if a driver didn't handle his car with respect. Even though a driver would be careful, accidents did happen—a blown tire or a bad spot on the road.

Sitting with his dad and friend with his arm in a cast and his broken ribs, Bill spoke about his recent accident. Trying to push his coupe beyond its limit, he said that speed had caused him to wreck his green coupe. He quickly lost control and rolled his car. All thought that Bill was fortunate to escape with only broken bones and a concussion as it was nearly a fatal accident.

Thinking again of his son, Bobby added, "Ronnie tended to drive too fast; he always wanted to drag race his Impala. I warned him to stop, but he wouldn't listen. Many times when he found someone to challenge him, he'd be out late at night drag racin' that car. I don't want to see that car drivin' around Riverside and be reminded of my son."

"I understand, Bobby. It's tough enough without seein' his car," Vic said.

"I'm just glad you found a buyer for his car, Vic. Thanks for comin' here and takin' it back," said Bobby. Time had slipped by the men as they talked.

Later that night, Bobby's daughter Torri came home from her waitress job at Bert's Café. Coming into the kitchen, she said 'hi' to everyone. They were reacquainted with each other.

"Why are you so late, Torri? Is Bert payin' you extra to stay this late?" asked her dad, looking at the clock on the kitchen wall.

"Kay had me work tonight's shift. Bert drove over to Hadley for a couple of days. I'm working an extra shift tomorrow, too. It's fine. Yes, dad, they're payin' me extra. Besides, I'm makin' good tips. You worry too much," said Torri as she gave her dad a quick kiss on the cheek. Bobby pulled her in for an affectionate hug. He looked up at her and said, "Luv you, sunshine."

She replied, "Luv you, too. Nighty night." She turned and left the kitchen.

As Bill watched her go, he recalled Torri from years ago. Bobby had named his daughter after his friend, Victor. He had hoped for another boy, but it turned out to be a girl who was named Victoria –Torri for short. Tonight, her long reddish-brown hair had been pulled up into a ponytail. She had bright hazel eyes with an hour-glass figure.

Bill had only met Ronnie's sister once before. But he remembered her as a smart-mouthed, freckled skinny girl who teased Ronnie about working on cars. Ronnie told him that she called him a 'grease monkey' and would dance

112

around like a monkey, laughing at him. Her brother would chase her away, but one time, catching her, smeared grease from his fingers all over her face. He told her that she was the 'grease monkey' now. Their dad had made Ronnie clean the gas station and garage for two weeks for treating his little sister that way. Tonight, she didn't look like that little sister he remembered. She had grown up into a good-looking girl who had turned his head.

After leaving the kitchen, Torri headed for her bedroom. She recalled Bill, her brother's friend, who visited here. She didn't like the way he looked at her tonight, like a wolf on the hunt. Besides, he wasn't her type. She really didn't know what type she liked, but he wasn't it. Even though her family owned the garage and her dad and older brothers were mechanics, she didn't want anything to do with that lifestyle. And Bill was a mechanic. Noticing that his arm still in a cast reminded her of his near fatal accident. That's what guys with cars did—drove fast, dragged, and wrecked. *No, thank you.*

She had left after high school and tried college just to get away from this small town and their gas station. But going to college, she had made some bad mistakes. She had dated and partied too much and didn't study enough. She had failed two of her classes, and after trying again one more semester, she had realized that she had fallen behind. She felt bad about spending her parents' money, but they didn't seem to mind. They were glad that she had at least tried. Then, with Ronnie's sudden death, Torri wanted to come home to help her parents get through this. After moving back, she had picked up a temporary waitress job at Bert's Café right away. She didn't know what she wanted to do in life, yet. But Bill was certainly someone she wanted to avoid.

After Torri left, the three men continued to talk and drink. Finally, tired from the long drive, Bill left the two men talking and went into the front room to sleep on the couch. After he left, the two friends talked about the Red Devil. Bobby also knew that his son had liked Matt's Red

Devil. He had told his dad that he wanted a Corvette for his next car.

Recalling the times he saw the car, Vic said, "I remember that red sports car that Matt drove around in Scottsville. His uncle Fred gave him the keys to it the day he graduated from high school. It had a fuel-injected engine in it. One fast car to be sure. Bill and Matt worked on that car several times in my garage." His son Bill had loved that red sports car.

"Unfortunately, my son was too impressed with that car," replied Bobby, shaking his head in sorrow. The conversation turned to another recent death.

"Say, we heard that the Fletcher's mom died. Do you know anythin' about it? They had the funeral last week at the Diamond V Ranch. No one at home knows what happened. Do you know?" asked Vic. Since they would be going out to Matt's family's ranch, he wanted to know a little more about the Fletchers' situation. *With their recent death, how would they feel?*

"No one here in town knows much, except someone said she was sickly. A few days before she died, they had come into town, shoppin' at the Mercantile and havin' lunch at Bert's. Someone said they bought paint that day. A few who saw her said that she looked thin and pale. Some figured that her poor health did her in," answered Bobby. The gossip about Beth Fletcher was still circulating.

Vic explained, "You know that the Fletcher brothers grew up with nothin' and were orphaned as teenagers. When Clyde married Beth, they moved out to her family's Diamond V. The mother-in-law never liked him, makin' it hard for him to stay and work their ranch. Everyone in town knows the Vanovers; they are hard people to like. Finally, Clyde had had enough and went to work for the coal mine. That's how he had money to buy a ranch. For them to buy a ranch over here was quite a surprise. Everyone thought that they'd buy a ranch near her folks. The Fletchers are good, hard workin' men. But no one in Scottsville knows how the wife died, either. Even as a young girl, she had been unhealthy, though." The mystery of her death remained.

114

"That's interestin'. The town people here have turned against them. They sound like decent men; they don't deserve the vicious gossip. I'll mention this to Doris, and maybe, let some people know. It's hard to change opinions after people get into their heads about somethin' like this," Bobby said. He had heard the gossip and didn't like it, but he had kept quiet. The news that the brothers were orphaned surprised him. He too didn't think they deserved the gossip. Tragedy hit everyone at one time or another. What people did after a tragedy is what counted.

The two men shook off their talk of death and moved to talk about pulling the engine out of the Red Devil. They discussed what needed to be done and what adjustments needed to be made. Bobby said he might drive out to the ranch and help; he'd liked a few days away from the station. Vic told him that he could use all the help he could get since his son Bill wouldn't be much help. The two decided they'd better get some rest, so they said 'goodnight' and went to bed.

Chapter 8

Out of the Ashes

Early the next morning, the sunshine had spread across the crystal-clear blue sky. The sharp snow-packed peaks surrounded the small mountain town and ranches which were nestled in the little valleys with rivers and streams snaking their way through the high mountain canyons. The chilly air warmed as the sun came up from behind the Rockies. The feel of the early spring filled the air, sending birds into nest building. The red-breasted robins were up first, loudly chirping in the early dawn. After sunrise, the tiny sparrows flew around tweeting as they carried twigs and grass in their beaks to make their round nests tucked in small openings. The time of renewal and rebirth came nearer each morning as time approached the spring months.

Before the big flatbed truck drove into the ranch that morning, the Fletchers were busy with their ranch work. The two brothers and Dave had been out feeding the herd. Twister and the heifers were fed with some hay and grain.

Fred had ridden up into the dark timber to look for signs of any predators roaming in the area above their herd. At this time, the end of March, the male grizzlies would be coming out of hibernation. And later, in April or May, the female grizzlies would emerge. He noticed many tracks near a spring. Fred found it hard to distinguish the tracks, but he did see one clear paw with claws which looked like a bear. Dismounting, he looked closer at the print. He would have to keep his eyes out and mention this to everyone. Mounting and continuing, he rode back down through the tall lodge pole pines, around downed logs, the underbrush, and the rocks. As the sunshine spread across the blue sky, the light shown through the tall pines, leaving columns of light and dark in the timber. The fresh smell of the pines filled the air. With the dark earth covered in pine needles and new green grass, a heavy moist smell came from the ground. Small birds and animals of the forest were coming

116

out of their slumber, making the forest come alive. Fred rode through the pines and made a wide circle.

Riding back down to the pasture and the hay wagon, the two brothers and Dave headed back to the ranch. They took care of their horses before going into breakfast. Clyde with Dave's help had unhitched the draft horse Jack. Walking him into the stable, Dave fed, watered, and brushed Jack down. Fred dismounted his chestnut horse Captain. He unsaddled him, taking off the bridle, and putting on a rope halter. Walking him into the stable, he fed, watered, and brushed his horse down.

The men checked the horses' hooves for debris which would jam up inside of the horseshoes. They inspected the horseshoes; sometimes, loose nails would push up from the hooves. The horseshoes needed to be replaced about every couple of months. Each man learned to keep an eye on his own horse's hooves for any problems. No cowboy wanted his horse to come up lame for lack of attention. Clyde trained his sons to pay close attention to their horses' hooves. If they didn't, they'd be walking instead of riding. He had no tolerance for an inattentive cowboy for his horse.

Before breakfast, Tom had milked the cow Sunny and had separated it on the back porch to the kitchen. He noticed that they had collected a lot of cream in the fridge. Living at the Diamond V all those years, he recalled his Grandma Nancy making it into butter. He'd have to talk to his uncle or dad about how to churn the cream. He didn't want to waste it. They drank up the milk just fine; maybe, they could use up the sweet, thick cream in their coffee.

Matt and Chet had been up, grooming their horses Diablo and Rusty. They needed to be fed, watered, and brushed down. After milking, Tom walked back out to the stable and took care of his grey stallion Brute. All the men had returned to the big kitchen, had fixed, and had eaten their breakfast.

They were drinking their second cup of coffee when the flatbed truck came down the dirt road to the ranch. Hearing a truck coming towards the ranch, Matt walked out of the house and stood on the porch, waving at his friend Bill in

the big truck. Tom followed his brother out with the dogs
Blue and Bandit. Walking down the steps, he told Bill's dad
to drive his flatbed truck over to their utility shed beyond
their corrals. The big truck rolled to a stop outside of the
shed. The men stepped down and said 'hello.' Excited to see
his friend, Matt gave Bill a handshake with a clasp of the
shoulder. The three Fletchers and Dave followed the two
out of the ranch house. They said their greetings. The two
dogs were happy to see the company. They ran around
sniffing the new men and the truck. Getting a few pats on
the head, the dogs' tails were wagging back and forth.

Looking at Bill's right arm in a plaster of Paris cast,
Dave smiled and asked, "When does the cast come off,
Bill?" The bulky white cast had names scribbled all over it,
hearts drawn with names inside, and little stick men
sketched in colors of black, blue, pink, and red—typical of
friends and family wishing him well.

Bill replied, "Not soon enough…in about two weeks."
Matt looked at his friend and noticed that his bruises had
disappeared, so he didn't look battered up. He walked stiffly
since his ribs were still wrapped tightly around his
midsection.

As the men looked up at the '51 Chevy faded powder
blue coupe on the flatbed, Fred said, "Hey, that's a good
lookin' car there."

Vic told how he had worked out a deal for it at the
salvage yard. They looked it over, walking around the
flatbed. The powder blue coupe had two-doors, a split
windshield, and a chrome front grill. Vic said the coupe had
the original inline 6-cylinder engine. The body had some
small dents around the handle and on the door, and the back
bumper had a small dent in the middle. Otherwise, the blue
coupe looked good.

Unable to contain his excitement, Matt jumped up on the
flatbed to open the driver's door. It was locked. Chuckling
at him, Vic pulled the keys out of his pocket and tossed
them up to see his excited face. He smiled *he's just like a
youngster with a new toy.* Looking inside, Matt saw a few
worn holes in the cloth bench, a faded metal dashboard with

a radio, and a clock above the radio imbedded in the dash. Dust layered everything inside. The steering wheel had a column stick shift. He'd have to get blankets to cover the bench seats, front and back. But other than a lot of scrubbing and cleaning, the coupe looked great to him. Afterwards, he jumped down from the bed.

"What do I owe you for this, Mr. Dickerson?" Matt asked. He knew he had saved his money and wanted to pay whatever he could.

"Listen, you're goin' to need your cash to get this car runnin', so I don't want anythin' for it," answered Vic. He felt awkward talking about money for this old car. As Clyde listened, he knew that he hadn't paid Matt his ranch salary, so he would give Vic his son's pay.

The men stood around and talked for a few minutes, and then, Clyde said they needed to get to work on the ranch. The three Fletchers and Dave left to drag their pastures to spread out the horse and cow manure from the stable and fields. They were also going to check out the irrigation ditches to see what condition they were in. Cleaning out the ditches would have to be arranged for another day, for it would take a long day or two to clear all the ditches around this big ranch.

Turning, Matt signaled for the other men to follow him. He took them around the back of the barn and showed them where his wrecked Red Devil sat. Protecting it from the weather, he had thrown a tarp over the broken-down car. He pulled off the tarp. Several times since the car had been towed here, he had walked out to look at it sadly. The worthless red fiberglass body looked crumpled and broken apart. The crushed front door lay beside the wrecked car, torn off during the accident. Until Bill had suggested taking out the engine, Matt thought his car was ready for the junk yard.

Today, when Bobby saw the wrecked car, the sight took his breath away. This wasn't the first time he had seen it, but seeing it again reminded him of his son's death. Vic looked at his old friend's shocked face and understood. They stood silently looking at the wreck.

119

That afternoon a week or so ago came rushing back to Bobby as he recalled the day his son died. He had been home with his wife Doris around noon talking on the phone to his oldest son BJ. After having dizzy spells a month ago, he had gone to Dr. Carter and found out that he had a heart problem. The doctor told him he had to slow down and to stop working long hours at the station. If he didn't, he could have a heart attack. Prescribing some medication, the doctor told him to get more rest.

He and his wife had decided to call their oldest son BJ that day and presented him with the idea of taking over the gas station and garage. His older son was more level-headed than his young son Ronnie who had a musical interest in his guitar and singing. BJ said he and his wife Sally would have to discuss it, but he knew he wanted to help his dad and take over their business as well as move back to Riverside.

When Bobby returned to the station that day, one of Ronnie's friend, George, was manning the station. He asked where his son was, and George told him he took a car out for a test drive. Normally, he would have asked for more details, but that day his mind was on BJ and his phone call. Anxious to leave, George had worked at the Johnson Ranch. He had left right after Bobby showed up. When the commotion about an accident circulated in town, Bobby didn't think anything of it until Sheriff Tom showed up. Now, this morning, shaking his head, Bobby pushed down his heartbreaking thoughts of that day. He needed to move on. Salvaging the engine had been his and Vic's goal for the day. He turned his mind to the job at hand.

Vic gently touched his friend on the back as they stepped towards the wreck. He knew by his friend's face that he still mourned for his son Ronnie. Vic recalled how he felt when he saw his son Bill's wrecked green coupe a couple of weeks ago. It took all he had to hold himself together. Bobby's reaction appeared to be the same as his. Standing beside him, he glanced into Bobby's water filled eyes and nodded. He whispered to him, "Hang in there, man. Let's look at the engine." The two walked over to the wreck, pulled the latch on the hood, and lifted up the smashed hood of the Red Devil.

Looking under the hood, the men checked out the V-8 Chevy orange engine which still looked like a beauty to them. They thought that the transmission could be pulled out with the engine. But they knew that the rear end would be too small for the coupe.

Finally, Vic reached in, pushed in the clutch, and put the gear into neutral. They pushed hard to move the wrecked Red Devil, but it didn't budge. Matt suggested pulling it with their old tractor. They agreed. Driving the old noisy tractor from their utility shed over and hitching it up, Matt pulled the wreck slowly into the shed. Afterwards, he parked the old tractor outside.

In the shed, there already was a block and tackle fixed to an overhead steel beam. To get to the transmission, Vic said they'd need to jack the car up. He asked the young men to get a jack and set the car up on wooden blocks. Matt and Tom hustled around, jacked it up, and set it on four blocks of wood.

Vic and Bobby grabbed their toolboxes from the cab of the flatbed truck. Putting them on the work bench along one wall of the shed, the two older men rolled up their sleeves and started. They first took off the hood. Since both were mechanics, they worked together. While Bobby worked above, Vic crawled under the car and worked. They knew how to proceed without much words: with an occasional 'hand me,' 'wait a minute,' and 'I got this.' The sound of men working with the tools filled the air. Matt and Tom stood by and watched. They were amazed at the magic that these two men seemed to have. With his right arm still in a cast, Bill had found a stool to sit on and watched from there. After a while, they were ready to strip out the engine and transmission.

Pulling the chain down from the block and tackle, the men secured it around the V-8. Working the chains, the orange engine and transmission emerged out of the old wreck and hung as the shed creaked at the extra weight. Matt and Tom worked the jacks to lower the car off the wooden blocks. They hooked the Red Devil again to the old tractor and pulled it out from under the suspended Chevy orange engine.

With the hood gone and the gaping hole in the front end, the Red Devil looked raped of its insides. Matt sadly looked at his car. Vic asked if they could use that tarp so they could set the engine down while they got the coupe off the flatbed. Matt went back behind the barn and picked up the tarp that had covered his Red Devil. Before taking it into the shed, he shook it out a couple of times. Outside, a cloud of dark dirt, twigs, and leaves caught in the air and settled on the ground as he coughed and sneezed from the dust. In the shed, he spread it down under the suspended engine. Bobby lowered it on the tarp. Vic went over to the Red Devil. Without a front door, he crawled into the front bucket seat and stripped out the 4-speed gear shift on the floor.

Satisfied, they turned their attention to the powdered blue coupe sitting on the flatbed truck outside. Vic unstrapped the two metal ramps that he had used to load the coupe. One by one, the men lined up the metal ramps at the back end of the truck bed. Since the car had been tied down with straps, the men untied those straps to free it. Under the front bumper, a chain attached to a manual come-along on the truck bed that held the car secure. Vic looked at Matt and told him to jump up and put the car in neutral. Without hesitation, he did. Then, as Vic turned the ratchet, the chain loosened, and the blue coupe was free to be pushed to the end of the truck bed. Easing the car down the metal ramps, Vic kept ratcheting as the car eased off the back end of the truck bed. The two metal ramps creaked with the weight of the heavy coupe rolling down. Finally, the car rested on the ground. The men unhooked the chain. To guide the car, Bobby got in and sat in the driver's seat as the other men pushed the car. Turned half around to watch the rear end, he maneuvered the steering wheel and guided the coupe into the shed. The men were ready for the next step in their work today. They had to strip out the old Chevy's blue-grey 6-cylinder engine and transmission.

But before they did, Bill sitting on the stool suggested they break for lunch. Smiling at each other, Bobby and Vic just shook their heads, just like the young men to think of their stomachs. Both were enjoying the work too much to leave and eat. They wanted to keep going. Matt suggested that he'd fix some sandwiches and bring them out to the barn. Bill joined him and Tom as the two left. After they had left, the two men took a short cigarette break. Walking around and looking at the blue car, they smoked and talked. After a few minutes, they both began working again.

Coming onto the back porch, the young men washed up in the big sink. In the kitchen, Tom went to the fridge and pulled out the fixings for sandwiches. Matt went over to the stove to brew some coffee. With only his left hand free, Bill asked what he could do. Both told him to get the bread in the breadbox sitting on the kitchen counter. Matt walked over to the fridge and pulled out a half jar of pickles. The three worked together to fix the bologna sandwiches with mayonnaise, mustard, and pickles. The coffee began to boil, so Tom went to the pantry to get the thermos for the coffee. Wrapping up the sandwiches in waxed paper, Matt put them into a paper sack along with a package of cookies. After adding some rich, sweet cream, Tom poured the coffee into the thermos, grabbing five tin cups from the cupboard. With lunch, the cups, and a thermos in hand, the three headed back to the utility shed.

As they were walking, Matt asked Bill, "I've got to get rid of the Red Devil's wrecked body and the old coupe's engine. Would your dad load and take them to our junk yard north of town? What do you think?" For days, his dad had been after him to get rid of that wrecked red car ever since the tow truck had brought it to the ranch. And he knew his dad wouldn't want an old engine sitting around either. His dad had insisted on a clean looking ranch without a lot of junk sitting around. After buying the ranch, he told his sons that he had wanted to keep the place as clean as the Seversons had maintained it over the years. Wanting to paint the older buildings, he would never let the buildings looked run down like his father-in-law's ranch.

"Sure. I'll ask him. What are you goin' to call your new wheels?" asked Bill.

"I hadn't thought about that," he replied. His friend always came up with new ideas.

"How about the 'Blue Devil?'" Tom suggested. He had been excited for his brother and had learned a lot today just watching the two mechanics work.

"How about ... the Demon?" suggested Matt. He wanted a different name for this car.

"Yes...yes...the Blue Demon...which rises out of the ashes of the utterly destroyed Red Devil. Doesn't that sound like a great legacy for your wrecked car?" Bill said, playfully. He slapped his friend's back as they walked towards the shed with the sack of lunch, the cups, and the thermos.

"I like the sound of that. Hey, I don't know how I'm goin' to repay your dad for doin' this," he replied, looking at Bill.

"Forget it. First, my dad wanted to help Bobby sell the Impala. And I wanted to help you. You helped me with the band when I was laid up. Besides, not everyone wants those old outdated cars. Most are into buyin' the newer models," Bill said to him quietly. Matt would never know how much he appreciated him helping with the gig. Bill wanted to keep the band together. Without his help, the band could have easily gone their separate ways. Now, with a second gig, he was stepping in again. Getting him another set of wheels was Bill's way of repaying Matt for his generous help.

The three walked towards the shed. As they entered, Vic and Bobby were deep into the blue coupe. Wiping the grease off their hands with rags, the two walked over to the bench. After setting down the lunch sack, the men dug in and took out the sandwiches. Matt opened the package of cookies. Tom poured each of them a cup of coffee. As the men ate and drank, they spoke about how everything was going as planned.

Finishing, the two men wanted to jack up the coupe for more 'elbow room' to work underneath the car. Since the coupe had a heavier body, Vic wanted a second wood block on each side. Matt and Tom jacked up the car and added wood blocks as he instructed. The men then began to position the block and tackle over the blue coupe. They had taken off the hood, so the blue-grey engine and transmission slipped out of the coupe with no problems. With the chain wrapped under it, they pulled out the old 6-cylinder blue-grey engine away from the coupe. Afterwards, they eased the engine onto the floor.

Sliding the block and tackle over to the V-8 engine sitting on the tarp, they put the chain around it. Pulling it up again, they slid the orange engine over to the blue coupe. The men eased it slowly into the car. The two were a perfect fit, sliding it in like a hand into a glove. Vic knew that a Chevy engine into a Chevy body always worked out the best. There wouldn't be as many problems. That's another reason he wanted the coupe from the salvage yard. He had spent some time comparing the two cars—engine sizes and such—from the auto manuals.

Again, working in silence, the two mechanics modified the engine mounts with a welder sitting in the utility shed. They soon bolted in the engine. The sounds of metal and socket wrenches turning filled the air. Vic crawled under the car and worked on disconnecting the rear end on the old coupe. They had to replace the pumpkin to fit the bigger engine. He also disengaged the links to the column gears on the old coupe. Taking a narrow saw from his toolbox, he cut a hole in the floor of the coupe for the gear plate. After a lot of muscle and sweat, the Red Devil's orange engine and transmission were in the Blue Demon.

As all stood back to look at the coupe, the men congratulated themselves on their hard work. About that time, the three other Fletchers—Clyde, Fred, Chet along with Dave---came into the shed to see how things were going. They were impressed with what they saw as they looked at the engine and car. Clyde then invited everyone over to the ranch house for a drink.

Walking over to the ranch house's back porch, Vic said, "You know, Matt. There's lots more that has to be done before you can drive it."

125

"Yeah, Bill did mention that he's stayin' for a while to help me work on the car," he said.

"I'll make a list of the work that's left. Take your time. Don't get in a rush," replied Vic.

Everyone stopped on the back porch as each took his turn to wash up. Vic and Bobby waited to the last since their hands and arms were the blackest with grease and oil from the engine and transmission. They soaped up. Next to the faucet sat a little brush to scrub off heavy dirt and grime. They both took turns scrubbing with that little brush: up and down their forearms, along the back of their hands, around the fingers and thumbs, and on top of the fingernails. But under their fingernails would take a small pocketknife to clean out the grimy dirt. After pat drying their hands, they walked into the big kitchen and sat down at the big kitchen table.

Clyde had taken down some glasses from the cupboard. From the whiskey bottle, he poured the dark amber liquid into each glass. Looking around at all the guys sitting at the table, he realized this was an exceptional day—a very special day. Along with his sons, Vic and Bobby had done a remarkable job of salvaging the wreck. At the back of each of the men's mind was the grief that they had faced a week ago—the death of a son and the death of a wife and a mom. But here they were, working today to make something good out of all that death and chaos. The men had been joined in their tragedies. Life had a way of pulling grieving people forward, ready or not.

Deep in thought, Clyde raised his glass and said, "Thanks, for today." Each man drank down his whiskey. Pouring another round from the bottle, he raised his glass again and said, "Here's to good friends." Again, each drank down his glass of the dark amber liquid.

Nodding, Vic added, "We've just got started. There's lots more to be done."

"Hell, it's a damn good start," said Fred. He knew their work had just started, but they had accomplished a lot in one day. Matt should be quite excited to get the engine out of his wrecked car.

126

"Son, we're goin' to wrap it up for today. We'll be back tomorrow. We'll load the ol' wreck and the coupe's engine before we leave today. After tomorrow, I'm headin' back home. Bill wants to stay the week if that's all right with you," said Vic, looking at Clyde and Fred.

"No problem. He's welcomed to stay," said Fred with Clyde nodding in agreement.

"Listen, we're goin' to get busy. We need to put new horseshoes on our string of horses," Clyde stood up. He pulled out his wallet and said, "I know we can't pay you for the work you've done, but here's a little maybe to cover your gas, drivin' all the way over here from Scottsville." This was Matt's pay for the month.

"Hell, man. That's not necessary," said Vic. He didn't want to take the money, but Clyde put it down on the table and pushed it towards him. Nodding at Vic and Bobby, he turned and with his brother, left the big kitchen and headed out to the corrals. Chet stood up, picked up their three empty glasses, and put them in the sink, leaving the whiskey bottle on the long table.

"I'm headed out, too. It's been nice havin' you all here. Have another drink or two if you want," Chet said. He left the big kitchen and walked out of the back-porched door towards the corrals to help his uncle and dad with the horseshoeing. These were the four horses that his uncle had traded for with the two steers. They would be using those horses to take guests up fishing or hunting. They needed to bring in some income for the ranch.

After coming back from the funeral at breakfast one morning, their dad had told his sons about the ranch's record book. The past owner Hans had told them how to set it up, but Clyde had only blank pages in his record book with the different categories written at the top. Feeling bad, he said he just didn't have the time to keep the records. Looking at the record book, his sons saw the bills and purchase tickets crammed and tucked in it, scattered throughout the blank pages. All three sons looked at their dad in surprise and confusion. After discussing the issue, Chet finally offered to take over and keep the records. Tom said he'd help too since he was interested in helping any way he could. It was decided that Chet would take over keeping the record books with Tom double checking his figures. It didn't hurt having two working the books—as a back-up plan.

Chet spent the next few late nights sitting at their small desk in their office, sorting the bills, recording the purchases, and adding and subtracting the figures. The blank columns in the record book started to fill up. After a week, he knew they needed to bring in some money to help pay for the mortgage later. Taking guests fishing in the summer and taking hunters in the fall, he figured that would help them until they could sell some of their steers in the late fall. But Chet also realized that they might need more income. He would gladly go find work, but he knew that his uncle would be headed out to the rodeo circuit for a month. He would need to stay and work the ranch. Maybe, Matt or Tom could find jobs this summer to bring in some cash. Matt wouldn't mind getting away from the ranch. With only summer off, Tom would be heading back to finish high school in the fall. He knew that his dad had wanted Dave to go and stay at the summer camp watching the herd. They would need Dave for the winter months when Tom was in school. Like his dad had said repeatedly, the ranch took everyone 'to pull his weight.'

Tonight, after everyone had left the big kitchen, Bobby took the whiskey bottle and poured himself another drink. His eyes questioned the others and they nodded. The men slowly sipped a third drink as they talked on about the car— the wiring, the new brake shoes, the wheel bearings, the fuel pump, the possible rusted gas tank, the radiator, and a new battery. The list went on and on. Writing down the repairs on a small tablet, Matt suddenly felt overwhelmed at the work still left on the powder blue coupe. Tom, too, sat surprised at the list. The two mechanics knew they would get a more repairs done tomorrow, but the young men would have to work the rest of the week to get the car running. All the men stood up and took their empty glasses to the sink and left the big kitchen.

Vic and Bobby headed for the flatbed truck to load the wrecked car. Matt walked around to the back of the barn and picked up the Red Devil's bashed-up driver's door. With the old tractor, Tom pulled the Red Devil over to the back end of the flatbed truck. Pushing and shoving it, they positioned the red car so that Vic could load it. He had hooked up the wrecked red car with a chain under the front frame and started turning the ratchet on the come-along. The wreck creaked and squealed as it moved up the metal ramps to the bed. The Red Devil seemed unwilling to go up the ramps. But the chain kept pulling it along with it groaning and screeching until it sat on the flatbed truck. The men secured the wrecked with straps to the bed. Bobby tossed the bashed-up driver's door under the wreck. The men went back to the shed and picked up the 6-cylinder blue-grey engine of the old coupe. With the men helping, they lifted it and brought it out to the flatbed. Vic secured it with a couple of straps.

Before Vic stepped into his cab, Matt stood in front of him and said, "Whatever money the junk yard gives you for the Red Devil and the old engine, you keep. Okay?"

"Hell, son. We may see only a little money for that wreck. The engine might bring us some. Don't worry about it... your dad gave me some money. Let's call it even," said Vic. He extended his hand out to him and they shook hands. Matt couldn't believe that Bill's dad had been so helpful.

Walking over to the truck, he stepped up into the cab. Starting the engine, Vic waved 'goodbye' to his son as everyone waved back. After driving to the junk yard, the two old friends planned to spend some more time together.

Matt stood watching as the flatbed truck drove down the dirt road from the ranch to the highway. Sadly, he thought of the pleasurable times he had driven his car, the Red Devil. He recalled all those days he cruised around with the top off when the wind whipped his hair around his head. He thought of the fun drive he had of 'shooting the canyon' through Blue Ridge Canyon with its tight curves and dark tunnels. Ronnie was sitting beside him, waving at the train's engineer on the other side of the wide river going through the canyon. His feelings for Ronnie hurt still deep inside.

Maybe, with the wreck gone, he'd get past his grief over his death. It had been odd with his friend's dad here today, but it seemed as if they had focused on the cars, leaving the grief buried. Now, with Bill staying the week, they'd work on the Blue Demon, do some drinking, and practice their songs. He needed to get his mind off the ranch work for a while, even though he still had to do some daily ranch work.

After the flatbed had disappeared down the dirt road and onto the highway back to town, the three young men headed back into the ranch house. Twilight had begun to descend on the mountains and the valleys. Long shadows started to stretch across the ranch. Walking into the big kitchen, the young men were reminded that dinner had to be fixed.

Since losing their mom, the Fletchers discovered that dinner was a sobering reminder of her absence. At the end of a day of hard work on the ranch, Clyde and Fred found it hard to come into the kitchen which stood cold and empty with no dinner cooking on the stove. So, the men depended more on the canned goods—bland and barely palatable. For meat, they would fry up hamburgers or cut up a roast and fry it up. Occasionally, Uncle Fred would prepare chili or ham and beans or maybe, a roast in the morning. The prepared meals were baked in a slow oven all day. Those special evenings felt like home again. Dessert became canned fruit or vanilla ice cream with chocolate syrup. There were no homemade cake, pies, or cookies. Sometimes, their uncle bought a package of cookies at the Mercantile. Uncle Fred kept hinting that they needed a woman back in this big kitchen. But the young men just kept quiet, neither wanted to get married yet. Their uncle's suggestion went unanswered. However, Chet had been thinking on it lately at night in his bedroom. He did want to find someone who would fit into his ranching life. At the end of a long day, he longed to come home to the comfort of a woman's arms--a warm, loving woman. He felt the time slipping by too fast.

130

Tonight, Matt and Tom were hustling around the kitchen and getting something ready for dinner. Coming in with them, the dog Blue settled under the table, waiting to be fed. Bill had taken a seat at the table and watched the two work at opening the three cans of baked beans and frying up two packages of ground elk meat. Matt made hamburger patties. As they fried in the hot iron skillet, he salted, peppered, and seasoned them.

Soon, the men came in on the back porch, washing up after working. The dog Bandit joined Blue under the table. The men were busy talking about the horses. Coming in, Fred walked over to the stove to get a pot of coffee started. Clyde sat down next to Bill. As the meal came together, Tom brought out the plates, silverware, and the cups to set on the kitchen table. As the food cooked, the big kitchen filled with the smells that made the men hungry. Matt came over to the table with the sizzling hamburgers. He flipped two patties on each of the seven plates. Tom brought over a hot pot of baked beans. He set the pot on a hot pad next to a bottle of ketchup, one of mustard, and one jar of dill pickles. Chet walked over the kitchen counter and pulled out a loaf of sliced bread to set on the table. The smell of hot food and freshly brewed coffee filled the air as the men sat down to eat.

Looking apologetic, Uncle Fred said, "Sorry, Bill. But we are a lit'l informal here. We cook and eat like we're out campin'." He glanced around the table and picked up the pot of beans and said, "Pass your plates down and I'll dish up the beans." One by one the six plates came down to him as he scooped beans next to their two hamburgers.

Smiling, Bill understood, "Hey, it's fine with me. Food is food, whether it's in a bowl or a pan." The hungry men sat silently eating as their stomachs filled. After a while, Fred stood up, walked over to the stove, and picked up the coffee pot. Bringing it back to the table, the men handed down their cups as he filled each one. Tom rose and moved to the fridge, taking out a mason pint jar of the fresh cream for the coffee. He also brought out the pitcher of milk to drink. Tom drank the milk and sometimes, Matt or Chet

131

would have a glass. They handed the thick cream around and stirred their black coffee as it turned a creamy brown color. Afterwards, Matt rose and walked into the pantry for a couple of cans of peaches. Once he opened them, he set them on the table, one at each end. As each finished, the men scooped a few slices of the slippery golden peaches on their plates. Tom and Matt took the empty cans and drank down the sweet juice left. The men poured the thick cream over their peaches.

As Clyde sipped his coffee, he said, "We finished shoein' today. I think the four horses will be fine for the dudes." He thought about this afternoon's work—a lot of hard work filing down their hooves, fitting the shoes, and nailing them on. With a new string of horses, the men needed to be gentle and firm with the horses as they became use to their new surroundings.

"Clyde, I noticed the horses will need some trainin' before we let folks ride them," Dave said.

Agreeing, Fred said, "Yeah, I noticed the two of Shawn's from Muddy Creek were a little frisky."

"What kind of horses did you get?" asked Bill, not knowing much about ranching or horses.

"Well, we have two mares, one gelding, and a stallion. I checked their teeth and they look to be about ten or so years old. Not a bad trade, though," remarked Clyde. It felt good to have a string of horses they could use. Yes, the horses needed some training. He didn't want any wild acting horses around a bunch of dudes who wouldn't know how to handle a horse.

"Do the horses have names?" again asked Bill, curious about the horses.

Fred nodded his head and said, "Yeah. They all came with names. The big brown mare's name is Honeysuckle and she's gentle...I think a broodmare. The other grey mare is Gypsy. The black gelding is Shadow, and the roan stallion is Legend. He is a little wild, too." Thinking of the four different horses that they shoed and groomed, each had their own personalities.

132

Thinking of the old saddles that Tom brought with him from the Diamond V, Fred said, "I've been working on the repairs of those three old saddles. They are nearly finished. I'm just about ready to brush out the dirt and grime and oil them down. They'll soon be ready to use."

As he thought about the old saddles, he wanted to get his rodeo saddles ready. He would be taking his horse Jinx and follow the rodeo circuit after they branded the calves this spring. With Dave hired and Tom back here from school, Clyde had enough men to work the ranch. He could take off, ride his broncs, and make some money. His name 'Lucky' meant something when it came to rodeos. Chet who usually came with him would have to stay and work the ranch. He smiled to himself as he thought how much he enjoyed the rodeos, competing against his rodeo friends, drinking with his buddies, and dancing with the cowgirls after a long day in the arena.

"That's great. I hope we get some people to take fishin' and huntin'. Those log cabins just can't sit empty all the time. We need some income," admitted Clyde. Hans told them about renting the log cabins to guest to take fishing or hunting. He had also given them a list of potential guests with addresses and had told them to write letters about how they could outfit hunters. The Fletchers still needed to work out that part of the business of their ranch. After the branding, he'd talk to his sons about all of this important business of having an outfitter's license.

"Dad, we're goin' to need some posters for the billboards in town...you know to advertise," Matt suggested as he thought of his trip up to Stewart's Lake not far from the ranch. He wanted to take guests up there to fish.

"Sure... Good idea. Make 'em up, " asked Clyde, pleased that his son had a good idea.

"Yeah, no problem. I'll even make a couple for the cafes to post," he answered. He'd buy a few colored posters at the Mercantile, write up the information, and take them in to town. Once the word was out, the people in town would let others know, too. If the logging job didn't turn out, he could make some money taking people fishing.

"On the poster be sure to put both fishin' and huntin'," add Chet.

"Before we get ahead of ourselves, we better inspect the cabins and see if any repairs are needed," Fred said. He knew they would need to be cleaned, to furnish them with bedding, and to supply them with other necessities. Up in the attic, the box of old blankets and bedding could be washed up and used for the three log cabins.

Dave nodded and said, "Just to add a suggestion, you can take people just for horse rides and charge by the hour. If you want, add 'Horse Rides' to your poster. Of course, I can help with fishin' and huntin'. Not only the lakes, but the river can be fished. As far as hunting, I've hunted around this area for years. A couple of times, we took hunters high up where the ramshorn sheep roam."

Living and working at different ranches, he knew the area well and had seen the antelope, deer, moose, and elk that migrated through the area. For fishing, he knew the kind of bait that would be needed to catch those rainbows, the browns, the cutthroat, or the lake trout. As a wrangler over the years, he helped ranchers guide hunters up into the back country.

"Yeah, that's great," said Matt. Chet nodded at Dave. Matt looked forward to fishing and getting away from the ranch. Chet looked forward to scouting for game and later, taking up hunters in the fall. With his knowledge, Dave had proven to be a valuable addition to their ranch.

Finishing with dinner, the men stood and took their plates and silverware to the kitchen sink. In the rotation of doing dishes, Dave took his turn at washing the dishes tonight. He rolled up his sleeves, filled the sink with hot water and dish soap, and began washing the dirty dishes.

As the men stood in the kitchen, Chet looked at his dad and said, "I need you to look at some bills that I found in the desk drawer. Come down to the office and let's look at them."

"Sure, I'm glad you've taken over the books." Clyde took the bottle of whiskey with him as Chet and Fred followed him down the hall to the office.

Feeling tired, Tom said, "I'm headin' to bed. By the way, I've worked on brake shoes before with Grandpa Paul. I can help do those. Good night." All said, 'good night.' Looking at Blue, he tapped his thigh twice. Blue followed him upstairs. Since moving to the ranch, Tom had fixed a folded blanket on the floor for his companion to sleep on.

After his brother left, Matt looked at his friend Bill and said, "I'm goin' to get our two sleeping bags from upstairs for the log cabin. I decided to bunk out there with you this week. Be back in a minute."

As he started to move out of the big kitchen, Bill called out after him, "Don't forget your guitar. We can practice a few tunes…not tonight, but later."

"Right." he replied. He went up the stairs to his bedroom, taking his sleeping bag and guitar from the closet. Walking into Chet's room, he took his sleeping bag. Yesterday, he had asked to borrow his bag.

As he came back into the kitchen, he said, "Bill, I'm goin' out to set up our cabin and put a fire in the stove. If you want, take a shower. It's just down the hall across from the office. Towels are in the hall linen closet. I'll be back." He walked over to one of the side cupboards. On the inside door were three sets of cabin keys, hanging from metal hooks. He took one set down and put it in his jean pocket. Carrying the two sleeping bags with his guitar slung on his back, he left the big kitchen, through the back porch, and out the back door.

After the sun had set, the evenings were cold and chilly. Temperatures were still below freezing during this first week of April. The dark night sky had only bright twinkling stars. The Milky Way spread across the vast cosmic sky like a swathe of scattered star dust. Only a slim, waning crescent moon hung in the distant horizon. The new moon would be in the night sky next week. Matt looked up and deeply breathed in the chilled air. This massive view of this night sky refreshed his soul. Walking up to the little porch, he used the cabin's key to open the door. Inside, he placed the sleeping bags on the two bunk beds and put his guitar up against one wall. Going over to the black heating stove, he

135

put in a fire. He then spread out the sleeping bags. Before he left, he turned on a small table lamp by the cabin's window. He walked back to the ranch house.

As Matt entered the kitchen, he saw Bill still sitting at the big table, talking to Dave.

"Did you take a shower?" he asked, curious to see his friend sitting there.

"No, not yet. It's quite an undertaking. I can't get my cast wet," explained Bill. He wanted to take a shower but didn't want to impose on anybody. He needed someone to help cover his cast.

"What do you do?" he questioned his friend. Bill explained that since he couldn't get the cast wet, his mom came up with the idea of using their empty plastic bags from their loaves of bread. Cutting holes at the closed ends, he'd slip his casted arm inside the plastic bags (his mom put two together for extra protection). Then, she would tape the ends closed with masking tape.

As he finished, he said, "My mom did pack the two plastic bags for me." His mom Cathy was a practical person who had helped his dad run the station and had taken care of their home. He had a special place in his heart for his dear mom who nearly went crazy when he wrecked his car.

"Hell let's get you fixed up. We have some tape somewhere," Matt said as he began looking for a roll of masking tape in the kitchen drawers. Bill stood up, walked through the living room, and next to the front door where he had set down his small suitcase of clothes. Bringing it into the kitchen and setting it on the big table, he sorted through the suitcase and found his two plastic bags.

Laughing, he held them up, and said, "Here they are. Might be silly, but they work." By then, Matt had found a roll of tape. As Bill unbuttoned his shirt, Matt noticed that the right sleeve had been cut open along the seam to allow him to slip it over the big cast. The sleeve had been rolled up above the cast. Dave had finished with the dishes, so he turned to help with taping the plastic bags.

As they worked together, Bill said, "Say, I'd like to go out and drink some beer. I'm off my pills, now, and I want to get stinkin' drunk. Do you have a place where you guys hangout? Maybe, we could call some gals, too," he asked both his friends. He needed to cut loose and have some fun. Bill enjoyed being around Matt; their friendship had never faltered.

"Yeah, we'll go up to Skyline. I'll give my friend George a call. We can call a few girls, too," said Dave, who knew a few girls who would go partying. Drinking up at Skyline, his friends had been out with the four cheerleaders--Suzie, Rebecca, Eveline, and Deirdre. *Not Eveline this time. She wasn't in town.* He wouldn't mind getting out and do some drinking.

"Hey, last night, at the McClure's, I met Torrie, Ronnie's young sister," Bill said.

"Ronnie's sister? I didn't know he had a sister," answer Matt. Since he had known Ronnie for only a short time, he had only met his parents. He knew his dad from the gas station. But now, he found out that there was an older brother BJ with a wife and two children and a younger sister.

Dave spoke up, "Yeah, I know her. Several years ago, I stayed with the McClure's when I first came to town. I didn't know Torri was back, though. She must have come back after her brother's funeral. What's she doin'?" Dave thought that Torri would like to go out with them. He'd call her to come and get acquainted with everyone.

"She's livin' at home and workin' at Bert's Café. That's all I know," he answered. But he certainly remembered how much she had changed.

"I knew her first when she was a young, skinny girl. But Torri's all grown up now," Dave added.

Bill agreed as he raised his eyebrows, "That's an understatement, Dave. She's a real looker."

"She's here in Riverside, now?" asked Matt, trying to catch up on who they were talking about.

"Yeah, she came home late from work last night. Evidently, she worked an extra shift at the café. The owner was out of town. Not sure...but Bobby wanted to know why

137

she worked so late," Bill answered, recalling last night's conversation with Torri and her dad.

"Wait a minute. Bert's daughter is Eveline who I dated until she left. The rumor is that she was pregnant. But on the phone, she told me she was going down to take care of her sick aunt in Colorado. Bert went out of town. Where did he go?" Matt asked. He knew the family and wanted to find out about Eveline.

"I can't remember," answered Bill. He couldn't remember the name of the town, but his interest perked up when Matt said he dated a girl who was pregnant. He didn't want his friend to get mixed up with a pregnant girl. "So, this girl...Eveline. Is she the kind to sleep around?" Bill continued. Standing ready to take his shower, he paused bare chested except for the bandage around his ribs.

"No. She's not like that. Eveline is shy, quiet and soft spoken," Matt explained, as he shook his head in dismay. Recalling that he had liked her, his heart had been crushed.

Dave agreed with him, "Yeah, she's real nice, but the rumor is that she is pregnant, and her parents sent her away to have the baby. She couldn't stay and go to school here."

"Oh, I see. That's really a shame," Bill said. They stood and thought for a minute about the terrible situation. Clearing his throat, he said, "Well, I better go and take a shower. Thanks for your help. I got this."

Nodding, Matt followed him down the hall, stopped at the linen closet, and pulled out a towel for him. He handed one to Bill who said, "Thanks, Matt." Bill went into the bathroom and closed the door. He turned on the shower. Then, he unwrapped the bandage around his ribs. This had been a long day for him. Still healing from his injuries, he felt the exhaustion in his body take over. Whenever he moved a certain way, his ribs pained him.

Stepping into the bathtub with the shower flowing, he carefully held up his right arm. Even though it was covered and taped, he didn't want to take the chance of getting it wet. He had learned to be extra careful after his injuries. He focused on shampooing his dirty, blonde hair. His curly hair had grown longer than he usually kept it, but he liked the longer look. Shaking his hair out of his eyes after shampooing it, he leaned up against the tiles. He stood and let the hot water run down his body. The heat soothed his aching ribs and back. With his right arm held up, it started to tire. Using his left hand, he quickly, scrubbed up, rinsed off the soap, and turned off the shower. Stepping out, he grabbed the towel and dried himself off.

Now, with his sore ribs, he had to slip on his jeans which took some time. Bending over, he had to stop a couple of times and catch his breath as the pain shot through his ribs until it subsided. As he finally finished putting on his jeans, he picked up the midsection bandage and walked down the hall to the kitchen where his friends sat, talking. Both realized that Bill still had a long way before he would be completely healed up from his injuries.

He indicated for his friends to wrap up his ribs for him. Both jumped up, and working together, they wrapped up his ribs. He slipped on his shirt and rolled up the opened right sleeve over his cast.

Shaking his head, he said, "Damn it, nothin' is simple. Thanks for helpin' me." Both were glad to help their friend.

"Let's head to bed, Bill," said Matt. The three left the kitchen. Dave headed toward the bunk house and the other two walked toward the small cabin. All said, 'good night.'

As they approached the cabin, a yellow light from the window shined out in the dark night, becoming a beacon to the two exhausted friends. They could smell the burning wood in the cold night air. They saw their breaths as they breathed in and out. As they opened the door, the cabin felt warm inside. Going inside, they undressed and crawled into their sleeping bags. Matt then turned off the small lamp, so the red and yellow fire in the black stove glowed in the dark log cabin. He pulled out his pint of vodka and took a sip. Handing it to his friend, he said, "Here, have a sip."

"Thanks, just what I needed…now that I'm off my pills. I could drink this whole pint, but with my dad comin' tomorrow, I better not. I need to keep a clear head," Bill said, as he sipped the liquor. He continued, "Listen, I want you to be careful with this girl Eveline. I've got a bad feelin' about her situation."

"You're right. I don't want to get mixed up with a pregnant girl," he agreed. "I just would like to talk to her and find out how she's doin'."

Bill handed the vodka back to his friend, and said, "No, Matt. I wouldn't even do that. It's best to forget about her. Hell, there's plenty of girls out there. You know, I'm still goin' with Denise. She's the first girl that I've met with a head on her shoulders. My ol' man is pushin' me to settle down and stop racin' my cars. My mom wants grandkids. Can you see me with a kid?"

"What?... Are you serious?" asked Matt. This side of Bill he had never seen. No, he couldn't see Bill with a child. That's not the Bill he knew.

"Hell, Matt. This wreck nearly killed me. I've had a lot of time to think. I'm twenty-one goin' on twenty-two. I don't know if Denise is the one, yet. She is the first decent girl that I've dated. You know, she won't sleep with me, yet... Says it's her faith," added Bill, quietly to his friend.

"I ran into that with Tammy on a date, too. Of course, we must respect them. They are not like those other girls who sleep around... I have had enough of the girls who like to flirt around, like those I've dated. They stroke our egos, but past that, they're phonies—like little devils after our hearts," answered Matt. He still felt the hurt from all the times he'd been betrayed by girls he thought were nice—Daphne, Suzie, and now, Eveline.

"Hell, man. That's deep. Of course, I'd like them to stroke more than my ego... just sayin'," said Bill, laughing. His mind hit the gutter as usual, but he had other thoughts about someone special.

His thoughts jumped to his girl Denise who managed to keep him at a distance. This was frustrating to him, but with his pain and injuries he had been sidelined in his sex life. For the first time, he looked at Denise as a person, not as a sex object. And with her, he wasn't a guy after a gal. They started getting together as friends.

They had real conversations about their lives—including his musical talent. Even though he couldn't play his guitar, she encouraged him to sing. She thought he had a strong voice. With her shoulder length brown hair and blue eyes, she was different than anyone he had dated. As a happy person, she smiled and laughed often. He liked her more every time they met. Since she had an apartment in Casper with Tammy, he didn't get to see her as much as he would like. With odd hours, she worked at a motel desk, taking reservations, and signing in guests. With her friend, she had taken a few college courses, but didn't have much money to go full time. Since he had been laid up with his injuries, she had driven down to see him often. She had continually cheered him up. He could see a possible future with her. But he wasn't sure she'd marry him. He'd take his time before taking that next step in their relationship.

"Let's get some rest. By the way, Johnny's goin' to call tomorrow and let us know more about the gig in Winston— you know, the senior dance. We'll be playin' this Saturday. We've got all week to practice and plan our set," said Bill as he closed his eyes, trying to position his body so he could go to sleep without his ribs hurting. He thought of his music and the band, and then, how much he cared for Denise. He had been thinking of her, and he missed her already.

"Yeah, that's great. I'm lookin' forward to playin' with the band. Goodnight," said Matt, setting the pint on the floor by his bed. As he turned on his side, he closed his eyes. The vodka had eased his throbbing headache after taking four aspirins at the ranch house. His headaches came on after a long day of work. Thinking of the gig out of town, he looked forward to getting away from the ranch. He still felt in his gut that he needed to find a job. Then, his mind spun with thoughts of Eveline—the whole story of her going away. And what about her being pregnant? Bill was right. He needed to put her in his rearview mirror, but he wanted to talk to her. He knew her problems were not his. As much as he liked her, his feelings for her had been trampled. He felt like a fool.

Clearing his mind of her, he thought of the Blue Demon. He looked forward to driving it and seeing how it performed on the road. He knew nothing would probably compare to his Red Devil, but maybe, with that special engine, the Blue Demon would spring to life and outdo other cars. The Blue Demon could again give him that freedom he so desired.

Chapter 9
The Grizzly

The next day, the Fletchers woke to an early spring day again with the sky clear and blue. As the sun rose, the ranch emerged from the grey morning with everyone turning to their daily work. Before dawn, Clyde, Fred, and Dave crawled from their warm beds to dress and head out to feed the herd. Hitching up Jack to the hay wagon, Clyde drove it toward the pasture. Bandit jumped up and rode on the wagon beside him. To save time in the morning, Dave had been loading the wagon at night with the hay bales. Fred saddled his chestnut Captain and Dave, his brown stallion Bullet. They mounted and rode out to the herd. They could hear the cows bellowing and mooing in the distance.

Riding out toward the herd in those chilly early dawns never stopped amazing the men. With the early spring, there was a layer of frosted dew blanketing the roofs, the trees, and the fields. The view of the rugged dark blue mountains, the vast expanse of the valley, and the willows and trees along the river capture their imagination and inspired the men to live and work on this land they loved.

The work moved along fast as Fred rode up into the timber above the herd to check for any signs of predators. Into the dark forest, he rode up to a rocky ridge, looking down through the lodge pole pines at a meadow. Suddenly, the hairs on his neck and scalp stood alert. He saw movement down below along the edge of the meadow. Captain started to stomp and dance around, snorting. Fred whispered, "Shhhhh," and rubbed Captain's neck. Reining him in, he stopped the horse. About five hundred yards below, he saw the dark shape of a brown bear moving along the edge of the meadow, in and out and around the pine trees. His heart started to beat hard realizing he was watching a grizzly, probably coming out of hibernation. Holding tightly on the reins, he guided Captain around behind some of the pines to watch the grizzly. With its head down, the grizzly moved around and seemed to stumble through the pines. Dismounting, he pulled out a pair of binoculars from his saddle bag. Lifting them to his eyes, he glassed the edge of the meadow. Slowly, he focused the binoculars. Breathing in and out slowly, he watched the grizzly for a few minutes.

Fred did not want to engage him, so he quietly slipped the binoculars back into his saddle bag. Then, he pulled out his loaded .32 Special from the scabbard. Even though the grizzly hadn't seen him, he wanted the rifle in his hands. He noticed that the grizzly appeared to be unaware of his surroundings. He mounted and turned Captain to circle wide around the grizzly. They headed back down through the forest to the ranch. Occasionally, he would stop, turning in his saddle to look behind him. Emerging out of the forest, he headed quickly towards the pasture and the herd. He stopped, looking up through the timber as he slipped his rifle back into the scabbard.

Coming up to Clyde and Dave working at throwing out the hay, he said, "I saw a grizzly about two miles up near a big meadow. We are goin' to have to watch the herd." He told them how he thought the grizzly was just coming out of hibernation and had not been aware of him.

Clyde said, "We may have to put a watch on the herd. Let's hope he moves on." Dave just nodded and thought that the days were going to be long, guarding the herd.

"After breakfast, I'll ride back here and watch the herd. I can check the fence lines for any breaks," said Dave. They knew that they didn't want to lose any cattle to a grizzly roaming around. Heading back to the ranch, Clyde turned the wagon as the men rode ahead.

At the ranch house, the young Fletchers fell into a morning routine of fixing breakfast. Tom came in from the barn after milking Sunny. Bill and Matt had walked over to the ranch house from the small cabin. Both felt good after a night of sleep. Bill asked what he could do, so they put him to making toast. Working together, the breakfast was nearly ready. As Clyde, Fred, and Dave came into the warm kitchen with the smell of coffee and bacon, they said, 'good morning.' With the eggs, toast, and bacon on the table, the men sat down, handed the food around. Their cups were filled with coffee and the sweet thick cream.

Looking around at his sons, Clyde spoke, "Fred saw a grizzly roamin' along a meadow up in the timber this mornin.' Be aware. Do you understand?" His concern for his sons made his heart pound this morning after hearing about the grizzly. Now, he had to worry about this.

"How far up was he, Fred?" asked Chet, concerned for their safety.

"About two miles up. I'm assumin' it's a male…too early for a female. There were no cubs. I watched him through my binoculars. He looked like he just came out of hibernation. He was movin' sluggishly around and he didn't see me. I was above him, lookin' down at him, about five hundred yards or so. Your dad's right. Take your loaded rifles and even your huntin' knives. Be aware of your surroundin's," added Fred. As all of them knew of the tragic death a year ago; none here wanted to face a grizzly.

"How about the herd?" asked Tom. Like all of them, he wanted to protect their cattle.

"We'll have to guard them around the clock for a while. Let's pair up and take a night watch. Will rotate that for a while. Maybe, the grizzly will move on or follow the deer herd that's been winterin' above the ranch," said Clyde. They talked a little more about watching the herd. Fred reminded them that they needed to clear the ditches for the next few days.

The men heard a pickup coming down the road to the ranch. After a knock at the front door, Matt answered it as Vic and Bobby stood on the porch. "Mornin'. Come in for a cup of coffee," he offered. They walked through the living room to the big kitchen with the smell of coffee and breakfast still hanging in the air. They said 'good mornin' and sat down. Matt made another pot of coffee as they talked about the plans for working on the car.

Glancing at the men, Clyde said, "We need to clear out the irrigation ditches. Oh, and Chet, go into town and pick up these supplies." He handed him a piece of paper with the list of items. Chet read over the list and nodded. They needed to reseed a few bare spots in the three pastures that they had dragged. He had listed four salt blocks for the cattle. Chet knew if they didn't have them in stock, he'd have to order them. After branding the calves in a few weeks, they'd be driving the herd up to the grazing lands and eventually to the summer camp. The herd would need those salt blocks.

Before he had moved, Hans had told them that his father-in-law Lars Nicholson had built a small log cabin up where the cattle spent the summer. Providing cover from the rain and weather, the little cabin just had room for a bed, a small table and chair, and a wood stove. A corral with a small lean-to stood next to the cabin. Clyde told Dave that he'd be spending the summer up with the herd in that cabin. Chet looked forward to going up to that summer camp while he scouted around for the mountain sheep reported to be up in the high country. His thoughts returned to the list and the men sitting around the kitchen table. He needed another cup of coffee before driving into town.

"We could use some groceries, too," added Tom as he stood. Taking out a tablet and pencil from one of the kitchen drawers, he started to write down what they needed.

Matt spoke up and said, "Get somethin' different for breakfast. How about some oatmeal? We're out of salt and maple syrup, too." Tom nodded and added the three grocery items to his list.

"Take that list of vegetable seeds on the fridge, too, Chet. I know it'll be a while before we can plant the vegetables but see if they have the packages out. If we wait until later, the selections will be gone. Ask about seed potatoes, too. We'll plant those earlier; they should grow well up here. Oh, I want that garden plowed with some cow manure put down. Tom and Matt, why don't you team up on that maybe this week sometime," ordered Clyde. As the coffee brewed, Matt stood up and took down two more cups from the cupboard. Between working on his coupe, he and his brother would have to take a few hours to plow the garden plot. He went around and poured everyone a cup,

146

giving Vic and Bobby each a cup. As the men handed the sweet thick cream around, they sat sipping their coffee.

Glancing at the two mechanics, Fred asked, "What are you plannin' to work on, today?"

"We have some light work to do today. We want to get the car wired. Of course, Bill, you can help with that. We brought some wiring from Bobby's garage if you need a little more to make the connections on that bigger coupe. That car needs new brake shoes, too. When you pull off the four tires, replace the shoes and grease the wheel bearings. While the car is up on the blocks, that would be a good time to do those two jobs, " explained Vic. Bill nodded his head at his dad. He knew they had a full day in front of them.

"Knowing the coupe needed a new battery, I brought a new one with me from my garage. I charged it last night. You can pay me for it when you get a chance. We're goin' to measure the drive shaft and make one. We need to finish that third member—the 'pumpkin' for the rear end. We talked to Nat at the junk yard last night about lookin' for a rear end for the coupe. He called back this mornin' and told us that he found a nine-inch rear end on an old wrecked '56 Fairlane. We stopped and picked it up before comin' here," added Bobby.

"Great. I'll pay you for the battery after our gig. Did you get anythin' for my wreck and engine?" asked Matt.

"Yeah, Nat wanted to pay us. Said he could make some money off the engine and wreck, He thought that the red leather seats would sell fast. I told him to keep the money to pay for the rear end and some parts to make the drive shaft. He sure has a lot of good old junk cars and trucks out there. Oh, let me give you your old license plates from the Red Devil and the papers for the coupe," said Vic as he left the kitchen and walked outside to his cab to get them. As most mechanics did, he looked at junk yards as a gold mine with the spare parts just sitting there, ready and waiting for some repair or replacement job. Coming back, he handed the plates and papers to Matt.

"Another thing that you guys might do is take out the gas tank on the coupe. It's probably rusted. After the Red

147

Devil's wreck, the radiator will need work. It probably leaks like a sieve. Take them both into town to Cliff's, a block off main. His house sets across the back alley from the Pole Cat Bar; he does radiators and can work on your gas tank, too. Go to his house, knock on the door. His wife Anita will answer. Tell her what you want done and she'll take down the information with your name and phone number. She'll let you into his garage where you can drop off the radiator and gas tank. While you're in town, stop at the auto parts store and get some new brake shoes for the coupe," explained Bobby.

Bobby had known Cliff and Anita Bradley for years who had a large garage next to their house where he worked part-time on radiators, his specialty. During the day, he worked at the sawmill in the winter and drove a logging truck in the summer and fall. Over the years, Bobby had sent him as many repair referrals as he could. Cliff had built up a good steady part-time business. Everyone in town knew him and depended on him for repairs.

As the men finished their coffee, they stood up and headed out to work. With their plans to burn out the irrigation ditches, Clyde and Fred left. Dave planned on riding the fence line and watching the herd.

With plans to work on the coupe, the others headed towards the shed. As they were walking out, Bill told his dad that Matt named his coupe the 'Blue Demon.' Shaking their heads, Vic and Bobby both remembered naming their cars special names years ago. Vic laughed and said, "Remember my Grey Ghost –the '38 Chevy?" That was his car's name in high school. Vic fondly recalled his Grey Ghost and those days with his friends, driving around and enjoying those days of youth with his dates with his girlfriend Cathy, their activities, and their parties.

Bobby said, "Yeah, I sure do. Things don't change much, do they Vic." The two laughed as they walked into the shed where the Blue Demon sat, ready for another day of work.

148

Chapter 10

The Affairs

After they had left the kitchen, Chet was left to wash the breakfast dishes and pans. As he rolled up his sleeves, he thought that they should get someone to do this work. He didn't mind stepping up and helping, but surely, they could hire someone to do the cleaning, maybe twice a month. Knowing that the ranch house hadn't been cleaned, the place looked dirtier and dirtier. This ranch house was much bigger than their small old house. With a second floor upstairs, each of them had a bedroom with two empty bedrooms and a second bathroom. Downstairs, the rooms were big and spacious. Nobody had cleaned the place since they had returned from the funeral. The floors looked scuffed and dirty, a fine layer of dust lay over all the furniture, and the living room fireplace was filled with ash. Next to the fireplace, the wood holder needed to be filled with split wood. Maybe after going into town, he'd clean out the fireplace and split some logs out back.

In the meantime, he'd get these dishes washed up and drive into town for the groceries and the ranch supplies. He thought about seeing Betsy Crocket at the Mercantile. He still didn't know anything about her mysterious past that she avoided talking about. *What could she be hiding?* He didn't want to get mixed up in another relationship like Lois's. That affair had burned him enough to stop him dating for nearly a year or two. But, that one night with Betsy still made his heart skip a beat. Her beautiful auburn hair and her cute smile had attracted him that night at the wedding reception. Maybe, they could go for a few drinks, depending on her work schedule. He hadn't been out since returning from the funeral, so he wanted to get out and relax a little.

As he finished the dishes, he wiped the kitchen table clean. He thought about another girl, Sophia—her beauty and her kindness. After calling her once, Chet had again called her a second time. While her phone rang and rang, he had sat and waited. Finally, she had answered. It was a short

149

call, but she had sounded pleased to hear from him. He liked hearing her voice which reminded him of the night they were together at Lookout Point before the funeral. They made small talk—about her and college, about him and the ranch.

She had asked for his phone number so that next time she said she would call him. His thoughts soared at the idea of her calling him. Then, she started to call him every three days. Not wanting to run up the ranch's phone bill, Chet had driven into town a couple of times late at night to use a pay phone. He had gone into the Pole Cat Bar and had used their pay phone in the back. While Sophia and he had talked, the jukebox had played the top hit songs in the background. She had laughed when she heard a song she liked. That time they talked about their favorite songs and singers. She said she loved the singers like Connie Francis and Elvis Presley. He said he preferred country songs like the ones that Marty Robbins and the Sons of the Pioneers sang.

During another call, they had talked about the time they met at the Dry Creek Bar. She reminded him that he had gotten drunk out of his mind that night. Since that night, he had been able to talk about his mom's death. It had become easier and easier as time moved on. He also told her how he had seen her taking the exam at the high school. He had liked talking to her, and she had felt the same. Their calls continued. A kind of excitement filled him as he wanted to see her. Many of her conversations had turned to getting a teaching job. With her wanting to teach, he didn't know how he would fit into her world. Maybe this was all that their relationship would be—continual phone calls and enjoyable conversations. He hoped not, for he liked her more each time they talked. He wanted to see her, take her out, and get her in his arms again. The next time he would be sober.

Finishing up in the kitchen, he rolled down his sleeves and walked back to the office down the hall. He sat at the desk as he pulled out the ranch's checking book. Taking a few minutes, he double figured the record book before he filled out the amount to the Mercantile. Folding it, he put

150

the check into his front shirt pocket. He thought that they had enough money for another month or two. Walking down to the kitchen, he picked up the two lists on the kitchen table, slipped on his sheep-skin vest with his jacket over it, and grabbed his pickup keys. Taking down his hat, he walked out through the back-porch door to his old white pickup. Driving down the dirt road, he left the ranch headed towards town, thinking about getting together with Betsy (his Elizabeth). He'd ask her out for drinks. Besides, Sophia lived far away.

In town, Chet drove down main street. He made his first stops to the Riverside Hardware store for the garden and pasture seeds and to the Brown's Grain and Feed store for the salt blocks and three sacks of grain for the livestock. He drove down the street and stopped in front of the Mercantile. Parking his white pickup, he stepped out and walked into the store. Behind the counter stood Betsy, smiling, and talking with a customer. When she looked at Chet, she dropped her smile and finished bagging the groceries. He thought that everyone must be in a bad mood today. In both stores, the owners seemed short with him.

Waiting his turn, he said, "Hi, Betsy. How are you?" He peered into her beautiful hazel eyes surrounded by her short auburn hair. She wore her usual silver and turquoise earrings, dangling from her ears. She looked good. A white apron tugged at her large bustline under a red western blouse.

"I'm fine. What can I help you with, Chet?" she asked. He stood tall and masculine in his ranch jacket and vest. As he reached inside his vest to his shirt pocket, she looked at his handsome face. Glancing down his face, she saw his blue-plaid shirt opened at the neck. Underneath that shirt, she knew of his muscled chest and strong arms. Her heart spun as she recalled her night with him.

Tired of waiting for Chet to call, Betsy had been dating around. She had a few dates with twenty-one-year old Craig Webster, who wrangled at the Johnson Ranch. He told her that he had spent time in the Army and wanted to get back

151

to civilian life. Driving a turquoise Bel-Air, he enjoyed drag racing his car and challenging the other drivers.

One time a few weeks ago, Craig had raced Matt Fletcher with his Red Devil and lost out near Carter's ranch, the Double D Ranch. That night, he'd been out with one of high school cheerleaders, Suzie Workel, who had a sassy attitude about her. With her short brown hair and light brown eyes, she was a looker. He liked her. She wore a short mini-skirt and had long, slender legs that wound up around him in the back seat of his Bel-Air.

While Betsy was working at the Mercantile, Craig had talked to her. Then he had been at the bar one night at the Dark Horse Tavern while she was bartending. He had asked her out that Saturday night. Unable to resist his advances, the two had slept together. *How was she going to tell Chet?*

She would have to be careful going out with Chet again. She didn't want to lose her chances with Craig, either. Going out with two different guys would be 'touch and go.' She didn't know either of them that well. They could be the jealous, possessive types. Then, she'd end up with no one. She had moved here to get away from an ugly situation with her ex-boyfriend a year ago. Being careful, she wanted to start life fresh here in Riverside.

"I've got of list of groceries to get plus I wrote out a check for last month's bill," he said, as he dug in his shirt pocket for the check that he had written that morning.

Taking the check, she said, "Let's go back to the office." She moved out behind the counter and walked to the office as Chet followed her. He noticed her swaying hips with the strings of her white apron wrapped around her small waist. She had on a pair of tight jeans and boots. His thoughts leaped to the night they spent together. Since he hadn't called her after they had returned from the funeral, he felt bad about not calling her and going out.

As they entered the office, she stepped behind the desk and pulled out their record book from a desk drawer. Betsy looked over the record book and glanced at the check. She noticed a difference.

"I think there's a little mistake here," she said, trying to keep it business-like.

"What are you talkin' about? Isn't that the total from last month's charges?" he asked, confused.

"Let me show you." She turned the record book around for Chet to look over their Battle Axe Ranch account page. He looked down the list of monthly charges and a total which was more than the amount on his check. He scanned the entries and saw some recent charges made by his dad Clyde and his Uncle Fred.

"Sorry. I just took over the books at the ranch. I didn't have those sale tickets with those charges. Do you want me to rewrite a new check for that total you have here? I could bring it in tomorrow. Would that be all right?" he asked, concerned that his dad and uncle had made charges without giving him the sale tickets. He'd have to talk to them about that so he could keep accurate records for their ranch.

"No, there's no need to do that. We'll just carry the amount over. I suggest that you call here and get the total before writing out a check each month. I'll make out a receipt and record your payment, leaving a carry over," she explained.

She knew that the store owner had done that with many of the ranchers who sometimes got short of money from time to time. The owners knew that she did the books for the Dark Horse Tavern, so they trusted her to handle the accounts here at the Mercantile. After the business was taken care of, Chet shook his head a little embarrassed and put the receipt in his front shirt pocket. He noticed that she recorded their carryover on the receipt. He'd have to call the Mercantile from now on. Betsy closed the record book and put the book back into the desk drawer.

Coming around beside Chet, she smiled up at him, "Don't worry about this. We work with the ranchers all the time. Sometimes, when the ranchers order cases of groceries, the ranchers' accounts are carried over until they pay. They're always good for it, though," she said and laughed. He liked her sweet voice. He reached out and put his hands on her arms and moved down to her hands, taking her small hands into his large rough ones. Looking down at her hands, he glanced at her face and, then, to her soft lips.

"Betsy, would you like to go out?" he asked, looking into her hazel eyes. She looked at him, but her eyes swung away from him. She shook her head.

With her hands in his, she said, "Chet, why haven't you call me before now?" He could tell by her eyes turning away from him that she was upset with him for not calling and asking her out.

"I'm sorry. I've been busy at the ranch. This has been a rough time for me," he said. He didn't want to tell her that after his mom's funeral he needed some time alone. She should realize that without him having to explain his situation.

"What do you want to do?" she finally asked. She still didn't know if she should go out with him.

"Let's just go out for drinks. We'll go from there," he said. He would like to spend time with her, but he felt her hesitation. This was not the Betsy he remembered, but, of course, she was working.

"I have to get back out to the counter. I'm workin'," she said, pulling her hands away and stepping around him.

"What about Friday or Saturday night?" he asked again, not wanting to give up since she hadn't said 'no.' He reached out with his hands on her waist and pulled her into him. He felt an old familiarity come to him. He felt her full breasts against him and smelled her sweet perfume. Moving his hands to her lower back, he gently pulled her closer to him so that he could feel her body against his. Her body stirred his desire.

She gasped and said, "Chet...please." He looked at her lips, wanting to kiss her. She turned her head and said, "No, Chet. Not here." As she said those words, he stepped back. Something had changed between them. He could tell when someone didn't want to be kissed. Catching her breath, she put her hands on his vest inside his jacket. She fingered his vest, trying to decide if she should go out with him. Both of their hearts were pounding.

154

"Listen, I'm workin' right now...I.." she whispered. Swallowing, she started to say more but suddenly, the little store bell out on the counter began ringing. An impatient customer had been waiting for Betsy to check her out. Jumping at the sound of the little bell, she pulled back from him. Releasing her from his arms, Betsy quickly left the office, holding her fingers to her mouth as she tried to get control of her emotions. She smoothed and straightened her apron, touching her hair as she walked quickly to the front counter.

After she left, Chet took a breath. She still attracted him, but her eyes showed that she had changed in her feelings towards him. *She must be dating someone.*

He waited a few minutes before walking out of the office. He pulled out a shopping cart, for he still needed to shop for groceries on his list. As he pushed the cart around and picked up items from the different aisles, he noticed that people would look at him and turn away. Again, it seemed everyone was in a bad mood. He managed to find everything on the list, so he headed towards the checkout counter and waited his turn as others checked out.

Betsy smiled and talked to everyone, quickly taking their money, ringing up the cash register, and sacking their groceries. Working efficiently, Chet recalled how she managed the drinks and people at the wedding reception. She seemed to like the social interaction which he found unsettling. He preferred the solitude that ranch work gave him.

As he moved closer to the checkout counter, he noticed that people were glancing at him and then whispering to each other. *Was this his imagination?* Being the last in line, he finally came up to the counter. Betsy rang up his groceries, wrote out a charge ticket, and sacked his groceries.

Watching her, he asked, "What's with everyone, today? Did somethin' happen that I haven't heard about?" She didn't want to tell him that people were talking about his family. This would not be the time to tell him. He would probably get angry. She didn't want to have an angry

155

customer standing in front of her. *Best tell him quietly on Friday night.*

"No, I haven't noticed anythin'," said Betsy. He noted that she ignored his two questions. He recalled that she did that often when he asked her questions. She continued, "Listen, I'm workin' at the tavern on Friday night until eight. Come there and meet me. We can have a few drinks and talk."

"What? You're workin' on Friday night? Why didn't you tell me?" he asked.

"I'm tellin' you now. I work here in the daytime and a few nights over at the tavern," she explained. The owner Dick Knutsen had hired her to bartend during the happy hours. Renting an apartment above the tavern from them, she liked Dick and his wife Arlene. Betsy did their books for the bar. They had been good to her ever since she had moved here a year ago. She'd been saving a little so she could buy a more dependable car than her grey jeep pickup. Her life now was busy, but she had a lot of bent up energy in her. She didn't know if she could ever just settle down, but she did want to find the right guy that would treat her right and love her. Craig seemed her choice right now; she would let Chet down easy and tell him on Friday night.

"All right. I'll see you then. Bye," he said as he picked up his groceries. His face revealed his confusion, but a least he'd get to see her. Walking out of the store, he put the groceries in his white pickup. He started the engine, backed up, and headed back out of town to the ranch.

He thought about Betsy and how she had acted around him. He figured that that one night together in her apartment didn't mean much to her. Feeling a little guilty that night, he had used her to forget about the widow Anna. But he thought that they could pick up from there. He liked her and thought they had a connection. Obviously, she didn't feel the same as he did.

As he drove out of town, his mind tangled up again with thoughts of the three women in his life--Anna, Betsy, and Sophia. He had mixed feelings about each of them. Anna, a widow still grieving, came with the four children whom he didn't want to raise. Betsy, always working with her mysterious past, had been distant today. Sophia, at college with only phone calls, lived far away.

Finally, he shook off all those thoughts and focused on the ranch and what needed to be done. They were working on burning out the dead grass in the irrigation ditches around the pastures and the ranch. Knowing that he bought the garden seeds today, Tom and Matt were going to plow the garden plot, mixing in some cow manure. They had to seed some of the pastures' bare spots. Their horses needed shoeing. He must be getting like his dad, always making lists in his mind. However, thoughts about work on the ranch settled him as he turned down the dirt road to their ranch. After putting away the groceries in the kitchen, he drove his pickup over to the barn to store the seed, the grain, and the salt blocks.

Going back into the ranch house, he cleaned out the fireplace, throwing the ash out onto the garden area. Around back, he swung an axe and split the logs. He liked the feel of swinging the axe, using his strong muscles in his arms and back to split the logs. Noting that the wood pile was getting down, they would have to go up into the forest and bring down logs before winter. Hans had told them how he used the mules to do the labor. Finally, he had a pile to take into the ranch house. The evenings were still chilly enough that a hot fire at night in the living room's fireplace warmed the entire house, especially upstairs. He then headed out to the stable and saddled his sorrel Rusty. Looking around for his dad and uncle, he mounted and rode Rusty out to help with the ditches.

157

Chapter 11

The Rumors

After breakfast, Matt, Tom, and Bill walked out to the shed where the Blue Demon waited. Vic and Bobby again brought in their toolboxes and set to work on the car. Tom and Matt rolled up their sleeves while Bill gave them directions. The men made some small talk, but they focused on the car. The noise of wrenches being turned, a hammer hitting metal, and a few sharp cuss words filled the shed. The morning went along smoothly as Bobby and Vic finished with their work.

They had accomplished a lot in the two days. The Red Devil engine was securely mounted into the Blue Demon, the transmission was linked to a drive shaft they made, and the rear end from the junk yard (the third member) had been completed. The last job they wanted to complete on the coupe was attaching the exhaust pipes. They used two-inch tubing, made two straight pipes, cut them, and bracketed them underneath the car. The two men gave a secret smile as they finished with the exhaust. With no muffler, the Blue Demon would have a deafening sound, coming and going. They wiped their greasy hands on two rags, cleaning off most of the grimy grease. Both wanted to head back to town.

Vic walked over to his son Bill and said, "We're goin' to leave you guys to work the rest of the coupe. I'm drivin' back home early this afternoon. Can't leave your mom runnin' the station too long. Now, do you have a ride home?" He had originally planned to stay until tomorrow, but he knew that his wife would have her hands full running the gas station without him. Vic wanted to make sure his son got home all right.

"Yeah, I'll get a ride back with the band after our gig. You drive back safely, Dad. I'll be home on Sunday," answered Bill as he hugged his dad 'goodbye.'

"Thanks again for your help, Mr. Dickerson...and you, too, Mr. McClure. I'm forever in your debt," Matt spoke.

He braced against the flood of emotions he felt for these men. Shaking their hands, they patted him on the shoulder.

"Be careful drivin' that Blue Demon after you get it runnin'," said Vic.

"I'll be seein' you around, Matt. Don't be a stranger. I look forward to seein' you drivin' down main street in that powder blue coupe. Thank your dad and uncle for makin' us feel welcome," Bobby spoke as he thought how glad he had met the Fletchers and realized how nice of a family they were. He would never forget how Ronnie talked about how he liked Matt. And even though his death still hurt deep inside, he felt better about meeting and working with Matt. Other than being a good friend, he had nothing to do with his son's death. The town gossip about the Fletchers needed to stop. He'd do everything he could to tell people how good these men were. They didn't deserve the bad opinions that had been circulated around town.

Waving goodbye, Vic and Bobby drove out of the ranch and towards town. After they had left, the young men turned back to working on the Blue Demon. Their next step focused on the rusted-out gas tank and busted up radiator. Dropping out the gas tank and disconnecting the rubber hoses to the radiator, Matt figured that they better take them into town. They could buy some new brake shoes. Needing a break, they could stop and have lunch.

After draining out the gas tank and the radiator, the three of them loaded them in the bed of Tom's red pickup and drove into town. Recalling the directions, they drove to the Pole Cat Bar and found Cliff's house across the back alley. As Bobby had told them, they knocked at the house until the wife answered the door. They gave her the information, dropped off the gas tank and radiator, and drove over to the Riverside Auto Parts. After charging the new brake shoes, they drove down to Bert's Café. Matt knew he'd have to use the money from the gig to pay for these parts and repairs.

Coming into the café, the three found a table and sat down. Bill looked around and saw Torri who was taking an order from another table. She hadn't seen them, so Bill jabbed Matt in the arm and nodded his head towards Torri.

159

Whispering, he said, "That's Ronnie's sister, Torri. She's workin' today." Matt looked over and saw the young waitress with a reddish-brown ponytail. He couldn't see her face; he looked around the café.

He glimpsed over at the front counter. Kay Merther, Eveline's mom, worked the cash register, handing a customer his change. As she looked at Matt, she dropped her eyes and turned away from him. She had recognized him as Eveline's date. He was the last person she wanted to face, and he would probably have questions about her daughter that she didn't want to answer. Her husband Bert had been very adamant about sticking to their story about her sick aunt, no matter what. She would not answer any of his questions.

Finally, after Torri had given the order to the cook, she came over to Bill, Matt, and Tom's table, bringing them the menus. She put them down as they handed them around.

Bill smiled at her and said, "Hi, Torri. You look nice today." He turned on his charm as he took a menu.

"Hi, Bill. I'll be right back to take your orders," said Torri. She left. After a while, she came back with three glasses of water. After setting the glasses down, she looked at Bill who winked at her. She figured he'd be the flirting type. She seemed to be his target today. He could just forget about it, for she didn't want anything to do with Bill.

"Hey, let me introduce you to the Fletchers... this is Matt and Tom. Guys, this is Torri," he said. She looked and nodded at each of them, gasping quietly to herself. She lost her smile the minute he mentioned their names. Ignoring their 'hi's', she took out her tablet and pencil from her apron pocket. She stood waiting to hear what they wanted to order for lunch. Noticing that she was all business, the three ordered as she wrote.

As she picked up the menus, she mumbled coldly, barely audible, "Nice to meet you." Walking back to place their order, she stopped at the cook's window.

As she took their orders, Matt's thoughts jumped to Torri who as Bill said was a 'looker.' As he glanced at Torri, her looks took his breath away. She looked a lot like her brother with her reddish-brown hair, her hazel eyes, and the tilt of her head. But she had her own attractive look about her. She had a gorgeous figure under that white blouse, short black skirt, and the red flowered apron. Expecting her to smile, he noticed that her body tensed up and there wasn't a smile when Bill introduced him and his brother. Her cold words surprised him as she left.

But Matt dropped his thoughts of her and focused on talking to Eveline's mom. His interest peaked at seeing her. He wanted to catch her attention. If not, he'd wait until they went up to pay. His thoughts were of Eveline and her predicament.

With her back to them, Torri closed her eyes, trying to stop her beating heart. She knew that it was Matt's car that her brother wrecked. Her mind whirled at the thought of him sitting there, alive and smiling, while her brother Ronnie lie dead and buried. *How could she be nice to these Fletchers?* As a waitress, she had to deal with all kinds of customers, but this took all her courage to not scream and tell them to get out of here. About this time, more customers came in for lunch. Torri busied herself taking care of them. She'd hustled around, got their orders in, and hopefully, the Fletcher brothers would leave before she lost it. She had to keep herself focused on doing her job.

As Tom looked around, he noticed the people sitting in the café were looking at them and whispering. He muttered quietly to Matt, "Everyone is lookin' at us. They're talkin about us." He had always been well-liked in school and this didn't feel right to him. He felt animosity in the air.

Matt said, "What the hell? You're imaginin' it." He took a sip of water from his glass, just like his brother to be worried about what people thought. He'd always been popular in high school. Being new in town would probably be hard on Tom for a while.

Looking around, Bill added, "They're just curious. That's all, Tom." *No*, Tom thought. *This is more than curiosity. Why us?*

Since the café filled with more customers, Kay began helping Torri serve the meals. Every table in the café was filled. So as Torri took orders, Kay went back to the cook's window and picked up the meals. She brought over the three orders of hamburger and fries to Matt, Bill, and Tom's table.

As she set them down, Matt spoke, "Hi, Mrs. Merther. Do you remember me? I'm a friend of your daughter's."

"Yes. How are you? Do you need anythin' to drink?" she asked the three of them.

"Oh, we ordered coffee and Tom ordered a cola. Have you heard from Eveline?" asked Matt. Bill gave him a quick kick in the shins under the table. Quickly, he looked at Bill who shook his head slightly 'no' and glared at him.

"I'll be back with your coffee and cola," said Kay who had ignored the question about her daughter. She came back with two cups and a glass of cola. She poured the coffee.

Matt pressed on and asked, "Could I get Eveline's phone number, just to call her? I really like to talk to her." Again, Bill kicked his friend in the shins under the table. His shins were getting sore.

"No. I'm sorry. I can't do that. She's too busy," she said. She didn't want to talk about her daughter at all. Even a few words could be misconstrued. She didn't trust herself to say anything.

"When will she be comin' back?" he asked.

"I'm sorry, Matt. Please, just stop askin' about her," she answered. Kay turned away and left their table. Obviously, she felt upset about her daughter.

Bill looked at him and said, "Hey, buddy. What was that about. We said to forget about her."

He replied, "No, *you* said to forget about her. I want to talk to her, that's all."

His brother Tom quietly spoke up, "Hey, Matt. What are you goin' to talk to her about? She isn't goin' tell you anythin' more than what you already know. I think her mom is right. Stop askin' about her." They sat silently eating their meal and drinking their coffee and cola.

"Yes, Matt. A thing like this would be a touchy subject for the parents. Think of the shame. I'd like to know who knocked her up. I may sleep around, but I'm careful not to get a girl pregnant. That's a rotten deal," said Bill softly. As he finished, Matt thought about what he said. Most guys he knew, including himself, knew how to protect themselves. Maybe some younger guys didn't know. Yes, he would like to know the guy who didn't. Leave it to Bill to see things differently than he did. From what Ronnie had told him, he knew it wasn't anybody from around here.

As they finished their lunch, the three stood up and walked to the front counter to pay. Tom felt the hairs on the back of his neck stand up as everyone glared at them. Matt and Bill were too busy talking about the car to notice the people's stares and whispers. They walked out of the café. Matt said he wanted to look for jobs on the billboard in the post office.

As they walked over, Bill asked, "What kind of a job are you lookin' for?" Matt told he had applied at the sawmill to drive a logging truck this summer, but he hadn't heard back.

In front of the post office, Matt noticed a pay phone next to it. Looking at Bill, he said, "I'm goin' to call right now to see if I got a job there or not." He pulled out his wallet for the phone number and dug into his pocket for some change to make a local call.

As he made the call, Tom and Bill went on into the post office to look over the billboard. Chet had mentioned to Tom that he might consider getting a summer job. Looking over the board, they noticed that the sawmill had an opening for a truck driver, an advertisement listed several summer road construction jobs, and a few openings for wranglers at different ranches. The billboard had other notices about rentals and announcements. The notice about the start of a local rodeo every Friday at the Double D Ranch interested Tom. He would love to go and ride some broncs or rope some calves. He wondered if they had any prize money. He'd have to tell his brothers about the weekly rodeos. They turned to look at Matt as he strolled into the post office. His face had a frown and he was muttering to himself.

"Son of a bitch!" Matt growled. No one else was in the building; the postmaster looked over and stared disgustedly

163

at him. He threw the note with the phone number into a trash can.

Seeing that Matt needed to vent but not here in the post office, Bill said, "Let's go. We'll talk about it later." Bill looked over at the postmaster and nodded his head and smiled, slightly waving his left hand 'goodbye.' They headed out of the post office and walked down to Tom's pickup in front of the café. They got into the pickup and headed out of town.

Bill looked at his friend, and said, "Okay. Spill it."

"Shit, Bill. I talked to the guy at the sawmill. He said they weren't goin' to hire anyone like me who drag raced and wrecked a car. They wanted safe, dependable drivers," he answered.

"Where did he get that? You didn't wreck your car," complained Tom. He felt bad for his brother, but he had his suspicion when people in the café were looking at them and whispering.

"Besides, I'm a cautious driver. You know, Bill. You had to push me even to drag race in Scottsville that time," said Matt. His frustration made it difficult to talk.

"Easy, buddy. You don't want to work for a guy like him. Obviously, he isn't interested in knowin' you. You and your family are new to this town. How long ago did you move here? About a month ago? You're outsiders. It'll take time for them to get to know who you are," said Bill.

"Yeah. But there must be some gossip runnin' in this town. I felt it today in the café," added Tom.

"Think about it, you two. Anyone seein' you drive that Red Devil would cause the town to talk," laughed Bill, trying to lighten his friend's mood. He liked the look of that red sports car himself and often thought he would like to drive or drag it. He never got the chance.

"I wouldn't be so upset, but the guy at the sawmill said if I passed the driver's test, he'd hire me. I passed it. This doesn't make sense to me, " said Matt. He had to shake off his anger. Recently, finding a job had too many disappointments.

164

"Listen, we looked at the billboard and there's still some jobs out there we can apply," mentioned Tom. Dropping the talk of the town and the sawmill job, they spoke about the other jobs listed. Then, Bill turned their conversation to working on the Blue Demon. Matt soon forgot about his anger. He wanted to get the Demon running so he could have some wheels again.

Chapter 12

Money Problems

After driving into the ranch, Tom parked his pickup near the shed. There was a smokey haze hanging in the air out near the ranch's pastures. The air smelled of burnt grass and debris from the men cleaning out the irrigation ditches.

The three men went into the shed to begin working on the car. Suggesting they needed to listen to music, Bill said he had packed a little transistor radio in his suitcase. He walked over to the small log cabin and came back with it to the shed. Turning to a local station, they listened to country music while they worked. Bill wrinkled his nose a little and laughed. Matt told him that they wouldn't be able to listen to rock n' roll hit songs until tonight when the big station out of Oklahoma could be heard. Up here in the mountains, the reception was bad during the day.

Just about that time, the dog Blue came running over to the shed and ran around sniffing the men. Tom squatted down and gave his dog a big hug and roughed up his body. He said, "Hey, Blue. What have you been up to?... out helpin' with the ditches? You smell like it. Lay down, we've got to get busy on the Blue Demon." His dog went over and found a place to watch the men work on the car.

The two brothers rolled up their sleeves and started working on the Blue Demon. Bill stood by, giving them helpful directions, and handing them tools when needed. Replacing the old worn out brake shoes, they worked on through the afternoon. Tom did most of the work on the brakes since he had done a brake job before. When the new brake shoes were in place, he had Matt jump into the driver's seat and push on the brake pedal, so he could bleed the brakes as he adjusted them. With Bill's help, Matt greased the wheel bearings. They managed to get a few items off the list that Bill's dad had given them.

In the late afternoon, they went over to the ranch house. Crowded around the back porch's big sink, they scrubbed their greasy arms and hands. They joked with each other,

166

playfully splashing water on each other. Taking towels to dry off, they snapped them playfully at each other. Dodging around, they each landed a good hit on each other. Bill had the advantage since his casted right arm could block Matt or Tom's towels with no effect.

Finally, Tom called for a truce, for he heard the phone ringing in the living room. It was Johnny calling. He confirmed that the Winston gig for Saturday night was from nine to twelve at the high school gym. Bill wanted to get together a few hours before the gig to work out their set. He asked Matt where they could meet. He replied that a drive-in at the edge of town would be a good place. Bill told them to meet him and Matt at the drive-in around seven Saturday evening. Both were thrilled that they would be driving down to Winston in a few days. The next few nights here at the ranch they decided they needed to practice their songs.

After the phone call, Tom asked, "Am I drivin' you to the gig? I'd like to go hear your band."

"Absolutely. But what about drivin' the Blue Demon? What do you think?" asked Matt, looking at his friend. Bill took a few minutes to think about the idea.

"Let's see how much we get done in the next two days. If we get it runnin', we could take it. Tom could follow us in case somethin' goes wrong," Bill suggested. If they did get the coupe running, the men thought that might be a good idea having Tom follow—a back-up plan. They didn't want to miss the gig.

Dinner time was approaching. The young men could smell something good cooking. Coming into the kitchen, Tom opened the oven and saw a big pot of chili cooking slowly. Uncle Fred must have mixed up the ingredients and put the chili on to cook while they were in town. As evening approached, Matt and Tom set the table. They both noticed that the fridge and pantry were filled again with groceries that Chet had purchased that day at the Mercantile.

After working all day on burning out the grass in the ditches, Clyde, Fred, Chet, and Dave came to the back porch, stopped, and washed up. Their jackets hanging on the back-porch hooks smelled of burnt grass. They chatted as they came into the kitchen and sat around the big kitchen table. Their stomachs growled at the thought of the chili that Fred had prepared. Tom put the box of saltines on the table while Matt pulled out a block of cheddar from the fridge. Each would have to cut their own cheese for the chili. Clyde asked Matt to get the bottle of hot sauce out of the cupboard. As Fred set the pot of chili on the table, the men handed down their bowls to be filled. Soon, they were all silent as they spooned and ate down the delicious, hot chili. For dessert, Chet went to the fridge and pulled out the vanilla ice cream and the can of chocolate syrup. Grabbing a big spoon from a kitchen drawer, he placed the ice cream and syrup on the table. Those ready for dessert handed their empty chili bowls down for ice cream. Dave and Bill wanted another bowl of chili, so they dished themselves another bowl.

Glancing around, Clyde spoke up, "We need to get that garden plowed...just a reminder."

"Yeah, dad. We'll get it tomorrow," answered Tom. His dad wanted to get the garden ready for the fresh vegetables that it would produce. He and his brother planned to get the old tractor and plow the large plot next to the ranch house on the south side where the sun shone brightly most days.

Their uncle spoke up, "How is the work on the coupe comin' along?" The chocolate syrup was handed around for those who had ice cream.

"Good. We hope to get it runnin' soon. Maybe, even drive it to our gig in Winston," said Matt, letting his dad know that he, Tom, and Bill would be leaving for a day.

"Who are you playin' for?" asked Fred. Matt's guitar playing astonished him. Proud of his nephew, he hoped that he had found something he liked to do. He knew that he needed the freedom a car gave him. That's why he handed him the keys to his '59 red Corvette when he graduated. Matt had a different view of life right now and it didn't include the ranch. Maybe, later he would see it differently.

"The band will be playin' at a dance for seniors. The others—Johnny, Rob, and Dan—are driving there to meet us. Tom is comin' along," answered Matt. Smiling at the thought of the trip and getting together with the band members.

"I'll hook a ride home after the gig. Thanks for lettin' me stay here at the ranch," said Bill. He had enjoyed his time getting to know his friend's family.

"But you guys be damn careful drivin' that coupe. Don't get stupid. I don't want to hear about another accident," growled Clyde. Getting up from the kitchen table, he took his bowl and silverware over to the sink. Turning, he glanced again at Matt, and said, "You can't drive that coupe anywhere until you get the license changed over. Don't be gettin' into trouble with the law."

The three looked at each other realizing they wouldn't be driving the Blue Demon to the gig. *The license plates were from the Red Devil.* Another fact they hadn't thought of. They knew that Tom would be driving them to the gig in his old red pickup Saturday.

Opening the cupboard, Clyde took down the half-emptied whiskey bottle and a few glasses. Turning, he headed out of the kitchen down to the hall to the office. His brother and Chet followed him into the office.

Clyde sat down in the chair in front of the desk, pouring out the dark amber liquid into the glasses. He needed a few minutes to himself as he thought about Matt, his car, and his gig. His son seemed focus on getting himself away from the ranch. *Let him. He'll be back*, that's what he hoped. Tonight, he recalled once that Beth and he had argued about Matt. She wanted their son to have his freedom to follow his own dreams. He would give him his freedom to dream if he kept up with his responsibilities here at the ranch. Matt's name was on the deed just like all of them.

Then, his mind spun around into thinking about his wife. Only at night did the nightmares return. He'd hope that some night he would sleep without those terrible memories. His brother told him that Time would heal the pain of losing her. Those were easy words to say to someone, but he felt that Time was taken too long. *How long would it be?* Taking a sip of his whiskey, the sting of the strong liquid on

169

his throat reminded him that there were more pressing matters about the ranch that he needed to focus on.

By then, Chet had come into the office and sat down on the chair behind the desk. Uncle Fred pulled up a chair from the wall to sit next to his brother. Looking seriously at them, he pulled out the record book from the desk. He tapped it, thinking for a few minutes before he said anything. He didn't want to hurt them or make them angry. This was a touchy but serious subject.

Picking up one of the whiskeys, Chet took a long gulp. He said, "Dad, Uncle Fred, we need to talk about chargin' groceries or supplies for the ranch. I discovered today that there is a difference in the total I'm runnin' here at the ranch and the one at the Mercantile. We need to be more careful. I need those charge tickets. Either bring them to me or put them on the desk here in the office. For our records to be accurate, I need them."

"Oh, Chet. I'm sorry. I washed my jeans without emptyin' my pockets. I found a wet, wadded-up paper in the bottom of the washer. It must have been one of those tickets. The writin' was all gone, so I threw it away," said his uncle as he took his whiskey and gulped it down.

"But, Uncle Fred. Give me the faded ticket. It'll have a printed number on it that can be traced at the Mercantile. At least, I would know that there had been a charge made. Do you see?" he explained.

"Damn it. I think my charge tickets are still in my jacket. I'll get them to you, later. What happened today?" asked Clyde, gulping down the rest of his whiskey.

"Nothin' bad. For the ranchers, Betsy said that the store often carried over the unpaid amounts into the next month. It wasn't that much, but I wrote out a check, thinkin' we were paid up for the month." He reached into his front pocket and pulled out the receipt and said, "Here's the receipt for this month with the carry-over amount written on the bottom. See here." He showed his dad and uncle as they both nodded and understood.

"Yeah, we'll be more careful from now on… How is Betsy?" asked Uncle Fred. He remembered dancing with her at the wedding reception. Knowing that Chet had been out with her, he wondered how things were going with them.

"She's fine, workin' days at the Mercantile and a few nights a week at the tavern," he answered.

"Why is she workin' both places?" asked Clyde. He didn't understand why a young woman would work at a bar. He felt a woman belonged at home, taking care of a family.

"I don't know, but I'm goin' to see her Friday night for drinks. Do you have any other charges out there at other stores?" asked Chet. Shaking his head 'no,' his dad poured each another round of whiskey. He looked at his uncle who shook his head 'no.'

"From now on, I want to know where we sit every day, every week. I don't want a surprise like this today. We're goin' to have to be careful, maybe, cut some corners this summer," said Chet. They had enough money, but it would be tight if they weren't careful.

Clyde spoke up, "I've mentioned to Tom and Matt to look for summer jobs to bring in some cash. After we sell the steers in the fall, we'll be okay." They eased back in their chairs and talked more about their cash supply, about the herd, and about other jobs that needed to be done around the ranch. After their second drink, they got up and headed out of the office. It was late and they needed the rest.

While Clyde, Fred, and Chet talked in the office down the hall, the others had stayed in the kitchen, talking about the Blue Demon. Earlier, Dave had made a call to his friend George who said they'd get together Friday night up at Skyline.

"That's sounds like fun, Dave. I need to get drunk and hold a girl in my arms," said Bill, looking forward to getting out. Shaking his head, Matt knew that Bill knew how to party better than anyone he knew. Then, they started to talk about getting the coupe to run.

As the three talked about the coupe, Dave sat quietly and listened. Today, he'd been busy with the herd, riding the fence line for breaks and keeping his eyes out for that grizzly that Fred told them about. He had taken a ride up into the timber about a mile in, circling the area and looking for fresh tracks. Riding his horse Bullet, he carried his .30-30 Winchester in his arms, loaded. He rode ready to protect himself if necessary. He knew how quickly a grizzly could come out of nowhere and attack without warning. Recalling the incident with Caden, he knew that if he had had his rifle in his hands, the outcome might have been different.

Anyway, the ride through the timber made him tense. Coming up on a little spring, he looked at the dark wet earth for tracks or claw marks. Nothing, but deer tracks. Today, the magnificent forest was filled with birds and small animals. Some of the aspens were starting to bud green against the white bark. He felt the heat of the sun on his back when he came out of the forest into an opening. Riding through the lodge pole pines, he heard a breeze whisper through the high branches. Around downed logs and underbrush, he rode Bullet in a big circle and down towards the herd. As he emerged out of the timber, he saw the green pasture stretching out before him. In the fields, sprouts of green were shooting up as the warm sun beat down on the fields. Hearing a meadowlark's musical song made his heart skip a beat. *How could you not love this land? He was lucky to be here and away from the sawmill.*

Looking closely through the willows, he rode over towards the creek that ran along one side of the ranch. The tall willows ran on both sides of the creek. Over the little bridge and down the other side he rode. Bullet faltered and tripped slightly with his right hind leg. Concerned, Dave dismounted, slipped his rifle into its scabbard, and walked around to his horse's hind back leg. He kept his hand on Bullet so the horse would know where he was. Lifting the hind leg and holding on to the hoof, he saw part of a pinecone jammed into the horseshoe. He cleared it out with a pocketknife. With his hand on the horse, he walked around to the front of the horse.

Giving his horse an affectionate stroke, Dave said, "There, old boy. That should feel better."

He then walked Bullet down to the edge of the stream as the horse took his fill of the cold water. Squatting down, he

172

too cupped his hand and drank the spring water. As he stood, he looked up and down the creek, hoping that that cow moose had moved on.

Abruptly, two young moose came charging out of the willows. They were chasing one another. With their long, spindly legs, their mouths opened, and their pink tongues hanging out, they sprinted around. Looking back, the calf in front looked as if he was laughing at his twin chasing him. Oblivious to Dave and his horse, the two chased each other farther away from the bridge down through the willows. Their reddish-brown bodies disappeared into the clumps of the deep willows. He smiled to himself at the sight. They looked like children chasing each other—so playful. He wouldn't bother them if they stayed down here and not in the fields. The cow moose would be somewhere around here. Mounting Bullet, Dave thought about how many young moose he saw hit on the highway. He hoped these twin calves stayed away from the dangerous cars and trucks.

As he finished his thoughts, Dave came back to the conversation at the kitchen table. They were talking about the coupe and getting it started. Tomorrow they were going to pick up the radiator and the gas tank. When they got up, Tom suggested that they plow the garden. Matt said he would scoop and shovel some cow manure out of Twister's pen for fertilizing the garden. They both knew that they needed to complete the garden so their dad would leave them alone to work on the coupe. With their plans made, the three decided to head to bed. Dave got up and headed out to the bunk house.

That night in the small log cabin, Matt and Bill practiced their songs for the gig on Saturday night. The songs sounded great with Matt using his sheet of paper with the chord progression written out for each of the songs. Since they wanted a mix of rock n' roll and country, Matt suggested they play and sing the songs that Ronnie had played at the other gig. The two recalled all the artists that they had played. There were nearly ten. He reminded Bill that Rob, the base guitar player, would be happy that they had added some country songs. As they practiced, Bill said he felt odd singing without a guitar in his hand. Matt told him that he sounded fine. Close to midnight, they finally turned off the light and crawled into their covers and fell asleep.

Chapter 13

The First Drive

At the Battle Axe Ranch, the next two days went by quickly with lots of work. Before starting on the Blue Demon, Matt and Tom worked at getting the garden plot turned under. Matt had mucked out the manure from the bull pen. Scooping it into a wheel barrel, he had made a couple of trips, dumping the rich, dried out manure onto the garden spot. He had spread it around with a shovel, pushing the wheel barrel from one end of the plot to the other end.

Coming from the utility shed, Tom drove the old tractor pulling the long plow blades behind him. Dropping the blades down, he then drove the tractor over the garden area. The rich, brown earth mixed with the manure turned up behind the old tractor. Working together, they had the plot turned and fertilized with the manure. Tom had gotten a little carried away with the old tractor, so the garden plot had been extended a little more. The two brothers laughed but knew that they would have to buy more seeds if they needed to plant more rows of vegetables. The whole family could benefit with fresh vegetable. The time to make the rows and plant the seeds would be later in May.

Finished with that job, Tom drove the old tractor and the plow blades back to the shed while Matt pushed the wheel barrel and shovel back to the barn. Again, Bill sat down on the back-porch steps and watched the two brothers work together. Amazed at seeing the two work, he enjoyed knowing more about ranching than he had ever known. This certainly was a world apart from his work in Scottsville with his dad's gas station and garage.

Focusing then on the coupe, Matt called Cliff's house and asked about the repairs. Cliff's wife answered the phone and told them that the radiator and gas tank were ready. The three drove into town and picked them up. Matt charged the work to the ranch. Tom voiced some concern about doing that, but he assured him that after the gig and with the money from the wolf pelt he'd have enough to cover the expenses. He told him he'd better tell Chet, so he could keep the records accurate. He had spoken to them about making charges to the ranch and how important it was for them to give him the tickets.

After talking with Chet about the money and the ranch, Tom and Matt had decided to put in for the road construction jobs that were listed on the billboard in the post office. They had called for the applications and had waited for them to come in the mail. Tom wasn't looking forward to working off the ranch, but Matt looked forward to doing something else this summer. The job applications had come a couple of days later and they had filled out the forms and sent them in. Everything was done by mail since the road construction company was from out of town. After hearing about the wages, they realized they could make more than working on the ranch.

After returning from town that Thursday, the three worked on connecting the hoses to the radiator. The gas tank was tricky to get reattached, but with a lot of cussing, they got it in. While in town, they had filled a small gas can with gasoline. After pouring the gas into the tank, they crawled under and looked for any leaks from the connections that they had made. No links. That day went by fast.

During the evening hours in the small log cabin, Matt and Bill practiced their songs; Matt played his guitar and Bill sang. They were getting the feel of each other, playing off each other. Matt learned to pace his chords with Bill's words as he sang. With Bill's sore ribs, he took shorter breaths in the songs which slowed down the pace. Matt timed his chords to Bill's words and breathing. Bill encouraged Matt to join him on the chorus lines. With two voices, the chorus lines sounded stronger. Alone, Bill's voice had a raspy sound which fit well with the rock n' roll songs. Matt's voice had a mellow, deeper sound. Together they created a richer chorus line to their performance. They both enjoyed playing together. After a long day and an hour or so of practicing, they crawled into their sleeping bags and fell to sleep, exhausted.

By Friday morning, the time finally came to turn the Red Devil's engine over. First, they jacked up the car a little and pulled out the wooden blocks, one by one. All noticed that the tires were a little low and would need more air in each. Sitting in the shed was a hand and foot air pump. Tom went around to each of the tires and pumped in a little air. With the Blue Demon setting on its own tires, Bill eagerly wanted to hear the engine and to tune it. As Matt turned on the key and pushed the starter button, the engine choked and sputtered. Pushing down on the gas pedal twice, he tried it again. Finally, the Blue Demon roared as the engine started. Without mufflers, the rumble echoed off the walls of the shed. They looked at each other with wide grins on their faces. Success felt good after days of working on the car.

The hood had not been attached yet, so Bill and Matt had plenty of room to work on the engine. As before, Bill checked and cleaned each of the spark plugs, changed the points in the distributor, and adjusted the timing. Matt handed him the tools. They looked at the water levels in the radiator and the new battery. After lifting the hood and attaching it to the car, the Blue Demon was ready for detailing. He ran his hand along the hood to the sixteen-inch ornament. Shined up it would look great, along with the front grill. With a little 'elbow grease,' he'd polish up that chrome.

With all the work that Bill had done the previous day, his ribs were hurting him. Too much leaning over and reaching made them sore, so he sat on the stool while Tom and Matt decided to clean the inside. Without mentioning his headaches, Matt was experiencing some intense ones. He quietly took his dose of aspirin, grinned and kept going.

Tom worked on the inside, dusted it, and swept it out. Matt filled a bucket with water. Pulling out the floor mats, he splashed water on them and scrubbed them with a brush. With a clean bucket of water and a rag, Tom washed down the dashboard, the steering wheel, the gauges, the clock, and the radio. The windows inside and out came next with Matt cleaning the front windows and Tom doing the back windows. The two light blue cotton blankets from the attic slipped over the seats, front and back. They matched the powder blue car.

Bill remembered the license plates and Matt put them on the Blue Demon. Bill couldn't stand it any longer, he said, "Come on. Let's take it for a drive."

Reluctant to go far, Matt agreed, "Let's just drive it down and back on our ranch road to the highway first."

Tom piped up, "Can I drive it once?"

Matt nodded, "Yeah, we each should take it for a spin." They deserved a chance to drive the car that they had worked hard on this week.

Not waiting until the car to be washed on the outside, they crawled into the Blue Demon. Matt started the engine up. With dual pipes and no mufflers, it rumbled loudly. He pushed down on the gas pedal a couple of times, revving the engine. He felt it come alive—the spirit of his Red Devil was back and running, only in a different body. After the wreck, the rumbling motor came alive. In this bigger car, that engine had a deeper, darker sound. This Blue Demon seemed angry at the world. Matt sensed his freedom descend on him; his soul soared as he thought about driving it. He knew that independence came with the Blue Demon. He again had a set of wheels.

Matt drove it out of the utility shed, past the ranch house, and on the dirt road toward the highway. Smiling at Bill, he said, "Maybe, we'll drive it just a little way down the highway." He couldn't resist seeing how it drove on a paved road.

They laughed together. Pulling onto the highway, he headed toward the Johnson Ranch turnout which wasn't far from theirs. The Blue Demon smoothly ran along the paved road. A few squeaks from the body made them smile. He pushed down on the gas pedal and the speedometer read seventy---eighty. The Blue Demon sat higher above the road than the Red Devil, but Matt liked the feel of this car which seem to have diabolical energy. Afterwards, he eased up and coasted down the highway. Making a U-turn at the Johnson's turnoff, he headed back to the ranch. He noticed that the Blue Demon turned wide while the Red Devil had

178

'turned on a dime.' The difference of driving the two cars made him aware he'd have to make the adjustments. For the next fifteen minutes, the three took turns driving the Blue Demon down and back on the ranch road. Tom loved the feel of a car since he'd only driven pickups. Bill knew this car would go faster than Matt had pushed it on the highway, but he didn't want to drive it fast today. Besides, with his right arm in a cast, he had a little trouble shifting the gears.

Finally, Bill said, "Let's go to town. We can drive to McClure's and show Bobby. I'll put a little gas in the tank." Eagerly, they were ready for a drive into town.

"Yeah, I need to get use to drivin' this car," said Matt. The cold tires at first gave them a bumpy ride but smoothed out after they warmed up on the road. They drove into town and stopped at the McClure's Garage. Bobby saw the car and came out of the station, smiling.

"Hell, I'm impressed. You boys did a damn good job to get it runnin'," he said. They got out of the car. Matt went to put a little more air in the tires, Tom went to the gas pump, and Bill stood talking to Bobby about how they finished up and how well it drove.

"How much do you want to put in, Bill?" asked Tom, holding the gas pump.

Pulling out his wallet from his back pocket, he looked at his money and said, "About two bucks."

"Let me take a look at the engine," said Bobby, pulling the hood latch, he lifted it up. He automatically reached for the oil dip stick. Cleaning off the stick, he stuck it back in and pulled it out once more. It needed a quart. Bobby went into the station and grabbed a quart of oil and a spout. As he was adding the oil, Matt told him that he'd be in to pay for the battery after the gig. Finishing with the oil, Bobby stepped back, using his rag to wipe clean the oil that had dropped on the engine. He put on the cap and threw the empty can in the trash barrel next to the gas pump.

"No problem, Matt. I know you're good for it. Start it up for me," said Bobby. He crawled in and started up the engine. Bobby listened and looked at the engine which had a solid sound, purring and rumbling. Smiling, he liked the

179

sound of no mufflers. As he reached up and closed the hood, he said. "Great job. Now, those license plates aren't legal yet. Go down to the county courthouse in Midler and get the paperwork done before you drive it anywhere. Do you hear? You're goin' to get a ticket if you don't."

"Yeah, I know, Bobby. Thanks again for your help," answered Matt. *Oh, the license plates.*

"And by the way, keep it on the road and out of the ditch, will you," he said looking at Matt straight in the eyes. Bobby's steel look told him he was being warned. He nodded, knowing that he had seen that same look from his dad and uncle. He had been careful with the Red Devil and he would do the same with the Blue Demon.

Driving back to the ranch, the three talked about getting together tonight up at Skyline with a campfire, drinking, and girls. Thick smoke swirled around the pastures as they drove into the ranch. Curious, Bill got out of the coupe and watched the men putting fire to the ditches. Even though the men were farther down by the fields, he could see the fire snake make its way quickly inside along the ditch. Smoke rose as the grass was eaten by the fire snake. Occasionally, the reddish orange flames could be seen leaping up the sides. A slight breeze pulled the grey smoke up into the sky. Bill had never stayed at a ranch like this, everything interested him—the talk of the horses, of the calves, of the grizzly, of the garden plot, and now, the fire in the ditches. His friend Matt lived in a different world than he did.

Turning back towards the ranch house, he joined the two brothers where it was time to muster up some dinner. Checking into the fridge, Tom saw a bowl of leftover chili from last night's dinner. He noticed two packages of bratwursts that Chet must have bought at the Mercantile. Matt and he talked about how to cook them—with their cast iron skillet. They both wished they had a barbeque grill that Fred talked about making out of one of their fifty-five-gallon barrels. Evidently, he had seen a grill at one of his rodeos last year. But he had yet to make one—someday.

Bill asked how he could help. Both replied 'nothin, just take a seat.' Tom put the leftover chili in a pan to warm up on the stove. Then, he brought out the cast iron skillet for the brats. Matt decided they needed some potatoes, so he gathered about seven from the pantry. He looked them over for cuts or bruises in the potatoes, cutting those out as he washed them off. He put them in a pot of water to cook. Over the last few weeks, they found that the potatoes tasted good with the skins left on, so they had stopped peeling them before cooking—either frying or boiling.

Feeling useless, Bill noticed the coffee pot, so he got up and took the coffee pot to the sink. Emptying the grounds into a garbage can under the sink, he rinsed out the pot and the tin basket. Then, he remembered the coffee can in one of the cupboards. Filling the pot first with water, he put the basket in. Holding the coffee can, Bill asked, "How much do I put in?" Looking at him, Matt said fill it to the second mark on the tin basket. Dinner had been started. The three talked about the coupe and about getting it registered and transfer the license plates. Against their wishes to take the Blue Demon, they decided to drive Tom's red pickup up to Skyline tonight.

As the sun plunged behind the rugged Rockies, twilight descended on the ranch, sending dark shadows across the valley. For a few glorious minutes, the sky turned a brilliant reddish hue, and the thin white clouds were etched in crimson. The men in the pasture raised their eyes to the mountains as the warmth left the earth. They had to stop burning the grass in the ditches, so they mounted their horses and headed to the stable where they unsaddled and groomed their horses for the night. As they were brushing them down, Clyde mentioned that they had to get some dewormer for the horses.

Smiling to himself, Dave said, "I have an interestin' story to tell about horses and deworming them. I bet you never heard of feeding a horse tobacco. Have you?"

Fred took the bait, "No. Where did hear of that?"

"When I was workin' on our ranch in Hadley, we knew of a rancher who used tobacco," said Dave. He laughed and shook his head, remembering the first time he had heard the story.

Exasperated, Fred said, "Are you goin' to tell us the story or what?" Clyde enjoyed hearing the two carrying on as he brushed down Chief who was munching on his grain.

Finally, Dave explained, "This rancher would buy a box of cigars. He'd break 'em up in the horses' grain—the whole box. He swore they loved the taste and it cleared out the worms faster than anythin' he had seen." Finishing with Bullet, he gave him his grain and water.

"Damn, that's a waste of a lot of good cigars... But I have heard of a guy feeding his goat cigarettes," said Fred. Neither Clyde nor Fred smoked; they never wanted to spend the money on them. However, if they were at a bar and someone offered a cigarette, neither turned one down. Over the years, Fred did like a cigar occasionally. After a day of rodeoing, his rodeo buddies would get together at a bar and buy a cigar to smoke with their drinks. *But to feed a cigar to his horse? Not likely.* Rubbing his horse Captain, he checked his hooves. He said, "We're about ready to shoe our horses before summer, Clyde. We have the new string done, but we need to do ours."

"Yeah, we'll get to it as soon as the ditches are done," said Clyde as he headed out of Chief's stall, closing the half door. The men left the stable and walked towards the ranch house. As they came onto the back porch, they could smell the rich food cooking. Washing up, they moved into the kitchen where the young men were cooking and setting the table. As they sat around the big kitchen table, the dogs Bandit and Blue came trotting in and laid down under the table, tired and stinking of smoke after a day of running around the fields.

After setting out the meal on the table, the bratwursts, the potatoes, and the chili were passed around. The hungry men filled their plates as they quietly ate, filling their growling stomachs. Cups were filled with coffee and a package of cookies were handed around. Matt went to the pantry and took out three cans of pears. He opened them and set the cans on the table. The sweet white pears were spooned onto their plates. Knowing how informal they were, Bill took one of the cans and drank down the sweet

182

pear juice. Tom and Matt reached for the other two, but Chet smiled as his long arm reached out and took one of the cans before Matt got one. The two brothers gulped down the sweet juice as Matt took another cookie.

Finishing their dinner, Clyde and Fred got up. Taking their dishes and silverware to the kitchen sink, they needed another cup of coffee.

"I'll make another pot if you want more coffee," said Bill as he took his dishes to the sink.

"No, we'll just mix a little whiskey in our half-filled cups," said Clyde. He walked over to the cupboard, pulled down the bottle, and poured the smooth liquor into their cups. Chet held out his cup out for a little. As he drank, he thought about going to town tonight to meet up with Betsy.

Dave held out his cup, too. Deirdre had called and wanted him to pick her up tonight. She lived the farthest out on the Lodge Pole Dude Ranch. After picking her up, he would stop and pick up Torri and take them both up to Skyline. Before going out tonight, Bill and Matt wanted to practice a few of their songs, so they decided to go over to the small log cabin.

Rolling up his sleeves, Tom started washing the dishes since it was his turn. As the men talked about burning out the grass in the ditches, they had noticed that they needed to dig some sections out. Nodding their heads, they knew it would be another day working at clearing the ditches.

Finishing their coffee, the men then moved into the living room as Fred started to build a fire. Dave eased himself into one of the chairs while Clyde stretched out on the old couch. After slipping off his cowboy boots, he swung his feet onto the coffee table setting in front of their old couch. Chet sat at the other end of the old couch. They watched as the small pieces of wood caught fire as the flames flickered and danced up the logs until they caught on fire. Soon, the fire roared and threw out hot sparks. The yellow, orange, and red flames filled the room with its warmth.

"I heard Matt and Bill say they were goin' to play tomorrow night in Winston," said Fred.

"Yeah, they've been busy this week practicin' their songs after workin' on the coupe," Chet said.

"Well, is Tom goin' to take his ol' red pickup?" asked Clyde. He knew they better not take the Blue Demon.

"Yeah, Say, I am goin' into town to see Betsy. I'll see you in the mornin.' Dave, I'll pair up with you tomorrow night and watch the herd," said Chet. He stood up to leave. Dave nodded.

"Say 'hi' to Betsy for me. Tell her she owes me a dance. Are you still sweet on her?" he asked. He remembered the two had spent a night together. She was a great dancer, the best he'd ever taken out on the dance floor. At the rodeos, he loved getting the cowgirls in his arms and dance all night. He couldn't wait to go on the circuit again.

"Uncle Fred. Yes n' no, I think she's been datin' around," said Chet as he shook his head in disappointment. He knew that she had been dating others. Of course, she was free to date who she wanted. He just thought they could pick up where they left off before his mom's death.

"How about that young gal who keeps callin' here at the house? What's her name…Sophia? What's goin' on with her," asked Fred. He loved to find out who his nephew was interested in.

"Uncle Fred, you are sure curious tonight," answered Chet. He knew his uncle was pushing him for information.

"Okay…Okay. I want to know what my nephew is up to in his love life. You're not gettin' any younger," he said, laughing. He got up and put another log on the fire. Before sitting down, he gave his nephew a quick punch to his midsection.

Chet blocked it and laughed, saying, "I'm still young and quick enough to stop you." As he left the room, Dave stood up.

"I'm headed out. See you both in the mornin'," Dave said as he walked out of the living room. He'd drive both Deirdre and Torri out to the party up at Skyline.

As the two older brothers sat comfortably in front of the fireplace, they looked at each other and smiled. They both were tired but knew they would have to get up and ride out tonight.

"In a few more weeks, we'll be brandin' those calves. Afterwards, I'm headin' out to the rodeo circuit. My friends have been keepin' me informed about the different ones. Some have some high stakes," said Fred, fondly thinking of rodeoing.

"You're goin' to break your neck someday. You talk more about the cowgirls than the broncs," Clyde said as he glared at his brother.

"What are you sayin'? I ride them both just fine," laughed Fred. He thought of one or two cowgirls he would have liked to have married. But again, he did not want to abandon Clyde. Now, with Beth gone, his brother seemed to need him again. However, his nephews were now grown up and Clyde wouldn't be alone if he did leave. He would have to think more on this.

"When are you goin' to settle down and get married?" he said.

"I've been takin' care of your sorry ass. I might find myself a cowgirl. You better do the same," Fred fired back.

"No, I've already tried that, and it didn't exactly work out," said Clyde quietly as he thought of his twenty some years of marriage.

"That wasn't your fault. Don't give up," he replied, encouraging his brother to move on.

"I don't know what I am goin' to do," responded Clyde. He didn't like being a widower.

"Are you gettin' any sleep at night?" asked Fred. His brother seemed tired and worn out.

"Not much...most nights I get a few hours or so. I feel that she's here, in this house, in our bedroom. I can feel her presence at night," he answered, quietly. He gasped as his eyes pooled with tears and blurred his vision. The nightmares had not gone away. Brushing his hand over his eyes, he took a deep breath, getting hold of his emotions. During the day, the ranch work kept his mind busy. But at night, his wife's death came rushing down on him. In the

185

darkness of his bedroom, he crumbled inside and couldn't sleep.

"You need to get her belongings packed up and out of your bedroom. They are reminders of her, that's all," he said.

"I can't touch her things, Fred. Can you take care of them?" he sighed, defeated. He had loved her so much that he couldn't imagine how she could do it.

"Listen, I'll take care of it... I can tell this is eatin' you up. Remember what you told the boys? Some things we cannot control. She did it to herself. Her addiction was out of control. You couldn't have stopped her. You know that. Accept it and go on... Sleepless nights are goin' to catch up with you. You'll ruin your health, brother, and that's not good," said Fred. He wanted his brother to be strong and healthy. No sleep would make him a weak man.

"Yeah, I know you are right. You know, after she lost those babies, she told me her sex life was over. We slept in the same bed for years. I couldn't touch her," he said. Every night he felt defeated, rejected, and lost. There were some nights when he couldn't take it and that's when he went into town.

"She told you that. My God, why didn't you divorce her, Clyde? I couldn't have lived like that," he said. He never knew the whole story, but this revelation surprised him. He felt sad for his brother who didn't deserve that. But then, he recalled that Beth was on drugs and not herself.

"Divorce? No, I couldn't leave her. We stayed together for the boys. She loved the boys. Sometimes she would let me in, but it was her mother who put the idea into her head about blamin' me. Nancy wanted us to fail. She thought that Beth would leave me. But the drugs took her out instead. We cared for each other more than anybody knew. I had hoped if I got her out of there, we could recapture our love," admitted Clyde. She had slept beside him for so long that it was hard to sleep without her. For years, her warmth had comforted him at night. He learned to accept her wishes.

"You tried. And here we are, with our own ranch. Clyde, we need to get drunk. We've done nothin' but work since we've been back from the funeral. Let's go out on the town tomorrow night. It'll be Saturday. We are too young to give up on livin'. Hell, we both need to look around for some women," Fred said, thinking of getting his brother out of his depressed state. A man needed a reason to live. Yes, a ranch could keep a man going, but sometimes he needed more— companionship and love. And Clyde needed that.

"Yeah, I liked to go out sometime, but I don't know about the other part. I'm not ready to get involved with anyone. Right now, we better go and get saddled up," said Clyde as he reached for his boots and slipped them on. Standing up and shaking off his thoughts of Beth, he said, "Let's go. I don't want any hungry grizzly eatin' up our herd. He'd better not come around here to our ranch." Fred thought *there's my brother. He's back.*

Fred stood up and went over to the fireplace. He poked the logs down to the hot, red embers. Sparks flew up the chimney as he broke up the burned wood, leaving the remnants of the hot fire to burn into ash. The fire had warmed the ranch house for the chilly night ahead. Both left the living room and headed toward the stable. The herd needed their attention tonight.

Chapter 14

The Skyline Party

With the chilly April evening, the group up at Skyline Campground had started a campfire to warm up the dark night. The party had already started before Matt, Tom, and Bill had driven up to the mesa. Two cars were parked near the campground which had an old wooden picnic table next to the campfire. George's two-tone green car was parked next to Craig's turquoise Bel-Air. They had gathered the wood and started the campfire. Craig had brought a case of beer with his own pint of whiskey in his car. As a friend, George had picked up Rebecca and her friend Melanie; Craig had a date with Suzie. The two cheerleaders, Rebecca and Suzie, brought some snacks—a couple of bags of potato chips and crackers. The beer and the snacks sat on the old wooden picnic table.

One of the girls, Melanie, a blonde, brown eyed junior, had brought a bag of marshmallows, thinking that they might want to roast them over the campfire. That Friday night, the three of them were having a sleepover at Rebecca's house. As a junior, Melanie Carter had never been out partying like this with her friends. As the youngest of her family, she had three older brothers. One was Denny—the town doctor. Her parents owned and ran the Double D Ranch. Her dad Mark Carter was the 'old man' who had called the sheriff when the guys would drag race their cars out on the flat stretch of highway near their ranch. She felt awkward around these guys who would drag race, knowing that her dad called them in whenever they raced.

The girls were sitting down on the benches of the picnic table, munching on the chips and crackers. Craig opened the case of beer and handed out a can to each of them. George and he walked over to the campfire, poked around the logs, and added more wood to the fire now that it had started. The two made small talk, waiting for Dave to come with Deidre.

Meanwhile, the girls were whispering and talking among themselves. They were curious to hear the rumors about Eveline.

"Eveline called me two nights ago. She sounded upset and miserable," whispered Rebecca. The whole high school knew about Eveline and her pregnancy. They knew that she had been sent off to have the baby, but they didn't know where. Her friends felt sad for her and worried about how she was doing.

"Did she say where she is staying?" asked Suzie. That had been the secret around town. Her parents insisted that she was with her sick aunt. But the town knew her absence was based on her pregnant condition.

"No, we didn't talk about anything particular, except how lonely she felt," answered Rebecca.

"Is she coming back afterwards?" asked Suzie.

"Sure. Her folks own the café in town. We didn't talk very long, but she said she couldn't call anymore because her dad put a restriction on her calls—only to her parents. She told me to write a letter and give it to her mom who would send it on to her," said Rebecca softly. The parents were protecting their daughter the only way they could—no contact with friends who would talk.

"Will she write us back?" asked Suzie. If Eveline wrote back, they would know her mailing address.

"I don't think so. We should write her though. She would like to hear from us. Don't you think?" asked Rebecca.

"Listen, if her name comes up tonight with the guys, play dumb. I think Matt Fletcher's coming and he might ask," said Suzie. They recalled that Eveline had liked Matt and talked about him all the time after they had met.

Melanie looked confused, "Why would he ask about her?" She had never met Matt or any of the Fletchers, although she had heard about them. She knew Eveline from school, but Rebecca and Suzie were cheerleaders, so they got around more than she did.

"Eveline had a few dates with him. Maybe, he won't ask. I don't know. Don't say anything. As far as the guys are concerned, we haven't heard from her. Okay?" said Rebecca. She looked at Suzie and then at Melanie. They both nodded and agreed. No one would want to be in Eveline's situation.

Rebecca felt particularly bad because she remembered when the Hadley High School basketball team stayed overnight in the Riverside motel. Along with the other cheerleaders, she had been at that motel. But they had gotten separated from Eveline, and they hadn't seen her again until school on Monday. Suzie, Deirdre, and she had enjoyed their little fling that night with a couple of basketball players, partying and making out. Because of their coach, the players did not have any liquor, so despite being teetotalers that night, they had had fun.

When they came to school, Eveline told them that she had made out with one of the basketball players, and that he had taken her home. Her parents had grounded her since she came home after curfew, but she played like it was nothing. Jokingly, she had showed them her hickies on her neck. But months later after hearing of her fainting in the doctor's office, they counted back and knew that that night something had happened to Eveline that she hadn't told them. Her best friends had defended her at school, but others spoke harsh words about her. Many classmates had spread rumors of her being a 'slut' and a 'whore.' *A vicious condemnation of a nice friend.* Silence fell on the three girls as they thought of Eveline's terrible situation and of how her parents must feel.

Finally, Craig came over to Suzie, and said, "What are you girls whisperin' about?" He came up behind Suzie and wrapped his arms around her. Looking down at her, he said, "Come over by the fire." He kissed her on her temple.

She smiled up at him and said, "Oh, we're just talking about school, but we're done. Ahhhhhh. Are you feeling ignored?" Suzie flirted with him, batting her eyelashes at him. Slipping her legs out from under the picnic table, she picked up her beer can and took a sip. They walked over to the campfire and he pulled her closer to him. Craig leaned down and gave her a kiss.

Smiling down at her, he said, "Don't get sassy with me, Suzie." As a young senior in high school, he liked her, but sometimes her mouth got in the way and took over. A few weeks ago, he had a date with her when he raced his car out at Carter's flats against Matt's red sports car.

Between that time and now, he had been out with Betsy who worked all the time. He rented a small apartment above the Dark Horse Tavern. Later, he found out that Betsy rented the other apartment down the hall from him. With her red hair and hazel eyes, Betsy was a beautiful woman who had a bustline that defined her. But she had held something back when they were together. He told her about his military experience, but she wouldn't talk about her past. She told him 'it was complicated' and deflected his questions. He wanted someone who was more open and honest. Suzie did have her faults, but she didn't hold back. In fact, he had to kiss her to shut her up. As he thought about getting her into his arms tonight, he smiled down at her and kissed her again.

The campfire roared as they huddled around it. Looking up, they saw a pair of headlights coming along Skyline road. Behind them was a second pair. An old red pickup parked next to Craig's Bel Air. Matt, Tom, and Bill stepped out of the pickup, walked over to the campground, and said 'hi.' The other black pickup parked next to the red one, and Dave with Deirdre and Torri stepped out. Walking over the campfire, they introduced themselves. For the first time, they met Tom and Bill. They found out that Tom would be a senior next year in high school and that Bill from Scottsville had totaled his green car. For the rest of the introductions, Torri was reacquainted with George. The four high school girls said 'hi' to Torri and the guys. Everyone noticed Bill's cast on his right arm and that his movements were stiff and careful.

"Hey, grab a beer over on the table there," Craig said, inviting everyone to have a drink.

"There's some chips and crackers over there, too. Help yourselves," said Suzie. A couple of the guys handed Craig some money for the beer. Dave went over to the picnic table

191

and called out 'Heads up!' and started tossing cans to Matt, Tom, and Bill who caught one with his left hand. Everyone shouted 'nice catch' as Bill smiled, popping off the top. Thirsty, he stood and gulped the whole can down as everyone watched. Tonight was his night to party.

Belching loudly after he emptied the can, they all laughed as they took sips of their beer. Bill said, "Sorry, but I haven't been out partyin' for more than two weeks. I need another one, Dave." He tossed him another one.

Craig raised up two fingers, for he and Suzie had finished their first cans. Dave tossed him two cans. He grabbed two extra cans and walked over to Deirdre and Torri and gave one to each of them. As they popped open their beer cans, they talked among themselves. Someone said they were going to need more beer, but then George said he had brought a pint of whiskey they could drink. Looking at Tom, Bill said he'd go for more beer if they needed any more. Although before driving up to Skyline, they had stopped at the liquor store and Bill bought two pints of vodka—one for him and one for Matt. Tom knew they wouldn't need any more beer.

As the party continued, the yellow bag of potato chips and the red box of crackers were passed around. Emptied after a little while, someone toss the bag and box into the campfire. Sparks floated up when the empty box hit the burning wood and the bag crumbled. The flames leaped high as it consumed the paper. The box soon burst into flames. Someone put another piece of wood on the fire. As the new wood caught fire, the sound filled the air—deep loud pops as the sap grew hot. As the crowd drank and ate, Matt glanced over at Torri who glared back at him. He found that she reminded him of Ronnie in some of her features. But her eyes did not look kindly at him. He quickly looked away.

Soon, the marshmallows came out and the girls wanted sticks to roast them on. A couple of the guys walked away from the campfire and into the grove of aspens, looking for sticks. Coming back with several, the girls soon had roasted marshmallows. They laughed when some of the marshmallows dropped into the fire, burnt to a crisp. The girls licked their sticky fingers as they mumbled words of delight at the sweet taste of the brown, crusted marshmallows hit their mouths. Most of the guys didn't want to eat the marshmallows, but at the insistence of the girls, Tom and Matt had a couple of the sticky delight.

The guys were gathered on one side of the campfire and the girls on the other side, except for Craig and Suzie who were wrapped together with their arms. For Tom, he noticed the young, blonde-haired girl whose name was Melanie. Having been popular at his old high school, Tom had no fear of crowds and eased around the fire to stand next to her. He asked her what year she was in school and from there, they started talking to each other.

Finally, they eased over to the picnic table and sat down, talking. He found out that this was her first party out drinking and she told him about her family and their Double D Ranch. At first, she was nervous, but after they talked for a while, she relaxed and felt comfortable getting to know him. He told her about himself and that he planned on playing basketball when school started. As they talked back and forth, he noticed that her blonde hair pulled up in a ponytail bounced around her head. Her eyes looked blue, but she would turn and look at the fire while she talked. A couple of times, he saw flashes of blue as she glanced at him.

Melanie seemed to shiver once in a while, so he asked, "Do you need my coat to warm you up?"

"No, then, you'd be cold. I am fine," she insisted. But Tom could tell she was cold.

"Well, slide over here. We'll keep each other warm together," he said, as he reached around her, she moved into his warm body. They came together, smiling at each other. He liked her. Cuddled together, they continued to talk.

Over by the fire, George and Craig were talking about their work out at the Johnson Ranch. They both worked under the foreman Wyatt Gordon who had shot the grizzly a year ago. Both knew the story. And everyone in town had retold that story. Wyatt's reputation as a good marksman

193

had been known for years. Matt wanted to hear the story, so they told him the most interesting part—which was how Wyatt shot the grizzly from about seventy-five yards away. According to him, the grizzly didn't know what hit him. As the two talked about their foreman, Craig mentioned that he saw a new rifle in the gun store downtown—a 270 Winchester Model 70. Wyatt had talked about getting one and Craig definitely planned to buy one, for he wanted to get back into hunting after being in the military.

Interested, Matt asked Craig, "You were in the military?"

"Yeah, I joined the Army right out of high school. I wanted to get out on my own and I did. I was stationed in Germany and traveled to Austria…Switzerland…Italy…France. I had a great time seeing Europe," said Craig.

"What did you do in the Army?" asked Matt. He never knew anyone who had joined the Army.

"Oh, I was a clerk—typed all day and played all night," answered Craig. He gave Suzie a squeeze as he spoke. Looking at each other, they kissed. All eyes focused back to the campfire.

As the guys talked some more, Bill brought up the subject of outer space and wondered if they were going to the moon. "I've seen those satellites cross the night sky. Maybe, we'll see one tonight," said Bill. They all gazed up at the huge canopy of sparkling stars against the dark unknown. They felt small and insignificant against that undiscovered universe.

Needing to drink some more, Bill took out his pint of vodka, opened it, and drank a couple of sips. The clear liquid stung his throat a little as he swallowed. A little tipsy, Rebecca walked around and came over beside Bill. She reached for the pint as he handed it to her. She took a long drink and then shook her head as the sharp alcoholic liquid slid down her throat.

"Wow," she grasped, "that's strong." She gave Bill a sexy smile and fluttered her eyelashes.

"Just like I like it," he said. She turned to walk back but stumbled. Bill caught her with his left arm and steadied her. As she regained her balance, he pulled her closer to him and whispered to her, "Stay." Rebecca liked Bill's looks with his long, curly blonde hair. She felt sorry for him because of his broken arm. As she stayed beside him, Bill wrapped his arm around her. George sent a few daggers his way. He knew that Rebecca had been dating around, but she had always come back to him. It hurt him to watch her flirt with Bill.

When Dave called him about getting together tonight, he had told him about how Bill and his dad had come here with an old car and that they had spent the week working on putting the Red Devil's engine and transmission into it. As he talked, George had listened with interest. *Another car he could challenge.*

Looking over at Matt, George said, "Dave told me how you pulled the engine out of your wrecked sports car. That must have been a lot of work." Then, Matt and Bill told them about what they had done all week and that the blue coupe was running. As the conversation turned to their cars, they had a few questions to ask about the coupe. Silence fell on those who recalled the wreck and the death of their good friend Ronnie. Some even remembered about Mrs. Fletcher's death the same night.

And then, Deirdre walked around the campfire and stood beside Matt. As he turned to look at her, she took her arms and wrapped them around his waist, saying, "We're sorry to hear about your mom. Everything seemed to happen all at once."

Surprised at the affection, Matt put his arms around her and hugged her. He didn't have any words to express his feelings, for he'd been working at putting that behind him.

Then, Torri, who had been quietly drinking her beer this whole time, finally had something to say. All night, she had been gradually becoming more upset as she glared at Matt. With an act of rage, she threw her empty beer can into the fire. Squinting her eyes at Matt, she stomped around the campfire, pointing her finger at him.

"You. You, son of a bitch. Because of you and your damn car, my brother is dead," she said as her strong words rang out. Keeping her eyes on the fire all night, she could not look at him without thinking of her dead brother. It was just like that other day when Matt, his brother, and Bill had showed up at the café. She had kept quiet that day, but not tonight. With a little liquor in her, her tongue loosened up and she wanted to have her say—right or wrong. She wanted to let him know what she thought of him and his red sports car.

Taken back by her words, Matt looked at this fire spouting girl, and said, "I feel bad about your brother, but I didn't have nothin' to do with that. That was all on Ronnie."

"You're a piece of shit in my book. Don't you look at me like that," she screamed. Everyone was shocked at her anger, but they did understand her anger at losing her brother.

"Listen, lit'l lady. For your information, I drove that sports car for nearly a year and never wrecked it once. And my uncle drove it before me and never wrecked it either. You're out of line talkin' to me like that," he said as he defended himself.

"Hold on, hold on, now. You two calm down. It was an accident, Torri. You've got to accept it," said Bill trying to bring some sense back to the party.

"I don't have to calm down. No one can tell me how to feel, especially you, Bill Dickerson," said Torri as her brown eyes blazed with fury. With her ponytail bouncing, her reddish-brown hair added fire to her words.

Breathing hard, Matt looked closer at her. She reminded him of Ronnie. As she screamed at him, he felt as if Ronnie had risen out of his grave and was shouting at him. Shaking his head and closing his eyes, he looked again at her. He needed to get away from her; she was pure poison to him. He felt the scrutiny from the others. Deidre who had stayed by his side looked at the spectacle that Torri created. Like Bill, she wanted to defend Matt.

Stepping in between Matt and Torri, Deirdre faced her, and said, calmly, "Torri, that isn't fair to say such things.

196

Matt wasn't even in town at the time of the accident. He not only lost his best friend, but he lost his mom on the same day. Have a little compassion for him."

As she said those words, Torri crumbled in front of her. The impact of Deirdre's words weakened her knees. As she started to fall, Matt quickly stepped around Deirdre and caught her. Even though she hated him, she held tight to his strong arms, steadying herself. Tears rolled down her face. Still mad at him, she struggled to get away from him, slapping her hands against his chest.

She cried as she sobbed, "Get away…get away from me. I hate you." He held her up.

"Listen, I know what you're goin' through, but I didn't do anythin'," he said trying to reason with her. She was past reasoning. Hitting and slapping his big chest with her opened hands, she sobbed against this tall man holding her up. For Matt, her hysterics reminded him of his mom's episodes. She screeched out her agony, "Oh Ronnie….Ronnie..."

Finally, Dave came over to the two of them, and called out to her, "Hey, Torri….stop." He wanted to quiet her down and for her to get hold of her emotions. The two men looked and nodded at each other as he took her into his arms, pealing her away from Matt. Turning to Dave, she stumbled into his arms as she sobbed against his chest. She clung to him, putting her face into his big chest. He walked her slowly over to the picnic table. Sitting down with her in his arms, he cradled her as she wept for her brother.

Rocking her back and forth like a baby, he whispered, "Shhhh. It's all right, Torri. Let it out." She cried until his shirt under his jacket was wet with her tears. The turmoil of her sobbing twisted inside of him as he felt her pain and anguish.

Those standing around the campfire stood in shock. Grief tasted bad in their mouths. They handed around the whiskey, trying to drown out their own feelings about his death.

Taking a few more breaths, Matt turn from the campfire and walked to Tom's pickup a few feet away. Leaning

197

against the pickup, he put his head down as his emotions swirled around. His head was throbbing as his stomach lurched. Stepping farther away from the pickup, he bent over as he retched a couple of times. Pulling out a handkerchief from his back pocket, he wiped his lips. *Damn those headaches!* He feared that he had his mom's affliction more than ever now.

Tonight, Torri had stung him deep with her words. Getting ahold of his emotions, he quickly stepped back to the pickup. Despite her accusing words, she looked lovely, fragile, but headstrong. Even though she had lashed out at him, he felt an unfamiliar tenderness toward her. His heart was pounding as he thought of her. *How could she be so endearing, yet so full of hate?*

Bill walked over to his friend, stood beside him, and said, "Hang in there, buddy. She didn't mean what she said." He noticed that his friend had been sick again. Curious, he thought that the liquor was too much for him. He put his left arm around his shoulders and gave him a quick squeeze. Then, Tom strolled over to his brother. Melanie stood by the fire, unable to move.

"Are you all right, Matt" Tom asked quietly. He had noticed his brother was sick. But he had heard Torri's words which cut him just as deep. He recalled in the café how people were whispering about them. This must have been the reason. *They blamed his brother for Ronnie's death.*

"I feel like shit. Damn it to hell...what can I say to her?" said Matt. He didn't want her to hate him.

"Let it go. She's upset. You know that," replied Tom. Nodding, he looked at his brother then at Bill who handed him the vodka. Taking a sip from the pint, Matt felt the sting of the strong liquor hit his dry raw throat. He gasped a little as it went down, clearing his mouth and throat.

"Hey, we came here to drink, guys. Let's go over by the fire," said Bill. The three walked back over to the group around the campfire.

By then, Dave had walked Torri over to his pickup and put her in the cab, shutting the door. Walking back over to the group, he said, "I'm takin' her home. Deirdre, you can stay. I'll be back. Do any of you want more beer?" All of them said 'yes' and a few dollars were handed over to him.

Craig said, "Let's get some more wood on this fire." The guys threw on two or three more small logs onto the campfire. With the new fuel, the fire smoked for a while and finally, burst into flames.

As Dave left, they finished off the rest of the beer in the case. Craig walked over to his car and got his pint of whiskey. Between the vodka and the whiskey, they were feeling really good by the time Dave had dropped off Torri, bought another case of beer, and drove back up along Sheep Creek up to Skyline and the campfire.

As Dave parked his pickup, Deirdre walked over to him as he got out.

"Is she going to be okay?" she asked.

"Yeah. It's been tough on her. She feels bad about what she said," he replied. Taking the case from out of his truck bed, Dave walked over to the picnic table, set it down, and opened it up. The guys came over and took a beer or two, moving back to the campfire that continued to roar, pop out sparks, and radiate heat to the group. They opened their cans of beer, drank down the cold liquid, and looked into the hot fire.

Glancing at him, Dave said, "Listen, Matt. I know Torri feels bad about what she said to you. We don't blame you. We know it was an accident." He wanted to smooth over her rant.

"Yeah, we know Ronnie was a little crazy about that car of yours," said George.

"Well, let's forget it. Can I ask about somethin' else that's been botherin' me?" asked Matt. Getting bold, he started to have a buzz with all the liquor. Knowing that Rebecca and Deirdre were Eveline's friends and fellow cheerleaders, he wanted to find out more about Eveline's situation.

George said, "Sure. What do you want to ask?"

"You know that I dated Eveline a couple of times. I've been wonderin' about her. Where did she go?" asked Matt. As he spoke, the girls looked at each quickly and then away.

The guys didn't want to talk about her, so they remained silent. No one spoke for a few seconds. The air filled with tension again.

Rebecca finally said, "Matt, we don't know where she is. Her parents aren't telling us anything other than she's with her sick aunt in Colorado."

"How can I get a hold of her? I just want to know how she's doin'. Tell me," he asked about Eveline again. With the alcohol running through his brain, he wasn't going take 'no' for an answer.

"We don't know anything more about her. She's in a bad situation. That's all," answered Deirdre.

Wanting to change the subject, George asked, "Bill, I hear you and Matt are goin' down to Winston to play at a dance tomorrow."

Bill turned to George, and said, "Right. We've got a gig for a senior dance. Matt's goin' to play lead while I just sing. I can't play my guitar with this arm."

"Rebecca, tell me about Eveline," Matt called out again, insisting on an answer.

"How many are in your band?" asked George, still trying to turn the conversation away from Eveline and her situation.

"The band has three other guys—one on drums, one on a base guitar, and one on a saxophone. I usually sing and play lead guitar. Matt, here, has been my backup guitar. We play mostly rock 'n roll songs, but we have added a few country songs for variety," answered Bill as he took a sip of his beer.

"You girls are ignorin' me. I can tell. You know more than you're lettin' on. You were her best friends. Come on, tell me somethin'," continued Matt talking to Rebecca and Deirdre. As he drank, he got more insistent.

Finally, Deirdre walked around to Matt, grabbed his arm, and said quietly, "Let's go over to your pickup. You've had too much to drink… You're drunk… Come on, Matt." She guided him towards the red pickup with her arm around his waist. She wanted him to stop asking questions about Eveline.

200

He leaned on her, put his arm on her shoulder, and stumbled a little as they moved towards the pickup. Along with Torri's hysterics, the girls had kept quiet about their friend. He felt that this party tonight had turned nasty. He was getting nowhere. Opening the door, the two slid into the cold cab.

After sitting in the cab and snuggling together, Deirdre thought about Ronnie who she had liked and dated. When he had played in the band over in Scottsville, he met a girl named Gail Gibson. He had gone out and spent the night with her. When he came home to Riverside, he had dropped her, saying that he had found someone he loved. She had cried herself to sleep until his death took her crying to another level. Emotionally, she felt vulnerable. But she wanted to let Matt know that no one really blamed him. They were just upset that he had died, and the town had turned their anger on him and his family. And now, he wanted to know about Eveline. *What should she tell him? He could write a letter.*

"Why won't you tell me about Eveline?" asked Matt, looking into Deirdre's brown eyes.

"Her parents don't want any of us to contact her," answer Deirdre.

"Yeah, I know. I even asked her mom the other day at the café. She wouldn't even talk to me," he said, as his head buzzed and started to throb.

"That's too bad, her mom told me we could write her," she said.

"Good. When you get her address, let me know," Matt responded, excited about the possibility of getting in touch with her.

"Sorry, you don't understand. We can write the letters, but her mom will send them. We don't have her address," she explained.

"Oh, I see. Her mom probably wouldn't send mine," said Matt, knowing how her mom had ignored him the other day. And then, Eveline had said to 'forget her.' *What a dilemma.*

"I think we should give Beth some time. Maybe, she'll want to hear from us, later," said Deirdre.

The two sat quietly thinking about Eveline and her situation. Deirdre put her hand up to Matt's dark brown hair, combed it through her fingers, and played with it. Looking at his handsome face, she wished that he would kiss her. His square, masculine jaw with his straight nose gave her pause to feel closer to him than when she first met him at the wedding reception. She recalled his tall warm body against hers, dancing together. *Could he ever like her? No, he still talked about Eveline.* Maybe, she could make him forget her tonight.

Deirdre leaned nearer to him as she fingered his hair. He looked down at her, and she raised her face to him, waiting for that kiss she wanted. With his head buzzing, he leaned down and sought out her soft lips. His arms moved around her, and he pulled her closer to him. Her warm, soft lips sent his emotions swirling. He moved his tongue along her lips and teased them open. As his tongue sought out hers, she tasted a hint of vodka. His hands moved up to her soft blonde hair. Pulling back, he looked into her eyes. With her head in his rough hands, he kissed her forehead, then her nose, and finally, back to her soft lips. He kissed her hard this time; his desire stirred within him. He'd had too much to drink, for his head was spinning.

After he had raced his car that one night, he recalled that he had driven her home and they had kissed. She had been drunk and upset over Ronnie's rejection. Those forbidden emotions that he had with her that night came flooding back to him. His head was throbbing, but that didn't seem to matter to him. He needed to feel her. Fumbling, he unbuttoned her coat as she unbuttoned his jacket. He could only think of feeling her warm skin. Finally, he pulled up her soft pink sweater and felt one of her breasts as his other hand went around to the small of her back. She shivered against his caresses. She pulled up his shirt and his t-shirt to move her hands over his warm chest and around to his back. Breathing hard, they felt their hearts pounding. As the two continued making out, their hands and lips sought out the warm and the affection they so desired.

Out by the campfire, Craig and Suzie had decided to leave, so they walked arm and arm to his Bel Air and drove away. With their heads buzzing, their desires had warmed them towards each other. Craig wanted to spend time with her at his apartment before he took her home.

With his ribs hurting, Bill wanted to rest on the top of the picnic table. He set the case of beer down on the bench of the picnic table. Crawling up on the table, he said that with all the work on the car, he couldn't stand up another minute. While he stretched himself out and relaxed, Rebecca came over and sat beside him on the picnic table. Soon, turning carefully on his side, he had his hand up her blouse as they flirted with each other. Since they had taken over the table, Tom and Melanie moved over to the campfire with George and Dave. Then, Rebecca scooted nearer to Bill as she leaned over and kissed him. They stayed there, making out on the table, with kisses, giggles, and whispers.

The others by the campfire ignored the two on the picnic table. The fire had been dying down and everyone felt that the party was nearly over. With Melanie's hand in his, Tom walked her over to his red pickup, dropped down the tailgate, and picked her up and set her down. He hopped up next to her.

They looked at each other and smiled. Tom asked, "Would you like to go out with me some time, just the two of us?"

She laughed, thinking of tonight, and said, "Yes, that would be nice."

"How about next week? We could go to the movies. Can I get your number?" he asked. She nodded as he dug around in his pockets and scrounged up a piece of crumbled paper and a stubby, short pencil. He handed them to her. Turning half around, she put the paper down on the bed of the truck as she wrote down her phone number. He took the pencil from her and wrote down his number for her. Carefully tearing the paper into two, he handed her his number and he kept her number.

She said, "Thanks. I have to clear it with my parents, but I'm sure it will be fine. You can meet them when you come and pick me up. Our ranch is beyond your ranch where the guys drag race their cars. It's the turn off to the right," Melanie explain. He knew it was getting late and they should be leaving, so he jumped down from the tailgate and lifted her off. Setting her down and with her still in his arms, he stopped, looked into her face. *Should he kiss her? Yes, definitely.*

Slowly, he leaned down and gave her a soft kiss, just brushing his warm lips over her soft lips and whispered, "I'll call you."

She blushed and quietly said, "Call at night. I'm in school during the day."

"Yeah, Melanie. Let's go," he said as they walked back to the dying campfire. He held her warm hand in his. They walked over to George's car. He helped her into the back seat. Closing the door, he smiled at her and lifted his hand and waved 'goodbye.'

Getting ready to leave, Dave and George were picking up the empty beer cans. George walked over to the picnic table where Bill and Rebecca were making out. He cleared his throat to get their attention, but they didn't notice him.

Finally, he said, out loud, "Hey, you two... it's time to leave. Becca, I'm ready to leave. Come on." As Bill looked over at George, he pulled his hand out from under her blouse. She took her hand out from under his shirt. With his right arm in a cast, she had to help him button up his shirt. Rebecca put herself together as she pulled down her top and buttoned up her coat. Crawling off the tabletop, she stood ready to leave.

"Oh...you're no fun, George," whined Rebecca. She had always complained.

"Do you want a ride home, Becca? Or do you want to walk?" asked George, disappointed tonight. Driving her up to Skyline, he wanted to make out with her, but she had left him and made out with Bill. Inside, he was burning up with anger. He had just about enough of her flirting around.

"But give me a minute to say goodbye," she said. Disgusted, George turned and took the case of beer to Dave's pickup. Bill slowly crawled off the table as he reached out for Rebecca to steady him.

He took her into his arms and said quietly, "Sorry, my ribs are hurtin'. Is George your guy?" She nodded as he looked into her beautiful face surrounded by her honey brown hair. At least, he had gotten a girl in his arms tonight. But for some reason, his blood had run cold with her. He had felt no pleasure in being with her tonight. Making out with her hadn't turned him on. Maybe, Denise had changed him. He looked forward to getting back home and seeing Denise—someone he cared for and could trust.

"You better treat him right, Becca. He seems to care for you... Goodbye," said Bill, giving her a final hug. He could tell that she played around with George's emotions. Her flirtations would anger any man. She had a wicked side to her that he recognized instantly. If George were his friend, he'd tell him to find another girl. Turning, he walked over to the campfire and helped Dave kick dirt on the dying embers.

Over in Tom's pickup, Deirdre and Matt heard everyone getting ready to leave, so he said, "We better stop." He pulled back from her as she pulled down her pink sweater and buttoned up her coat.

"I'm busy this week, but do you want to go out next week?" he asked, looking at her as she patted down her short blonde hair. Pulling out a tube of hot pink lipstick from her pocket, she flipped down the visor with a small mirror. He watched her apply hot pink to her lips. He liked kissing those soft lips. Flipping the visor up again, she turned to him and smiled.

"Yeah, Dave has my number," she answered. She doubted he would call her. She could hope, but he had been concerned about Eveline. To her, it seemed as if he still cared for her. After Ronnie dumped her, she had had many disappointments that she had to guard her heart right now.

He sensed her coldness. He didn't like leaving her this way, so he took her back into his arms. He held her close, and said quietly, "Hey, what's the matter? Did I say somethin' wrong?" His sensitivity made him aware of her indifference suddenly.

"I don't know. You seemed interested in Eveline. Will you really call me?" Deirdre asked. She would like to go out again with Matt. He was a kind, sensitive man. She liked him a lot.

"Yeah. Do you want to go out? I'll take you for a drive in my Blue Demon."

"Sure, I want to go out with you. The Blue Demon? Is that what you named your car?" she asked.

"Yeah," he answered, and he drew her in closer so he could kiss her again. "I'll call. I promise," he whispered. As they were kissing, there was a tap, tap, tap on the side window.

Outside, Bill said, "Okay, lover boy. We've got to go. Come on...it's cold out here."

They couldn't help but smile at each other; they separated. She took her fingers and wiped off the hot pink lipstick over his lips. As she did that, he looked at her smeared lips. He took his fingers and wiped her lips clean. Smiling at her again, he pulled the door opened, let her out of the pickup, and walked her over to Dave's black pickup. He gave her a final kiss as he wrapped his arms around her. He whispered in her ear, "Goodbye. See ya' next week." Chills went down her spine as his tenderness made her turn warm all over. She whispered back, "Goodbye, Matt."

Everyone said their 'goodbyes' and drove down the Skyline road and back home.

****

Earlier that evening, Chet got ready to go into town and to meet Betsy at the Dark Horse Tavern. He took a quick shower since he'd been working all day. Thinking about her, he hoped that they could talk more. After driving into town, he parked in front of the tavern on main street. He

206

opened the door of the tavern and the loud music from the jukebox came rushing out. He was a little early, so he looked around to see if she was waiting on a table near the back. Not seeing her, he walked over to the bar and ordered a draft beer. Maybe, she was in the back working on the books. He waited and sipped his beer. As the time slipped by, people came and went from the tavern. That night the owner Dick was working the bar. Smoke filled the room as people smoked, drank, talked, laughed, and listened to the jukebox.

Two couples came into the bar, put some money into the jukebox, and punched in their favorite songs. They went to a table and ordered some drinks. When one of their selected songs played, they jumped up and danced on the small dance floor in front of the jukebox. Their mugs of draft beer came to their table. One of the guys walked over and paid for their beer. Then, he went back to dancing. The couples danced another four songs when finally, they decided it was time for a break. They walked over to their table. Sitting down, they drank their mugs of beer, talking and laughing.

As he drank his draft beer, Chet kept looking around for Betsy. Obviously, she wasn't here. As Dick walked by behind the bar to mix a couple of drinks, he asked, "Hi, Dick. Did Betsy work tonight?"

"You know, she didn't show up," Dick said, concerned.

"Would you tell her I came in tonight? We were goin' to meet for drinks. I am Chet, by the way."

"Sure will. I know who you are. You're one of the Fletchers. I bet she finished work over at the Mercantile and went up to her apartment and fell asleep. She's done that a couple of times. You know, she gets up an hour or two before that store opens to stock those shelves. Then, she opens and works a full day over there. I don't know how she keeps goin' some days," said Dick as he finished mixing the drinks. He smiled and nodded at him.

"Thanks," said Chet. He paid for his beer and left. Going out into the cold night made him shiver for a second. He could see his breath as he walked over to his white pickup. He started up the pickup, let it idle for a while, and turned on the radio. As he listened to Elvis Presley sing (one of Sophia's favorite), he thought about Betsy. If she was up asleep in her apartment, he wasn't going up to wake her. He could give her a call, but it sounded like she needed the rest, working those two jobs. He decided to drive down to the Pole Cat Bar and call Sophia.

The dark April night chilled everyone who was out. Since it was Friday night, many people were headed for drinks at the local bars. Chet had to drive around the block to find a parking place near the other bar. Finally, he found one on the next block. Parking, he stepped out into the cold night again, walked down the street to the bar, and entered. The smoke-filled room was packed tonight. He strolled slowly through the throng of people to the back where the pay phone was. He picked up the receiver, put in his coin, and dialed the number. While the phone rang at the other end, he dug in his pocket for more change. When he heard Sophia answer 'hello,' the operator told him to put in the money for the call. He pushed his change into the slot and heard them clink down to the bottom of the phone. The operator said, "Thank you."

"Hi, Sophia. It's Chet," he said.

"Hi, Chet. How are you doing?" she asked. She sounded good.

"Oh, fine. Just workin'. How are you?" he asked.

"I have some good news. I have an interview in a town near you," she answered.

"Oh, where?" he asked.

"It is in Hadley. It's a junior high position. I don't know why they even called and wanted me to interview. I want to teach high school," she said. He heard her disappointment in her voice.

"You never know. Maybe, for your first job, you start there. I don't know, Sophia," said Chet. He wanted to encourage her, but he didn't have any knowledge about schools or teaching.

"I just don't know if I'd liked teaching at a lower level. I am certified to teach seventh grade to twelfth grade, maybe. I don't know what subjects I would be teaching in the junior high... Oh... don't I have to drive through Riverside to get to Hadley?" asked Sophia.

"Yes, you do. Maybe, we can see each other if you want to stop. I could meet you here in town," he said. He felt his heart skip a beat as he thought of seeing her again.

"I'll have to make some arrangements, but I'll call and let you know," she said.

"What day is the interview?" he asked.

"It's next Friday, so I think I may stop on the way back through on Saturday. Will you be around?" she asked.

"Yes, I'll be here. I'd love to spend some time together," Chet said. Her answer was interrupted by the operator asking him to put in more money. He grabbed some coins and slipped them into the phone. He heard them clink down into the phone, one by one, and then, he heard her voice again.

"I have to go now. I'll call you next week about my plans. I miss you," she said quietly.

"Yes, I miss you, too," he replied.

"Well, goodbye, Chet. Thanks for calling tonight. It's great hearing your voice," she said quietly.

"Yeah, goodbye. See you next week," he said. He heard the line go dead as she hung up. He put the receiver back into its cradle, and he stood there thinking how much he wanted to see her again. Her words gave him hope. Chet turned, moved slowly through the crowd at the bar and out through the door. Walking down the street, he didn't even notice the cold. He hurriedly crawled into his white pickup a block away. As he started the engine, he thought about how great it would be to see her and spend some time with her. He drove down main street and back to the ranch.

Chapter 15

Settling the Score

Ever since Eveline had discovered her pregnancy at the doctor's office last week, the Merther family had to deal with this terrible situation. Sitting for hours in the kitchen, her dad Bert had forced it out of Eveline. He wanted to know the name of the guy. Both parents were shocked when they heard the story. They found out that it was a Hadley's star basketball player named Devin Banes. Bert flew into a rage. Eveline cried and said he forced himself on her. He simmered for days as his daughter sobbed in her bedroom, ashamed to face her dad. Too mortified to let Eveline go anywhere, Kay called the high school and said she was sick. She stayed home for a week. Her parents wouldn't even let her attend Ronnie's funeral.

That following week one evening, Dr. Carter met with her parents and Eveline at their home. Bert had decided that his daughter would have to be sent away. Showing them a brochure about the convent, the doctor went over their services and costs. He asked if they had any questions. Her mother Kay worried about her daughter's health, but he assured her that the nuns were associated with a hospital and that she would receive the best of care. Her dad Bert wanted to know about her schooling. Again, the doctor reassured him that the convent ran a private school in which Eveline could finish her senior year there. Her mom worried about her daughter being by herself. The doctor told her that she would have girl companions who were in the same situation.

There was nothing more to decide; their daughter would have to leave Riverside soon by herself. Eveline wanted her mother to come with her, but her dad said they needed to keep the café opened. Sending her away would cost them, and they couldn't afford to close the café, even for a few days. He told her not to phone them unless it was an emergency. Long distant phone calls cost too much. She could write letters and let them know how she was doing.

The arrangements were made, and the next day, Dr. Carter picked up Eveline early in the morning.

As they left Riverside, the doctor had two hours with Eveline in the car to counsel her about her pregnancy. As a doctor, he spoke to her as a patient and slowly gave her medical information about her pregnancy. He didn't want to overwhelm her, so he'd talk and then he'd be quiet for a while so she could take in the information. The doctor told her that as a young woman, having a baby was a natural process and there was nothing for her to fear. He told her more about the convent and again reminded her that there would be others like her; she wouldn't be alone. He emphasized the important of keeping herself healthy, physically and mentally.

Concerned about the baby, Eveline wondered about the adoption procedures. The doctor explained that some married couples couldn't have babies and that the convent carefully found good couples who would love to raise their babies. The process took time, but the convent handled everything. After the baby was born, the adoption would be final. He told her that the records were sealed for the protection of her, the new parents, and the baby. The doctor gently told her that after the baby that she could return home and start her life again. Dr. Carter felt bad for Eveline and her situation. He did not know the whole story, but the parents didn't even bring up the option of marriage. There were situations like this that came up in his practice, but an unmarried pregnant girl always surprised him.

As the doctor talked, Eveline quietly listened to his advice, realizing that she had a lot to think about. The thought of living at the convent frightened her; she had never been away from home—even away from her parents. Feeling the pressure, she knew she had to be strong and brave. Arriving later that morning in Winston, Dr. Carter had arranged for her to travel by bus to the convent in Colorado where she would stay until she had the baby. She thanked him for his help and for driving her here. She knew that he didn't have to take her, but he had been driving back to Winston that morning—back to his main practice. Before

211

she boarded the bus, he told her that he would call and check on her progress. He'd let her parents know that she got there and how she was doing.

After Eveline had left that morning, her dad Bert raged on at home. He got on the phone and started calling people he knew in town who might know the people in Hadley. In order to get information, Bert concocted a story about a customer who had left a leather jacket in his café. He fabricated a story that he knew that the guy's last name was Banes and that he was from Hadley, but nothing else. Shaking her head at her husband's phone calls, he surprised Kay when he came up with a business address.

Kay asked, "What are you going to do?" She feared what her husband could be planning.

"I'm goin' to let that son of a bitch know what he did," spat out Bert.

"How is that goin' to help? It'll only worsen the situation for us here if someone finds out," she said. She thought he would be calling attention to their terrible situation.

"I don't give a damn. No guy is goin' to do this to our daughter and get away with it. That kid's goin' to realize he can't mess with us," he shouted. He was getting angrier by the minute.

"Bert, stop and think. What are you really goin' to do?" she asked again.

"I'm goin' to punch that kid's lights out. It ain't goin' to be pretty, but I'm goin' to settle the score," Bert hollered. Grabbing his coat and keys, he started to leave. Turning to Kay, he said, "Keep the café opened. I hired Bobby's daughter Torri to help at the café since our daughter isn't here. I'll be back tomorrow. I've gotta do this, Kay," he said. He gave her a quick kiss on the cheek and left.

Only his wife knew the reason that Bert left town for two days. As he drove over Tepee Pass to Hadley, he thought about his daughter being sent away. As a parent, he felt totally helpless, but with this decision to find this guy, he felt better doing something—right or wrong. He found out that the family name 'Banes' was well-known in

Hadley. The father owned a real estate business. The two-hour drive helped him settle his anger a little as he made his plans.

As Eveline was stepping up into a bus in Winston, her dad arrived in downtown Hadley. He found the real estate office with no problems; it was right on main street. Parking his car in front of the office, he sat and looked around for a few minutes. Bert was a large, bald man with a big belly. He could intimidate most people with just his size, his big hands, and his dark, black eyes. As he stepped out of his car, he flexed his muscles under his jacket.

Going into the real estate office, he strolled by the front desk with a woman talking on the phone and walked straight back to an office where a man with a grey suit and maroon tie sat behind a big, fancy desk. Bert closed the door to the office, turned, and stared down at the suited man.

"Mr. Banes? I'm Bert," he growled. He stood with his feet spread apart in his old clothes and dingy jacket.

"Yes. What can I do for you?" said the tall man as he stood up. He had a slick nature about him, greying hair and manicured manners. Bert didn't like him immediately.

"You have a little problem. Is your son's name Devin?" asked Bert. He would enjoy twisting this fancy guy around his little, fat finger.

"I'm not sure why you're here. What do you want?" asked Mr. Banes, but mentioning his son got his attention. He could smell this large man with a big belly standing in his office. He stunk and smelled like a greasy café.

"I need to talk to your son Devin," Bert said in his gruff voice.

"He's not here. He's in school. Tell me what you want," said Mr. Banes.

"Hell, it seems that your son's been foolin' around, gettin' into trouble," said Bert. Again he wanted to take this slow, not giving out too much information right now.

"Listen, you better start making sense or I'm calling the sheriff," Mr. Banes, answered. Trying to remain calm, his temper was slowly rising.

213

"That's okay. I'm leavin'," said Bert. He turned and left the office, walking out of the building and got into his car. He started up the engine, backed up, and drove down the street.

As he drove away, he noticed that a café sat across the street from Mr. Banes' office. After driving down main street, he turned around, came back, and stopped a block from the café, where he turned off the engine and waited. Deciding that he needed lunch, he strolled down and stepped into the café. He found a table near the window where he could watch the real estate office. He could eat, drink, and sit there, waiting. He knew that sooner or later that either the son would show up or he would follow Mr. Banes home. Since he didn't know what Devin looked like, he had to wait.

After ordering off the menu, he asked if the town had a local newspaper he could read. The young waitress brought it to him. The waitress sadly reminded Bert of his daughter. *Eveline is probably at the convent today.* His eyes pooled with tears a little as he thought of his lovely daughter and her unfortunate future. She had been a good daughter; he had tried to protect her. He found out that some things in life couldn't be controlled. Fate had dealt her a hard road to travel. He hoped she would come out of this and could make a good life for herself. As a parent, he felt he had failed her. He shook off those thoughts. He needed to get focused and make this kid pay for what he did to his innocent daughter.

He sat looking through the headlines; nothing caught his attention. Since he heard that this kid played basketball, he turned to the sports page. The basketball season had ended, so the sports section featured the track events and a photo of the team members. He scrolled through the names listed under a photograph. Finally, he saw the guy's name 'Devin Banes.' His heart pounded in his big chest as he read the name. Counting the faces with the names, he landed on the face of 'Devin,' smiling, tall in the back row. The face was small. Bert's eyes weren't that good. Squinting closer at the small face, Devin had a smug look on his face like his dad.

214

He got madder as he looked at the photo. He had to settle this score or else he'd go mad for the rest of his life, thinking of his daughter.

Soon, the waitress brought out his meal. As he folded up the newspaper, she set his plate in front of him and poured him some more coffee in his half empty cup. He ate automatically, not tasting the food. His mind focused on this guy; his anger simmered deep inside.

About this time, a car pulled up to the real estate office with a young man wearing a blue suit and hat. He got out of the car and took a drag on his cigarette before tossing it into the street. He stepped into the office and disappeared. A few moments later, he and Mr. Banes came out of the office. They were deep into a private conversation; they kept looking around. Their tense body language told Bert that they were talking about something serious—maybe, about Devin. Mr. Banes pointed his finger in the chest of the young man who kept shaking his head. Disgusted, Mr. Banes turned and went back into his office. The young man got into his car and drove off. *Interesting* thought Bert.

After finishing his meal, Bert signal to the young waitress. He told her that he wanted a piece of pie--- whatever kind they had for dessert. She smiled and brought him a piece of apple pie. Then, he asked her for the bill. Bringing over the bill, she handed it to him as he pulled out his wallet and handed her the cash for the meal. He told her to keep the change which amounted to a big tip of over a dollar. He asked her for more coffee, saying he was waiting to meet a friend. Looking at his watch, he knew he had to wait here another hour until around three-thirty. School would be out, and he'd bet that the young kid would be showing up at his dad's office—at least that's what he hoped.

As the clock ticked the time away, the afternoon went slowly by. Bert drank several cups of coffee and read more of the local newspaper. He read the want ads in the back of the paper and scanned the paper for a real estate ad. Sure enough, the Banes Real Estate had a medium sized ad along the bottom of the third page of the newspaper. The ad mentioned they managed and sold all types of properties such as homes, ranches, office buildings, and rentals. Bert got the impression that they were successful here in Hadley. He felt good that he was here today to put a little fear into their comfortable lives. *Yes, he was ready for a good fight.*

Being the underdog for years, he knew how to be a bully and how to street fight. As a fat, unpopular kid, he had fought against those who had hated him and who challenged him many times. Guys learned to stay out of his way. He never dated in school. After many odd jobs, he ended up as a fry cook in a café one time. Uncommon for him, he liked the hot grill, the tubs of hot grease, and the sharp knives that sliced through the food. He ruled the kitchen, bullying anybody who tried to take over. Then, one day, a young, cute waitress named Kay Rosley walked into his kitchen. She shied away from him at first, but after a while, she learned to handle him in her sweet way. He finally asked her out one weekend and after three months of dating, they married. Afterwards, he and Kay had worked hard together to start and run their own café in Riverside.

Today, this fancy guy from Hadley was going to remember he shouldn't mess with their daughter—their pride and joy. It was close to four o'clock now, so Bert got up and left the café, walking down to his car a block away. He sat in his car, watching and waiting.

Soon, a polished white and red Chevy drove up to the real estate office. The loud radio played a hit tune by Ritchie Valens which sounded up and down main street. Bert rolled his window down a little to hear the popular tune. Just what he thought, the son had shown up here at his dad's office. This young kid wore a leather and wool varsity jacket, got out of his car, and walked into the real estate office. The green and yellow varsity jacket had the school letter H in yellow on the left side and some award metals pinned on the right side. Bert got out of his car and headed towards the office. Finally, he would get to face this snot-nosed kid. This bastard named Devin would remember this day for a long time.

216

Coming into the office, he walked straight past the front desk again and went to the back office. He stepped into the office, closing the door. He looked at the young kid sitting in a chair. Mr. Banes stood up behind his desk. Bert didn't wait for an introduction. Grabbing that varsity jacket, he lifted Devin up out of the chair and pushed him up against the nearby wall.

"You're the son of a bitch who can't keep his pecker in his pants," shouted Bert. With his right hand, he drew back and punched him in the midsection, right in the solar plex. Devin gasped, bent over, grabbing his midsection. Bert's left hand came up with an upper cut to his jaw. Then, with his right hand, he smashed his nose and heard the crunch as Devin cried out. Bert stepped back and let the kid fall, holding his nose as blood poured out over his varsity jacket, turning that 'H' to red.

By this time, Mr. Banes grabbed Bert by his arm and spun him around, facing him. He shouted, "What's the meaning of this? You can't come in here and hit my son. I'm calling the sheriff."

"Fuck you, Mr. Banes. I just did. And you go right ahead and call the law. I have a complaint I'd like to file," threatened Bert with anger in his gruff voice. Mr. Banes took a step back as he heard the threat. He had a reputation to protect and whatever this fat man had to do with his son, concerned him. His youngest son must have gotten into trouble again.

"Listen, whatever your name is, we need to take a few minutes to talk about this. What in the hell are you doing here?" said Mr. Banes. He still didn't know the situation since his older son Doug who was here earlier hadn't told him anything. Now, his youngest son Devin had just walked in and he was just about to discuss this matter with him.

"My name is Bert and I'm from Riverside, where I have an underaged daughter who got pregnant by your snot-nosed son. There's nothin' else to say," growled Bert. Finally, he had said it.

The woman who sat at the outside desk came to the door, knocked, and opened it and asked quietly, "Should I call the sheriff, Mr. Banes?" She had heard loud noises and voices coming from her boss' office.

"No, no, Jane. That won't be necessary. There seems to be a small disagreement. Go back to your desk," Mr. Banes said. She left and closed the door. He turned to his son who was nursing his bloody nose.

"Okay, Devin. What is this man Bert talking about? Do you know his daughter?" said Mr. Banes.

"What? I don't know any girl from Riverside. Why would I be there," said Devin, trying to sound innocent. He sounded like a sniffling kid with his nose held closed shut. He had forgotten that he was on the basketball team and would have been there for a game.

"Damn it to hell. You're a liar. You were there with the basketball team this winter, playin' a game at our high school. My daughter's a cheerleader. We had a snowstorm that night and your team stayed at a motel in Riverside," said Bert, knowing he caught the kid lying.

Listening, Mr. Banes looked surprised at his son and said, "Tell me the truth. This is not the time to lie to me. Did you go out with his daughter?"

Bert noticed that the young son had no guts to stand up to his dad as he started to whimper.

Caught with no way out, Devin cried out, "Yeah…sure. I went out with someone…yeah, a cheerleader. I don't even know her name." He clearly remembered that cute cheerleader named Eveline, but he wouldn't admit it to his dad.

With his cocky attitude, he pulled at his varsity jacket, and continued, "What about it? Listen, it wasn't her first time. That lil' darlin' knew what she was doin'." Looking at Bert, the kid squinted his eyes in a shrewd look that told Bert that his daughter wasn't that innocent. He just stood there, shocked. *Eveline hadn't been innocent? She had kept a secret from them.* Parents were the last to hear about such matters.

"Oh, Devin. What have you done? What about your basketball scholarship to college? Now, you'll have to marry this girl, who you don't even know," said his dad in agony at the thought that his son had just destroyed his future.

Bert jumped in really quick and said, "Hell no. That ain't happenin'. No way do I want this son of a bitch to marry my daughter." Obviously, Devin felt relieved that he wouldn't have to marry the girl.

"What are we going to do, Bert?... Sit down and let's talk?" asked Mr. Banes, happy to hear that Bert wasn't here for his son to marry his daughter. He now wanted to get this smelly guy out of his office and out of town before anyone else heard about this.

"I'm fine standin'. What do you have to say?" asked Bert.

"Dad, I need to take care of this bloody nose. Can I leave?" asked Devin. He knew that his dad would take over and take care of this problem. His dad nodded and Devin slipped out of the office.

Concerned, Mr. Banes asked some questions about Bert's daughter and how were they handling this situation. Bert told them that they were sending his daughter to a convent to have the baby, giving it up for adoption. He asked a few more questions to clarify the situation with the daughter.

With his son gone, Mr. Banes said that he was sorry about the unfortunate situation. He said he admitted that his son had made a big mistake, but the young sometimes did get into trouble. As he spoke, he pulled out his check book from the desk drawer. Thinking for a few seconds, he wrote out a check to Bert after asking for his last name.

Handing Bert the check, he finalized the meeting with these words, "I hope this will help with the expenditures. I'll send you a check each month for this amount for next six months. I have only one condition. Please keep my son's name out of it. He's got a chance for a scholarship to college. I don't want anything to ruin his chances. Do you understand?"

Bert took the elegant looking check with his name written on it. Several times in his lifetime, he'd seen how big men like Mr. Banes got around and covered up their

219

problems with money. Mr. Banes' smooth manners and the big check triggered Bert's anger even more deeply inside his gut. His daughter's future had been tainted. No money could change that. Looking at Mr. Banes with his dark, beady eyes, he took the check and tore it up into pieces, tossing them into the air as they floated and scattered down onto the floor. The check was now nothing more than tiny bits of paper. Then, he took a step towards Mr. Banes behind the desk who looked both surprised and frightened.

"I've met your kind before. Money isn't the answer. Let me tell you somethin'. That son of yours is no good, and the truth will come out. You can't keep his name a secret for very long. Every time you look at his crooked nose, I want you to remember me and what he did to my daughter.... It's curious, Mister Banes.... Did you notice that if you change the last letter of your son's name, it spells 'Devil?' I hope your son rots in hell," whispered Bert in his gruff voice. Turning he left, slamming the door to the back office. As he came out, Devin walked out of the restroom, with a tissue stuck up his nose, carrying his varsity jacket.

Stopping and looking up and down at Bert and his big belly, Devin said grinning, "Did my dad take care of you, mister?" His cocky attitude had never changed, even after a broken nose.

Smiling at the young kid, Bert balled his big right fist, took a swing, and smacked him in the mouth, blood poured as Devin fell backwards, hollering for his dad. Turning to see Mr. Banes come out of his office, he said, "Sorry, I had just one more thing to say to your son." Bert flexed his fists and his muscles under his jacket and left. Devin lay on the floor, holding his mouth with one hand and in the other hand, holding a bloody, broken front tooth.

Driving down to a motel for the night, Bert felt exonerated. After eating a couple of hamburgers and a vanilla malt at a drive-in for dinner, he called his wife Kay from a pay phone and told her he'd be home tomorrow. In the motel room, he took a quick shower, noticing his bruised knuckles. Slipping into bed, he relaxed as he thought of the events of the day. That money would have helped with the expenses at the convent, but he didn't care. They'd figure it out; he could open his café a little earlier or stay open a little later. Summer and the tourists would be coming to Riverside soon. He couldn't wait to tell Kay how he handled that fancy Mr. Banes and his son Devin. He decided not to tell his wife about Devin's accusation about Eveline—that she was not that innocent. It didn't matter what had happened before. Devin was responsible for getting their daughter pregnant; the hatred and anger landed on him. Bert realized that a parent could protect a child only so far. The rest was up to fate.

Chapter 16

The Winston Gig

The next day, Saturday, had a clear blue sky. The routine of the ranch continued, feeding the herd, Twister, and the heifers before dawn, milking the Sunny, and cleaning out the ditches. Clyde, Fred, Dave, and Chet were saddled up and were working at digging out sections of the ditches around their big ranch.

For Matt, Bill, and Tom, last night's party had left them with throbbing headaches in the morning hours. Upstairs at the main ranch house, Tom took a morning shower to clear his head. Matt and Bill slept in a little longer over in the small log cabin. But eventually, the morning sun woke up the two through the small cabin window. Both came over to the ranch house for showers. Matt helped Bill cover his cast again, and he showered and shampooed his long blonde hair. Afterwards, he took his shower. With his head pounding, he stayed in the shower longer and let the heat and steam ease away the pain. As he finished, he took some aspirin. Finally, the three met in the kitchen. Earlier, Chet had fried up bacon, so some were left for them. Matt took out the eggs from the fridge and scrambled up the eggs for them. Bill made toast as he did once before. Sitting down at the table, the three hungrily ate their breakfast.

Today was a special day for the three of them. Everything pointed toward their day preparing for the gig that night in Winston. Sitting at the breakfast table that morning, Bill planned out their set. Before coming to Riverside, he had Denise pick up some new sheet music in Casper. The other band members were practicing those new songs. He wanted the same songs along with a few new ones that they played at the charity dance. The band would play songs by Bobby Lewis, Chubby Checker, Elvis Presley, and Buddy Holly for rock n' roll songs. A few songs had good saxophone solos that had appealed to Dan. For Rob, they would play a few country songs by Claude King, Sons of the Pioneers, and Marty Robbins. He liked the Western ballads for they had stories. Bill and Matt worked up two songs from the Everly Brothers. Somehow, Matt harmonized naturally with Bill on a few bars in the songs, so their voices blended for a new sound. Bill became excited when they practiced at night in the small log cabin. Without his guitar, he felt lost, so he made a quick call to Johnny, telling him to bring his guitar to the gig. Even though he couldn't play with his cast, he could sling it over his shoulder as if to play. He just needed the prop to sing.

After having breakfast that morning, Bill and Matt went over the small log cabin and practiced their songs once more. Tom came over with them to listen. Recalling when Matt first began playing his guitar, he noticed how much better he played now. Not only did he play well, but he sang with Bill. His brother's musical talent made him proud of him. Now that Tom was older, he could understand how his brother had fallen in with Bill and the band. The excitement of playing together and performing for a dance made his head spin. He felt thrilled that he would be going with them to the gig, driving them down in his old red pickup.

Noon came. The men working on the ditches rode to the stable. They eased the cinches under the saddles, fed, and watered their horses. Walking over to the ranch house, they fixed up sandwiches, brewed a pot of coffee, and ate their lunch. The young men at the cabin came over for lunch. As they strolled into the kitchen, they all said 'hi.'

Glancing at his son, Clyde asked, "Matt, I hear that you and Bill have a gig. What are your plans for tonight?" He wanted to keep abreast of what his son was doing.

"The band has a gig in Winston. We're leavin' this afternoon. Tom is drivin' us down. The dance starts at nine and goes until midnight," explained Matt.

Bill spoke up, "I want to thank you for lettin' me stay this week. Matt's always tellin' me all about how much work a ranch takes. Now, I've had a chance to see it for myself. I really enjoyed my time here." He genuinely admired these men. It took a special breed of men to work every day at a ranch.

223

"We enjoyed havin' you. I hope you get your cast off soon," said Fred as he sipped his coffee.

"Tom be careful drivin' down there. Just a reminder—take care of your horses before you leave today. Matt, clean that cabin—sweep it clean and take out the ashes from the wood stove, " Clyde said. He wanted to get back to cleaning out the ditches. He stood and took his empty coffee cup to the sink. The sink was filled with the dirty breakfast dishes.

Turning, he looked around, and gruffly said, "Who's turn was it to do these dirty dishes?" He had to keep an eye on the boys. The ranch house was unclean enough without dirty dishes sitting in the kitchen sink, smelling up the place. The irritation about the condition of their ranch house only concerned him when he was here. Outside, he soon forgot about it and focused on the work to keep the ranch running.

Looking at each other, Chet pointed his finger at his brother and said, "Matt, it was your turn."

"It couldn't be my turn again," said Matt.

"Yeah, it was," answered Dave, laughing. He stood and took his coffee cup over to the sink, putting his cup on top of the pile of dirty dishes.

"Better get on it. Those dirty dishes don't clean themselves," chuckled Fred.

"Okay…okay. I've got it covered," he said. Without any more complaining, he rolled up his shirt sleeves, filled the sink with water, and squeezed in some dish soap. The others got up and left to go out to the fields again.

Tom looked at Matt, and said, "I'll go take care of our horses. I'm goin' to take Brute out for a ride." His brother nodded a 'thank you' as he scrubbed the dishes with a dish rag.

"Take your rifle, Tom," suggested Matt. He didn't want his brother riding around without one.

"Oh, I don't need my rifle. I'm not goin' to be long," said Tom.

With his wet hands dripping on the floor, he turned his brother, with a serious look in his eyes, and said, "Tom, when you least expect it, that grizzly will likely show up. Take your rifle."

Tom held up his hands, nodding he said, "Yeah, yeah. I will." He had forgotten that they were keeping a watch out for that grizzly that Fred had seen about two miles up from their ranch. But Matt was right. Dad was concerned about that grizzly. He went up to his bedroom upstairs and took out his own .30-30 from his closet. In his dresser, he pulled out the cartridges and loaded the rifle. Coming back down, he left the ranch house and went over to the stable.

As Matt continued to wash and rinse, the two friends talked more.

"Man, what a party last night," said Bill. He still couldn't get over the drama that went on last night with Torri. His making out with Rebecca was uneventful. She had nothing he wanted. Again, he thought of Denise. He missed her and couldn't wait to get home and see her.

"Yeah, it didn't go so well, did it?" answered Matt, recalling Torri's accusations, and getting nowhere with Eveline's situation. He couldn't write a letter; he didn't know what to say to a pregnant girl anyway. *How are you? I am fine.* Those old lines wouldn't do much good, considering the seriousness of her situation. It would be better not to get tied up with her. He needed to look around for a girl to date, not someone miles away. He had done that once before and it didn't work out for him. *He felt like a broken-down fool.*

"We have to look at the big picture. You have the Blue Demon, now. And I did see you makin' out with that cute blonde-haired girl. What was her name?" Bill said.

"Deirdre. She used to go with Ronnie. I'll see how it goes with her. I do like her. But you're right. I've got my wheels now. Bill, I can't thank you and your dad enough for helpin' me. When are you goin' to get yourself a car?" asked Matt. Last night, he had been with Deirdre. He liked kissing her. She interested him, but he hesitated in going steady with her. She reminded him of Daphne, with her teasing ways. He didn't know if he could trust her with his heart.

"After the cast comes off. However, I have been out lookin' at the salvage yard a couple of times. You know, Johnny has been helpin' me get around. I know the guys are worried about keepin' the band together. Tonight is important. And I have you to thank for steppin' in and takin' over when we needed you--like before and now," said Bill. He would never forget how Matt with Ronnie drove all the way over to Scottsville to be with him right after he got out of the hospital. Being in bad shape, he thought the band was finished. But with Matt and Ronnie playing that gig, the band had stayed together.

"What are friends for if not to help each other," said Matt. The two paused and thought about the events of the last month. They had both been through a lot—Bill, nearly died when he wrecked his green coupe and Matt, lost his mom when Ronnie wrecked the Red Devil.

Matt thought about his wrecked sports car. "Did you know I raced against Craig's Bel Air and I beat him with the Red Devil out at Carter's flats?" Smiling, he looked at his friend, "What do you think about Craig being in the Army?" he asked.

"What are you sayin'?" Bill asked, curious.

"I mean consider it—it's a chance to get away," he replied.

"Hell, no. That's not for me. I don't want no sergeant up my ass givin' me orders," said Bill.

"I don't know. Sounds interestin' that's all," Matt said as he finished the dishes. Silence fell on the two as he thought how lucky he was to have a friend like Bill.

"Man, it seems like you guys need some help around here," Bill said. He noticed that the ranch house looked dirty—the floors, the stove, and the bathroom.

"What?" said Matt confused. He had never given it any thought. To him, the house looked great.

"Just sayin'," replied Bill. He didn't want to make Matt feel uncomfortable. Anyway, they had more important things to talk about, so he switched their conversation to their songs and the gig. Then, Matt grabbed a broom and a bucket from the pantry and said he wanted to clean the

226

cabin and get their sleeping bags. Bill came along to pack his suitcase and help.

By late afternoon, the three were ready to load up and head out. They planned to stop in Riverside, gas up, and check the oil on Tom's old red pickup. After seeing and talking with Bobby at McClure's Garage, Bill said 'goodbye' to his dad's best friend. Bobby told Bill to tell his dad to come later this summer and they would go fishing again. Matt told him that they could stay at the ranch and he'd take them up on horses to a nice lake and catch all the fish they wanted. They finished talking about fishing when Bill said he'd talk to his dad when he got home.

Crawling into the old red pickup, the three took off to Winston and the gig. Their hearts were filled with excitement and joy, thinking of the night to come. Matt's soul soared at the thought of playing his guitar with Bill and the band. Tom felt lucky to be included in this brother's world of music, and Bill couldn't wait to get his hands on his guitar and sing his heart out. Thrilled at hearing a live band playing their favorite hit songs, the senior class filled the gymnasium with laughter, fun, and pleasure. That night proved to be the best performance for the Platte River Band.

227

Chapter 17

The Search

On Sunday morning, the sun rose behind the tall white peaks with the brilliance of the eastern sky. The peaks looked like tall sentinels against a crimson background. The robins were out early chirping, searching for worms, and flying to their nests. In the garden plot, many blackbirds were out pecking the upturned dark brown earth for worms, the bugs, and the old seeds. Clyde, Fred, and Dave had been out feeding the herd, the bull Twister, and the heifers.

They came over from the stable just as Chet had fried up some sausages. After the gig Saturday night, Tom and Matt decided to drive home, so they got in around three in the morning. Even though he was tired, Tom came downstairs and went out to the barn to milk Sunny. She could not go through a day without milking her in the morning. Matt finally came down after smelling the food cooking. He put on the coffee pot. The men sat at the big kitchen table while Chet mixed up some pancake batter. They made small talk. Matt took over making pancakes on the grill while Chet set the table and set out their cups for coffee. Going into the pantry, he took down the maple syrup.

"So, you drove home late last night. How did it go?" asked Fred, looking at his nephew.

Carrying a bucket of milk from the barn, Tom came onto the back porch and put the milk through the separator. Coming in with the fresh milk and cream, he put the milk in the fridge and put a pint of fresh cream on the table for coffee.

"The band played really well. The seniors danced for three and a half hours with only one thirty-minute break for the band," said Tom. He thoroughly enjoyed listening to the band, and he even danced with the senior girls who quickly liked him and his friendly manner. Plus, it didn't hurt having his brother up there playing in the Platte River Band. During their break, the girls flooded around Bill who had his casted arm and long blonde hair pulled in a short ponytail at the back of his neck. He gained their sympathy, and they liked his radical new look. The other band members—Johnny, Rob, and Dan—were also asked for autographs. Matt managed to slip off to the restroom and avoided the attention that the others liked. After returning to the band, he did have to sign a few autographs. But that was last night. Today, he was back here on the ranch.

"Yeah, all of the guys played well. I'm glad I could play my guitar last night," responded Matt as he flipped over each of the final three pancakes on the grill. Finishing up the pancakes, he brought them over to the big table. The men handed around the food while Tom poured the brewed coffee. They sat quietly and ate their breakfast.

"Chet and I watched the herd last night. How long do you think we need to guard them at night?" asked Dave. When he rode up this morning into the timber above their pastures, he hadn't seen any tracks other than deer and small game.

"I want a night watch for a few more days. I know we are not gettin' our sleep, but if it protects the herd, I still want us to be there," said Clyde. He didn't want to lose any more steers, heifers, or calves to the predators. The pack of wolves had taken three of their steers. That was enough.

Recalling that it had been about two months ago that they had last shoed their horses, Clyde added, "Our horses need shoeing. We've done those four older horses. Now, we need to do our regular mounts."

Just about that time, the phone rang in the living room. Clyde got up, walked into to the living room, and picked up the receiver.

"Hello," he said.

"Clyde, this is Sheriff Tom Lindon. I am formin' a search party and I am askin' for your help. Brad Johnson and the boys from the Johnson Ranch will be there, but I need you and your boys, too."

"What's goin' on?" he asked.

The sheriff explained, "Remember Betsy Crocket that young woman who works over at the Mercantile. Anyway, her folks called me and asked that I do a wellness check. It seems that she has an old boyfriend who just got out of prison. Betsy was the one who turned him into the authorities in the first place. Her folks have been trying to contact her for several days and have been unsuccessful. I went over to the Mercantile and asked about her. They were concerned. It seems that about midday a man in a dark grey pickup, both not local, showed up and parked in front of the store. Betsy went out to talk to him, got in the pickup, and left with him. Then I went over to the Dark Horse Tavern where Betsy worked. Dick and Arlene Knudson told me Betsy had not shown up for work on Friday night. I ran into one of the forest service guys and he said that he had seen a dark grey pickup drive up to the trailhead parking lot. It's the trailhead near your ranch. I am suspicious, Clyde, really suspicious. I need men on horses to conduct this search."

"Of course. I'll bring my boys and we will help out," he replied.

"Thanks Clyde. I really appreciate it. Can you meet up with me and the Johnsons at the trailhead say about ten o'clock?" asked the sheriff.

"Okay. We'll be there," said Clyde.

"Good… and Clyde, bring your rifles. I don't know what we are goin' to come up against," the sheriff replied.

"Will do. Bye," he said as he hung up the phone. Walking back into the kitchen, he sat down at the kitchen table. Looking at everyone sitting there, he took a deep breath because he was still sorting the news of the search in his head. They needed to get organized and get up there.

"That was Sheriff Lindon on the phone. I told him we'd help in a search. The Johnsons will be there, too. Get the horse trailer, saddle your horses, and bring your rifles. Fix some lunch and fill your canteens. We might be gone all day," ordered Clyde.

"What is this all about, Clyde?" asked Fred. This sounded serious.

"It's a missin' person. The sheriff will tell us more when we get there. Dave, you stay and take care of the ranch. I need you all to get ready, now. We have to be up there by ten," he replied. With their dad's cold steel look in his eyes, this was not good. Shocked, they sat for a second thinking of going on a search. Fred, too, felt the impact. Then, they got up and went to work getting ready. Dave said he would make them some lunch. The boys went upstairs and picked up their rifles with extra ammunition.

Fred got his pickup and hitched up their big horse trailer. He threw in a bale of hay in the pickup bed for the horses if they were gone all day. Clyde went over to the stable and saddled his buckskin Chief, tying on his scabbard. The three young Fletchers came into the stable, saddled their horses, and tied on their scabbards. With their loaded rifles, they looked at each other and wondered how this day would turn out. Dave came out with the sack lunches; each put one in his saddle bag. Clyde then saddled Fred's chestnut horse Captain while he backed up the horse trailer near to the stable. They slowly loaded the five horses. Chet went to get the keys to his white pickup since they would need another vehicle to ride up to the trailhead. Then, they grabbed their rifles and got in their pickups. Fred drove the big horse trailer with Chet following as they drove down the dirt road out of their ranch. Turning left, their little caravan headed toward the parking lot of the trailhead.

Around ten o'clock, everyone showed up at the national forest trailhead above the Battle Axe Ranch. After pulling into the parking lot, Clyde and Fred crawled out of the pickup and greeted Brad Johnson and his four boys from the Johnson Ranch. The young Fletchers got out of their pickup and said 'hi' to Johnson and his boys.

Sheriff Lindon and his new deputy, a medium height, thirty-year-old Chad Bentley stood by the sheriff's car. Bentley had moved from the Hadley Police Department to Riverside where he had been on the job here only a couple of months. Close to retirement, the old sheriff needed the help and wanted to train someone to take over for him when he retired. This morning, Bentley had driven his pickup and a small horse trailer up to the trailhead. In the timber next to the parking lot, his black mustang from the Pilot Butte herd stood tied to a big pine tree in the shade. Saddled, the black

231

mustang Blackjack munched the grass around the tree ready for the search.

Sheriff Lindon cleared his throat to get everyone's attention, and said, "Let's gather over here and I will explain. First, it was reported that a person, identified as Betsy Crocket, was abducted by a man in an unknown dark grey pickup. The guy from the forest service said he saw a dark grey pickup drive up here to this trailhead. What we need to do is search these two trails from here in about a mile." The sheriff took a second to let those words sink in before he went on.

When her name was heard, there was a quiet gasp. The whole town knew Betsy from her working at the Mercantile and bartending at the Dark Horse Tavern. The dreadful news impacted Chet as he thought of her. *Oh, Elizabeth.* Fred felt the shock. Matt and Tom looked at their brother, concerned. But with the business at hand, they all set aside their feelings. They were here to help in the search.

The sheriff went on, and explained, "Now, I ordered you men and your horses for the search because of the rough terrain. But also, sitting up on your horses, you'll have a better view. Go up the trail about a mile in, pivot, and come back down. If you guys don't find anything, we'll set up a grid search then." Again, the sheriff paused to let the words sink in. His mouth was dry from talking, so he paused to take a sip of water from his canteen. The Fletchers and the Johnsons were anxious to get ready as they shuffled their feet, making a few quiet comments to each other.

"You probably all know my deputy Chad Bentley. He and I will be here at the trailhead. If you find somethin', send someone back here. With his horse, Bentley will follow you back to your location. Now if and when you do find somethin', stay out of the immediate area. I don't want to mess up any evidence or tracks that might be there with those of your own. Keep an eye out. If you find anythin', send someone back for my deputy. Understand?"

Nodding their heads, everyone understood.

"Okay now, this is how we will proceed. Johnsons, you take the trail to the left. Fletchers, you take the trail to the right. Follow the trail with a man in the middle and flankers out on both sides. Stay close in and move slowly and examine the ground around you. The man in the middle should keep everyone in a straight line. If someone gets way ahead or falls behind, you could miss something. Keep in line. Moving slowly is very important. Do not get in a hurry; take your time. You should be close enough to talk to each other. Understand that?" said the sheriff. He waited for a few seconds while the men waited for him to finish his briefing.

"Are you ready to start? Unload your horses and let's go. Johnsons go left; Fletchers go right. Have at it?" the sheriff said.

The men move to their horse trailers. For each of the saddled horses, the men had to maneuver one by one out of the trailer. The smaller horses came out first. Fred had trouble backing up his chestnut Captain. His horse never liked the horse trailer. Clyde brought out his buckskin Chief. With skill, Chet backed up his red sorrel Rusty. The last two big horses came out last. Tom took his grey stallion Brute and then, Matt brought out his huge black stallion Diablo. The horses were all happy to get out of the hot horse trailer.

As the men talked to each other, the horses neighed and snorted, shaking their heads. The smell of leather mixed with the smell of pine filled the air. The jingle of the bridles sounded as the horses bobbed their heads up and down. The Fletchers checked their saddles and tightened the cinches. They put their loaded rifles into their scabbards and mounted their horses. Matt's Diablo pranced around eager to go as Tom's Brute dropped a pile of manure.

The Johnsons followed suit. By the time all the horses were unloaded and mounted, the search party had become a sizeable group of ten men riding horses. They were ready to start the search. As they split up and went their separate ways, a few raised their hands and waved a 'goodbye.'

As Clyde started on the trail to the right, his boys rode out to their positions—Tom and Fred, on his left flank with Matt and Chet, on his right flank.

"All right. Let's line up. I'm in the middle, ridin' the trail. Keep together," Clyde ordered.

They started to move, slowly, at a snail's pace. There were a few pines around the parking lot, but soon after passing through this small stand of pines, the men moved out into the open with tall sagebrush and lush grass in between. Each looked down and around on both sides of their horses. The hot morning sun high in the sky beat down on the backs of the riders. Sweat poured down their faces as a few took off their hats, wiping their foreheads with their sleeves.

As they rode, Tom rode out to far in front, and Clyde hollered at him, "Slow down, Tom. You're not in line with us." Hearing his dad, he stopped and waited until they were even again. Settling down, the horses finally realized that they were just walking slowly. Their riders kept a tight rein on them. Soon, the line moved into the timber where it was cooler, but the undergrowth was thicker. They had to move slower as the men guided the horses around downed logs and shrubs, all the time keeping their eyes out for anything. The chatter of small forest animals could be heard. A breeze high above the lodge pole pines swayed the branches. The trees creaked as they moved with the wind, cooling the forest below and the men on their horses.

Clyde noticed that they were getting to far apart, so he cried out, "Let's get closer together. We're missin' some of the areas between us." So, the men moved in closer. As they went through the thick forest, they looked closely at every shrub, every downed log. They had found nothing so far. As time slipped by, Clyde knew they had ridden in about a mile, so stopped, and said, "Let's turn around and head back to the trailhead. Stay close and go slow." He hadn't seen anything, so he wondered if they would be setting up a grid.

As Chet rode, his eyes stun from staring at the ground, the thick undergrowth, and around the old logs. His mind stayed focused on the ground even though his heart pounded in his chest, thinking about Betsy. He was hoping that since they hadn't found her, that she was all right. Maybe the Johnson boys on the other trail might come up with something. His brothers felt the strain of riding and searching through the rough forest. Fred was praying that she was all right. So far, they had come up empty in their search.

Suddenly, Chet on the far-right flank saw something. He wiped his strained eyes with his hand as he squinted, guiding Rusty around a boulder as he looked ahead. Just a glimpse of white. He called out, "Hold on guys. I might have somethin'." He dismounted and took a few steps forward.

Clyde hollered out, "Everyone halt and stay where you are. What do you see, son?"

Holding his reins, he took another step, and there, he saw a white cloth under a big log. He called out, "I can't tell yet." As he stepped a little to his left, he saw her. He froze as his mind reeled at the sight. He gasped....*Oh, my god. It's her!*

"Go slow, son," his dad yelled out, seeing his son move.

The sun beat down on Chet's back and he felt the sweat trickle down his back. He swallowed, trying to catch his breath to tell everyone that he had found her. His tongue seemed to be stuck. He didn't want to say the words, but he had to get it out.

"It's Betsy, dad," he finally said, glancing up at him with a look of horror. "Her throat is cut...she's dead." His voice cracked as he controlled his emotions.

"What?... all right... Stay where you are, Chet... Don't move. We don't want to mess up any tracks.... We'll send for the deputy," Clyde called out, looking from Chet to the others.

Seeing the horrible look on his brother's face, Matt wanted to go over to his brother but stopped as his dad ordered. Evidently, her body rested partially under an old log. That's why they hadn't seen her before when they swept through the area earlier.

Chet was the only one who could see her. Insects were buzzing above her—the flies were busy. Her throat had been sliced opened. Her opened hazel eyes had that vacant stare of death. Her blouse was soaked with dried blood.

Spotted with drops of red, she wore her white apron from working at the Mercantile. She had on her blue jeans and he could see her cowboy boots. His eyes moved back up to her head. Her auburn hair surrounded her small, pale face. There were purple bruises on her face. Chet could see one of her silver and turquoise earrings dangling from her ear. She lay at an odd angle as if she had been shoved under the big log.

Standing and looking at her, Chet took off his cowboy hat, in respect to the woman he knew. He combed his fingers through his dark brown hair, as he whispered, "Damn... it... to... hell." Turning, he stepped towards his horse. Chet couldn't look at her body anymore. He took another deep breath. Stepping closer to his horse Rusty, he stroked his neck, thinking of Betsy. Closing his wet eyes, the grief washed over him. He buried his head in his horse's reddish-brown mane. Rusty neighed and snorted as he felt Chet stroke his neck and head. A couple of tears ran down his cheeks. He quickly wiped them away with his sleeve as he put his hat back on his head. *How could this have happened?* This was a woman he had held in his arms and made love to---Elizabeth. Now, she laid dead at the hands of someone who had murdered her. Her brutal death hit him hard in the gut.

Looking over at his brother, Clyde said, "Fred, ride down to the trailhead and get the deputy up here quick...and hurry," he dismounted, stood, and said, "We can't get any closer, boys. Stay put until the deputy gets here."

Chet quietly said, "We need to cover her body, dad." He wanted to protect her against prying eyes.

"No, no, son. We can't touch her. It's a crime scene. We gotta stay put until the officials come. Hold your position," exclaimed Clyde.

"Damn it, Dad," Chet cried out. His voice was filled with sorrow.

Dismounting, his brothers stood in shock at the thought that Chet had found her. Fidgeting with his reins, Tom stood in the sultry hot forest. He was on the other side of his dad and couldn't see anything. Only Chet could see the body. As they waited, the horses munched the grass. Looking lost at what to do, Matt stood next to Diablo. Thirsty, he unhooked his canteen from the saddle horn and drank the fresh, cool water. The heat in the forest was getting unbearable as they stood and waited.

"How long do we wait, dad?" asked Matt. He was anxious to go over to his brother.

"We wait until the deputy gets here. Just don't move from your positions," answered Clyde. Looking up above their heads to the sky, he said, "It's around noon. Go ahead and eat your lunches if you want."

Chet softly said, " Shit, who could eat now." He had taken down his canteen and took a sip. With a breeze shifting his way, he could smell death in the air. *Damn it, Betsy, what happened?*

With their stomachs growling, Matt and Tom pulled out their lunch from their saddle bags. Both were hungry, so they ate their sandwiches and cookies quickly, barely tasting them. Finally, each took out an apple. After eating them, the two fed their horses the apple cores. Matt's Diablo nudged up against him as he fed him the core. He stroked his neck as they stood together in the hot shade of the forest, waiting. Tom also unhooked his canteen and drank the cool water to quench his thirst. Even though the men stood silently waiting, the birds chirped deep in the forest. The bees and bugs buzzed, and the horses munched and snorted, shaking their heads and swishing their tails against the flies.

As the two ate their lunches, Chet and Clyde stood by their horses and waited. Chet kept his head down, not wanting to engage in any conversation with his dad or his brothers. As he looked down at the forest ground, he watched a bunch of black ants scurrying around the pine needles, moving here and there. Still in shock, his mind was filled with images of Betsy and the tragic scene. *Who could have done this? And why?*

Soon, the sound of hooves coming up through the timber made the men to turn their heads toward the sound. As Fred appeared riding his horse, Bentley came behind him riding his mustang Blackjack. The deputy dismounted and tied his

237

black mustang to a nearby pine tree. Looking at the ground, he stepped slowly closer to the body and marked his path to the body. He stood looking down at the body. In his hand, he held a black walkie-talkie. Clicking it on, he called the sheriff, "Lindon, this is Bentley. Call the coroner. It is Betsy and she's dead."

At the other end, the voice spoke, "I'll call the coroner. Chad, send someone down here to get him."

He replied back, "All right, Tom. I will send someone." Bentley carefully stepped back the same way he walked over to the bloody scene.

He turned to the Fletchers and said, "Will one of you go down to the trailhead and wait for the coroner Robert Cowan? He'll have to ride up behind one of you. He doesn't have a horse."

Wanting to do something, Tom raised his hand and said, "I'll go down, wait for him, an' bring him up." The deputy nodded at him and said, "Okay." Then, looking at the rest of the Fletchers, he said, "I need to record what you saw and when. Let's move over to the trail, and I'll ask you some questions." They all nodded and understood. Finally, they could move.

Walking over to the trail, they tied up their horses and strolled over to the deputy who had found a fallen log to sit on. He set down the walkie-talkie and pulled out a small green tablet and short yellow pencil. He proceeded to ask them questions as he jotted down their information.

First, he asked what position they each had ridden and when they had spotted the body. Clyde mentioned that they had ridden past by her body going up the trail. When they were coming back, that's when his son saw the body. Then, the deputy directed his questions to Chet who calmly answered them. Although his voice sounded steady, his body trembled inside as he thought of her. *Elizabeth was so lovely and beautiful.*

The deputy asked, "Did any of you approach the body?"

Clyde said, "No. I had the boys stop where they were. Nobody moved from where you found us."

Chet said to the deputy, "We should cover her body, damn it." He didn't like leaving her like this.

"No. We have to wait until the coroner gets here. I don't want anyone walkin' around her body, Chet. We need to keep that scene untouched. Listen, we'll take good care of her after that." Bentley noticed that he was a little edgy.

People reacted differently upon seeing a dead body. For some, they remained distant and unattached. For others, they had feelings that showed. Even though Chet had controlled his voice, his eyes and body had told the deputy that he had been stunned at seeing her.

Time seemed to stand still while the men waited for the coroner. This was a longer wait. The sun rose high in the sky above the forest. Sunbeams streamed down through the tall pines. The hot deep forest still had the sounds of the birds and small animals scurrying around. A hawk flying high above called out. The natural world was still alive as death hung in the air. The men sat, stood, waited, and waited.

Eventually, Tom with the coroner Robert Cowan riding on the back of the grey stallion Brute came up the trail. Dismounting, the coroner grunted as his feet landed on the ground. He never liked riding a horse, in the saddle or on the back of one. He stood for a few seconds, looked at the men, and nodded.

The coroner said, "Chad, I will take it from here. We can let the Fletchers go if you've gotten their information. Thanks guys." Carefully walking over to the body, he squatted down as he looked around and examined her body.

The deputy asked a few final questions and jotted down their answers. Folding his green tablet closed, he slipped it and the short yellow pencil back into his shirt pocket. He said, "Thanks, you guys can all leave now."

Clyde asked, "Will you keep us informed of what you find out?" He wanted to know what happened here to this young woman that they all knew. He would like to know who did this.

Shaking his head, the deputy said, "Sorry, Clyde, I cannot do that. You guys might be called to testify and that would contaminate your testimonies if I told you anything more than what happened here, today. I am afraid this is the last you will hear from me or the sheriff. Thanks, again. We appreciate the time and effort you put into this search. You did good work."

With those final words, the Fletchers walked over to their horses, mounted them, and headed back down the trail through the timber. Coming up the trail earlier, Clyde noticed a small creek flowing down through the trees. He guided them over to the stream to let their horses drink some water. They dismounted for a moment, allowing them to take a drink of the icy, cold water. Chet squatted down by the cold stream. Taking off his hat, he bent further down. He cupped the cold water in his hand and splashed water over his face and head a couple of times. The smell of death still filled his nostrils. Dipping his hand into the stream, he sipped the icy water from the palm of his hand. The water helped clear his head of the grizzly scene. Combing his hand through his wet hair, he put on his hat and stood up.

Refreshed, they all mounted and headed back to the trail through the tall sagebrush and the small stand of pines next to the parking lot. When they got to their horse trailers, Clyde noticed that the Johnsons had already left. Deciding to eat, Fred and Clyde sat on their tailgate and ate their lunch. Chet's lunch sack remained in his saddle bag. He couldn't eat. While his dad and uncle ate, Matt, Tom, and Chet slowly loaded their big horses—the grey and black stallion. Then, the other three horses were loaded. Finally, they were ready to take off.

No one said anything. They had all been through an emotional morning; words were meaningless for them. Small talk would be ridiculous. *What does one say after discovering a dead body?* They needed to get back to the ranch and put this search and tragedy behind them.

As they drove into the ranch, storm clouds gathered up in the high country. Thunder echoed in the far distance. Streaking from the dark clouds, white lightning strikes could be seen. The Fletchers' little caravan pulled up to the stable. The men quickly unloaded the horses, unsaddled them, took them into the stable to groom them. The horses were frisky after riding in the trailer. As they talked to their horses to settle them down, the men brushed them, fed them grain, and watered them. Finally, they headed toward the ranch house.

As they stepped into the kitchen from the back porch, Dave sat at the kitchen table, eating a sandwich. The smell of brewed coffee hit the Fletchers' noses. Bandit and Blue under the table came out to greet the men. Fred brushed Bandit's head as Tom went down on one knee to hug his dog Blue. The coffee was a welcome smell as Chet went to the cupboard and pulled out some cups. Clyde went to another cupboard and took down their bottle of whiskey. This bottle was nearly empty. They would have to get another bottle next time someone went into town. All the men sat down at the big kitchen table. Tom went to the fridge, brought out the pitcher of milk, and the pint of heavy sweet cream as Matt poured the coffee. Finishing his lunch, Dave waited, wondering how the search had gone.

Finally, after finishing their coffee, Clyde poured some whiskey into his coffee cup. Passing the bottle around, the others did the same. When the bottle came to Chet, he looked at it and drank straight from the bottle. With the strong liquor going down his parched throat, he gulped a little. But then he took another long swig of the dark amber liquid. As he set the bottle down, Fred grabbed it and poured some into his coffee cup.

"What a freakin' day this has been," Chet growled. He wanted to drown out those images and memories of Betsy.

"Can someone tell me what happened?" asked Dave finally.

Everyone sat quietly for a minute. No one wanted to talk about it, but Clyde finally told him about the search and about finding the body of Betsy up in the timber above the trailhead. Dave was stunned at hearing the news. He wanted to know more, but Fred told him that's all they knew. The sheriff and deputy wouldn't tell them anything more because of the investigation.

Since Dave was a local man, Chet recalled that he had known Betsy before, so he asked, "Dave, did you know her?"

Surprised at the question, he cleared his throat, and replied, "Yes n' no. I knew of her when we were in high school. I had just moved here after my dad lost his ranch in Hadley. I didn't get involved with school much since I worked after school and on weekends to get enough money for my own place. Then, after graduation, I heard that she and her folks moved away... not sure, but I think somewhere in the Midwest. After three or four years, she moved back here. Workin' part-time at the tavern, she kept to herself and didn't date much. She then got the job at the Mercantile. That's when she started datin' around. I heard she was datin' Craig Webster and, of course, I knew you dated her, Chet. That's about all I know. I don't know who could have done this to her." The men listened to Dave's information about Betsy. Chet realized that he had dated a woman he knew less about than he thought. She had always said that her life was complicated. Evidently, she had been hiding something from everyone here since moving back.

As Clyde looked around at his sons and brother, he said, "Listen, I'm proud of how you handled yourselves today." He did not want to reveal the information that the sheriff had given him. He knew what the sheriff had meant about their possible testimonies. They had only done the search, nothing else.

"I hope I never have to go on a search again," expressed Matt as he tried to forget about the long, slow search and then the long wait.

As the men sipped and finished their coffee, Clyde spoke up, "We better get busy. I mentioned shoeing our horses this mornin'. We have time to get started, might even finish by night fall. The weather looks like it might rain, so let's go set up in the barn."

Most of them wanted to get back to work and shake off their thoughts of finding Betsy. Dave mentioned that his horse had a loose shoe on the right hind hoof. The men took their cups to the kitchen sink and left the kitchen.

242

As they moved out of the kitchen, Fred took Chet's arm and held him back for a moment. Looking into his nephew's dark brown eyes, he said quietly, "Are you goin' to be okay?" He knew that Chet and Betsy had dated and that they had spent a night together. He affectionately took hold of his nephew's shoulder and pressed it. He himself felt the terrible loss of someone so beautiful. *Who could do something like that?*

"Yeah, I hope they catch the bastard," Chet spoke out harshly. He had to stop thinking of the gruesome images of her. Now the anger started to burn inside him. The two moved together out of the ranch house and walked over to the barn where the men were setting up to put new horseshoes on their horses. He had to keep his mind off her and keep himself busy. Bringing their horses into the barn, the men all worked on their horses' hooves, trimming them, and putting on their new horseshoes. The physical labor of working with their horses kept their minds off the long, hot search.

By twilight, the tired men headed back to the ranch house. Dinner that night came from cans opened and warmed up—a bland meal of beans that filled their stomachs. The terrible events of the day had left them feeling empty. They ate, drank, and finished their meal. After dinner, Clyde and Fred walked down to the office to talk about the ranch. Dave and Tom would be going out to watch the herd tonight, so Dave left to take a quick nap over at the bunk house.

The three young Fletchers moved into the living room. Matt started the fire to warm up the ranch house on this chilly night. As Chet had settled on their old couch, Tom sat in the old chair next to the fireplace. He waited for the small twigs to catch fire and watched as the flames danced up to the split logs. A silent tension filled the air except for the popping and snapping of the pitch in the wood.

"That was some search. I've never been around the sheriff or deputy in a situation like that, " said Tom, looking at Chet.

243

"That's the way it's done," he answered. Staring at the fireplace, he just shook his head as his anger rose inside of him, thinking of who could have done this. The fire in the fireplace matched the anger he felt. Chet had a dark shadow hanging around him. Ever since he had spotted the body, he hadn't said more than a few words. Of course, his brothers knew that he had dated Betsy.

Just then, the phone rang on the table.

The phone kept ringing. "Answer it," growled Chet. Tom stood and walked over to the phone.

He answered it and said "Hello." Chet stood to leave and go upstairs, but he turned to him and said, "Wait, Chet. It's for you. It's Sophia."

Turning back around, he strolled over to the phone. Taking the receiver from him, he covered it with his hand and said, "Can I have some privacy?" He looked at his brothers.

"Yeah," said Matt. The two left the living room and went up the stairs to their bedrooms.

Sitting down on the chair next to the phone, Chet took a second or two, taking a deep breath. His eyes looked at the floor as he shook his head. He had to collect his thoughts before he spoke to her. Clearing his throat, he answered, "Hi, Sophie."

She replied, "Hello, Chet. How was your day?" Hearing her voice made his heart jump.

He hesitated and answered, "I had a rough day…don't ask… How are you doin'?"

She answered 'fine,' and they talked for a few minutes. She wanted to tell him about her plans for the interview Friday in Hadley. He told her that he looked forward to seeing her on Saturday. Cutting their conversation short, she said she had to work on a final paper. Chet told her he missed her and couldn't wait to see her again. She whispered back that she missed him, too. They said 'goodbye.'

Chet hung up, walked over to the couch, and sat down again. While watching the hot fire burn, he thought of Sophia. His desire for her stirred as he thought of her.

Hearing her sweet voice gave him relief from his sad thoughts. The anger he had felt all day started to leave him. He had to be strong and put that terrible search behind him. His eyes started to feel heavy and his head fell back against the couch as the exhaustion took over.

Later that night, Clyde walked into the dark living room. The fire had burned down to only the hot, glowing embers. Seeing his son asleep, he walked down the hall to his bedroom and brought back the old red quilt with him. Chet felt someone gently lay him down. He felt someone take his legs and swing them up onto the couch. He felt his boots come off. And then, a warm blanket covered him. Too tired to open his eyes, he felt the love and gentleness from those big hands. He heard his dad whisper the words, "Good night, son."

Chet mumbled back, "Good night, dad." He fell back to sleep.

Clyde quietly walked down to his bedroom where he closed the door and went to bed. Even though he was known as a tough man, he had a tender side—a vulnerable side that he closed off most of the time. Tonight he knew that his son was hurting, but Chet had a solid character in him that he recognized in himself. That streak of toughness would help his son get over this tragedy.

That night, the rainstorm had stayed up in the back country. By morning, the streams and the river would be overflowing with muddy water coming down from the mountains. The spring runoff had started, and the rainstorm would only add to it.

Later, with his eyes closed but not asleep, Clyde heard his son Tom come down the stairs and leave the ranch house. Soon he heard horses' hooves leave the ranch, disappearing into the night. Even though most of the nights were sad and lonely for him, he felt proud as he dozed towards sleep. The search today had tested all the Fletchers. His sons were growing into such strong men who would live and work this ranch---the Battle Axe Ranch.

Chapter 18

The Challengers

For the next four days and nights, the time went by fast. The herd was getting fed, the cow was being milked, and Twister was humping the heifers. The work around the ranch continued. The Fletchers moved through each day without much conversation. The impact of the search still hung in the air. Each day the memory of her death got lost in the hard ranch work.

After getting paid for the Winston's gig, Matt decided to pay for the charges he had made in town, repairing the Blue Demon. Cliff's wife accepted the money for her husband who had worked on the radiator and gas tank. Stopping at the gas station, he paid Bobby for the new battery. While Tom and Matt were there, they met Bobby's son BJ who had since moved to Riverside to take over for his dad. BJ, a tall, muscular man with reddish-brown hair, had the same friendliness that his dad had. Bobby thanked him and told Matt if he needed a final tune-up on the Blue Demon, he'd could bring it to the garage any time. Jumping at the opportunity, Matt said he'd be in as soon as he could.

At night, after work on the ranch was finished and dinner had been eaten, Matt would walk out to the utility shed where his Blue Demon sat. He had started it up each night to keep the battery charged. He also wanted to listen to the devil engine rumble as he revved it. Without mufflers, it was loud. His body reverberated from the noise as he sat in the driver's seat.

One night, he drove the coupe out of the shed to wash it. Tom had walked out with him and said he'd help him. They filled two buckets of soapy water and scrubbed the hood, the fenders, the doors, the trunk, and the top, cleaning off the dirt and grime that it had collected sitting in that salvage yard for years. With a couple of trips to the water pump, they rinsed off the coupe. The powder blue didn't shine like his red sports car, but it didn't matter to Matt. The chrome on the front grill, the back bumper, around the headlights,

246

and the hood ornament sparkled as he rubbed and shined each area. Tom worked alongside him. Matt then started the engine and drove it back into the utility shed.

The Blue Demon sat and waited for another chance to roll down the highway. The new fiendish spirit in this powder blue coupe wanted to feel Matt's hands on the steering wheel, his foot on the gas pedal, and hear the tunes on the AM radio. With the windows rolled down, the car wanted to feel the wind flutter the old headliner inside. The blue coupe had escaped the salvage yard and found a new driver. The Blue Demon felt the love and care that this new owner had for it. He even felt the devil engine inside of him with its diabolical energy. This new driver had spoken to him. Yes, he liked this new driver and looked forward to spinning his way down the highway soon.

Earlier that week, Matt told his dad that he needed to take a day and get the papers settled for the Blue Demon. On Thursday, Tom and Matt drove down to the county courthouse in Midler, a small town next to Winston. Since they were driving all the way there, Clyde had had a short list of ranch supplies they needed. After arriving at the courthouse, they stood in line waiting to get the license plates transferred from the Red Devil to the Blue Demon. His wallet seemed to be getting thinner and thinner. Afterwards, they made their stop at Bob's Feed and Grain, picked up the ranch supplies, and charged them to their ranch. While they were driving back to Riverside and the ranch, Matt and Tom listened to the radio and talked.

"We should call that road construction company and find out when they will be hirin'," said Matt.

"Yeah, we better. With dad only paying us half, I could use some money for gas. I want to take Melanie Carter out on a date," answered Tom. He needed to call her sometime this week.

"Carter? Is she related to the doctor?... Do you like her?" asked his brother.

"She's really nice. Yeah, the doc is her older brother. She's the baby in the family. We'll both be seniors in the fall. I'd like to date her this summer," said Tom, thinking of her and how she liked marshmallows that night up at Skyline. She had nice blonde hair, and he liked blondes.

"Yeah, my money from the gig is gone, but I still have a little left from my wolf kill. I'm goin' to take Deirdre out. I told her I would take her out for a drive in the Blue Demon," said Matt. He couldn't wait to get home and drive his coupe. Now, they would be legal and not have to worry about getting a ticket.

The warm spring day slipped into twilight as the sun dipped behind the peaks, leaving the few grey clouds tipped with orange and pink. Later, the long night sky filled with bright stars twinkling and the Milky Way strung across the darkness with its unique clusters. Still the early April nights were cold. The living room fireplace took the chill off of the ranch house. Everyone covered up and, in their beds, fell into deep sleep after a day of work.

The next day was Friday. The pre-dawn brought a few clouds hanging above the mountains. The aspen trees, cottonwood trees, and the willows were starting to leaf out. Along the northern side of the log ranch house, a row of lilac bushes stood at the edge of the lawn just starting to leaf out. They provided a wind breaker and would be in full bloom by the end of May. The morning birds were up early—the robins and sparrows. Over on the south side of the log ranch house, the turned-up garden spot had the blackbirds scurrying around pecking at the brown earth.

After a night of watching the herd, Chet and Fred came in from the pasture, tired and ready for an early morning nap before breakfast. Even though they hadn't encountered a grizzly yet near the herd, Dave had ridden up into the timber about two or three miles and found big claw marks left in the soft dark ground by a spring. They knew that a grizzly was still roaming around up in the mountains above the ranch.

That morning as Clyde fed the herd, he noticed one of the calves seemed sluggish. The calf was not running around with the others and the mother stood as if to guard her young calf. He took a few seconds and watched the calf.

He heard what he thought was a cough. It was hard to tell, so he decided to come back later and check on the calf.

As the men came into the ranch house for breakfast, they smelled the bacon cooking. Matt and Tom had started cooking as soon as they rose. They cooked eggs, toasted the bread, and brewed the coffee. Sitting down at the big kitchen table, they devoured the food as they talked about finishing the ditches today. Since it long hard work, Fred suggested that next year that they borrow a backhoe to do the ditches. He said he was tired of shoveling the fine silt out which took so long. They needed to finish shoeing the horses. A busy day stood before them.

When Chet had gone into town a week ago, he had purchased the seed potatoes that needed to be planted today. He told his dad that he'd take care of planting a row or two of them. Years before, he had helped his mom plant the garden when she was herself. Some years, they had good gardens that produced a lot of their vegetables. In the fall, his mom would can some of the vegetables for winter, putting up pickles, beets, creamed corn, and tomatoes. As he thought of those past years, he realized that his Grandma Nancy and Aunt Josey were always there helping her in their small kitchen on the Diamond V Ranch.

After working on the ditches, Clyde decided to check on the calf. He saddled his horse Captain and rode back out to the herd. Bandit and Blue ran out with him to where the calf lay. The mother cow stood beside her calf, nudging her. He dismounted and walked over to the downed calf. He inspected the calf's eyes, nose, and mouth; her nose looked fine and normal. But she didn't act normal, so he decided to take her and the mother back with him to the barn. It could be nothing or it could be serious.

He fixed up a rope halter for the mother cow, tethering the rope to his saddle. She would need to come with her calf. She bellowed at her little calf. He lifted the calf carefully up and put her across his horse in front of his saddle horn. Quickly, he mounted, holding the little calf in place. Obviously, she was not feeling well since she did not even struggle when Clyde lifted her up onto the horse. He noticed as he lifted her, he felt her ribs.

Concerned, he headed slowly back to the ranch. Riding up to the barn, Dave came out of the stable. Seeing the calf and cow, he walked over and reached for the calf as Clyde dismounted. Together, they set her down on her shaky legs. She bawled as the mother mooed back.

"We better put them in the barn and see what we can do. I don't know if the calf is sick or not. She's thin," said Clyde. Guiding the mother and the little calf following, the men guided them into the warm barn and put them in a clean stall.

"We need to get some hay and water for them. What do you think, Dave?" he asked, as he carried one of the hay bales from the side wall of the barn, breaking it up into the stall next to the mother and calf.

After Dave looked her over, he said, "We could watch her for a day or so. Maybe, we should check her temperature. We could supplement her feedin'."

Nodding, Clyde said, "Dinner will be ready soon. Let's go and come back after dinner."

The men came from the barn and walked over to the ranch house. Stopping on the back porch, they washed up. The two men came into the kitchen and sat down at the big kitchen table.

In the kitchen, the young men were fixing up dinner. Soaking the northern beans the night before, Uncle Fred had put on a pot of ham and beans to cook in the oven that morning. Dinner was warm and ready by evening. The brewed coffee pot sat on the stove while Matt set the loaf of bread on the table. Going into the pantry, Tom picked up two cans of sliced pineapples, opened them with the can opener, and set them on the table. Dave helped set the table and poured the coffee. Tom reached into the fridge and put the pitcher of milk on the table. Then, setting the big pot on the table with a couple of potholders under it, Uncle Fred served them as each man handed down his plate to be filled. They ate, had second helpings, and filled their empty stomachs after a long day of work on the ranch.

As they finished their meal, Clyde leaned back and said, "I brought a calf and the mother into the barn. The little calf is actin' sick and I thought I heard her cough. I don't know if it's serious or not."

"What can we do?" asked Tom.

"Make sure she has water, check her nose for mucus, and take her temperature. Dave thought she mind need more milk....Did you get your car's paperwork done, Matt?" asked his dad.

"Yeah, I got it done. We brought back the supplies, too. They are in the utility shed," he answered.

"Good. I want you, Matt, to paint that barn in the next two weeks. Do you think you can get it done before brandin'? And since you'll be near the barn, check on our sick calf, in the morning and at night. Take her temperature for a few days. If she worsens, let me know," ordered Clyde. He looked at his son.

"Dad, can I help Matt? It's a big barn," said Tom. He'd volunteer for anything to help at the ranch.

His dad said, "Sure. Any one can step in and help, but it's Matt's job."

The big task of painting the barn would be a major project for them to complete before branding in the next two weeks.

That evening, the young planned on going out on dates. Calling Melanie Carter earlier that week, Tom drove way out to her family's ranch, met her parents, and drove into town to the movies. With the Blue Demon ready, Matt had called Deirdre (after getting her phone number from Dave) and wanted to take her out for a drive. The young men in town had heard about the Blue Demon. After last week's party at Skyline, they heard that Craig wanted to challenge Matt to a drag race out at Carter's flats later that night.

Deciding they would all go up to Skyline for a few beers, Matt asked Dave to call their friends. When he called, George didn't know if he wanted to call Rebecca. After she spent last weekend flirting with Bill, he felt angry at her. Dave told him it was up to him, but maybe, she wasn't the girl for him. He asked him if he had told Rebecca that he

251

like her. George said he hadn't and didn't know if he liked her that much. Right now, he didn't want to go steady, but just wanted to date around. Girls were too complicated.

Dave then called Torri again to see if she wanted to go out. She told him 'no' that she needed to catch up on her sleep. Besides if Matt would be there at the party, she didn't want to see him. She felt embarrassed after last week when she accused him of her brother's death. She felt like a fool that night. He told her that Matt understood and wouldn't hold that against her. She couldn't hide from him forever. But Torri didn't change her mind about coming out. So then, Dave gave Suzie a call and asked her out. She said 'great.' She had been waiting to hear from Craig, but he hadn't called her.

The group met up at Skyline Campground. They built a small campfire since they were only going to drink a few beers and then go drag racing. Their vehicles were parked alongside the campsite. After Craig drove up and parked, he stepped out and brought the case of beer. Driving up in his turquoise sport coupe Bel Air, he had come alone. Even though it had been a week since they found Betsy's body, he couldn't get her death out of his head. He didn't feel like going out with anyone. Tonight, he wanted to drag race against Matt.

George had come with Rebecca in his two-tone green Fairlane. She seemed more attentive to George tonight. In his black pickup, Dave came with Suzie who was a little upset when she saw Craig there. She had expected him to call her, but he hadn't.

As the powder blue coupe approached the campsite, the fiendish rumble of the Blue Demon became louder. Matt parked it and revved the motor before turning it off. Without any mufflers, it loudly roared. Along with Deirdre, he stepped out of his car. Putting his arm around her they walked over to the campfire as everyone said 'hi.' They were handed two cans of beer; Matt opened one for Deirdre first, and then, one for himself.

The group made some small talk for a while. The girls were looking forward to Easter in another week. George and

Craig again talked a little about the work at the Johnson Ranch while Dave talked about the Battle Axe Ranch. Feeling a little awkward, Matt kept out of the conversation about their family's ranch since he'd been doing everything he could to get out of working. He looked around the group to see if Torri had come. Not seeing her, he wondered why she hadn't come.

Finally though, Craig glanced over at Matt and said, "I heard that you Fletchers found Betsy's body last week." The town had been gossiping about her death.

"Yeah. Have you heard anythin' more about who did it?" asked Matt. He didn't want to talk about the search at the trailhead or about Chet finding her.

"No. Nothin'," answered Craig. Since he and Betsy were just starting to date, he wanted to know more details about her death. He thought that Matt would know.

"I heard they sent her body to Ohio where her parents lived. They had the funeral there," added George. Along with Dave, they had been an old high school classmate. He was shocked when he heard about her murder.

"Neither the sheriff nor the deputy has said anythin' about the case," said Craig frustrated. He had searched the newspapers for information, but nothing had been written about finding her murderer, just her obituary. He hoped they would catch the guy who did it.

Wanting to change the subject, Matt asked Craig, "So, you think you can out race my Blue Demon tonight?"

Laughing, he answered, "Is that what you call your car? Why those diabolical names, Matt? First, the Red Devil and now, the Blue Demon. Why?"

"My dad named my first car. He said it didn't belong on a ranch. Now, with this car, it has the Red Devil's engine and transmission in it, so it seems right to name it the 'Blue Demon.' I just like the idea of a car that can create a little chaos in the world," he explained. He took a long drink of his beer. After emptying the can, he threw it into the fire.

He looked at Deirdre and asked, "Are you ready for another beer?"

"No, I'm fine," she answered. He then stepped over to the picnic table where the case of beer set and took out another can. Looking over at the group, he asked, "Anyone else need another?" Both Dave and Craig raised their hands. He grabbed two more and walked over to the campfire and handed them each one.

"Didn't you name your cars? Craig? George? Dave?" Matt asked, looking at each of them.

"Yeah, my car is named the Tank. It drives like one," replied Craig, laughing.

"I first named mine Peppermint because it's green. But, later, I shortened it and call it 'Pepper.' That really describes my hot car," replied George. Everyone snickered at the name 'Peppermint,' but the second name came with more of a warning about his car.

"My pickup is the Junker because it's a piece of junk," replied Dave, opening his beer can.

All the girls were listening to the names and wondered about why guys were into their cars. Most of the girls didn't own a car but drove their family's cars to get their driver's licenses.

The campfire had burned down to glowing red embers, so the guys thought it was time to go. They wanted to drive down to Carter's flats and drag race. Kicking dirt on their campfire and picking up their half case of beer, they crawled into their vehicles and took off.

As they were driving down the road off the mesa and along the Sheep Creek road, Matt thought about his friends' cars. Even though their cars were not the typical model hot rods that Matt had seen over in Scottsville, these men who lived here just hopped up their engines in their regular cars to race. Thinking about the cars parked beside the campsite, he knew that his fuel-injected devil engine in the Blue Demon could come close to outrunning them. The blue coupe had a similar weight to Craig's Bel Air, but a little more horsepower. Against George's Fairlane, it would be a close match with the same weight and horsepower.

They parked along the highway near Carter's ranch. Craig and George parked at the ranch turnout with the single mailbox sitting on the side. With the moon in its waxing phase, the night was black with only a small crescent moon and two bright stars, Venus and Jupiter. The cars' headlights were the only real light to see by. Craig decided to race first against George, so they lined their cars next to each other. Each revved up their engines.

Standing between the two, Suzie asked, "Are you ready?" They both nodded. Finally, she gave the signal and the cars 'laid rubber.' The colors turquoise and green zoomed by those watching on the sides of the highway. The roar of the engines filled the air as they both raced to the finish line. The two cars were neck and neck most of the way, but George's Pepper pulled ahead near the finish line. He beat Craig's Tank. The two cars slowed and turned around, coming back to the starting line and the crowd standing around watching.

Wanting to race Matt's Blue Demon, Craig lined up again. Matt crawled into his coupe, started the devil engine, and drove over to the starting line. He revved it a couple of times. It sounded hungry for a race. With his friend's Bill's advice in mind, Matt decided to really punch it, pushing the Blue Demon as fast as he could. He wasn't going to hold back like he had done before. He wanted to get off the line quickly, so that the Blue Demon could open up.

Again, Suzie gave the signal. With a 'squat and a fart,' the Blue Demon leaped forward ahead of the Tank. The engine's wicked power put the car ahead of the Tank by a car's length. Matt never looked back. He just hung tight to the steering wheel, shifted, and flew down the highway. Craig cussed as he pressed down on his gas pedal trying to catch him. He closed the distance a little as they raced toward the finish line, but he never could overtake him. The two drivers turned their cars around and headed back to the turnout near the starting point. As they parked, the two got out of their cars. Seeing Matt win, Deirdre ran over to him and excitedly hugged him. He hugged her back with the thought that Bill would be proud of how the Blue Demon performed tonight.

Craig came over and said, "Man, you sure had a quick start off the line. I couldn't catch you after that." Nodding, Matt smiled. One time with the Red Devil, he'd had a slow start, but this time, with the Blue Demon, he had a fast start.

George walked over to Matt, and said, "Okay, buddy. Let's see if you can beat my Pepper."

Nodding, Matt got back into his car, started the devil engine, drove over, and lined up at the starting point. George drove his Pepper over and lined up next to him, smiling he revved his 352 V-8 big block. Matt knew this would be a close race. He gripped the steering wheel, waiting for the signal.

As Suzie gave the signal, the two cars roared off the starting line. The crowd saw the green and the blue of the cars zoom by as they drove. The Pepper pulled ahead as George stomped down on his gas pedal. The Blue Demon was wide opened but couldn't catch Pepper which hit the finish line first. Both cars slowed down, turned around, and came back to the turnout.

Parking their cars, both drivers walked over and started to talk to each other. Rebecca came running up to George and put her arms around him. He lifted her up with his strong arms as she put her legs around his waist. They kissed a long kiss as he turned around with her in his arms. Setting her down, everyone opened another round of beer. They drank the cold fresh liquid as they talked about the races tonight.

They were busy talking that they didn't notice Sheriff Lindon's car with red lights flashing until they turned and heard the unmistakable siren coming right at them. They were caught; there was nowhere to run. The girls who were underage quickly handed their beer to the guys who threw the cans behind the sagebrush over by the mailbox. The girls huddled together while the guys stepped forward to meet the sheriff.

Driving up, the sheriff car parked behind Matt's Blue Demon. He left the engine running and the lights flashing red. Walking toward the guys, he pulled out his ticket pad.

Standing looking at the guys, the sheriff said, "You boys have a problem. I observed two sets of headlights drag racin' here on this state highway headin' right toward me. I want the two drivers who just raced to step forward." Everyone gasped and held their breaths. George stepped forward as Matt hesitated but stepped forward. "I need your driver's licenses and registrations." No one said anything. The air held a tense silence as the crowd looked on.

Both went to their cars, pulling out their registration papers, and opening their wallets. As they handed the sheriff the papers and licenses, he explained, "A citizen called my office tonight and reported the noise and the racin'. You guys know there are cows out here. You could hit one. There is a statue on the books about drag racing. It requires that you to be issued a citation."

He looked over the names and recognized both of them---Fletcher and Weaver. Getting old and close to retirement, Sheriff Lindon didn't want to drive out here late tonight. He had hoped that he would make it to midnight before he went home. But it wasn't to be. 'Old man' Carter called and reported the drag racing again. His calls were getting to be regular every other week. Tonight he had caught them and needed to issue the tickets, hoping to deter these young guys from racing out here. The rancher Mark Carter feared that one of his cows would get out and get hit. He worried not only for his livestock but for the lives of the young men driving those cars. After the sheriff filled out the details, he handed back the licenses, registrations, and the tickets to Matt Fletcher and George Weaver.

Looking over at the other guys standing around, he called over to Craig. "Mr. Webster. I'd like to talk to you.... I am surprised to see you here. You should be an example for these guys." Standing without a word, Craig just stared the sheriff in the eyes.

Glancing at the girls behind the guys who looked too young to be out here, he warned them, "I want to remind you that we have a ten o'clock curfew for those who are underage. Some of you should be home." Finally, he turned, walked over to his patrol car. Getting in, he switched off the bright, flashing red lights, turned his car around, and drove off towards town to do the paperwork on the two citations. He'd be late getting home tonight.

Thinking about the tickets that the two received, Craig said, "And that's the reason I left this fuckin' place and joined the Army." He kicked a small rock on the ground in front of him, turned to his car, got in, and drove off. He peeled out, kicking up dirt as he pulled onto the highway.

Seemingly unaffected, George just put the folded ticket into his wallet and went over to his two-tone green Pepper. Rebecca followed him and together they left. He spun out, but he honked his horn four or five times as he left. *Wake up cows. We're leaving. Old man Carter—are you listening?*

Shrugging his shoulders, Matt felt bad, never having a ticket before. Dave was gathering up the beer cans they had thrown behind the sagebrush, pouring out the contents. Suzie complained that she wanted to drink some more beer. He told her he'd get her a fresh one out of the case.

Dave looked at him and said, "Guess we'd better find another place to drag race. Hey, it's just a ticket, Matt. See you tomorrow mornin'." He handed Matt two left over beer cans as he took two for himself and Suzie. They both got into his car and drove off.

Matt and Deirdre were left. Handing her the two cans, he opened the door for her and went to his side of the car and got in. He still had the ticket in one of his hands. He wanted to crumble it up and throw it out the window, but that wouldn't be a wise decision. Almost out of cash, he'd have to figure out how to pay for this ticket.

"I'll drive you home, Deirdre. Sorry, about tonight," he said as he folded the ticket and put it into his wallet. Leaning across in front of her, he reached and opened the glove compartment, slipping the registration paper back into it. He started the engine as the motor rumbled. Turning on the radio, he turned the dial until he found the Oklahoma station that they could get at night. A hit song by Bobby Vee was playing. Listening to the song, he wanted to forget about the ticket.

"There's nothing to be sorry about. I had fun," she said.

"Gettin' a ticket isn't fun, Deirdre," he answered.

"No, I guess not. But it was just a citation. Everyone gets those once in a while," she admitted.

Matt was getting ready to pull onto the highway when he saw a car approaching the turn off on the highway. He waited for it to pass, but instead, it signaled and slowed down to turn right. He recognized the old red pickup as Tom's. Rolling down their windows, the two brothers looked at each other for a second, and Tom said, "What are you doin' out here, Matt?"

"Nothin'. Just takin' Deirdre home. What are you doin'?" he asked.

"I'm takin' Melanie home. We've been to the movies in town. What's goin' on tonight?" he asked, curious to know if his brother had raced the Blue Demon. Then, Tom realized that Melanie Carter sat next to him in the car. He had heard that her dad was the one who called the sheriff several times when the guys would race out here by his turnoff. He felt bad asking his brother with her here.

"We'd better go. See you later, Tom," he said, avoiding his question. Then, he revved his engine, smiled, and drove out onto the highway. He watched his brother head away from town. Smiling at Melanie, he continued up the dirt road that led to her parents' ranch—the Double D. He drove up their ranch house.

Turning off the engine, Tom looked at Melanie and said, "Thanks for a great evening. The movie wasn't that good, but the popcorn tasted good."

"Yes, thanks for taking me out," she said quietly. She looked at him with her blue eyes and smiled. He leaned over nearer to her, taking her in his arms he kissed her soft lips. He tasted a hint of popcorn. She put her arms around him as he pulled her nearer to his body. They kissed as he fingered her blonde hair. Pulling back, he looked into her blue eyes, looking at her lovely facial features—her small nose, her full lips, and her beautiful blonde hair surrounding her face. He kissed her again teasing her lips to open. As her small tongue touched his, he gently deep throated her. She moaned and chills went down her spine.

When he was looking at her, she looked at this handsome guy who had taken her out. This had been her first real date and she felt her heart skip a beat when he kissed her so deeply. His kisses moved to her neck and she gasped as he nibbled on her ear. Now, her chills turned to goosebumps as he spoke sweet words into her ear. His warm breath made her lean closer to him as she moved to kiss his neck. Her wet lips on his neck stirred his desire and his mind emptied while they continued to kiss each other.

As they were kissing, the porch light blinked off and on a couple of times. With their eyes closed, neither saw the signal from her dad. Mark Carter had been up waiting for her to return from the movies. Her mom Eloise had gone to bed. Earlier, they had met Tom and liked him with his friendly manners and smiling face. As Mark peeked from behind the curtain, he saw the two making out in the red pickup. Recalling his younger years, he felt protective of his daughter sitting out there in the arms of that guy. She was just a junior with another year of high school before she would be on her own. Right now, he wanted her to come in. He went over to the switch again, and turned the porch light off and on a couple times.

Out of the corner of his eyes, Tom noticed the porch light go off and on this time. He pulled back, and said, "I better go, Melanie." She took a breath and nodded. Taking his hands away from her, she tried to finger her hair back to normal. He had messed up her hair while they had kissed. Melanie reached for her small purse sitting on the floor, took out a hairbrush, and brushed the tangles out of her hair.

"Sorry, I didn't mean to mess your hair," Tom said, watching her brush the soft blonde hair.

"Oh. That's no problem," she answered smiling at him with her sexy blue eyes. She took a tube of rose-colored lipstick as she quickly applied the color to her wide, full lips. With her hair in place and color on her lips, she looked gorgeous. Her cheeks flushed pink told him that she had felt the same feelings as he did.

He came around to her door and helped her out. Holding her hand in his, he walked up the porch stairs and stopped before the front door. He asked, "Can I call you sometime this week?"

"Sure, I'd like that. I better go inside. Thanks again," she answered. He leaned down and gave a quick kiss on her forehead and said, "goodbye." She opened the front door and disappeared into the house. He turned, skipped down the steps quickly, and walked to his red pickup. Getting into his truck, he started the engine. He let it idle for a few seconds before he backed up and drove down the dirt road to the highway. He glanced at his rearview mirror and saw Melanie standing in a window, watching him drive away. He had warm feelings thinking about her and her kisses.

Glad that he had met someone, he wanted to call her and get to know her. He recalled that the Double D Ranch held weekly rodeos during the summer. Maybe he could come out to their ranch and ride a bronc or rope a calf and see her. Knowing she would be in his class, she would be a good friend to know when he started back to school. He did look forward to his senior year and hopefully, play basketball on their team. Being a new guy in school didn't sit well with him. His brother Matt told him not to worry that with his height of six feet, the team would be glad to have him. *But would they? Would he be on the first string like his old school?*

He made the right turn at their ranch's turnoff, drove down the dirt road, and into their ranch. Parking his red pickup, he got out, walked into their log ranch house. Taking two steps at a time, he went upstairs to his bedroom. Walking down the hall, he noticed that Chet was still up reading his paperback like he always did. He stuck his head into his brother's room, and said, "Hi, there. What are you readin'?"

"Hi, Tom…just another western. How was your date?" he asked his brother.

"Melanie's a great girl, pretty. Her folks run the Double D Ranch. They have the summer weekly rodeos out there. Maybe, we could go sometime. What do you think?" he said.

"Yeah, you bet. We'll plan on that," said Chet. He turned back to reading as Tom moved down to his bedroom.

****

Meanwhile earlier that evening, Matt drove Deirdre home in his Blue Demon. Listening to the radio, they didn't talk much since the encounter with the sheriff. His success at drag racing seemed miniscule to the problem he now faced—paying for the ticket. Deirdre tried to talk to him; she wanted to erase the hurt feelings he was experiencing as he drove her to her parents' ranch – the Lodge Pole Dude Ranch. As he made the left turn at their turnoff to the ranch, he slowed down, drove over the bridge, past the barn and corrals to their ranch house. She had been drinking her can of beer and finished it. But he hadn't opened his, so it sat on the seat between the two of them. He parked the car, leaving it idle as they continued to listen to the radio and the hit songs. The Oklahoma radio station had a countdown going, so if people stayed up late, they could hear the number one song in the country. Now, Elvis Presley's top song played on the radio.

"I better go. Will you be all right, Matt?" asked Deirdre. She sat and looked at him.

"Sure. Thanks for comin' out with me tonight. I better take off," answered Matt. He turned to her, looking into her brown eyes. She leaned toward him to kiss him 'goodbye.' He didn't move, instead he sat with a cold look in his eyes. His mind was still stuck on the ticket.

"I like being with you. Will you call me?" she asked quietly, afraid that he wouldn't want to go out again with her. He obviously was too sensitive to just let this night go. He should just consider the ticket one more experience to add to his life.

"Sure," he said. She thought she heard a hesitation in his voice. He got out of the car, walked around, and opened her car door. As she stepped out, he took her into his arms. He didn't want her to leave without kissing her.

Closing the car door behind her, he pulled her into him as he pushed her gently up against the car. The car was still running with the radio playing. With the side windows opened, they could hear the music. Leaning down and cupping her blonde head in his warm hands, he gave her a kiss. With her back up against the Blue Demon, his strong body pinned her there. He gently grounded his hips against hers as he continued to kiss her. She pushed her hips into his. When he first met her, he recalled those hips of hers grinding against him as they had danced at the wedding reception. He whispered in her ear as he kissed her neck, "I'm sorry about tonight. I feel like a fool."

"No, Matt. It's okay…" she tried to tell him more, but her words were smothered with his mouth as he kissed her, running his tongue over her soft, wet lips. She wrapped her arms around his shoulders and neck. As he kissed her soft, warm neck, she nestled her head against his head. He turned and kissed her lips. Another song came on the radio.

Deirdre felt lightheaded from the liquor and her heart was racing as he stopped kissing. He looked into her eyes which had a distant look to them. She wasn't looking at him, and she wasn't responding to him, except for her hips. He took a breath and just held her tight against him with his strong arms. She breathed in his masculine smell as she felt his warm breath on her neck. Her fingers moved through his dark brown hair. Playing with his hair, she seemed distracted.

With a raspy breath, he whispered, "Deirdre, I've got to go." He stepped back. Smiling, she swallowed and collected herself. Taking her in his long arms, he guided her towards the steps to the porch. She leaned in against him as they walked together. They took one step at a time. Standing on the porch, he kissed her temple, and said, "I'll call. Good nite."

He moved down the steps, walked over to his Blue Demon, and crawled in. Putting the gear shift into reverse, he backed up, and headed away from the ranch house down the dirt road, over the little bridge, and to the turnoff. Staying on the porch, she leaned against the wooden post, watched Matt back up and drive away. She raised her hand to her lips as she recalled his passionate kisses. With her emotions swirling inside, she thought of Matt. For a brief moment while he was kissing her, she thought about Ronnie. She turned, opened the door, and disappeared into the ranch house.

Matt had stopped the Blue Demon at the turnoff. Glancing back at the distant ranch house, he revved the devil engine. Looking both ways, he pulled onto the highway. With another hit song on the radio, he drove back towards the Battle Axe Ranch.

Getting that ticket still bothered him. Maybe, someone up there was telling him to watch it. He felt that the ticket was a warning to him. Even though he loved getting his wheels, he never really wanted to drag race. Bill had encouraged him to race the Red Devil in Scottsville and he liked racing. But here, in this small mountain town, the situation was much different. He didn't think people would mind if they drag raced their cars. Obviously, they did. His mind jumped as he thought about getting away from here. He recalled that Craig had joined the Army. Bottom line-- the ticket would have to be paid. Maybe, he'd talk to his brothers and borrow some money from them.

Turning right, he drove down the dirt road to the ranch. Against the dark night, the log house stood like a dark shadow. The porch light shone brightly on. From an upstairs window, a yellow light glowed into the dark night. He parked the Blue Demon in the utility shed. Turning off the engine, he stepped out of his beloved car. As he walked away, he patted the back fender with his hand, and said, "Goodnite, ol' Demon." He heard the hot engine begin to cool while he walked out of the shed.

Like he had always done, he looked up to the dark sky, decorated with all the twinkling stars and the vast cosmic world above him. He breathed deeply in the icy, cold air. Walking towards the ranch house, his boots crunched the ground. Going up the porch steps, he pushed open the front door. Silence met him as he entered the house. Taking two steps at a time, he strolled down the upstairs hall, passing

Chet's room. Sleeping with a little snore, his brother lay on his bed with a paperback on his chest. Matt smiled, flicked off the light, and walked down his bedroom. He walked by Tom's bedroom and heard his brother's unique snore which sounded more like a little motor running.

Matt was so tired that he didn't even turn on his light. Pulling off his boots, he slipped out of his clothes. He reached into his back pocket for his wallet and set it on the small table next to his bed. That ticket in there still plagued his mind. Thinking of Deirdre tonight, he liked her, but something just didn't feel right. Once when he was kissing her, he had a flash of Ronnie's face. Before his death, she had been his girl. *Was she thinking of Ronnie as she kissed him?* Confused, he didn't know, but somehow, he felt he needed to be cautious. She probably didn't realize that is why he came off moody tonight. *Did she really like him? Was she playing him?* He been with too many girls who had betrayed him. He had to guard his heart. Crawling under his covers, he stretched out and closed his eyes. His mind whirled and throbbed. Sleep overtook him into a dream world of chaos—a dream in which he seemed to be fighting a losing battle.

High up in the mountains, storm clouds had formed. High winds tossed around the branches of the tall pines, the aspens, and the old cottonwoods. A strong breeze whipped down through the canyons into the valleys. Lightning tore through the dark sky as thunder rumbled in the dark clouds. The April rain came pouring down from the dark heavy clouds as the storm moved quickly into the valleys, covering the Battle Axe Ranch with a drenching rain.

Earlier, Clyde rested in his bed, covered and had heard his three sons come home, one by one. Tonight, he thought of Beth. Without her warm body by his side, he felt cold and lonely. Some nights he slept; other nights he would have a nightmare. Waking up in a cold sweat, he could still feel her presence in their bedroom. He didn't know when he would be free of these feelings and nightmares.

As the storm moved down to their ranch, he listened to the pitter-patter of the rain on the windows as the wind swept the drops against the glass. Turning on his side, his mind finally closed shut. With the rhythm of the raindrops, he fell into a deep sleep throughout the rest of the dark, stormy night.

Chapter 19

A Visitor

Before dawn, Dave and Fred rode back to the ranch from watching the herd through the stormy night. After Dave had been out last night and watched the races, he came back to the ranch. He had saddled his horse Bullet and rode out with Fred. When the wind and rain came down from the mountains, they had to put on their slickers to keep dry. The night had put a chill into their bones. As they came riding up to the stable, they dismounted and unsaddled their horses. Hanging up the bridles, they led them into the stable with rope halters. They brushed their coats dry, gave them grain and water, and checked their hooves which were caked with mud and debris. The two walked over to the bunk house. They were going to take a nap after being out all night. Bandit had been out with them, so he too wanted to get inside where it was warm and dry.

Over at the ranch house, Clyde rose, dressed, and headed for the barn. Chet came along to help his dad. In the barn, the little calf and mother seemed to be doing okay. Chet lifted another bale of hay and spread some of it for the mother cow. As he did, he heard a definite cough from the calf. His dad heard it too and the two of them looked at each other. Clyde thought about the phone contacts that Hans had given him when they bought the ranch. One of those numbers was a veterinarian. He might call Hans about the vet since he noticed that the number was not a local call. When he got back from feeding the herd, he'd call him. In the meantime, they left the mother and the calf in the barn for another day. The two walked over to the stable to get ready to feed the herd. The draft horse Jack seemed ready to pull the hay wagon. Chet saddled his horse Rusty and rode alongside the wagon as Clyde drove out toward the pasture.

After the storm late last night, the muddy ground had puddles of rain in low spots along the two-track road. The pre-dawn air made the men see their breaths. Keeping him warmer, Chet had been wearing his sheep-skin vest under his jacket ever since his dad bought them when they first moved here to this mountain ranch. The white misty clouds hung around the mountains, touching the tops of the timber. As the sun started to dawn, the sky brightened in a pale reddish color, taking away the grey morning sky.

The herd bellowed loudly as their breaths could be seen. They were hungry and had started moving towards the hay wagon as Clyde drove it into the pasture. The little calves were cuddled down but jumped up. Tethering his horse to the wagon, Chet had dismounted and helped his dad break up the hay bales on the wagon and toss the hay to their hungry herd. Clyde drove the wagon over nearer to the barbwire fence to throw hay over to Twister and the heifers.

As his dad continued to feed the herd, Chet mounted Rusty and headed towards the timber to look for tracks. Fortunately, there hadn't been any cows break out of the pasture since they had spent weeks repairing the rotted-out fence posts. With this large of a ranch though, the barbed wire fence stretched out far. Other posts could still need to be replaced. As he rode out of the pasture, he rode Rusty over towards the willows where Dave said there were moose—a cow with twins. He glanced around as he rode, but he didn't see the moose nor did he see any tracks in the soft ground. They most likely had moved up into the forest or had moved down further along the creek covered in willows.

Before going any further, he stopped and pulled his rifle out of the scabbard. Loading his rifle this morning, he checked that the safety was on. He felt safer having the rifle in his hands, ready for any circumstances. Turning, he rode up toward the timber and into the dark shadowed forest. The moisture hung in the air as he smelled the rich wet earth with a heavy pine scent. A whiff of decay and mildew tickled his nose. The morning birds were chirping, busy nest building, and mate calling. He rode around the logs, the rocks, and the bushes. Watching the ground, he glanced through the tall, lodge pole pines as the sun started to lighten the dark shadows. He rode along a creek filled with muddy water from the rains looking for tracks along its soft banks. Nothing, so far.

He rode higher up to the big meadow with the lily pond. Coming to the edge of the meadow, he stopped and looked around before going out into the open. New green grass in the meadow was sprouting as he rode toward the pond. He stopped. At the edge of the forest, he saw the cow moose. In front of her were the twin calves with their little bodies and long, spindly legs. They were moving towards the pond. Not wanting to disturb them, he turned around, left the meadow, and moved back into the forest. Besides, Rusty didn't like the moose. After another loop through the pines, he rode parallel to their pasture below. He hadn't seen any tracks. Emerging out of the forest, he pulled Rusty to a stop, leaned over, and put his rifle back into the scabbard.

As he moved towards the ranch, he thought of seeing Sophia today. She said she would call when she came to town. He would meet her somewhere there. Anxious to see her, his chest tightened at the thought of the time they were together the night of his mom's wake. This time when he met her, he wouldn't be drunk, acting like a fool with her. He felt a strong attraction to her. With their phone calls, he knew more about her than anyone he had dated before.

He came to the stable, dismounted, took out his rifle, and unsaddled Rusty. Taking his horse into his stall, he brushed his reddish-brown hair, cleaned his hooves, fed him some grain and water.

"Rusty, I'm goin' to see a special girl today. Maybe, I'll bring her out here to the ranch to meet you. Wish me luck," he said as he affectionately stroked his horse's neck from ears down along his red mane. Rusty neighed in response, nudging Chet in the chest with his muzzle. He then turned and left as Rusty continued eating his grain. Closing the half door, he walked out of the stable and over to the barn. The calf had worried him this morning with her little cough. His dad was there, looking at the calf. Seeing his son, he motioned him over to look. The calf's nose had a little yellow-white mucus coming out and her breathing was heavy.

Shaking his head, Clyde said, "We're goin' to have to call the vet. She has a temperature. I think she probably has pneumonia. I hope we don't lose her." He stood up. The two left the barn to walk over to the ranch house.

As they stepped onto the back porch, they smelled breakfast. Washing up, they went into the big kitchen and said, 'good morning.' The two brothers, Matt and Tom, were up fixing breakfast. Along with a pot of coffee and a pitcher of milk, they had fixed oatmeal, bacon, and toast. The men sat down and ate. As they ate, Dave and Fred came in from the bunk house to have breakfast after a short nap. Silence fell on the men as they filled their hungry stomachs. They talked about the ranch and the work ahead.

Concerned, Clyde said, "With the rain last night, you boys will have to wait a day for the barn to dry out....The little calf is sick with a temperature and had mucus in the nostrils. I'm goin' to call Hans about the vet."

Fred spoke up, "Let's work with our new horses. Who would like to help train them?"

"I can," said Tom. Dave said would help. Matt needed to put horseshoes on Diablo.

"My friend Sophie is comin' through today, so I'm waitin' to meet with her in town. Is there anythin' we need? at the Mercantile? Or the hardware store?" Chet asked. Nodding Fred thought of a few grocery items as he got a tablet and jotted them down.

"Okay, I'll go make that call to Hans," said Clyde as he took his bowl and silverware to the kitchen sink. Taking his coffee with him, he walked down the hall to the office and made the call.

Waiting, Clyde heard the phone ring a couple of times. On the third ring, Hans answered, "Hello."

"Hi, Hans. It's Clyde over at the Battle Axe. We have a sick calf. Looks like pneumonia. Tell me about the vet. Does he live around here?" he asked.

"Oh, sorry to hear about your calf. The vet, Steve Kullens, lives outside of Midler. If you make a call, he'll put you down on his list. When he gets enough calls, he'll drive up. Of course, if it's an emergency, he'll come," explained Hans.

"Thanks. How are you folks doin'?" asked Clyde.

"Fine. I'm lookin' at buying a new place. We don't like livin' here in town. There's no room for the two fillies and our mare. They need a pasture, not stuck in a corral all day. If I get that place, I wondered if one of your sons, or maybe two, would be interested in workin' for me this summer. I'd pay them. I could sure use some help, repairin' the ranch" he said.

"Oh, what place are you buyin'?" asked Clyde.

"We're still decidin', but we hope to purchase a section of a ranch from Jared at the Lodge Pole Dude Ranch. It comes with an old ranch house, a barn, and some outbuildin's. If we do buy, it'll be in a few weeks before I could use some help. By the way, could you use some help brandin'? I'd like to bring my grandson Andy over to give him some experience. When I suggested helpin' you, Ingrid and Anna got excited and said they would like to fix lunch and dinner that day for the whole crew. What do you think? Could you use some help?" asked Hans.

"We sure could. I plan to brand in about two weeks. Thanks," answered Clyde.

"I heard about the search you and your boys conducted last week. That must have been quite an experience searchin' for that missin' person," said Hans.

"Yeah, the boys did a good job. I hope they catch the guy who did it.... I look forward to havin' you help with brandin'. I'll call you a couple of days before we brand," he said.

"Great. I hope you can get the vet to come," said Hans. The two hung up. Clyde sat at his desk for a few moments before he made the call to the vet. His son Chet walked into the office as he hung up. Clyde filled him in about the vet, about Hans buying a ranch, and about him want to help with branding.

"Do we have enough to cover a vet?" asked his dad. He had to keep Chet abreast of everything to do with money, spending and charging.

271

"Yes, we'll be okay if you can charge it and pay next month," he said.

"I don't want to lose the calf, Chet," he said.

"I understand. I'm glad you made the call." He walked out of the office and back to the kitchen. It was his turn to do the breakfast dishes. As he came into the kitchen, everyone had finished eating and had left. He rolled up his shirt sleeves and started washing the dishes. He knew that Sophia would be calling any time. While he finished with the dishes, his dad came back into the kitchen.

"The vet said he had several calls from ranchers around here this mornin', so he is drivin' up. He'll be here later this afternoon," said Clyde. "I'm goin' out to help Fred with the horses."

He left the ranch house and headed towards the corrals where the men had the horses separated, working, and training them. Tom worked with the two mares, Honeysuckle and Gypsy. In another corral, Dave was working with the gelding Shadow. In the third corral, Fred had the stallion Legend. The training involved getting the horses re-acquainted with the saddles, the bridles, and a few commands. Patience and a firm hand made the horses respond to the men. The old mares were easy, but Shadow and Legend would need more training.

The men kept working while over in the stable, Matt was putting new horseshoes on Diablo. Every time Matt came around the black stallion, his beauty and size amazed him. He recalled how strong and dependable he was when he rode him up the steep mountains to Stewart's Lake and out again during a heavy rainstorm.

At the ranch house, Chet sat waiting for Sophia's call. The nervous energy he had waiting turned his insides to a brewing storm. Sitting at the kitchen, he looked around. The dirty floor needed another mopping, so he went into the pantry, grabbed the broom, and picked up the mop and the bucket. Within thirty minutes, the floor looked clean without the dirt and scuff marks. Dumping out the bucket in the kitchen sink, he saw the dirty, water after mopping the floor. Just as he finished, the phone rang. He walked quickly into the living room and picked up the phone.

"Hello. Is Chet there?" asked the sweet voice of Sophia.

"Hi, it's me, Sophie. Are you in town? Where can I meet you? How long do you have?" he asked in a series of questions.

She laughed at the other end, "Yes, I am here. I'm at the phone booth by the post office. I have about an hour, maybe more. Can you come meet me?"

"Of course. Do you see Bert's Café down the street from you? I'll meet you there in about twenty minutes or so," said Chet.

"Yes, I see the café. I haven't eaten. Do you mind if I order?" she asked.

"No, go ahead and order…I can't wait to see you," he whispered in the phone.

"See you soon. Bye," she said. The phone went dead. He put the receiver back and went up the stairs two at a time. He needed to wash up a little and to change into a clean shirt. She sounded good. Going upstairs, he walked past his bedroom and into the bathroom. As he looked at himself in the mirror, he thought of seeing her. Shaking his head, he washed his face and hands. Seeing his sheets on the floor in his bedroom, he recalled his nightmare.

Last night, he had dreamed about finding Betsy's body. He had managed to keep that terrible day locked safely inside him, but in his sleep, it all came bubbling up—the dried, black blood, the throat cut, her death like stare, her bruised face, her silver turquoise earring. With a parched throat, he had screamed into the dark night: *Elizabeth, no…no…no.* His sheets were wet, and down the center of his muscled chest, sweat ran. He stumbled out of bed and headed for the bathroom.

With all their bedroom doors opened, his brothers heard him shout, and both woke up. Tom called out to him, "Chet, are you, all right?"

In the bathroom, he splashed water into his mouth and onto his face, and answered, "I'm fine." As Chet walked back to his bedroom, Matt hollered out, "Do you need help?" He mumbled, "No, go back to sleep." In his bedroom, he pulled off the wet sheets and wrapping himself into a blanket, he crawled back onto his bed. Closing his eyes, he tried to forget his nightmare. It took a while before he fell asleep.

Now, today, he combed his hair, put on a little shaving lotion, and slipped on a clean shirt and jeans. Going downstairs and into the kitchen, he picked up the list on the table and unhooked his pickup keys on the key rack inside the pantry. He carried his jacket since he wore his sheep-skin vest. He desperately needed to see Sophia-- his anchor in more ways than she would ever know. She had helped him through his mom's death by her tender understanding. And with their phone calls, she had been on his mind every day since he had met her.

Driving into town seemed to take longer than ever before. His pickup couldn't get there fast enough. He pulled up and parked in front of Bert's Café next to her red and white car. He walked into the café and saw her sitting at a table near the front. Without thinking, he strolled up to her, reached out, and pulled her from her seat. Taking her in his arms, he held her in a tight hug—he didn't want to let her go. Overwhelmed by his affection, she turned red as she blushed. People in the café looked at them and smiled.

Pulling away, she said, "Hi, Chet....uh...let's sit down." He smiled at her and kissed her on the forehead. He reluctantly let her sit back down as he pulled out the chair next to her and sat down himself. She collected herself, smiling she looked into his dark brown eyes and she felt her heart racing. She could never get enough of him—so handsome and ruggedly masculine. As she reach for her glass of water, he took her hand before she touched the glass.

Holding her soft hand with her pink fingernails in his calloused hand, he said, "Hi." So simple, but his eyes with that certain gleam told her more. Words couldn't capture how they felt towards each other. He caressed her hand, and said, "Hi, Sophie. How are you? How did the interview go?"

She shook her blonde head, "Not well, I don't want to talk about it... How are you?"

The new waitress Torri interrupted them as she brought out Sophia's lunch. As she set down the lunch plate in front of her, she asked him, "Do you want a menu?" looking at Chet.

Looking up at her, he said, "No, I'll just have coffee." She must be new here for he had never seen her before.

"Are you one of the Fletchers? You look like your brother Matt," said Torri as she stared at Chet who had similar features with a few differences. He was older and had a rougher look to him.

He looked confused at her, and asked, "Do I know you? I'm Chet."

"No, I'm sorry. I am Torri McClure. I know your brother Matt. Let me get your coffee," she answered hurriedly. He frowned *Oh, Ronnie's sister?* She left to get his coffee.

Meeting Chet just now made Torri think of a week ago when she first met Matt. Dave had to drive her home that night. She had broken down and cried up at Skyline. Her dad was still up waiting in the kitchen. He asked her why she was upset. She told him what had happened that she had lashed out at Matt Fletcher because he owned the car that killed her brother. Then, her dad took her in his arms and told her that they needed to talk. He wanted to help her deal with her grief. He said he understood her anger, but he explained that Matt had nothing to do with Ronnie's accident. That the Fletchers were good people. As it grew late that night, they had talked more about her brother and his death. She finally realized that she needed to apologize for her harsh accusations.

Today, as she walked away, she decided to write a note to Matt. Maybe she could smooth over her accusations. Before taking out Chet's coffee, Torri went into the back for a piece of paper. Since she didn't have his phone number, she thought this would at least show that she was sorry for her words. Her dad had told her that her brother and Matt had been good friends, playing their guitars and fixing their cars together. She did not know that he had made friends

275

with this new guy named Matt who probably grieved for his loss. After taking a few minutes to write out the words, she folded it and put it in her apron pocket.

When she brought the coffee pot and a cup out to their table, she handed him the note and said, "Would you give this to your brother Matt?" The note was addressed to 'Matt.' Chet nodded and put it in his shirt pocket. She poured his coffee and left.

Glancing at Torri, he noticed that she looked a little like her brother—with reddish-brown hair and a few similar facial features. But her shapely figure took him by surprise. Maybe, his brother found someone to date rather than those young high school girls he heard about.

Pulling his gaze and attention back to Sophia, he said as she ate, "We could go for a short drive up on the mesa above town. You could see what the area looks like from up there. Would you have time for a ten-minute drive?"

She wiped her mouth with a napkin as she swallowed, and said, "Okay....sounds nice. But I do have to get on the road again." He nodded as he sipped his coffee. She continued eating. He sat quietly and watched her. Looking at her as she ate, he saw her kissable lips and her short little nose. Her blonde hair was longer, and her brown eyes sparkled. She wore a casual grey sweatshirt that had the college logo with a pair of tight blue jeans and her white tennis shoes. As he drank his coffee, his mind filled with the images of her when they had been together and kissed before.

Finally, she sat back with her hand on her stomach, and said, "I'm full. Do you want some of this?" Her plate still had another half of a sandwich and some potato chips with a dill pickle. He grinned at her. He felt his empty stomach growl a little.

"How about dessert? They make good pies here. What kind do you like?" he asked.

"Oh, I love cherry. But I couldn't eat any more. You go ahead," she answered.

"I'll get a cherry pie and we can share. Okay?" She nodded as he waved his hand to Torri.

276

"What can I get you?" she asked, taking out her pad and pencil.

"Oh, just one cherry pie. We're goin' to share it," he said.

"Do you want it a la mode? With ice cream?" She looked at him and then at Sophia who nodded her head.

"Yes...a la mode," said Chet. When Torri left, Sophia pushed her plate in front of him. He quickly picked up the sandwich and wolfed it down with the few chips. He took a knife from her silverware and cut the dill pickle.

"Here's half of the pickle," he whispered as he leaned over to her, holding the half pickle for her to take, elbows on the table. She started to reach for it, but he shook his head, and said, "No...Open your mouth."

She smiled at him, opened her mouth, and he slowly put the half pickle up to her lips. Even though it was a small pickle from the start, she bit the pickle. As she chewed it, she squinted her eyes at the bitter taste of the dill. Chet still had the other piece ready for her. "Come on...just one more bite," he said, teasing her. He smiled at her with a hearty laugh. She felt people looking at them. Her faced flushed pink. She took the last of the pickle and chewed it. Afterwards, she took a sip of water to clear the dill pickle taste from her mouth. Leaning back in his seat, he took his half, popped it into his mouth, and winked at her.

Torri then brought over a plate with a piece of cherry pie and vanilla ice cream. She placed two forks next to the plate. They both picked up a fork and ate the delicious dessert. Despite the fact that she felt full, she did enjoy sharing the pie with Chet. She liked this playful side of him. Her feelings toward him were growing inside of her. Her mind flooded with the memories of him and all of the conversations with him. She liked him and hoped that they could get together. *But he lived here.*

He finished his coffee as the last bite of the cherry pie went into her mouth. Smiling at her, he said, "Ready?" She nodded, stood up, and started to put on her jacket. He walked around behind her and helped her with her jacket. Hugging her from behind, he leaned down and gave her a

277

quick kiss on the temple. He smelled a fresh scent coming from her blonde hair.

Putting his hand into his pocket, he dropped a few quarters on the table for the tip. Together they walked to the front counter to pay. He said, "I've got this." She started to protest but realized that she didn't want to create more fuss, so she kept silent. People had been watching them ever since he first hugged her. She had never been around someone like him who showed his affection. His passion astounded her and made her like him even more. He emitted confidence. Everyone she had dated had been proper and distant in public. She had been surrounded at college with guys who had 'put on airs' and who came off as fakes. Here was a handsome, broad framed man with raw power and a rough style. He certainly didn't imitate anyone. He was genuine from the top of his head to the bottom of his cowboy boots.

After paying, they walked outside where their vehicles were parked. She almost suggested that they take her car, but he didn't let her get a chance to say it. He held the door open for her to his white pickup. She stepped up and sat down, and he closed the door. He got in, started the engine, and backed up. Driving down main street, he turned near a bridge and drove up a dirt road. Big cottonwoods lined a creek—Sheep Creek. She said, "This road looks muddy. Should we be going this way. I hope we don't get stuck." Worried, she didn't like driving on dirt roads. Her adventure days were over—no more silly back roads that ended in trouble for her and her car.

He looked at her and said, "Yeah, we had a big rainstorm last night. Trust me. We'll be fine." He told her about the area as they drove to another turnoff. The white pickup climbed up the second dirt road to the big mesa—Skyline. Chet drove along the mesa until he came just above the town. He stopped, turned off the engine, and got out. Going to her side, he opened the door for her. She stepped out as he took her hand and he led her near to the edge.

Before them was a sight to catch the imagination. The breathtaking view took her by surprise---so vast were the

278

forested mountains and small was the town below. The beautiful colors of the sharp blue sky, the dark green forests, the sparkling river flowing around the town made her take a second look. She had never seen such a view. All of her life had been spent living on the prairies—the flatlands. There were no such mountains as these where she had lived. He pointed to the north where he said, "That's where our ranch is. At the end of that long, green valley down there." She looked where he pointed to. Glancing beyond, she saw the steep peaks capped with white snow behind the mountains.

"Wow, it's gorgeous," she exclaimed. A cool gust of wind blew into their faces. She felt her hair being swept away from her face. He turned to her, stepped towards her, and pulled her into his arms.

"Yes…gorgeous," he said, seriously looking into her face. Leaning down, he kissed her soft lips that he'd been watching while she ate, talked, and smiled. He teased her lips with his tongue. She tasted like cherry pie as she teased him back with her tongue. Her arms went up and around to his neck. He felt her fingernails moving along his neck and into his hair. He pulled her closer to him. With the wind, her blonde hair blew around their heads as they kissed. He brought up his hands and smoothed her long hair behind her small ears where her little, white pearl earrings were. She felt his strong hands around her head and her lips sought out his mouth as she deep throated him. He moaned. Catching his breath, he whispered, "Your hair is longer…Come with me."

Together, hand in hand, they moved to his white pickup and got in. He put his arm around her and pulled her into his chest. She snuggled her head against him. Breathing in, she smelled a scent of pine. Her cheek felt his broad chest rise and fall as he breathed. His warm breath brushed against her face. His other hand went to her head and he felt her soft blonde hair. He smelled a faint sweet smell of perfume as he leaned down to kiss her again. She raised her head to meet his kiss. They kissed and kissed. He wanted to touch her, to feel her naked skin against his hands, but he recalled that she had pushed him away the last time he tried to move too fast with her. He tapped down his desire as she continue to kiss him. She could feel that he was holding back. She didn't understand why he didn't push for more. After the phone calls, she had waited so long to be here with him. She had made the arrangements just to feel his raw desire for her. Yet, here he was—holding back.

She pulled back for a moment and looked into his dark brown eyes. Yes, she saw his desire. He closed his eyes and breathed. He wanted to stay here forever, but he wanted to show her where he lived. Opening his eyes, he whispered, "Sophie, I want to take you to see our ranch and meet my family."

"What?" she asked. *His ranch? Why can't we stay and kiss?*

"I know…I'd like to stay here and…um….but…while you're here, let me show you our ranch," he replied. He looked into her bright brown eyes to see her reaction. "It won't take long."

"Yes, I'd like that…but I don't want to leave my car parked downtown. Could I follow you there? How long will it take?" she asked. There again came her assertiveness—her taking charge.

"You can follow me. It's just a few miles out of town," he answered. He moved over to the driver's side, started the engine, and backed up as he turned the pickup back onto the Skyline road. She slid over beside him and snuggled against him again. He kept his hands on the steering wheel as they headed down the mesa on the slippery muddy road. Soon, he turned down along Sheep Creek. Chet noted that the creek was nearly full, running close to its banks with muddy water. When he got to the bridge, he made a right turn onto main street.

Stopping at the café, he waited while she got out and started up her car. He kept an eye on her car in his rearview mirror. While driving through town, she glanced around at the businesses. Further on, she noticed the school buildings. *Maybe, I should apply here.* When they were on the highway, he picked up his speed. Coming to the ranch turn off, he signaled a left turn. She followed him down the muddy dirt road to their ranch. He parked in front of the stable as she parked her car next to his. The dogs Bandit and Blue had come out of the barn to meet the new visitor. He noticed an unknown pickup parked by the barn, but he first wanted to take her in to see the stable and their horses--- particularly, his horse Rusty. The two dogs ran around sniffing her as she squatted down and petted them. Wagging their tails, they were happy to see someone new on the ranch. Chet reached down and stroked each of their dogs. They ran back to the barn to keep a watch on the others there.

As they walked toward the stable, he took her hand, telling her about their horses. She looked around as she walked, amazed at the beautiful log ranch house she saw driving in. And there were three small log cabins. *So many buildings.* Strolling into the stable, she smelled the horses, the hay, and the manure. She held her nose for a while until she got use to the strong smell. He pulled her over to one of the stalls with a reddish-brown gelding. He reached out his hand as Rusty moved toward him, putting his muzzle into his outstretched hand. Chet said, "Hi, o' buddy. Here's my gal." He pulled her hand up for her to feel his muzzle, "Say hi to him, Sophie." Rusty snorted and neighed deep in his throat. At the sound, she pulled back her hand and jumped back—a little frightened. "No, no...he's just saying 'hi'," he said quietly.

Chet then strolled over to the sack of grain that sat against the wall and scooped a couple of handfuls into a bucket. He said to her, "Here, put some grain in your hand. Keep it flat and opened. He'll nibble the grain off." He took her hand, sprinkled some grain in her hand and moved it nearer to Rusty who quickly muzzled the grain into his mouth. She felt the muzzle and the wet tongue against her hand. Sophia laughed as it tickled. While she was feeding Rusty, he leaned nearer to his horse and stroked his neck.

"He's beautiful, Chet," she said as he gave her more grain and she let the horse nibble the grain. Feeling more comfortable around the horse, she moved her hand up to his long neck and stroked him.

"Have you ever ridden a horse?" he asked as they both caressed Rusty. He put his muzzle against Chet's chest.

"Yes and no. Years ago, as a child, but no, not recently," she answered.

"We'll have to do somethin' about that. Maybe, next time, you can stay longer, and I can take you ridin'. There are some beautiful places above our ranch that I liked to show you," he said. Rusty had eaten all the grain, so he put the bucket back. "Come on, I think my dad and uncle are over in the barn. I'd like you to meet them." She leaned in and gave the red sorrel a little kiss above his muzzle. He liked it as he neighed again.

Chet pulled her into his arms, and said, "Can I get a kiss, too?" He bowed his head as she lifted her head to kiss him. She kissed him as her arms wrapped around his neck, pulling him into her. Goosebumps went down her body as he kissed her lips. He breathed in her faint perfume as he moved to her neck and kissed her again. She laughed sweetly, as she turned and kissed his neck. Rusty interrupted them with another neigh. Nodding to his horse, he said, "Yeah, she's a good kisser... jealous ol' boy?"

He leaned down again and kissed her hard with a crushing kiss; she could feel his desire for her. As he drew back, he was breathing hard. She gasped and relaxed into his arms. Her knees weaken and she felt a warmth deep within her. He didn't want to leave, but he whispered, "We better go."

Turning, they strolled slowly down past the other horses in their stalls and out of the stable. She looked at each one, thinking how magnificent they were. He mentioned all of their names as they moved past each one---Chief, Captain, Brute, Honeysuckle, Gypsy, Shadow, Legend, and finally, Diablo. Out in the pasture were Jinx and Thunder. Oh, he also mentioned their bull Twister, their milk cow Sunny, and their two mules, Tabasco and Baby Doll. Dave's horse Bullet was still saddled and tethered to the corral near the water trough. She listened amazed at all their livestock not to mention the herd out in the pasture.

Walking arm and arm, they moved toward the barn. A dark green pickup sat next to the big barn door. As the two stepped in, they saw that the men were talking while they stood in front of the stall with a mother cow and her calf. The cow mooed for her calf. Uncle Fred broke more hay from a bale and tossed some of it into the stall for the cow to eat.

"Hi, everyone. How is the calf doin'?" asked Chet, walking over to his dad with Sophia.

"Oh, Chet. This is the vet Steve Kullens. Steve, this is my oldest son, Chet," said Clyde.

Chet shook his hand and introduced Sophia to the vet, his dad, his uncle, and Dave. They all said 'hi.' Matt and Tom remembered her from the funeral. Dave liked her immediately.

His dad and uncle looked at this lovely, blonde-headed girl that Chet had his arms wrapped around. *This is the one who kept calling Chet. She must be the college girl.*

But the whole family was concerned about this sick calf here in the barn.

Clyde said, "Steve's just examined the calf. She has a high temperature of a hundred and two. He gave her a shot of an antibiotic. He thinks we caught her pneumonia early enough."

"Yes, I'm glad you brought the calf into this dry warm barn for a couple of days. Last night, the cold and rain would have weakened her condition even more. Of course, time will tell," said Steve while he closed his medicine bag.

"How long should it be before she's better?" asked Chet.

"It depends. The antibiotic will help within twenty-four hours. It'll take ten days before the antibiotic is finished. Nature takes its own course with animals," the vet replied. "Take her temperature for a few more days to make sure the fever goes down. Watch her nostrils for more white mucus. Right now, it's not much. I've listened to her lungs, and I don't think there has been any damage."

"Good. We don't want to lose her. Thanks for comin' today, Steve," said Clyde as he shook the vet's hand. Everyone in the barn said a word or two of thanks.

283

"I best be goin'. I have a few more calls to make before I head back to Midler. It's been nice meetin' all of you," said the vet. He headed out of the barn to his dark green pickup and drove off.

The Fletchers stood looking at the small calf as it rested in the hay while the cow ate. With her arm around his waist, Sophia stood beside Chet and clutched his sheep-skin vest. She had never seen so much fuss over a calf. She figured out quickly that the loss would impact the ranch.

"Clyde, I'm headed up to that new pond one mile up on our west end. There's a beaver dam cutting off that stream that comes down towards our fields. Do you have a stick or two of dynamite?" said Dave.

"Yeah, they're in a wooden box in the back of the utility shed on that long shelf. Be careful, Dave."

"Will do. I've blasted beaver dams before," he answered as he headed out of the barn.

Tom followed him and said, "I'll come with you, Dave." Dynamite interested him. He had never seen a beaver dam blasted apart.

Clyde called out, "Don't forget your rifles." He turned and looked at Chet and Sophia. "Do you want to come up to the ranch house for coffee or tea?" He recalled that Beth liked a cup of tea in the afternoon.

She nodded her head, smiled, and said, "Yes. Tea." She like Clyde, something about him reminded her of her dad Art. They left the barn, walked to the ranch house, and into the big kitchen. Recalling that he had mopped the floor, Chet felt glad that the floor looked clean.

Uncle Fred had put on a pot of chili that morning, so the kitchen smelled like warm food cooking in the oven. Clyde put on the tea kettle for Sophia, and Matt made a pot of coffee for the men. Carrying his rifle, Tom came downstairs and through the kitchen.

"See you later. Nice seein' you again, Sophia," said he as he left the kitchen to the back porch.

Chet pulled out a chair for her as she took off her jacket and hung it on the back of the chair. As she sat there, all of the Fletchers realized this was the first woman in their

kitchen since they had come back from the funeral. A
silence hung for a second. Walking over to the cupboard,
Chet took down five cups. Clyde looked for the tea
cannister in the cupboard. After opening several cupboards,
he found Beth's little pink cannister shoved in the back.
He'd have to buy more tea if Chet were serious about this
girl. She looked good sitting in their kitchen. He would be
happy for his son if he had found someone to marry. *And
just think, his own grandkids. Damn, he was getting ahead
of himself.*

The tea kettle whistle. Chet poured the steaming water
into a cup while Clyde threw in a tea bag. Taking her cup of
tea over to the big table, he sat next to Sophia. He smelled
the mint from the hot tea which reminded him of his mom.
In the past, she had sipped mint tea along with other spiced
teas.

Soon, the coffee perked, and the smell of brewed coffee
filled the air. Going into the pantry, Matt came out with a
package of cookies. After the coffee cups were filled, the
cookies were passed around. Sophia took one, just out of
courtesy. She sipped her tea and nibbled at her cookie. The
others drank their coffee and gobbled down two or three
cookies each. Chet drank his coffee, slowly, watching her.

They sat and asked her about the college, her family, and
her recent interview. Chet barely listened to his dad or Fred
or Matt. He focused on her and her sparkling brown eyes,
her soft lips, and her lovely face as she answered their
questions. He knew all of her answers for they had spent
hours talking to each other over the phone. Answering their
questions, she had so much poise and grace. He recognized
a strength in her; she faced the unknown with a mature,
curious nature. For a moment, he wondered how she could
like someone like him. He felt himself lucky beyond words.
Time was slipping by and getting later by the minute.
Sophia needed to get on the road. Chet saw her tense up as
she glanced at her little wristwatch.

Glancing at Chet, he knew what that look meant and
said, "Sophia needs to go."

285

"Why don't you stay here for the night, Sophia?" asked Fred, knowing that Chet could use more time with his girl.

"No, thanks. I really need to get back today. I have a big paper due on Monday and I need to type it up tomorrow. With graduation so close, I can't risk missing that deadline," she explained.

Chet could tell by her voice and her words that she needed to leave. He rose, picked up her jacket from the back of her chair, and helped her put it on. She thanked everyone again. The two left the kitchen. They walked wrapped in each other's arms towards her red and white car. Pulling out her keys, she paused and turned to Chet, and said, "Would you want to come to my graduation in two weeks? I'd like you to meet my folks.... Your ranch is magnificent. I had no idea."

Looking at her, he considered it. "I'll let you know. Afterwards, maybe, you could come here for a couple of days--stay here in one of those little log cabins. I'll take you for that ride. Call when you get there." They slowly kissed as he moved her up against her car. His heart ached with the thoughts that she was leaving. While they kissed, his tongue sought out hers. The taste of mint tea and coffee mixed. His idea of coming for a couple of days after graduation took seed in her mind. *Just two more weeks*. She could hardly wait to be with him again. Finally, pushing him back with her small hands inside his vest, she had to leave, or she would lose her resolve to get back to college.

He complained, and said, "I'll miss you...." as he breathed hard and kissed her again.

"Chet...Chet...I've got to go." He finally stepped back.

"Okay.... Be careful, love," he whispered as she turned from him and opened the car door. She got into the car and he closed her door. Rolling down her window, she smiled at him, "I'll call." Starting the engine, she let it idle for a minute. "Thanks for everything. I like your family." Backing up, she turned the car around and drove down the muddy dirt road to the highway. Stopping at the turnoff, she turned and waved goodbye to him. Did she hear him use that endearing word 'love?' It was just a whisper, but she knew she heard him say it—*love.*

He stood with his hands in his jean pockets while she drove away. Lifting one of his hands, he waved back at her as she stopped and waved out her opened window. He watched her red and white car drive down the highway and disappeared into the distance. He took several deep breaths as his heart throbbed in his chest. *Just two more weeks.*

Chapter 20

An Apology

Up somewhere in the distant mountains, they heard a blast which sounded like a shotgun going off. Dave and Tom must have dynamited that beaver dam. When Chet looked toward the barn, he saw his brother Matt standing on a tall ladder, painting. Walking nearer to him, he called out, "Be careful up there, Matt." His brother had started painting at the very highest point and had finished painting a few feet from the top.

He turned slowly around, looking down, "It was nice seein' your girl again," he said.

"I have the night watch, so I'm headed in for an afternoon nap," Chet said.

"Sophia is nice. I like her. Is she comin' back, soon?" he asked.

Suddenly, Chet remembered the note for Matt. "Oh, I forgot. Here's a note from Ronnie's sister Torri. She gave it to me when we were at Bert's Café," he said as he pulled out the folded note in his shirt pocket. He also pulled out the list of groceries. With Sophia here, he had forgotten to stop at the Mercantile for the groceries. *Tomorrow.*

Surprised, Matt carefully moved down the ladder. Reaching the ground, he asked, "What did Torri say?"

"I didn't read it, Matt. It's addressed to you." he said. He held out the small folded paper as Matt placed the paint can on the ground and the paint brush across the can. His fingers were sticky with the paint. Frustrated he said, "Open it for me, will you?"

"Yeah….here it is." Chet unfolded it and held it up for his brother.

"Hold it closer so I can read it," he insisted. He squinted as he got closer. The neat handwriting scrolled across the white paper said:

Matt, I am so sorry for the other night. Forgive me. Torri

At the bottom she had written down her phone number. Shocked, his mind leaped to that night when she had gone crazy. He hadn't forgotten her firestorm that she had created that night. He felt her misplaced wrath aimed at him. Wanting to forget about her, he didn't think he'd ever hear from her again. *What changed her mind?* He didn't care and he wouldn't ever call her number.

"Fold it back up and slip it into my back pocket, Chet," ordered his brother.

"Oh, do you need your ass wiped, too?" he laughed as he folded the note. Reaching into his brother's back pocket, he felt his wallet. He took it out and opened it to put the note inside it. As he did, he noticed another piece of paper. He unfolded it and read the citation for drag racing.

"Smart ass. You try holdin' a piece of paper with paint on your hands," Matt retorted, laughing. He glanced at his brother as he pulled another piece of paper from his wallet. *Shit, my ticket.*

"When did you get this ticket? So, you got caught drag racin'. Son of a bitch," said Chet staring at his brother, waiting for an answer.

Angry at his brother that he had discovered his ticket, he shouted, "Put that back. It's none of your damn business." The air got tense as the teasing disappeared between them.

"Listen. You better tell dad yourself or I will. Do you hear me?" he said firmly.

"No...no. I don't want dad to know about it. It's just a ticket. I'll pay it. You know that dad will ride my tail if he hears about this. I'm in a bad spot, Chet. Please, keep quiet," pleaded Matt.

"Do you have the money to pay for it?" he asked.

"Not all of it ... I have a little, but I wanted to ask you and Tom for a couple of bucks. I'll pay you back," he answered.

"Where did your money go? Oh....don't answer that...I know, the Blue Demon," said Chet.

"Sure...I need wheels just like you and Tom have. I'm waitin' to hear about a job with the road construction company. Any day they should call. I'll pay you back," he replied.

"We're in a real tight situation here at the ranch. We now have to pay for the vet, not to mention this paint. It goes on and on, Matt. It takes money to run this place. We have to tighten our belts. Do you hear me?" he shouted. His anger increased as he thought of how irresponsible his brother could be, fooling around racing his car like a teenager. He needed to grow up; he was tired of covering for him over the years.

"I hear you, loud and clear," he shouted back at his brother.

"This is the last time…the *very last time*, I'm goin' to cover your ass. Grow up, Matt," were his parting words as he handed him his wallet back—painted fingers or not. He turned and left his brother standing there.

After Chet left, Matt's insides shook at his brother's words. *Yes, he knew they were tight on money. And he wasn't a kid.* He had made a mistake. He'd find some job to bring in some cash—somewhere, somehow. Slipping his wallet back into his back pocket, he noticed that it now had red fingerprints all over it. He climbed up the ladder with paint can and brush in hand. As he leaned against the ladder to paint, he slapped the paint on the side of the barn. More paint fell to the ground than on the side, so he finally took a couple of breaths. Afterwards he leaned over, he worked the paint into the old wood. The barn would look great when he finished. He felt the strain on his arms and his back muscles. His head ignited with a throbbing that turned his stomach. He gulped down the bile that threatened to come up. Ignoring the pain, he stayed up on that high ladder. Painting this barn became his goal for the next two weeks. He needed to prove himself. *His money had not been wasted.* The Blue Demon sat in the utility shed waiting---waiting to free his troubled soul.

Clearly upset, Chet headed back to the ranch house and upstairs to his bedroom. From the night before, his dirty sheets were still on the floor. He picked them up and grabbed a few dirty clothes that needed washing. Since their mom's death, each of them had to do their own washing. He went downstairs to the back porch where the washing machine sat. Starting the washer with a load of dirty clothes and sheets, he left and went back upstairs. Throwing a blanket on the mattress, he laid down, stretching his long body out. Dozing, he thought of Matt. *Idiot.* Today was going so well until he saw that ticket. The money issues were bothering him.

Reflecting on Sophia, he looked at the small clock on his bedside table. Estimating the time, he figured she'd be at her apartment just after dinner--four to five hours. *Did he really call her 'love?'* It slipped from his lips naturally. She probably would think of him as crazy or think of him as a fool to call her that so soon in their relationship. He wanted to take it slow with her. But he felt that his feelings for her were barreling down—uncontrollable—like a locomotive on the rails, speeding faster and faster. It could derail in any second and throw them apart. He hoped that it wouldn't. He replayed the events of the day again, and eventually, sleep took over him as he relaxed.

Twilight approached as the sky started to fade into grey except for the west where the sun had dropped behind the mountain peaks. Everyone finished up their work and moved toward the ranch house where the warm chili in the oven waited for them. Going up the stairs to his bedroom, Tom carried his rifle after being with Dave as he blasted loose the beaver dam. He put his rifle into his closet after unloading it. Before going downstairs, he walked over to Chet's door. He heard him snoring and knew that he needed to get up and eat dinner.

Knocking on the opened door, he called out to him, "Wake up, sleepy head. Time to eat."

"What?" he mumbled as Chet sat up in bed and rubbed his head. Looking at the small clock, he said, "Okay...thanks." Standing up, he left his bedroom and followed Tom down the stairs.

"Man, Chet. You should have seen that beaver dam blown to smithereens—sticks, mud, and water went everywhere. That's the first time I have ever seen that," Tom said excitedly as he went down the stairs.

"Great. We'll be gettin' water down here in our fields," Chet replied.

The two walked into the big kitchen. Matt came in from the back porch complaining that they were out of turpentine to clean the red paint from his hands. His shirt had spots of red paint all over it. Fred said to add it to the shopping list. Chet told everyone that he forgot to stop at the Mercantile, but that he would go tomorrow.

Fred had brought out the pot of chili from the oven, setting it on a hot pad on the table. Bowls were set down with the silverware. The loaf of bread, the saltine crackers, the pint of sweet cream for the coffee, the pitcher of milk, and the three cans of sliced peaches found their way onto the big table. Tom found the cheese in the back of the fridge and set it on the table. They sat down, passing their bowls down to Fred as he dished up the chili. Filling their hungry stomachs they sat silently and ate. Dave, Matt, and Clyde asked for seconds on the chili while Tom and Chet spooned out the sliced canned peaches into their bowls. Chet recalled the package of cookies that they had opened, so he got up and went into the pantry to bring it to the table. A few cookies with the peaches would make a tasty dessert.

Dave finished up quickly, and said, "I need to take a little nap before the watch tonight. Come and wake me up, Chet. Thanks for dinner," He stood up, took his bowl, and cup to the kitchen sink. Everyone noticed that he always thanked them for dinner, so polite of him. But they knew that he had had a rough time when his family lost their ranch. Dave knew the value of a good meal and a roof over his head. He would some day like to settle down, but that would come with time. He liked working for Fletchers.

"Will do" Chet said. They were lucky to have Dave who was dependable and knowledgeable about ranching. After he left, the family thought about the day.

"We've had a busy day. Did Sophia enjoy her visit to the ranch, Chet. She seemed nice," said Fred. Pleased with his nephew, he hoped that this was *the* girl for his nephew.

After the search and finding Betsy dead, his nephew seemed different, more focused. An experience like that would affect anyone. Now, this college girl seemed interested in him.

"Yeah, she really liked the horses. She wants me to go to her college graduation. If I do, I'd like to bring her back here afterwards for a couple of days. She could stay in one of the log cabins, maybe," said Chet. He wanted to see what his dad would say.

"Sure, son...that's fine. It'll be a little while longer before we get guests," replied Clyde. "By the way, I talked to Hans today. He told me he's buyin' another ranch—near the Lodge Pole Dude Ranch. He and Ingrid don't like livin' in town. I guess Anna and the kids are movin' out with them into an old ranch house. He asked me if one or two of you would want to work for him this summer. What do you think? ... Matt? ...Tom? Or both of you? He said he'd pay regular wages."

The two sat thinking for a few minutes. Finally, Chet spoke, "If one of you or both go work for him, it would make it easier on us this summer. I'm a little worried about the money."

"One thing---no matter what, I want to keep Dave on. He's worth every penny we pay him. He'll be goin' up with the herd to the summer camp," said Clyde.

Thinking of working for Hans, Tom said, "I'd like to do ranch work for Hans this summer. What about you, Matt. We could team up and work together. We know the people, so it would be easier than workin' for strangers."

"I need to think about it. If the job with the road construction company doesn't come through, I guess I better do somethin'," said Matt. Disappointment could be detected in his answer. They knew his feelings about ranch work, but what option did he have? They lived in a ranching community with many ranchers needing help.

"What was the temperature of our sick calf?" Clyde asked, looking at his son.

"Oh, it was one hundred or so," he answered.

"What? Listen, son. You need to be accurate. How much over one hundred? Check it again tonight." Clyde told him Matt. He nodded, keeping his mouth shut. The calf had fought him when he tried to use the rectal thermometer. The mother cow didn't like him in the stall with them either. She kept bumping him around with her head. His dad didn't realize that he had tried his best.

The Blue Demon seemed to be calling him right now. He needed to take a drive, maybe up to Skyline and relax away from here. Tomorrow night, he'd be on watch. He got up, put his bowl, cup, and silverware in the kitchen sink. Taking down his keys from the hook in the pantry, he walked to the back porch, put on his sheep-vest and then his jacket, pulled his hat on his head. He stuck his head back into the kitchen and said, "I'll check the calf's temp again. I'm goin' for a ride. See you all later." He left. He wrestled with the calf in the barn again. Then, he went to the utility shed. Everyone heard the Blue Demon start up and leave the ranch.

The men decided to move to the living room and put in a fire before nightfall. Spreading out around the room, Clyde took a seat on the old couch with Fred. Chet sat in the old stuffed chair by the fireplace, waiting for the call from Sophia. Tom swept the ashes aside and started to stack the small twigs underneath the split logs. Fred had brought with him the whiskey bottle and four glasses. He set them on the coffee table in front of the couch. He filled the glasses about one finger of dark amber liquid. Handing each a drink, they raised their glasses in a salute that ended another busy day at the ranch.

The phone rang and Chet jumped up and answered it. Sophia had made it back safely. Being exhausted after the long drive, she made the call short. After hanging up the phone, he said he wanted to read a little before going out to watch the herd. Remembering his washing, Chet put his wet sheets and clothes into the drier. He was tired of the housekeeping stuff. Going upstairs to his bedroom, he picked up his paperback novel, stretched out on the bed, and read.

As Clyde and Fred had another finger of whiskey, they talked about looking forward to branding those calves before driving them up to the summer camp. The cold, chilly night descended on the ranch and the surrounding mountains and valleys. Inside the log ranch house, the fireplace took the chill off and warmed up everyone in it. As bedtime approached, the men left to go to bed. They said 'goodnight.' The fire had burned down to a bed of hot embers.

As Clyde lay in his bed, wide-awake, he listened to the quiet ranch house. He waited until he heard Chet leave to watch the herd. Hearing the horses' hooves disappear into the distant fields, he could stop worrying about the herd. Chet and Dave would build a little fire out near the herd to keep them warm. Once in a while, they would take a ride around the pastures. With their presence there, any bear or grizzly would most likely stay away. They couldn't lose any cattle. Thinking of the herd, Clyde hoped that the little calf would survive her bout of pneumonia.

Finally, he heard the loud sound of Matt's Blue Demon coming back to the ranch. It disturbed him that his middle son still had hard feelings about ranching. He thought that by now he would have settled in like his brothers, but it seemed that he still resisted the ranch work. As Beth argued, Matt should be allowed to follow his dreams. *What were his dreams?* He felt that Matt really didn't know what he wanted. That's why he floundered around. Despite what Beth had argued, he never had kept any of his sons from following their dreams. Yes, he voiced his opinion and displeasure from time to time. But Chet and Tom were committed heart and soul to their ranch. Today, with Chet's girl, he noticed that something serious was brewing there. He hoped his oldest son had found happiness with someone. After finding Betsy's body, he had worried about his son. But he seemed to have put aside that horrible event and had moved on.

Now, for himself, he hoped that he would get over this loneliness that plagued him at night. His heart still ached at the thought of Beth taking her own life. He knew he would never understand how she could do it, especially with so much to live for. Closing his tired eyes, he turned on his side, reached out and touched the empty pillow beside him. He yearned for the night that he didn't think of her. *Time...Time...Time to forget.* He had to keep his focus on the ranch—their Battle Axe Ranch. At last, he breathed deeply and fell into the sleepy world.

Chapter 21

Getting Ready

A couple of weeks later, the May night was edged out as
the early dawn sky turned bright orange as the sunlight
peaked through the heavy white clouds. The low hanging
clouds were filled with moisture from another evening of a
spring rainstorm. The wet ground had soaked up the rain
turning it to a dark muddy color. The wet fresh smell of
long grass, sagebrush, and pine filled the morning air. All of
the old cottonwoods, the aspens, the willows, and the lilac
bushes were green with leaves popping out every day. At
the Battle Axe Ranch, the smoke from the ranch house and
bunk house filled the air with the smell of burning pine.

The day before the young Fletchers with Dave divided
the cows from the calves. The herd resisted the separation
with their usually dodging, dashing, and sprinting. A good
cutting horse needed to be quick and persistent to battle
these stubborn calves. Riding his stallion Brute, Tom helped
cut out the calves along with Chet on Rusty, Matt on
Diablo, and Dave on Bullet. Working together, the work
was intense in getting the calves into a separate pasture and
settled. The calves wanted to stay with their mothers.

In the predawn hours before the sun came up, Clyde and
Dave had risen and headed out to the herd with the hay
wagon. With his arthritis acting up, Fred slept in that
mornin, so just the two went out to the pasture. He would be
late, but he'd be there later. Dave saddled his brown stallion
Bullet to ride above the pastures into the forest. Tracks of a
grizzly were still observed a couple of miles above the
ranch. No steers or calves were missing, but everyone had
been on alert. After feeding the herd, Clyde drove the hay
wagon over to the pasture where Twister was humping a
heifer. He brought a bucket of special grain out to them as
they munched the tasty treat.

This morning the Fletchers were busy thinking of the
day ahead, branding the forty calves. The little calf who had
pneumonia had survived and now stood with the other

calves waiting to be branded. During those first days in the barn, Matt figured out how to take her temperature. He'd been doing it all wrong. He finally took charge and used his body to keep the calf from running from him. Being sensitive, he had been too gentle and not forceful enough to get the little calf's temperature that first day. But he managed to satisfy his dad with more accurate readings.

Matt had finished painting the barn. Every day for two weeks, he (sometimes Tom helped) had painted until he couldn't stand the color of red anymore. Fred had purchased a pint of turpentine so that he could clean off the paint from the brush and from his skin, but his fingernails were outlined with a thin red line along the cuticles. It would be a while before that paint would fade. The painted red barn looked great. His dad told him that he'd done a good job of finishing it.

As the kitchen filled with the smells of breakfast, their dad and uncle with Bandit came in from feeding the herd. Bandit took his place under the table with Blue until they could get fed. Stretching out, Bandit sighed. Getting older, he tired quickly from running around the herd. Returning from his ride in the timber above the ranch, Dave came in a few minutes after Clyde and Fred had washed up in the big sink on the back porch. He came into the kitchen after washing up.

Today, the whole family would be involved in branding the calves. Even the former owner of the ranch Hans Severson and his family were planning to be at the ranch. Hans was bringing his grandson Andy to help. Anna along with his wife Ingrid had made plans to fix the meals for the whole gang. Knowing how important the first branding was, the Seversons wanted to help wherever they were needed. After the death of Beth, Hans had kept in close contact with Clyde, hoping that that they would continue with the ranch. He worried since he knew how devastating a death could be. But he had noticed that all the Fletchers had been able to continue with their lives on the ranch.

For themselves, the Seversons had another big adjustment to make. Even though they had moved into town after selling their ranch to the Fletchers, Hans had purchased a section of land (160 acres) from the Lodge Pole Dude Ranch. For two weeks, they had been moving and getting settled into their new home—their own ranch again. Surprisingly, the move had been easier than he and his wife had expected. Ingrid figured that it was because they had gotten rid of the old stuff from their move into town. Anna and the grandkids were excited about moving out to their new ranch and they settled in quickly.

The old house had been built out of planks cut from a sawmill. They were two-inch-thick cross layered which gave a four- inch-thick wall. Inside the old house, the walls had horizontal planks. The roof consisted of wooden shakes. Several outbuildings included a small barn, a tack shed, and another old log cabin used as a bunk house (the original home). There were a couple of corrals and a windmill that pulled water up from a deep well. With an older place, there would be some repairs needed. Hans had made some plans that he hoped that they could get completed before winter.

With four bedrooms, the Seversons had plenty of rooms for the children, Anna, and the grandparents. All were happy to be together again, in fact Anna was able to get her own bed back with her dressers. The two girls Heidi and Bridget still were together as Andy and the baby Cade were separate in their bedrooms. The bedrooms were small, but they were happy to be out of town and on a ranch again. The quiet, solitude of a ranch descended on them at night. The children again rode the school bus into town. The mare Rhapsody and the two fillies Jewels and Moonbeam were happy to have an open pasture to run.

As promised, Hans hired Chuck Nubben to help run the ranch, but he still needed more help this summer. Charles (as he now wanted to be called) had already moved into the bunk house. Hans wondered if he was sweet on Anna. While they lived in town, Ingrid had told him that Anna and Charles had had lunch together several times. He'd have to watch to see if anything came of their being together on the ranch.

Needing more help, Hans had asked if one or two of the Fletcher boys wanted to work for him. He had been waiting to hear what they had decided, for he had a long list of repairs for his new ranch—the Norsemen Ranch. He named it after their Norwegian ancestors whom they had admired more than anything. Their new ranch still had paperwork to be completed at the bank. Hans had to register a new brand for his ranch. But today, the Seversons were focused on helping the Fletchers with their first branding of their new calves at their ranch.

Branding the new calves every year represented a legacy to all the ranchers, along with their reputations. After purchasing their ranch, Clyde had sent in the paperwork to change the registration of their brand from the name of 'Severson' to their name, 'Fletcher.' Experience counted, for the hot branding irons needed to leave a crisp, clear image of the ranch's signature. For them, that was a Viking axe image, using two branding irons. One iron was a straight line and the other had two opposing triangles, the tops pointing at each other. The image appeared as an axe, like a tomahawk. Coordinating the roping, the wrestling, the branding, and the castrating of the young calves would be important in completing the hard task of work.

The young, feisty group of calves had been driven into a separate pasture for branding. Neither the mother cows nor their calves were happy with that separation and kept calling to each other, filling the air with their bellowing. The young calves had to be watched for they kept wanting to break out of the pasture. Luckily, many of the weak places in the fence line had been repaired since the Fletchers moved here. Over the last month, Clyde, his brother, and his son Chet had worked much of the fence lines near the main ranch, replacing the old rotted out fence posts with new ones. Even with those repairs, those young calves had a knack for finding a way out of the barbed wire fence.

After the past month of April, the big log ranch house started to feel like a home to the Fletchers. The barn had been painted. A plowed garden plot had been made ready for planting in another two weeks. Chet had already planted two rows of the seed potatoes that he had purchased. Some hints of an everyday life took hold.

Today like every morning, they were fixing their own breakfast. As each woke, they fell into a routine. With the first up, Chet had brewed a pot of coffee. Then, he had cooked up some sausages in the big black skillet. Tom had milked their cow Sunny in the barn. By the time he had finished with the milking, Matt had come downstairs. He had taken out the eggs to fry up on the grill. Tom had set to work on making some toast with their eggs and sausages.

"Mornin' boys. Those calves and mommas are sure makin' a noise. They don't like bein' separated," said Clyde. They said "mornin'." Each poured his own cup of coffee. Chet grabbed the platter of fried sausages and put it on the long kitchen table as Tom set out the plates and the silverware. The men pulled out their chairs and sat down as Matt brought over the plate of fried eggs. Silence fell on the group as they passed around their breakfast. They were hungry as they devoured the food.

As the six men ate and drank their coffee, they talked about the work ahead of them. Today, they talked about getting set up to brand, the different tasks, and the equipment needed.

"The Seversons will be here soon. Hans wants Andy to have a part in this brandin'. Guess he helped last year. I don't know what he can do. We've got to be careful he doesn't get hurt. The rest of the family is comin'. Ingrid and Anna will be fixin' our meals," said Clyde sipping his second cup of coffee. He felt glad that they were coming to help.

Thinking of Anna, Chet wondered how she was doing. He had never called her after she had moved into town. He had heard that she had been dating the doctor. He recalled that when they first moved to the ranch, he had been struck by her beauty—this blonde, blue eyed beauty. He quickly became attracted to her. As a widow though, she had still been grieving. Their relationship never blossomed past passionate hugs and kisses. Plus, he never wanted a ready-made family; she came with four children—Andy, eight years old, Heidi, six, Bridget, four, and baby Cade, Jr., eight months old. He'd also heard in town that Anna had been dating the wrangler Chuck Nubben. At least, she was dating and getting around as he had suggested. He hoped that maybe Anna would find someone to love her along with her four children.

But now for him, Sophia's number in his wallet meant more to him than anything in his life. After her visit a couple of weeks ago, they continued calling each other. She had finished her college exams just the other day. Leaving tomorrow, he had planned on driving down and seeing her college graduation. She wanted him to meet her parents. Then, they planned that she would come back with him and stay here at the ranch for a couple of days. When she came to stay at the ranch, he wanted to take her riding up to that lily pond near that big meadow in the forest above their ranch. He found it hard to stop thinking about her while he thought of seeing her, kissing her, and getting her into his arms. But today, he had to keep his focus on those calves that needed to be castrated—that would be his job. His belt buckle carried his sharpened knife in its sheath this morning. The ranch work came first.

Wanting to know their plans for branding, Dave asked, "So, where do you want me this mornin'?"

Clyde sat for a moment thinking. With this new hand, he wanted to utilize his abilities as a wrangler. "I figure you can lasso the calves while Tom here can rope their hind legs. I'll brand them. Chet here castrates the males and can cut off their little horns. Hans will be around to help. Matt, you can help wherever someone needs to switch. We can work together, dividin' up the lassoin', holdin', and the cuttin'. I figure we'll do about half the calves before we break for lunch. We'll see how it all goes," answered Clyde. He eagerly wanted to get started.

Not forgetting something important, he continued, "Matt, we bought a sack of dewormin' to mix with the horses' grain. Why don't you take care of mixin' them together first? Check the directions on the sack for the correct amount. Then, mix some up for the young calves. Wasn't there a feeding trough in one those pastures, Fred?"

Then, Tom reminded his dad that their milk cow Sunny needed some of that deworming mixture. Matt felt like he always got the unwanted jobs, but at least, he'd be away from the rest of them for a while. He didn't like the brutality of the branding, the castrating, and the dehorning the young calves. When he joined them, he'd lasso the calves for he didn't mind that part of the branding.

"Yeah, it sets in the field next to the one the calves are in now. We could move the freshly branded calves into that field and leave them to feed on the grain mixture there. Don't forget to get a special bucket for the testicles and I'll fry them up, tonight," answered Fred. The traditional Rocky Mountain oyster fry was his specialty. Before he left the kitchen, he'd grab one of the big cast iron skillets, some lard, and a small sack of flour and ingredients for seasoning. He would use the campfire for cooking them outdoors at the end of their branding.

"Good deal. We left Jack hitched to the wagon this morning, so load some wood for the fire and a few bales of hay for the horses. I'll get the branding irons. Oh, get those cuttin' sheers in the tack shed for the little horns. Get the little straight iron to burn the base."

As Clyde and the rest of men continued conversing about the branding, a knock came at the front door. Chet went down the hall through the living room to the front door. Both dogs Bandit and Blue followed him. He opened it and smiled. Silver headed Hans Severson and his eight-year-old grandson blonde-haired Andy stood on the porch.

"Mornin.' Come in. Did Anna come?" he asked, looking around them to see if she was behind them coming up the stairs. As soon as Andy saw the two dogs, he bent down and gave each a hug. The dogs were glad to see Andy, waging their tails and sniffing him.

"Mornin' Chet. Oh, she drove around back with the food. Ingrid and she cooked all day yesterday," answered Hans. Together, they walked to the kitchen as Anna knocked at the back door. Matt jumped up and answered the back-porch door.

"Hi, Matt. Help me with a few things from the car, would you?" she asked as he stood looking down into her bright blue eyes. She didn't come in but turned around and went back to the station wagon. Matt gladly followed her out, helping her bring two big bowls into the kitchen. Going over to the fridge, she bent down and moved a few items around so the big bowls would fit in there.

As she stepped into the kitchen, there wasn't one Fletcher man who didn't gasp silently with seeing this beautiful, blonde haired, blue-eyed woman walk into the kitchen. For them, this was the second woman in their kitchen since the funeral—first one was the lovely Sophia, now Anna. She turned to look at everyone as her long blonde braid down her back swung around with her slim body. As she turned, Chet smelled a clean fresh scent coming from her. Under her jacket, she had on a red-plaid shirt tucked in her tight blue jeans with her cowboy boots. She looked like she was ready to work.

"What are you doin' in here? I thought you'd be out in the pasture by now," she said, looking at the men staring at her and admiring this attractive woman.

Clearly his throat, Fred spoke up, "We were just gettin' ready to head out. Wanted to wait for you guys to show up." Quickly to cover their amazement, the men nodded, picking up their plates, the silverware, cups, and put them in the kitchen sink.

Before leaving the kitchen, Clyde turned to her and said, "Anna, would you drive the wagon out around noon with our lunch. And, keep the dogs inside. I don't want 'em around the calves today." The dogs would stir up the calves and he wanted them calm. He wasn't one to mince with words.

"Sure. Will do," she answered. That's Clyde--giving orders. She went over to the dogs, bent down, and gave each a hug. Again, the dogs were happy for the attention, wagging their tails.

Matt picked up the rest of the breakfast plates from the long table. Today was his turn to wash the dishes. He would gladly stay here in the kitchen with Anna. He liked her caring attitude.

As she looked up and smiled at Chet, he just nodded his head at her and left the kitchen. She sought his eyes, but he lowered them. He pushed down his initial emotions that had stirred up seeing her. His heart had been taken by Sophia. Today, the ranch work called to him. Tomorrow he would see Sophia. Shaking off his thoughts of both women, he walked out the door and headed for the stable and his red sorrel Rusty.

Looking over at Matt instead, she said, "I have a few more sacks of groceries and two large skillets in the back of the car. Would you get them for me?"

"Of course." Smiling at her, he left the kitchen.

Chapter 22

Returning

Taking off her jacket and slipping it on the back of a chair, Anna looked around at the big kitchen that she had missed so much. So many years of memories of cooking and eating here. As they had driven into the ranch this morning, she had glanced at the newly painted red barn, the stable, the fields, the timber, the rugged mountains surrounding the big log ranch house. She missed this. But as she looked around the kitchen, she noticed that the dirty floor needed to be cleaned. Yes, the counters and table were clean, but the stove top looked greasy and had old baked on food around the burners. *Oh, my. Without a woman, this house probably needs a good cleaning.* She needed to talk to Fred about getting a housekeeper at the ranch.

Going into the pantry, she found Beth's blue apron. Her memory of her death was a horrible one. She had haunting images of her tragic suicide. Obvious, there must have been something wrong that had made Beth do that. There were no answers for her. Suicide frightened her. She couldn't think of a time in her life when she would want to kill herself. Yes, her own husband's death nearly destroyed her. But she still had her children that she lived for every day.

The town's people still didn't know about the suicide; they just knew that she had died. Such a secret would never be known. Those who knew were only a few and they had closed their lips against speaking of her suicide. They spoke only of her death. But a few people in town had turned against the Fletchers. The tide had turned a little as more people in town became more acquainted with the family.

When Ronnie had been killed in the car, Anna had heard a few comments made when she bought groceries at the Mercantile. Some women were upset that none of Fletchers had come to Ronnie McClure's funeral. Of course, they knew they were out of town since the wife's body had been sent to Scottsville. The people had been alarmed that the family hadn't buried her here. Why bury her so far from her family? Was their cemetery not good enough for the Fletchers?

Then, they turned their gossip to the young Matt Fletcher. They faulted him for bringing that red sports car into their town. Who names a car after the devil—the Red Devil? If the car hadn't been here, Ronnie would never had driven it and wrecked it on that dangerous curve up near Grady's ranch. He would still be alive. But Bobby had been talking about how the Fletchers were decent men who had had a tragic death of their own.

The gossip didn't end there. What about Bert and Kay Merther's daughter? By now, everyone knew that she was pregnant. But her dad and mom still said that their daughter Eveline had gone down to Colorado to be with their sick aunt. The gossip on that story still had legs on it. Words had been whispered about Bert finding the kid who had gotten his daughter pregnant and had punched and knocked him out. They knew that the kid was not from around here; a few knew that he had come from Hadley—a basketball player. She had been a cheerleader, so that made sense.

Another recent event that had the town stirred up more than anything was the brutal death of Betsy Crockett—a murder in their own backyard. Still no word from the sheriff's office if they had found out who had done it. And word got around that Chet Fletcher had found her body with the search party up at the trailhead above their ranch. Again, her funeral was held in Ohio where her parents lived, not here in Riverside where she had gone to school and had returned to live and work.

Thus, events like this hadn't happened in their town for years—not until the Fletchers showed up. Three were dead with a young girl pregnant. What an outrage in their minds. *This new rancher and family had brought all this bad luck to their little mountain town.*

Their irrational minds didn't care for the truth, just the spectacle of the events. Typically, rumors were ridiculous and unfounded. But again, a few people were finding out that the Fletchers were just caught up in the unexplained consequences. In the gossip, only a sliver of truth remained.

The town started to believe that Fate had handed Fletchers a bad hand of cards since they had moved to their Battle Axe Ranch.

More personal and pressing issues took over Anna's mind today. As she recalled the last month, her days had been a whirlwind. Weeks ago, Hans told her that he was looking for a small ranch to buy. Both he and Ingrid didn't like living in town. Particularly, he wanted the horses to have a pasture, not just a corral. And he again wanted to raise some cattle. *Guess you can't take the 'cow' out of a cowboy.* He said Anna could move out of town with them. Sleeping on her uncomfortable rollaway, her little rental house made her feel sore and lonely.

Her heart soared when they moved out of that crowded small town with its rumors and gossip. In town at night, barrels of stinking garbage burned. The children jumped at the chance to move out of town. They were resilient as children are, but she could tell they wanted to live at the ranch with their grandparents. Andy and Heidi had one month of school left. Bridget and the baby kept her busy during the daytime.

Thinking of her love-life, in the last month, she had been out with Denny Carter. His family owned the Double D Ranch. She asked him why he didn't stay and help his dad with the ranch. He told her that he wanted to see the world, so he joined the Army. The Korean War came along, and he became a paramedic with a MASH unit, flying with a helicopter pilot. After getting wounded, he was discharged. With the GI bill, he went to medical school, did his internship, finished as a doctor.

"Wow, I didn't realize you were in the war and were wounded," said Anna, surprised that she had never asked about his background in all the years that she knew him. But as a doctor, she wouldn't have asked.

"Yeah. In fact, my military buddy Jack East has that helicopter business south of town, past the lumber mill," Denny said. He felt glad that Anna was interested enough to ask about his past. Many people in Riverside didn't know much about him. His medical practice here in Riverside, in

Winston, and on the reservation had kept him busy. *As he knew, a doctor's work never ended.*

As she listened to him, she had begun to feel an attraction to him. Denny and she had kissed several times. She knew that he had strong feelings for her. Being a gentle and kind man, the doctor was easy to be with. Over the few weeks, they had gone on short, afternoon horse rides. Both of their horses were kept at the same corrals in town.

Then, one day he had called and said he didn't have any patients that afternoon. He suggested they go for another ride. They had met at the corrals down by the river, had saddled their horses, and had ridden out of town up towards the Skyline Campgrounds. The day was cold, but she loved getting out and a chance to exercise her brown mare Rhapsody. Denny had ridden his white stallion Ghost who pranced around like a dog in heat. The two had laughed because it was true with her mare and his stallion. She had told him to keep his stallion separated from her mare. He had understood so he told her he'd put Ghost in a different corral since there were several corrals. But Denny thought it was too late. Her mare was probably already impregnated. Time would tell.

As they rode up to the long flat mesa Skyline overlooking the town and the valleys, she was struck by the vastness of the dark forested mountains surrounding their little town. Stopping at the edge of the mesa, the expansive landscape took her breath away. She had never seen this view of the tall peaks, the small town nestled down in the valley from up here. Looking up the valley, she could see the highway running through the fenced pastures of the ranches. She had smelled the fresh breeze as it caressed her face. *What a splendid view from up here.* That view had made the ride up here worth it.

Then, Denny had turned Ghost around and had headed towards a stand of aspens with their stark white trunks. He had dismounted near one of the camp sites, leading his horse over to one of the aspen trees. Loosely tying the reins, he let Ghost graze on some of the dry grass. She had followed, tying Rhapsody to another aspen tree near Ghost.

He had pulled out a brown grocery sack and a bottle of wine from his saddlebags. Smiling at her, he had motioned for her to sit at the old wooden picnic table.

Surprised, she said, "What is this?" He had a quiet, subtle nature about him.

He had smiled again at her, and said, "A little surprise. I brought us an afternoon snack." As he spoke, he pulled out a little blue 'n white-checkered tablecloth and spread it on top of the picnic table. He next pulled out some wrapped cheese, a bag of crackers, and two apples. As he twisted the corkscrew into the cork, he had asked how she and the children were doing this week. Turning the screw into the cork, he pulled the cork out of the top of the bottle—pop.

"The children are fine. Andy and Heidi will be out of school soon. Bridget spends a lot of time at Grandma's. And Cade is fussy with his teeth, but he's talking …just single words," she answered. He always asked about them. If she married him, the girls and the baby would probably accept him easily. Her oldest son Andy was her only worry since he had been so close to his dad. But there would be a big compromise for her to consider. As she had thought of marrying him, she knew that she would have to move to Winston away from these mountains and valleys. She just didn't know if she could leave her in-laws either. For eight years, she had lived with Hans and Ingrid. They were very close to her, and she couldn't imagine how the children would feel without them around.

Pulling out two tin cups from the sack, he had apologized for not bringing wine glasses. He had poured a little wine into both cups. Taking the apples, he had cut them into fourths with a pocketknife that he had pulled out from his jean pocket. The wrapped cheese had been sliced, so taking a few crackers with the apple pieces, Anna had put them on a napkin he gave her. She tasted the crisp, juicy apple, the soft cheddar cheese, and the dry cracker. They had talked, ate, and sipped the wine. This romantic side of Denny had been a new revelation to her. She had never been courted like this before. He had told her about his long days taking care of people, of the monthly visits to the reservation, and his responsibilities at the hospital. Being a doctor had to be rewarding. She couldn't imagine what his long days were like—some nights, too. *Where would she fit into this life of his medical world?*

The afternoon had grown late as time seemed to fly. Looking at his watch, he had said, "We should ride back to town. It's getting late." Anna agreed. Gathering everything up and putting them into the brown sack, Denny said he really enjoyed the time with her.

Pushing the cork back into the bottle, he said, "I look forward to seeing you every week." He wished he could see her more since he thought of her often.

Standing, he had taken her hand into his as they walked towards the two horses tied up to the white aspens. Turning towards Ghost, he had opened the saddlebag and slipped in the bottle of wine and the brown sack. They stood between the horses. The two were munching the grass and moving around. With their rumps, the horses had pushed them together. They both had laughed as he pulled her into his arms. Looking down into her blue eyes, he had leaned down for a kiss. He had brushed his lips gently over hers. Closing his eyes, Denny's heart pounded in his chest as he kissed Anna. She kissed him back, putting her arms up and around his neck. She felt a little shiver as he had deepened his kiss. Her thoughts were whirling in her head. She had many emotions and doubts.

Holding her in her arms, he had walked her back gently up against an aspen tree. With her back against the trunk, he had kissed her again. Stepping towards her, he had pressed his strong body against her slender one as she looked up into his brown eyes and his greying temples. She had seen the desire in his eyes as she closed her eyes and relaxed into his arms. She had goosebumps all over her body. They had been going out for over a month now. With his professional manner, he had respected her and hadn't gone beyond kissing.

But this afternoon, it was obvious that he wanted more. Under her jacket, his hands moved over her full breasts to her waist to the small of her back. He breathed hard as his

311

desire stirred. Kissing her again on her lips, he moved to kiss her on her soft, sensitive neck. He whispered soothing words as he kept kissing her. She gasped for air, as her hands moved to his chest. *No, no, not yet. Oh, Caden.* He felt her warm hands on his chest pushing him away. Denny took one step back from her, but still holding her at arm's length. He had been taking this affair as slow as he could. He had controlled his emotions around her for a long time. *She won't let me love her yet.*

Finally, he asked, "How long, Anna?" He tried to look into her blue eyes, but she had closed them.

"I don't know... I'm sorry," she whispered quietly, looking down, avoiding his questioning eyes.

"I love you, Anna. You're in my thoughts when I wake and when I go to bed. I dream about us. We could build a life together with the children. Why can't you?" he had asked her pleading.

"Oh, Denny. This is too much, too soon for me," she answered.

"Let me guide you. Trust me. Relax and let me love you," he explained. He had been losing too much sleep over her. He had to convince her, somehow.

"Maybe....maybe. But I don't know," she quietly spoke. *He would be easy to love, but did she love him? She just wasn't sure.*

"We aren't strangers, Anna. We've known each other for years. Let's find out if we feel the same for each other. You're making this far too hard," he said. He knew he couldn't wait much longer. He wanted to love her, to make her his wife, to raise her children, and to have a lifetime with her. But she had pushed him away and had rejected him. She didn't realize that her sorrow for her dead husband was driving him away. Denny felt it rise out of her like a dark shadow, killing any desire he had for her. Right now, he needed to get away from her.

Shaking his head and frustrated, Denny had turned to his white stallion, untied the reins, and walked Ghost away from her. Pulling her jacket around herself, Anna ducked under her horse's long neck to the other side. She had felt bad about pushing him away. As she stroked Rhapsody, she put her head against the mare's warm neck. She breathed deeply, smelling the horse's comforting presence. Her emotions were raging inside her. She had many doubts about her life that she couldn't commit to anything.

She had realized that she might lose Denny if she didn't respond to him and let him in. That afternoon he had surprised her, and she had been overwhelmed with her emotions. But as Denny had held and kissed her, the memory of Caden had come rushing over her. Caden was still in her heart, even though it had been over a year now since his death. *I must get over losing him.*

Taking the reins in her hand, she had mounted her mare, turned around, and rode over to Denny who had mounted his stallion and waited. He sat tall, and handsome on his beautiful white stallion, making a striking figure of a man. As she rode up to him to speak, he had ignored her, had turned his horse away from her, and had headed out of the aspen grove. He couldn't look at her with his hurting heart pounding.

"Denny, wait," she had called out to him. "Can I see you again next week?" She had ridden towards him.

He drew up the reins on his white stallion and stopped. Turning in his saddle, he had frowned at her for a moment. *She still wanted to see me.* He had nodded—he'd see her next week. She had given him a little hope. Turning back in his saddle and clicking his tongue, he told Ghost, "Let's go." Her rejection had cooled his desire. He had been torn apart inside that day. Trying to get near her and showing her his affection, she had rejected him. He would break it if off soon if she didn't let him in to love her.

Oblivious to his feelings, she had followed him down the dirt road for a while, and then she pressed her heels into Rhapsody to catch up with him. Still riding fast, she had come up beside him and shouted, "I'll race you." Flashing a smile with her white teeth, she had ridden away from him. She again had pressed her heels into her mare. She had felt the breeze against her face as they raced down the road. Her long braid had bounced up and down on her back as she stood up in the stirrups and leaned forward, encouraging her mare to gallop faster. The sound of the white stallion's big hooves pounding the ground behind her had encouraged her to shout to Rhapsody, "Run, girl. Come on, run…run."

The white stallion easily had galloped past her while Denny had smiled and shouted, "I've won. You're like a little fox, Anna." Pulling them to a gradual trot and to a stop, the two horses had stomped and pranced around, huffing, puffing, and snorting from the race. Glancing at her with his serious brown eyes, he said, "This is not a game."

Laughing, she had loved the excitement of the chase. *Was she a temptress? Was she playing with his feelings?* She thought of Chet and their night in the stable. She had cut him off too when he tried to love her. *Maybe I am a temptress.* But no, she wanted a meaningful relationship. She would need to think about the possibilities of marrying Denny. His intensions were clear that day.

But her next marriage had to be different than her first with Caden. Years ago, having too much to drink after their graduation, Caden and she had gotten carried away and had a one-night stand. Her marriage to Caden had been forced upon them when she became pregnant. The two had been fond of each other, but they weren't in love. Married for eight years, Anna had done the best she could to make a life for them. Her four children had given her and Caden a reason to stay together. But if she were to marry again, it had to be for love.

Since that romantic afternoon up at Skyline, Denny had taken her out to dinner each week. Their affair had been the talk of the town. Thoughts of their times together had filled her days recently. He still pressed his desires for her, but he had held back waiting for her to decide.

****

Today, standing in the kitchen of the Battle Axe Ranch deep into thoughts, she hadn't noticed that Matt had made two trips with all the food in from the station wagon. He stood looking at her, just staring. Her natural beauty hit him in the chest. She probably didn't realize how attractive she looked. He quickly looked down as he felt his face flush. He needed to get her off his mind. This would not be good for him to feel this way. She was five years older than him.

As he cleared his throat to get her attention, she turned to look up at him. He stood tall like Chet and his familiar handsome face struck her. The two brothers looked very similar, but Matt had a different personality. He was a quiet, sensitive man, more naïve and playful.

"I'll finish these dishes if you want to go join the men," she said, smiling at him. He needed to keep his mind off her mouth and her lips. Any man would notice her beauty, and he admired her.

"Oh, no. It's my turn. Besides, I wanted to ask about Moonbeam. How's she doin'?" he asked about the filly, trying to focus on another subject.

"I don't know. The kids were concerned the other day that she was not her usual frisky self. It's probably nothing," she answered. Washing and rinsing the dishes, she set them on the rack for Matt.

"Why? Has the vet seen her?" he asked. Concerned about the little white filly, he didn't want anything to happen to her. As an orphan, she could still not survive. Moonbeam would be only a month old now. Most ranchers knew the possibilities of their young foals and calves dying. He picked up a towel and started drying the dishes.

"I don't know. Talk to Hans about her. He can tell you more than I can," said Anna.

As he dried the dishes, Fred and Andy came into the kitchen from the back porch. Andy felt excited about being here on the ranch again. He noticed that his mom loved coming to the ranch.

Fred looked at Matt, and said, "I came to get you. Andy and I are goin' to help you with mixin' up the grain. We came in to get a measurin' cup from the kitchen. I have the wagon outside all loaded. Why don't you and Andy head out?"

Andy looked up at Matt, "You do dishes?" He thought he looked silly drying the dishes. As he grew older and took

315

on more responsibilities, his mom had been at him to help sister Heidi with the dishes.

Several years ago when he was six, Andy recalled that his dad and mom had an argument. His parents thought he had left the ranch house that morning, but he stood on the back porch. He heard his dad point out that his mom needed to stay in the kitchen where she belonged. She told him that she wanted to help with the ranch. He argued that ranch work was no place for a woman and that it was too dangerous. She should take care of the kids, cook the meals, and do the dishes. Sobbing, his mom became so upset that she ran upstairs and slammed the door to their bedroom. Andy creeped quietly out of the back-porch door.

Recalling that argument, he strongly felt that doing the dishes with Heidi was girl's work; he didn't want to do that kind of work. He took care of the horses and the cattle— a man's work, just like his dad had done.

"Hey, a guy sometimes has to step in where he's needed," replied Matt, smiling, as he snapped the towel at Andy in a playful manner. The young boy laughed as the towel hit him in the chest. Then, the two played at snapping and dodging for a few minutes, both chuckling. Anna laughed at the sight of the two, but said, "Enough, you two." They were dashing around the big kitchen.

Andy called out, "Okay…okay. I give. Hey, will you play your guitar for us today?"

Caught off guard by his request, Matt thought for a minute. He looked at Anna to be rescued. Raising her eyebrows, tilting her head, and smiling, she said, "Sure, he will…won't you, Matt." She winked at him. "By the way, Grandma and the kids are coming out here to the ranch later this afternoon. After dinner, maybe, we can all sit around the fireplace in the living room and sing while Matt plays. How does that sound?"

"Great. Let's go, Matt. I want to help you." He nodded at him as Andy headed out of the kitchen to the back-porch door. Matt looked around in the cupboards for a big measuring cup. Finding one, he followed Andy out. Anna called out to him, "Thanks, Matt." He turned and looked at her with a big grin. He enjoyed being around Anna and the kids again. Since being back from mom's funeral, the big ranch house seemed empty. This morning, the three of them had brightened and warmed up the place as he had recalled the days before the Seversons had moved into town.

As Anna turned back to the sink to let the water out of the sink, Fred quietly sat down at the long kitchen table. He wanted to talk to her about an important matter. She thought he had left, but turning she saw that he was sitting in one of the table chairs. He had a serious look on his face.

With a frown on her face, she came over to the long table, and said, "What is it, Fred?"

"Sit. We need to help Clyde with somethin'."

Sitting down, she looked into his worried, dark brown eyes, and said, "What?" This sounded serious.

"It's about Beth. Well, not exactly her, but her clothes and belongings. They are still in the bedroom. While Clyde's busy brandin', would you mind doin' me a favor?"

"Of course. What do you want me to do?" she said as her hands grasped his rough, calloused hands. He explained that the dresser and the closet with her clothes needed to be boxed up. He'd come back before lunch and store them in the attic. Clyde didn't need to know about it; they'd get it done, quietly.

Anna understood and asked, "How is he doin'? And the guys?"

"Oh, Anna, as you know only too well, it's been hard. We are really doin' okay. My brother always looks tired, though. He's havin' trouble sleepin'. Beth's funeral did not go well." He hesitated to tell her. But he ended up going on and told her about the fiasco that went on with the Vanovers. Fred went on to describe Beth's wake and funeral—the pine box coffin and the dropping of it in the grave. He told her about the nasty words that were said. He probably told her too much, but he needed to get this off his chest to someone. After he had finished, she just sat there, amazed at what he had told her. She blinked and shook her head in disbelief.

317

"My, God. How did you manage?" she asked. *How could such things happen at a funeral?* She felt sad that the Fletchers had such a horrible time during their time of grief.

"We got through it 'n left. There was nothin' we could do after we got there. Everythin' had been arranged. I wished we had never agreed to have her funeral over there. It was hard on the boys. Chet and Matt even got into a fight. Of course, Tom didn't know how she died. So, that left him in the dark. When the boys told him, it shocked him. But Anna, I need your help, today. I can't ask the boys...and Clyde can't do it," explained Fred. Then, he quietly said, "I can't do it either." He bowed his head, holding back his grief that threatened to break him. His fierce love for his nephews and brother made it especially difficult for him to deal with this. He gripped Anna's hands tightly as he took a breath.

"Of course. It'll take no time at all for me to pack her things," she said. He nodded, getting up he walked out of the kitchen. After a few minutes, he came back with three empty boxes. Setting the boxes down, he walked over to Anna, took her into his big, strong arms, and gave her a warm hug. She felt warm and natural in his arms. She put her arms around his waist, and she held him for a few minutes.

Anna and Fred had become close on the night that Hans had burned the grizzly rug up on the mountain. The grizzly that had mauled her husband had been shot by Wyatt Gordon who had the taxidermy make it into a rug. Hans had rolled boulders and rocks into a circle around the ground that his son had lain mauled and bleeding. His son's blood had poured from his body and soaked the earth. Hans decided to set up a ritual around this sacred place. He then built a huge pile of old dried logs and twigs in the center of this circle. When everyone slept at the ranch house, Hans had ridden out one moonlit night up to the sacred spot. He had lit off a roaring fire with the grizzly's hide on top. As in the old Viking tradition, the thundering fire had honored his dead son. As the smoke rose from the fire, his son's spirit rose up to meet the gods. The old silver-haired father had called on the one-eyed Odin, the Scandinavian god of wisdom and death, to carry his son's spirit to Valhalla—an old belief for those ancient warriors who had died fighting courageously. That night on the mountain had been an emotional one. Riding up to the mountain on his horse to see the fire, Fred had comforted Anna that night. A tear slid down her cheek as she recalled that emotional night on the mountain.

As Fred and Anna separated, he kissed her forehead and whispered, "Thanks, Anna. If you need another box or two, they're up in the attic. I'll drive the wagon back here for you." He moved away, thinking he wished he were younger. He would marry her and take care of her and the children in a second, but it wasn't to be. There would be someone else who'd step in and love her like she deserved. Her next question really threw him.

"Fred, have you and Clyde thought about gettin' a housekeeper? This kitchen floor is filthy. And I bet the rest of the house needs a good cleaning," she said, hoping he'd understand her concern.

"Oh, I don't know. We've been focused on the herd and the ranch. We've managed to get our meals on the table and work. That's it," he answered, as he looked down and around at the dirty floor. He knew that the bathrooms were a mess and he could only guess what the boys' bedroom upstairs looked like. The place did look dirty.

"I think I know someone who could cook and clean. Since I've been reading the billboards in town, I noticed an ad for work by someone everyone knows in town. It's Violet Olsson. She's an older lady. For years, she has worked as cook and housekeeper at the Circle G Ranch. But since John and Janet Grady were married, they moved out at their uncle's ranch and Janet took over that position. Violet has been looking for a position. What do you think?" said Anna.

"I don't know, Anna. I don't think Clyde would hire someone to do the house. Besides, I don't think we could pay her," he admitted.

She looked at him puzzled, and said, "Violet's ad says she'd work for room and board and a small allowance. I think she'd be perfect. You could call and arrange for an interview, first. Don't tell Clyde until you've talked to her," she said. By the look of this kitchen, she knew they needed help.

"Let me think about it. Don't talk to anyone," said Fred. Maybe, he could just consider the possibility and talk with the woman, like she said. She nodded.

"Don't wait too long. Some rancher will hire her; she comes cheap. I'll call tomorrow and give you her number. In the meantime, I'm cleaning this kitchen floor," she said, shaking her head in disgust.

Nodding, he left the kitchen to join Matt and Andy outside, waiting at the wagon to mix the grain. As she watched him leave, she wondered why he never married. He was such a kind, caring man. Something about these Fletcher men made her flush. She shook her head and walked into the pantry to find a broom, a bucket, and a mop. At least, she would clean the dirty kitchen floor. Then, she would prepare their lunch.

Chapter 23

The First Branding

As the sun on this spring May morning warmed the earth, the Fletchers began the long day of branding their forty calves. With the spring rain last night, the ground looked dark and muddy. A thin layer of white mist hung above the river that ran through the valley. As the sun warmed the air, the misty fog disappeared. Parts of the fields had puddles of rainwater in the low spots. The two-tracked roads around and beyond the ranch were also filled with rainwater. Rising higher, the sun warmed the herd and men alike.

After eating breakfast, Clyde had given his long list for their different duties today. Going into the stable, each of the Fletchers saddled their horses. Chet had saddled his red sorrel Rusty while Tom saddled his grey stallion Brute. Dave saddled his brown stallion Bullet. Since Hans came out to help with the branding, Chet had caught their brown gelding Thunder from the pasture. He had saddled the gelding for Hans who looked forward to doing something productive. He did miss working on a ranch. The men checked their ropes and coiled them for the roping.

As the men waited by the stable with their saddled horses, Clyde said, "We're goin' to have to find some high ground to brand today. While we fed the herd this mornin', we noticed that there's puddles of rainwater in the pasture."

"We'll be in mud up to our eyeballs," commented Hans, recalling times before on the ranch.

"Yeah, let's go set up. Fred and Andy are drivin' the wagon out," said Clyde as he looked over at the ranch house. With his brother in charge, he knew he didn't need to worry about the mixing up the grain and the dewormer. He kept poking Matt to keep his focus on the importance of working the ranch.

The men mounted their horses and rode toward the pasture to the young calves waiting. The two stallions were frisky and ready to run. Looking at each other, Dave and Tom smiled at the idea of a challenge. They each let loose their reins, pressed in their heels, and the two horses trotted into a full gallop. Head to head they galloped along the grass that paralleled the muddy road to the pastures. They continued around the pastures all the way to the edge of the timber. Slowing down the horses, the two riders pulled on the reins and turned their heated stallions around. Prancing around, the horses breathed heavy and snorted, shaking their heads. The two young men smiled and laughed at the race. Dave's brown stallion had won. They chatted as they rode slowly back to the pastures, cooling down the horses after their race.

Working together in the pasture, the men quickly set everything up. A fire had been started, surrounded by rocks. The branding irons sat on the hot embers, ready to brand. The other small iron for the little horns rested on the embers. Early that morning, Chet and Clyde talked about the rain last night, making the calves' hides wet. They would have to wipe dry a spot on the calves' hips before branding. Chet had taken a bag of rags from the tack shed. Also, Clyde suggested clipping the hair a little. That would help dry the spot a little more. Chet found a pair of sheers to clip the hair along with the bag of rags. Drying the spot would add another step or two to their branding today.

Untying his coiled rope, Dave rode over to the calves, milling around. Swinging his rope, he lassoed one calf and dallied the rope around the saddle horn. He then started to pull the calf towards the branding area. On his horse, Tom quickly threw another rope to catch the hind legs, putting the calf on its side. Hans came over and grabbed the calf's hind legs, pulling it nearer to the branding area. Clyde picked up the two ash grey irons from the bed of embers. As the calf lay on its side, Hans held the calf down as Chet clipped the area and dried the spot on the calf's hip. Then, Clyde branded the calf with the first hot iron, putting a long line on the hide. The second hot iron put the two horizontal triangles, the points touching, at the top end of the line. The battle axe clearly marked the calf. The stinking black smoke from the burning hair filled the air. With its eyeballs rolling in fear, the calf bawled. Feeling the hot breath of the calf, Hans comforted the calf with words, "Hey, take it easy. It'll be over in a minute."

Since it was a male, Chet quickly pulled out his sharpened knife, squatted down, and went to work to castrate it. Pulling down one of the testicles, he cut it off with a swift motion. He avoided cutting the skin on the calf. He did the same to the second testicle. There was a metal bucket off to the side he threw them into. The calf continued to bawl and grunt. Hans still had a hold of the calf as Chet then grabbed the cutting sheers and dehorned the calf. Clyde followed with burning the buds at the base with a soft touch of the small iron. Finally, the men finished with the calf, pulling off Tom's rope around its hind legs and then Dave's rope around its neck. The calf stood, grunting, bawling, and kicking, ran away towards the other calves.

Fred now mounted on his buckskin horse Captain cut off the calf and moved him towards the side gate that led to the next pasture with the feeding trough full of grain and a dewormer. Andy took his position on the wooden side gate, opening it when the branded calf came towards him. Waving his hat, he helped guide the calf into the next pasture. He repeated this over and over. A few times he came over and sat on the calf, helping Hans. He let him help a few times but told Andy to stay at the side gate. Most of calves were frightened and kicking all the time, trying to get away. As a young boy and inexperienced, Andy could easily be caught off guard with an unexpected kick. Hans didn't want him to get hurt.

This process went on calf after calf until the men had completed around twenty of the calves. A few were friskier than others and it took Hans to sit on them to keep them still while they were branded. The ground was muddy and got churned up in the branding. The sweating men had mud caked on their boots and jeans. The horses' hooves were caked with mud. Hustling to brand, castrate, and dehorn the calves kept the men in continual motion—muscled men dominating the reluctant, struggling calves. Clyde had to scrape the irons clean occasionally. The mixture of smoke, sweat, blood, and burning hair filled the air. It was brutal and rowdy, but a necessary part of ranching.

Earlier, after Matt helped mix the grain for the horses. He placed a big mixed bag in the stable. Then, he moved over to his black stallion's stall. Lifting his hands, he stroked his beautiful head.

"Are you ready to go to work?" he said. He liked the look of this big stallion, so strong. Matt leaned into the horse's neck, feeling the warmth against his face. Bringing over a bucket with him, he fed him some of the grain mixture. Diablo snorted and munched the grain down quickly. Leading him out with a rope halter, he saddled Diablo, putting on his bridle. He, then, mounted and rode to the pasture. Matt ended up taking Dave's place at lassoing the young calves. Dave had dismounted and helped Chet with the calves on the ground. He took over the dehorning.

Tired, hungry, and needing a rest, Clyde looked around. He saw Anna driving the wagon out from the ranch house. He called out to the men, "Let's stop and take a break. Grub's on its way." Clyde walked over to the campfire, pulling the branding irons and the single iron out of the fire, and setting them on the ground. He scraped the branding irons clean as he did throughout the morning. The scorched hair and skin clogged up the branding irons. He needed to keep them clean for a clear mark.

Chapter 24

The Lunch Break

Before driving the wagon out at noon, Anna had taken the empty boxes and had walked down the hall into Clyde's bedroom. She had met Beth only once when they came to pick up the orphaned filly Moonbeam for Heidi. That day she had tea with her and had a short chat in the kitchen. Recalling her frail body, she felt sad for her. Both dogs followed Anna down to the bedroom, sniffing around and finally, resting on the rug by the bed.

As she started to pack the clothes from the dresser, she felt strange touching them. She left the bottles and the hairbrush and comb on the dresser. Seeing the little carved jewelry box, she opened it. A rose brocade cloth lined the inside. A gold chain, a silver broach with a delicate flower pattern, and a pair of small silver earrings, matching the broach, filled the bottom. On one side lay two gold rings on top of each other—one large and one small band. She picked up the small gold band with the three little diamonds fixed in it. They were dull, clouded with scum. Holding the ring, she walked down to the bathroom and cleaned the diamonds with a little soap and water. Both dogs followed her down the hall and watched her as she stood in the bathroom. When she finished, the little diamonds sparkled brightly between her fingers. Anna thought about her own wedding band without any diamonds. Walking back into the bedroom, she put the ring with now twinkling diamonds back into the carved jewelry box and closed the lid. *Clyde must have a tender heart inside his gruff exterior.*

After emptying the dresser, she double checked the drawers and found a tarot deck of cards tucked in the back in one of the drawers. Opening the pack, she noticed that they were well-worn. Curious, she shuffled them in her hands, looking at the individual cards. She had heard about these cards before and the superstition about playing them, but she had never seen a deck. Shrugging her shoulders, she slipped the cards back into their case. Instead of putting them into the box, she laid them on top of the dresser, thinking she would ask Fred about them.

As she moved to the closet, she folded up the clothes and packed the shoes and the one pair of cowboy boots. On Clyde's side of the closet, she saw an old pair of canvas bib overalls. There was an odd smell coming off of them. *Must be his old overalls.* As she looked further down into the closet, she noticed a pile of men's shirts lying on the floor. Picking up the shirts and grabbing some hangers, she planned on tidying up the closet. But as she hung one of the shirts on a hanger, she noticed that it was missing a button. Glancing through the rest of the shirts, she saw a torn pocket, more missing buttons, and a few worn out elbows on the sleeves. *She should sew and fix up these shirts.* Anna folded them into a pile to take home. Maybe, she would ask Fred if there were other shirts that needed mending. Going into the kitchen, she found a paper sack and put the folded shirts into the sack. Back into the bedroom, she carried the packed boxes and set them in the hallway for Fred to store in the attic. She found a pencil and marked the three boxes with the name 'Beth' on the side, so the family would know. The dogs had followed her around as she busied herself backing Beth's belongings.

Then, she recalled how she had to have Ingrid pack up Caden's clothes after he was killed a year ago. *Odd that two widowers had emerged from this ranch.* Brushing away those disturbing thoughts, she walked down to the kitchen to fix the lunch for the guys branding out in the field.

****

The morning flew by as noon approached. Anna fixed lunch by making sandwiches and cooking a pot of baked beans. She had filled a big camping coffee pot with water, adding coffee grounds. She loaded the wagon with the food and the camping tin plates, utensils, and cups. Driving the wagon out to the pasture with the two dogs, she brought lunch out for the men. As she pulled the big draft horse Jack

326

to a stop near the branding area, the men all dismounted and coiled their ropes.

On the wagon in the early morning, Chet and Tom had also loaded a few hay bales for the horses to eat. The two men each lifted a hay bale and spread it out for the horses. Tying their horses up by the water trough, the men loosened the cinches under their saddles, allowing the horses to breathe easier, eat, and drink. Even though the men were tired and hungry, they took care of their horses first. They even checked the mud caked hooves and with pocketknives, cleaned out the horses' hooves. They kicked or scraped off the dried mud on their cowboy boots and jeans.

The two dogs Bandit and Blue were happily running out around the calves and then over to the main herd. Sniffing the ground, they ran around the herd. Both dogs saw a small animal which took them running into the timber. They had spotted a black and white skunk dashing away from the open pasture to the cover of the forest. They chased it, leaping over logs and through the underbrush. But the skunk found his safe hole in the trunk of an old log and disappeared deep into the dark round hole. Barking, they realized the game had gotten away. Bandit started to move into the dark hole, but soon got a surprise for his efforts.

Just then, the skunk turned around and sprayed the dog. Backing up too late, he yipped loudly with his eyes stinging. He tried to clear his eyes by rubbing his face on the leaves and dirt. He rolled and rolled on the forest ground, trying to rub off the spray. Running back to the men, they chased through the herd and the calves. Finally, the two dogs with the strong smell of a skunk came near to the men and sat next to Fred and Tom. They laid down with their tongues hanging out, huffing after the chase. Bandit took his paw, licking it, rubbing it against his eyes and face a couple of times. He'd forgotten how dangerous a skunk could be defending his hole. Soon, the smell of the skunk hit the noses of everyone there. All sounded their dismay of the sick skunk smell; some held their noses closed.

Fred shook his head, "Hell, Bandit. You can't stay here." He pointed to the ranch house and told Bandit to go. The dog stood up, looked around in confusion, but he put his head down and headed for the ranch house, smelling like a skunk.

Waiting for Anna to spread out the food, the men came over to the wagon for lunch. Anna dished each man some baked beans. She had fixed up a plate of cut cheese and brought a jar of dill pickle spears that the men added to their plates of sandwiches and beans. After filling their plates and bowls with the food, the men wolfed down the food in a few minutes. Some had their own canteens with water to drink. Clyde picked up the coffee pot from the wagon and set it on some hot embers at the edge of the campfire. The coffee would taste good after it had boiled and brewed.

The muddy ground had dried after the morning sun had reached its zenith. Matt and Tom rolled two big log stumps from the wood pile next to the fire. Sitting down on the up-turned stumps, they stretched out their tired legs. Seeing another big stump, Andy copied the two Fletchers and rolled a log out and sat next to them. Chet sat down on the ground, cross-legged next to the campfire. Dave sat down next to the wagon wheel and leaned up against it. Hans, Clyde, and Fred sat on the wagon after shoving the extra food back away from the edge. All the men in some way wanted to rest their legs, arms, and backs after their hard morning of branding.

Anna walked around and handed the men the apples and offered them a few cookies that Heidi and Bridget had made with their Grandma the day before. Seeing her son Andy sitting on the stump, she went over and offered him a cookie from the tin. He asked if she wanted to sit down on his stump, but she shook her head. Walking over to Chet, she sat on the ground next to him, cross-legged. She had eaten a sandwich already before loading and driving the wagon out to the pasture. Looking at the campfire, she pulled out an apple and munched on it.

She glanced at Chet who sat beside her. Thinking about him, she knew from his eyes that his feelings towards her had changed. That was fine. They had become more like good friends. He looked at her for a moment, noticing how

328

beautiful she looked sitting crossed legged beside him. He smiled at her. Having another apple in her pocket, she pulled it out and offered it to Chet who hadn't taken one. He nodded 'yes.' She handed him the apple. Pulling a small pocketknife out of his pocket, he cut a piece of the apple and chewed it. He continued to cut and eat until only the core was left, and then, he tossed the core towards Blue who quickly snatched it from the air and chomped down on it. Folding the knife, he slipped it back into his pocket.

Quietly, she said, "How are you doing? I haven't seen you in town."

"I've been busy here on the ranch," he said.

"I know it's been hard on all of you." He looked at her and then nodded his head as he lowered it, staring at the campfire. Taking a deep breath, he didn't say anything for a few moments. No words were needed for they both remembered that night when his mom died. She had been there.

Glancing up at her, he asked, "I heard that Hans bought that ranch. Are you pleased?" He wanted to change the subject.

Excitedly, she answered, "Yes. We've already moved into the old ranch house. After moving into town, our move to the Norsemen Ranch went much easier. We're still getting settled."

"It'll take time," he said. He had heard that she had been dating and wondered how she felt. He sat silently, looking at the embers in the campfire.

"We love it much better. I've been ridin' my mare Rhapsody. The kids have been concerned about the filly Moonbeam. Maybe, one of you could look at her," she said.

"Why? What's wrong with her? Is she eatin'?" he asked, concerned about the orphaned filly.

"Yes, as far as I know. But Heidi said she hasn't been herself lately. It could be nothin,'" she added. She saw Andy looking at the two of them sitting together.

As a growing boy, Andy had noticed that his mother had been going out on dates. He wondered what she was thinking. *Did she want to get married?* All of this confused

329

him, but he wasn't stupid about girls and boys. Going to school, he had a few girls he liked. But he tended to be shy around them and didn't know how to talk to them. One girl Bonnie was really nice, but she was so popular that he froze when she came near to him. His tongue seemed to have a mind of its own when he was around her. He ended up saying the stupidest things to her. He needed help to figure this girl thing out. In the meantime, he knew that his mom had been out with the doctor. He didn't know what that meant and felt confused about seeing his mom with another man, even though he was a doctor.

Knowing that Andy was watching her, Anna stood up and walked over to her son, putting her hand on his back. She noticed that he had been acting strange since she had started dating. He needed a father someday soon to explain the things about girls and boys. But she was afraid he probably already knew a little. She would have to be careful in marrying. He seemed to stare at her with curiosity that she hadn't seen in his eyes before. She worried about what he would think if she did marry.

"Did you get enough to eat, Andy?" she asked. He told her he did and handed her the rest of the tin of cookies.

Chet spoke to her, "Thanks for lunch, Anna." Everyone around the campfire echoed his words. She acknowledged them with a nod of her head. Smiling to herself, she walked over to the wagon.

Most everyone rested after eating, so it was a quiet time. The air filled with the smell of freshly brewed coffee as the pot boiled. Fred reached for one of his gloves from out of his back pocket. Walking over to the pot, he picked it up with his glove protecting his hand and took it over to the wagon. Anna had noticed the coffee had started to boil, so she had set out the tin cups as he filled them. Then, walking around, he handed the men each a cup. A few came over and took the filled cups. All said 'thanks.' As they sipped and finished the coffee, the conversation began about how to take care of the skunk smell on a dog. Many of them had had numerous occasions dealing with this situation. Several home remedies had been tried.

"I've heard that tomato juice will take off the smell," offered Dave. That was an old solution that never worked, but some tried it anyway.

"No, I heard that dish-soap will take it out, but it always stings the dog's eyes," Hans said.

"Does anythin' really work? " asked Fred. They questioned the remedies, and some had tried those without much luck.

"Someone told me that mouthwash worked on his dog. Maybe we should try that on Bandit tonight. I hate to waste good tomato juice. No matter what we do. Bandit won't like it," commented Clyde. Several laughed at the suggestions, knowing that the smell would wear off after a few days.

Chapter 25

The Dilemma

Finally, they decided to get back to branding. The skunk problem would be there tonight. Putting their dirty tin plates, bowls, and cups over onto the wagon, the men walked over to their horses. Anna mentioned that dinner would be up at the ranch house tonight. Walking over to their horses, they cinched up the straps and mounted their horses. Clyde walked over to the temporary woodpile and picked up an armful of cut wood. He put some more firewood on the hot embers of the campfire. Picking up the three irons, he put them into the campfire.

Mounting their horses, the men found it easy to lasso the unbranded calves since those that were branded had been moved to the next pasture. Other times when they had branded, the calves were mixed together, so the sorting took some time. But here, the selection was certain and quicker. The lassoing began, the branding went on, the castrating continued for the males, and the cutting off the little horns followed with a quick iron to the buds. The calves kicked, bellowed, rolled their eyeballs as the men wrestled with them. The afternoon progressed smoothly as the men worked hard at finishing up before evening.

After everyone had eaten, Anna decided to get back to the ranch house with the wagon and the dirty dishes. She called to Blue to come with her. He did and jumped up on the wagon, riding beside her back to the ranch house. Her mother-in-law and children were coming. She wanted to be there. They were frying up three chickens for dinner. She had enjoyed being on the ranch and helping with the lunch, but she felt underfoot here with the men today.

A year ago, she had helped Hans and the men brand their calves, but this year, no one encouraged her to stay and help. They seemed oblivious to her. She stepped up onto the wagon. She waved her hand 'goodbye' to her son. Those others who had a hand free, waved back at her. Turning on the wagon seat, she slapped the reins and clicked her tongue for Jack to head out. Anna looked forward to spending the afternoon with her beautiful girls and her happy baby.

As she drove the wagon back, she thought of seeing Chet, sitting next to her around the campfire. He seemed relaxed around her but didn't say much. She felt that they had slipped into just being good friends. Once he said that he would call her after she moved to town. But he never did. She recalled that Chet had dated Betsy Crocket who had been murdered. She wondered about how that had affected him. She hadn't heard if he had been dating anyone else in town, but she had heard that he had been stopping in at the Pole Cat Bar a couple of nights each week. *He must be out drinking—drinking away his hurt feelings of losing Betsy.*

Her mind shifted to Denny who had been seeing her once a week when he came to his office in Riverside. She felt the pressure of deciding if she wanted to marry him or not. That day up at the aspen grove at Skyview, he had made it clear that he would not wait forever. However, she couldn't decide. It didn't seem right to have a timer put on her feelings—ticking down. *Tick-tick. Tick-tick. Yes or no.* How could she decide? She felt uneasy; the pressure overwhelmed her.

Then, a few weeks ago, an old acquaintance, Chuck Nubben, had met her at the Mercantile while she was shopping for groceries. The two talked and he asked her to go to lunch with him. She said 'yes.' Chuck had been one of Hans' ranch hands who had been present when her husband had been mauled by the grizzly. After finding her husband, he had driven the wagon to bring Caden back to the ranch. They both recalled the day that her husband's horse Diablo returned without his rider. Chuck and Jim with Hans had ridden up to find him. They had found his mangled bloody body; he was conscious for only a little while. Chuck and Anna had a connection with each other from that experience—a mutual sense of loss.

That first meeting at lunch with Chuck had felt awkward for a few minutes, but soon, Anna had relaxed and enjoyed talking about what he had been doing since her husband's death.

"Would you mind callin' me 'Charles'? That's my name. Only my ranch buddies call me 'Chuck,'" he said.

"Of course, Charles. I like that better, too," she said.

After leaving the Battle Axe, he told her that he had hired on at the Lodge Pole Dude Ranch as a foreman. He had a circle of ranching friends she knew. He was still friends with Jim McDob who now worked at the Double D as a foreman. Another friend was Wyatt Gordon who shot the grizzly while he worked at the Johnson Ranch.

At twenty-six years old, Charles was a tall, thin man with curly black hair and dark brown eyes. His parents, Jess and Sue, lived in Midler on a small ranch. He had a married younger sister, Emma (who married Felix Zahner), and two nephews, Joe and Al. She listened to him speak fondly about his extended family. He knew his nephews ages and talked about how fast they were growing. Charles had worked for Hans at the Battle Axe Ranch for four years, so he knew Anna's family well—her children, her husband, and her. He had recalled children as little kids, but she told him they were growing up fast. He had always liked Anna, and now that she was a widow, he had begun to have thoughts about her. He had called on her a couple of days later and they had gone for lunch again.

She recalled their conversation during their second lunch. As they were eating, Chuck told her about talking to Hans recently. This had been the first time she had heard about Hans's plans to start ranching again.

Charles said, "He surprised me when he said he wanted to buy a piece of land from the Lodge Pole where I work. He asked me about it."

"Oh, yes. Hans and Ingrid don't like living in town. I'm also having second thoughts. I knew that Hans had been asking around for some land," answered Anna.

"Yeah, I had dinner at their house one night. Evidently, Jared at the Lodge Pole wants to sell a section of his ranch—160 acres," said Charles.

"Why is he selling?" she asked.

"He told me that he and his wife wanted to build a bigger house. He built a new house up on the mesa this last year. It's a beautiful spot with a great view of the mountains. This past year, I've been buildin' new corrals and sheds for the horses up there," he explained. He had put in long hours of hard work both building and taking care of their herd. He didn't tell her that Hans said if he bought the land that he'd hire Charles to help run his new ranch.

"So, now what?" asked Anna. She listened carefully since Hans hadn't told her about this before.

"Jared and his wife Mary have moved into their new house. They want to sell the bottom section. By the way, the highway cuts through a small part of the acres, so it's split. The land they are selling has an older ranch house, a barn, a few outbuildin's, and a bunk house. I thought that the deal sounded good," he said. As the two finished their lunch, they talked a little more. He wanted to know how the children were doing. She told him they were looking forward to the Easter break. Then, they left. He drove her home. As she stood on the porch ready to go inside, he asked her out again for dinner and some drinks that weekend. She said 'yes' and would arrange for the children to stay with their grandparents.

During their lunches, their date out to dinner, and their conversations, her beauty had struck him in the gut every time he looked at her. At first, it was hard to look into those blue eyes of hers, knowing her past. But as they became more acquainted, he had begun to stare into those blue orbs and easily got lost in them. He couldn't believe how easy they fell in together. He had thought of her often. His mind had whirled as his desires stirred for her. He had felt confident around her. *This felt so right.*

Being a quiet, shy man, he hadn't made any advances. In fact, they hadn't even kissed. He didn't want to push her. Something had sprung up quite unexpected between them as they dated. To him, she wasn't ready, for there seemed to be a shadow around her as she still mourned for her husband. And he could wait. Charles had a silent, strong personality about him. Confidence exuded from him—the way he carried himself. He had told her he wanted to settle down and hinted at marriage. He had never come out as directly as

Denny had, but the offer stood there between them. Surprised at his unexpected interest, she had spent sleepless nights thinking of him. He had spent nights thinking of her.

Now, she had an unforeseen dilemma. Here were two men who wanted to marry her. Her life seemed complicated beyond belief. How could she decide? Both were good men. Her future was in her hands. But since they had moved in again with Hans and Ingrid, she didn't feel lonely. The children and she felt comfortable with them again. She just shook her head and cleared her thoughts of this complicated situation.

Chapter 26

Devotion and Sacrifice

As she drove the wagon up to the back door of the ranch house, the smell of the skunked Bandit hit her nose. The strong smell made her gulp as she held her nose closed. Blue jumped down from the wagon and the two dogs ran off to meet Fred coming down the dirt road from the pasture. Stepping down, she smiled at him as he rode up on his horse Captain.

Dismounting, he said, "Let me help you, Anna. I'll take care of the wagon and Jack."

Grabbing most of the dirty dishes, she said, "Thanks. I hope the men got enough to eat."

"Oh, it was mighty fine, Anna," he said as he picked up the rest of the dishes and an empty pot. Together, they walked through the back porch and into the kitchen.

After putting the dishes into the kitchen sink, she said, "Beth's clothes are packed in boxes in the hallway. By the way, I found a bunch of shirts that need mending. Do you or the guys have any more shirts? I want to sew on buttons and cut off the torn sleeves for you. Oh, and I left Beth's lotion, perfume, and her hairbrush and comb on the dresser. Did you want me to pack those, too?"

Fred thought for a few moments, then said, "Why don't you take those for the girls. Maybe, they could use them. I'd like to clear out all of the reminders."

"Are you sure? I left the carved wooden jewelry box," said Anna.

"Yeah...we'll leave the jewelry box. Are their weddin' rings in the box?" asked Fred.

Feeling a little embarrassed at looking inside, she said, "Yes, both are there."

"Yeah, those rings are pretty special. My brother and Beth really loved each other. They had a beautiful life together for years, but it all fell apart. Their marriage died years before her death. I don't mean to talk so openly, but

337

it's the truth," he said quietly, tapping down his own feelings about his brother's marriage.

Anna couldn't say anything. Words couldn't capture her sad feelings about what Fred had revealed to her. She nodded at him and turned around to look out the kitchen window at the ranch. She had heard the anguish in Fred's voice and knew the heartache that the family must be feeling after Beth's death.

Those tragic memories of her own came crushing down around her. Turning on the faucet, she started to fill the sink to wash the dirty lunch dishes. She had to keep busy. Coming back here today was troubling her. Everything in this house, this kitchen, the stable, and the pastures had reminded her life with Caden. During the last year, she realized that grief had dominated her while she had lived on this ranch. Now, she needed to look more to the future for her and her children—and to the two men who wanted to marry her.

Seeing Anna busy with the dishes, Fred turned and left the kitchen. Picking up the packed boxes in the hall, he took them upstairs to the attic. There were only three medium sized boxes—meager belongings for a person. *How could one's total belongings fit into these boxes?*

Since Beth's death, Fred had been sizing up his own life. He had wanted more in his life, but he had devoted himself to raising his younger brother when they had been orphaned. Several times, he had had a chance to marry, but he didn't. Trying to balance Clyde's life and his own life didn't allow for him to go off and get married. But he reminded himself that his life wasn't over. He still lived and breathed. They owned this mountain ranch which had fulfilled their dreams. His rodeo friends had been calling him in the last few weeks about hooking up at the spring rodeos. Fred wanted to go and be with his friends. Everything around the ranch was getting settled, so he felt that he could leave soon for a while.

Coming back downstairs, he walked down the hall into his brother's bedroom. On the dresser, he saw the bottles of lotion, the perfume, the talc powder, and the brush and comb that Anna had left. But what caught his attention on top of the dresser was a worn-out deck of tarot cards. He wondered where Beth had gotten them. Clyde told him about her wild ideas and her superstitions. He wondered if his brother knew about these tarot cards. Thinking about what he should do with them, he slipped them into his inside jacket pocket. Knowing that his brother didn't need them, he didn't want to give them to the young children either. As he picked up all the items, he checked behind the bedroom door. There hung Beth's old faded yellow robe which Anna had missed. He rolled everything up into the robe and headed for the kitchen. He came back to the kitchen and walked into the pantry, where he found a grocery paper sack and slipped the robe with the items inside the sack.

As he came out of the pantry, he said, "I think the girls will enjoy havin' these. Don't you? You forgot her yellow robe that hung on the back of the bedroom door. Take it with you. Find someone who could use it."

Anna turned and smiled at him, "Oh, sorry. Yes, the girls could use the lotion. I might wait until they are older for the perfume, though." They both had a short laugh.

Reaching around her, he turned on the faucet and filled himself a big glass of water. Exhaustion was already getting to him today. He drank it down and said, "Thanks, Anna. I better take care of Jack and get back to the brandin.' See you later for dinner."

After tethering Captain to the back of the wagon, he stepped up and sat down on the seat. Releasing the brake, he took up the reins and turned the wagon around towards the stable. He took care of Jack, brushing him down, watering, and feeding him. The draft horse Jack was old like him. Affectionately, he stroked Jack's big head. The whiskers on Jack's muzzle were turning white. "Well, o' boy. We're just about ready to pasture you," whispered Fred to the horse who snorted and nudged him. "Oh, so you say 'no.' You might be right, Jack. We both have a lot of kick in us, yet."

Turning, he walked out to his chestnut horse Captain. He mounted him and headed back to the pasture to help with the branding. He thought how good it was that the Seversons had come to help today, not only helping with the branding but with Anna packing up Beth's belongings. Friends like them were hard to find. But they had been lucky to have them. He hoped that he could repay them their kindness and support someday.

Chapter 27

The Secret

As twilight descended on the rugged mountains, the setting sun left the skies a reddish orange, and the blue mountains with their white peaks of snow standing out. The dark shadows started to cover the timber, the ranch buildings, the pastures, and the big log ranch house which sat with its windows casting a bright yellow into the early evening hours.

Out in the field, the men had finished with the branding. They had gathered around the warm campfire as Fred prepared his specialty--the Rocky Mountain oysters. Since Chet had castrated the males, he helped his uncle with preparing them. He first took the calves' balls out of the skin sack and pounded them flat. Fred took and tossed them in a paper sack with the seasoned flour. He then popped them into the cast iron skillet with the hot melted lard. He let them fry on one side, and he flipped them over with his long hunting knife.

While they were cooking, Chet walked over to his saddle bag, pulled out his pint of whiskey, and handed it around for the men to have a sip or two. As they enjoyed the fresh taste of whiskey, the men made small talk about the different calves and how the branding went. The pint of liquor skipped Andy who was handed a canteen of water. He frowned, wishing he too could have a sip of the whiskey, but the men said, 'no' and 'you're too young.'

As the tasty oysters were cooking, Fred nodded to Chet to come with him as he walked over to the last few pieces of wood. He picked up a small piece of wood. Then, he took out the worn pack of tarot cards from his inside pocket. He carefully handled the pack so that only his nephew could see it. He looked at his uncle surprised and said quietly, "Those are mom's. Where did you get them?" With his back to the men around the campfire, he handed them to

Chet who had followed his uncle. He slowly turned his back to talk to his uncle.

With their backs to everyone, Fred said quietly, "I had Anna pack up your mom's belongings today. I took the boxes up into the attic. But she found these in one of your mom's drawers. We need to get rid of them. Did you know about these?"

Realizing what his uncle had done, he said, "Yeah, we knew about the cards. She used to play them when we were still in school. We kept them a secret from dad. Mom didn't want him to know. What do you want me to do with them?"

Seeing the deck, Chet recalled how his mom had played and played those cards. As kids, he and his brothers would come home from school when she'd be at the small kitchen table, setting them down and turning them over. She would quickly put them away and tell them not to say anything to their dad about them. She had said it was their little secret. Their mom then would get out the cookies and milk. Even though they were curious, they had never told their dad about them. Their mom had made them promise to keep it a secret. Over the years, she played them quite a bit. Sometimes he had watched her shuffle the deck and start over, setting them face down and turning them up, repeatedly.

"I don't want to keep them or give them away. They're nothin' but trouble. How about burnin' them? After we're done, everyone will be headin' back to the ranch house. You stay around and put out the campfire. After everyone has left, throw them into the fire," his uncle said. He turned and walked back to the campfire, putting the little piece of wood on the campfire. Taking out the cooked oysters, he put them on a tin plate. Chet nodded at his uncle, indicating he would burn them later. Before turning, he had slipped the tarot deck into his inside pocket.

As he waited for the Rocky Mountain oysters to cool a little, Fred thought about the night weeks ago on the mountain with the grizzly hide burning. He recalled how Hans had destroyed the grizzly hide in memory of his son's death. Maybe, in some small way, burning these tarot cards would be the same thing. He knew that Beth's suicide was more about Matt's supposed death than the tarot cards, but he knew she did get wild ideas about dead spirits. After years of listening to Clyde's concerns, he'd heard about how Beth had believed in those occult practices. Those cards were no good. Letting someone have them didn't seem the right thing to do. He wanted them destroyed so they wouldn't give someone else wild ideas, especially the young children.

Fire was a way to purify—to clear away the bad. Every man respected the ever-powerful force of fire. In the forests, fire burned out the tangled undergrowth and the dead wood. Afterward, new growth of trees sprang from the black ashes. On the ranch, the ditches were cleared of dried dead grass, small twigs and dead leaves, and other debris that were left after the water was pulled. *Yes, burning those tarot cards would be best. Fire would destroy those dangerous cards.*

As his special oysters were ready to serve, he stood up and handed the tin plate to Clyde who took a few and handed the plate around. Being a tradition after branding, the men ate the delicate appetizers. They thanked him for cooking them up. They enjoyed the taste as they talked about the long day of working together at branding the calves.

Encouraged by Matt who stood next to him, young Andy took one of the oysters. He had a dubious look on his face, so he said, "Don't nibble at it, Andy. Pop it into your mouth, chew it, and swallow it down. It tastes great."

Unsure, Andy instead took a small bite. Then, he spit it out, "Sorry." The men all laughed and joked about the tradition; they knew it was an acquired taste.

After the Rocky Mountain oysters were eaten and the whiskey nearly gone, the men walked back to their horses. After their uncle took care of the iron skillet, the tin plate, and the empty bucket, he mounted Captain. Their dad picked up and cleaned off the cooled branding irons, tied them to the back of his saddle, and mounted Chief. Mounting his stallion Bullet, Dave said he'd take a ride

343

around the calves and the herd to see if they had settled down for the night. Hans mounted Thunder while holding out his hand for his grandson to ride with him. Andy easily swung up and sat behind his Grandpa with his arms wrapped around him. His grandson had had the best day of his life being here today with his grandpa and with the men branding those calves.

Only the three Fletcher brothers were left to put out the fire and clean up anything left from the branding. Chet motioned for his brothers to join him by the campfire. Taking out the deck, he squatted down. As Matt started to kick dirt on the campfire to put it out, Chet said, "Wait, Matt. We need to talk. Uncle Fred had Anna box up mom's belongings out of the bedroom today while we were out here brandin'. It's somethin' that needed to get done. As Anna packed, she came across mom's tarot cards. Remember them?" Looking at the worn pack of cards, they stared at them.

"Yeah, I do. What are you goin' to do with them?" he asked. Tom walked over to the campfire.

"Do you remember them, Tom? They were mom's," said Chet.

"Yeah, they were our little secret," he replied. They remembered them.

"Uncle Fred wants us to burn them. And he doesn't want dad to know about this."

"Why do we have to get rid of them? We could keep them and hide them from dad," suggested Matt. He didn't like destroying something of their mom's. He knew that her belongings were meager. They lived sparingly for years at the Diamond V Ranch.

"No, Matt. These cards are nothin' but trouble. People get weird ideas when they play them. I agree with Uncle Fred. They need to be destroyed," said Chet. Tom nodded his head in agreement. Their brother always had opposing views about some issues. But Matt understood and nodded in agreement. He wanted something to remember his mom by, but certainly not those tarot cards. Years ago in school, he'd asked his friends at school about them. They all told him that they were crazy and stupid cards. One guy told him they were cards of the devil. *No, he didn't want them.*

Without any more words, Chet took out of the cards and tossed two or three at a time into the campfire. After all seventy-eight of them were nestled on top of the embers, the boys took a few small pieces of twigs and grass beside the campfire and covered the cards. With the flames dancing around them, they watched as the colorful figures and numbers turn
black and curl at the corners. Then they burst into flames. The ash flew around as the fire ate them up. When they had disappeared, the three kicked dirt on the dying embers of the campfire, burying the ashy remnants of that deck.

The three mounted their horses and headed toward the ranch house where dinner awaited. Each would remember this night as they burned up their mom's secret tarot cards. As they rode towards the ranch house with its warm yellow lights streaming from the windows, their stomachs growled for dinner.

Chapter 28

Song and Storytelling

After Anna had come back to the ranch house, Ingrid and the three children had driven to the ranch and joined her in the kitchen. Ingrid carried the baby Cade in, and she said, "Anna, I brought his play pen and a folding table and chairs. Would you get them." She nodded and told Heidi to help her. They went out to the car and brought them in. Setting the play pen up in the kitchen, Cade was happy to see his mom as she took him from Ingrid.

"There's my baby. How are you doin'?" Anna said, giving Cade a kiss, as he babbled out, "Mama … mama." In one month, he had grown bigger. His blonde hair was longer, and the front bangs needed to be cut to keep it out of his blue eyes. Pulling some toys from the diaper bag, she gave him one as he reached and giggled. She set him down into the play pen. The girls were excited to be back in their old house, so Anna sat them down and gave them a few words of caution. Ingrid helped set up the folding table with the folding chairs.

She explained, "Now, girls. This isn't our house. I don't want you running through this house like you did when we lived here. Stay downstairs—in the living room or here in the kitchen. Did you bring something to do while we cook?"

Heidi pulled out a book she was reading, and said, "Yes, mom. I'm reading my book of fairy tales." She had gone to their local town library and found a few books that interested her. With a library card now, she could get more books there this summer.

Bridget pulled out her coloring book and crayons, and said, "Oh, Heidi. I'm coloring fairies in my book. Tell me what color I should color them?" She crawled up and sat on a chair, setting her coloring book and box of crayons down on the folding table. Looking at her sister, she waited with her big blues eyes. Bridget adored her sister; she knew so much more than she did.

"Are they good fairies? What are they doing? I think the lighter colors would be best," she suggested as looked into the box of crayons. "Mom, Bridget needs a better box of colors. Now, they have crayons that come with many more shades. Some of her crayons are only stubs."

Anna looked at Heidi; she nodded and made a mental note to get her another box of crayons. Bridget loved coloring. In fact, Grandma Ingrid had bought her a set of watercolors one day at the Mercantile. They had spent an afternoon painting with those—painting barns, houses, trees, mountains, horses, and dogs. After that day, Bridget wanted to watercolor almost every day.

While the girls were busy with reading and coloring, Ingrid and Anna started to cut up and fry the chicken. With the two of them working, they had the pieces of chicken frying in two skillets on the stove in no time. The two had made potato salad and a fruit salad yesterday. Anna had baked Andy's favorite, a chocolate cake. Ingrid thought that biscuits would taste good with the fried chicken. Opening the fridge, she noticed several pints of cream were in the back.

"Oh, my, Anna. Look at all the cream they have. We should take them home with us tonight and churn some butter. I'll use a little for the biscuits," exclaimed Ingrid. Going into the pantry, she brought out the flour. The cupboards were disorganized, so they had trouble finding the cookie sheets. Anna helped her find the baking powder and a measuring spoon. She could tell that a little re-organization was needed in the cupboards. She hoped that Fred would take her advice about hiring a housekeeper—particularly Violet.

Soon the day slipped on into late afternoon. The girls had finished their books and had gone into the living room to stretch out and to take a short nap. Anna had given Cade his bottle while Ingrid moved the play pen into the living room. Taking a blanket, she laid the sleepy Cade down for his nap, holding her finger up to her lips for her girls to be

347

quiet. As the children took their naps, Ingrid and Anna sat in the kitchen while they waited for the men. Anna saw the tea kettle, so she put it on and looked into the little pink tea cannister for the tea bags. When it had whistled, she poured them each a cup of tea while they quietly chatted about their new ranch, the house, the mending, and the children.

The fried chicken and the biscuits had been cooked and were left warming in the oven. The table had been set with plates, silverware, and cups. The coffee pot sat on the stove waiting for the men to come in from the fields. Finally, they started coming onto the back porch to wash before eating. As they filed in and sat at the table, Anna went to the fridge and pulled out one of the big bowls and set it on the table. She followed with the second one, taking off the covers of both. Ingrid took out the two platters of fried chicken and the biscuits.

Placing them on the table, Dave said he'd get a jar of jam from the pantry. Ingrid recognized one of her jars of apple butter as he popped off the lid. When they had moved out, she had left them a few jars in the pantry. She noticed that all the quarts of pickles she had left were gone. Without a woman in the house, she knew that the men had enjoyed the homemade pickles and the jam.

The last men to show up were the three Fletcher brothers. They moved around the table and found a place to sit. Clyde waited for all of them to sit before he started passing around the food. They filled their plates. Anna went around and filled their cups with coffee. Tom got up, brought over a pitcher of milk for the girls and Andy, and a pint of cream from the fridge. Coming in from the living room, the girls shyly walked over to the folding table where their plates were set up. Anna took their plates and stood at the end of the table. As the food was handed around, she filled her daughters' plates.

Matt looked at the girls and said, "Hi, girls. What did you do today?" They just smiled as the other men looked up from their food and smiled at them.

Little Bridget shyly spoke up, "I colored fairies."

"Oh, that sounds fun. And you, Heidi? What did you do?" said Matt.

She proudly answered, "I'm reading a library book."

"What was your book about?" asked Chet. He himself read a lot and respected others who did.

"It's a book of fairy tales about a big, bad wolf, a prince charming, a magic mirror, and a wooden puppet," said Heidi, smiling as she thought of all the folk tales. She could never get enough of them. She would have many books to read this summer. Everyone listened to this young girl and her enthusiasm. They recalled their childhood enjoyment of learning to read.

"Will you play for us tonight, Matt?" asked Heidi. The children were anxious to hear him play his guitar and sing like he did one night weeks ago. They had had so much fun.

"Sure. Later. Eat up," he answered. Tired as he was, he knew he would have to play a few songs for them. His head had started to throb, so he would need to take some aspirins again.

About that time, Cade in the other room, woke up from his nap, crying for 'mama.' Anna excused herself and left the kitchen with the diaper bag. After a few minutes, she came back in with him. The Fletchers noted how big he was getting.

Hans reached out to his little grandson, and said, "Sit, Anna, I'll hold him while you feed him." He was sitting near the end on one side of the table. She slid her chair beside Hans off to the side and opened a baby jar of turkey and one of carrots. Taking a bib out, she tied it around his neck. She scooped a little meat with carrots on his baby spoon. He opened his mouth, gummed it, and swallowed. She managed to get quite a bit of the baby food into him. Finally he had had enough, he reached and grabbed Grandpa's spoon in his little fisted hand. Pounding the table with the spoon, the loud noise got everyone's attention.

"I have some milk for him," said Anna. Taking out a covered cup for him, she filled it with milk and handed him the cup. He took a couple of sips. Trying to talk, Cade babbled with delight as he sat on his Grandpa's lap, looking at all the men and his brother Andy around the table. Inquisitively he reached for everything that was within reach of his tiny little fingers. The men laughed as Hans attempted to keep the baby's hands from the silverware and from the food on his plate. Without a highchair, Hans did his best. He had eaten most of his dinner, so just a few bites were left. Little hands to his mouth--that's how Cade ate the bits of fruit and potato salad.

Sitting next to his other grandson, Hans said, "Well, Andy, how did you like brandin' today?"

"It was great. I want to learn how to lasso those calves," he said. Everyone chuckled for they knew when they were young, it took a lot of practice. But they admired his effort today. The men passed around the fried chicken and biscuits again as many took seconds. The potato and fruit salad nearly disappeared from the two large bowls.

When the food all but disappeared, Anna got up and brought over the chocolate cake. Andy's eyes smiled as his mother cut the cake. She had made his favorite. The men handed down their plates to get a piece. Knowing the men would like more coffee, she put on a fresh pot on the stove. Chet, Dave, and Andy asked for a second piece of cake while the others relaxed while they drank their coffee. Finally finished, they got up and took their plates and silverware to the kitchen sink.

"Let's go down to the office," said Clyde as he went to the cupboard for the bottle of whiskey. The men followed him, keeping their unfinished or empty coffee cups.

Before Dave left, he turned to Anna and Ingrid and said, "Thanks for dinner....best one I've had in a long time." The others agreed and thanked them.

Hans handed baby Cade to Anna and said, "I think he got more on him than in his mouth. Be good, lil' cowboy." He gave his youngest grandson a kiss on his golden head. Anna took him to the kitchen sink and washed his little pudgy face off with a cloth. He reached out with his sticky hands and splashed water from the faucet until she turned it off. His hands were now as clean as his face.

Going down to the office, the men waited while Clyde opened the whiskey bottle and poured a little dark amber liquid into each of their cups. With the chairs in the kitchen, they stood around, leaning up against the wall.

"Here's to us…our first brandin'," he said. They all raised their cups in acknowledging the work and effort. This was the first time that the Fletchers had branded their own calves with their own brand. Clyde got a little choked up thinking about it.

Fred stepped in and said, "Yeah, thanks Hans for givin' us a hand. We managed to get 'em all branded in one day." They had worked hard and now were exhausted. Clyde filled their cups up with another round. They drank the next round without ceremony.

"Let's go sit down in the livin' room, get comfortable, and relax," Fred suggested.

They walked down the hall, went into the living room, and sat down in the old comfortable couch and chairs. Chet went over to the fireplace and put in a fire for the evening.

Going upstairs, Matt took four aspirins for his headache. He felt more and more that he had his mom's headaches. It left him feeling strange and alone. If she were here, he could talk to her about them. But he didn't want his dad to know about them, although his brothers had noticed when he had become nauseated from them. Even though he had made light of the headaches, he felt they had their suspicions. Quickly, he came down with his guitar to play a few songs for the children.

After a while, the women and children came into the living room. The men stood up and moved around the room to give the women a place to sit. Anna carried Cade in and set him on the floor. He crawled around for a while, but eventually crawled over to his mom to sit in her lap. There were strangers around and he wanted his mom. Anna sat on the couch with Ingrid beside her. Hans sat on the couch next to Ingrid.

The children sat down on the floor in front of Matt. Again, like last time they were excited to hear him play his guitar—strum the strings and change the chords. He let them each play the strings with their small hands as they took turns. Bridget giggled while Andy looked curiously at the guitar itself. He had asked his mom for a guitar and she told him they could put an ad on the billboard at the Mercantile. He wrote it up saying 'Wanted. A used guitar,' with their phone number. He hadn't heard anything yet, but he was anxious to get a guitar and play like Matt.

Anna told them to sit back, so that Matt could play. As he thought about the songs he'd like to play, Matt remembered that they like the country songs, and particularly those that had a chorus line that they could sing along with him. So, he started out with one of the Sons of the Pioneers. They loved the song and sang with him. Matt next played one of his favorites by Jimmie Rodgers. Clapping afterwards, the children wanted another one. He played around with some of the chords before starting a song by Bobby Edwards. Since he had played with Bill on their last gig, Matt had added this country song to his repertoire. He also played one of the songs by the Everly Brothers that he and Bill had worked up. As he finished, the girls said they loved that song the best.

Finally, Matt recalled that in school when he was young, they had folk songs. He asked them to sing a couple of their songs from school and that he would play along with his guitar. Heidi knew one and sang one with little Bridget listening quietly. As she sang, Matt noted that Heidi had a nice, clear voice. He told her that when the song ended. She said that she took her music class more serious since he had played for them a month or so ago.

Anna noticed that Matt looked tired after singing, so she suggested that they let him rest while Grandpa told them one of his Scandinavian folk tales. The girls grew excited to hear one of Grandpa's stories.

Hans looked at his granddaughters and smiled, "Yes. What story do you want to hear tonight?"

Bridget said, "I would like to hear about the little fairies." She had been coloring them today.

Heidi responded, "Sis, the Vikings didn't have fairies. Did they, Grandpa?"

Hans took a few minutes to decide how to approach both of the girls without getting one or the other upset. He said, "Many people lived back in the ancient times. There were the giants who were very big and tall. Then, there were the little people who were known as fairies, elves, and trolls. But the most well-known were the dwarves. My grandpa told me stories about them. Here's the story that your great-grandpa Lars told me...."

Once long, long ago there were little people who were called dwarves. They lived in stone halls down in the dark underground. Their beautiful halls were lined with gold and silver. In this time of long ago, the ancient people of the north believed that four dwarves held up the corners of the sky. The first little dwarf held up the corner of the north where the northern lights dance. The second little dwarf held up the corner of the south where the sun travels in the summer. The third little dwarf held up the east where the sun rises. And the fourth little dwarf held up the west where the sun sets.

Now along with these four dwarves, many other dwarves were known. There were long lists of their names. Some of the dwarves were light; some were dark. The light ones were beautiful, like little elves or fairies. Most of them were craftsmen. They made strong weapons and tools for the ancient people like their swords and axes. They were like our blacksmiths who fashion things from metal, including gold.

Some dwarves were skilled at making something special. One dwarf could make meade out of honey, fruits, spices, and grains to drink. Another made a magic staff that could be used as a weapon. Some made different horns-- to drink from or to blow. Blowing the horn was a way to communicate or to warn if an enemy came to their shores.

A few dwarves made special things for the gods. One made the most beautiful golden ring that the god Odin wore. One dwarf made the god Thor his hammer which sounded like thunder. Another made a magical spear that always returned. And one made a magical sword that could cut through stones. One special dwarf made a big ship that could sail on the sea. That big ship could magically be folded up into a tiny ship that could be put into a pocket.

But the magical dwarves that were the most unusual were the shift changers. With their magic, they could change their shapes to become different animals. One dwarf could become an otter, and one a fish. Another dwarf could change into a huge fire-breathing dragon. All of these dwarves were known through the ancient stories about them. And that's the end of the tales of the dwarves.

As he finished, everyone had listened with interest. The Fletchers had never heard such tales before. Curious, Heidi asked, "Grandpa. Are these stories in a book for us to read?"

"Yes, one ancient book is called the *Edda* which tells of these dwarves and other tales. Some day when you go to a big library, you might be able to find these kinds of books. Many of the ancient manuscripts had to be translated for us to read."

"I will do just that," said Heidi. She had a keen interest in reading about magic, fairies, and now dwarves. Her Grandpa's stories had opened up new ideas to think about.

"What does it mean to be 'tanslated'?" asked Bridget.

"That's 'translated' with an 'r.' Not everyone speaks our language. Across the ocean, people in foreign countries speak different languages—such as French, German, or many others."

"Oh, how do we know what they are saying then?" questioned Bridget further about languages.

"In school we study those languages. Maybe, one day you will take a foreign language."

"But, Grandpa, did the four dwarves get tired of holding up the sky?" asked Bridget, curious how they could do such a thing.

"Now, Bridget. The ancient people had a big imagination. The story about the dwarves holding up the sky helped them explain the natural world to them. When the wind blew, they imagined a giant eagle moving his broad wings back and forth. When a rainbow appeared, the ancient people said that it was a bridge from earth to heaven. They didn't have science like we do now to explain the natural world. When you go to school, you will begin to learn all about our world," explained Hans.

After hearing about this, Bridget's little eyes grew wide with surprise. She asked, "Mom, when can I go to school?"

"You'll be starting next year in kindergarten. Remember, we talked about it." Knowing that her girls would ask more questions, Anna added, "It's late, children. Thank Matt for playing his guitar and Grandpa for his story of the dwarves. We need to go home." She held Cade who had fallen asleep in her arms while Grandpa told his tale. Along with the lull of storytelling, the warmth from the fireplace had put the men in a relaxed state. The children thanked Matt, and the girls hugged Grandpa and thanked him for the story.

Before leaving the living room, Hans glanced around, and spoke up, "I have a lot of work to do at our new ranch. Do one of you boys want to work for me this summer? I would pay you." He wanted to ask the young Fletchers before they left tonight.

Not hesitating, Tom answered, "Yes, I would like to work for you." He looked at Hans as he waited to hear if his brother would join him. But Matt held back, thinking. He didn't know if he wanted to work or not, but he did like the idea of working for the Seversons.

"Sure, but I wanted to take people out fishin'. But, yes, I can help," he said.

"Good, we'll put you on a part-time basis. Is that what you want, Matt?" asked Hans.

"That would be great. I may have a few gigs with our band," he answered. He did have commitments. And he didn't want to stop playing his guitar. Bill would be expecting him to play back up lead since he had his cast removed.

Hans replied, "That's fine with me, Matt. I plan to pay you boys weekly, since some days or weeks I may not need you. I'll let you know when you show up what my plans will be." Tom and Matt both thought that sounded good since that would allow them some time here at their ranch and for Matt, time for other activities.

When the children, Anna, and Ingrid, got up to leave, they moved into the kitchen. Hans asked for help to load their stuff that they had brought today.

Chet and Dave helped load the play pen, the folding table, and the big empty bowls. While they were in the kitchen, Ingrid told them to keep the leftovers. She was sure they'd liked them.

"Could I take your pints of fresh cream with me? I'd like to make some butter," asked Ingrid. She hated to see so much cream wasted.

Tom had been milking their cow and knew that he had to throw much of their cream away after it soured, so he eagerly said, "Yes. We don't have a way to make it. How much do you think you can make from the cream?"

"From those in the fridge, it'll make about two pounds. I will keep one and bring one to you folks," she explained.

"That's fine. We'd like some fresh butter," said Tom.

The children, Anna, and Ingrid said their 'goodbyes'. Anna gave Ingrid the paper sack filled with the Fletchers' shirts that needed mending. Fred had brought a few more to add to the others. She quietly told Fred she'd call him in the morning and give him Violet's phone number.

When they had all gone out to the cars, Hans stayed behind to talk to Clyde and Fred who were sitting down at the big table.

"First, you know that I've purchased that ranch land near the Lodge Pole Dude Ranch. I have room for a small herd. I was wonderin' if you might want to sell me a few of your cows. Would you fellas be interested?" asked Hans.

Nodding Fred added, "Some of our cows are still nursin' their calves for a few more weeks."

"I don't know. How many do you want?" asked Clyde.

"I'm not sure how many—maybe five to ten. It depends on Brad Johnson. I've asked to buy some of his cows, too. After I hear back from him, I'll let you know. I would be buying at the market price," said Hans.

"That's fine. We'll wait until we hear from you. In the meantime, we'll think about it some more," he said. He wasn't sure what to say just now. His brother kept abreast of the market prices, so that had to be figured into their decision to sell or not, along with Chet's record keeping. *So much to consider* thought Clyde.

"Thanks again for your family's help today, Hans," said Fred. They said their goodbyes and Hans left. From their porch, Clyde and Fred watched the two cars drive away from their ranch onto the highway and into the dark night.

Chapter 29

The End of a Day

The ranch house stood quiet with all of the Seversons gone. The two older brothers, Clyde and Fred, sat at the big kitchen table, talking about their first branding and the selling of their cows.

Tired, the three young brothers came into the kitchen and decided to head to bed. They went upstairs to their bedrooms. Carrying his guitar, Matt leaned it against the wall next to his bed. He had enjoyed playing for the children tonight. He'd been thinking about following Ronnie's example of playing at the local bars. He needed to pay back his brothers for the money he had borrowed to pay for his ticket.

Matt had received a call from his friend Bill. Surprised, he said he and Denise were getting married sometime this summer. His friend had finally decided to settle down like his dad wanted. Denise was doing the arrangements, so he'd let him know the date when it had been settled. *Bill married?* He wondered if Bill would keep the band going after he married.

Dirty, sweaty, and exhausted from the branding, Matt wanted to shower first, so he called out to his brothers, "First to shower."

Chet replied, "I'm second." No answer came from Tom.

Matt walked down to his bedroom to check on him. Tom was resting on his bed, clothes on, and had fallen asleep. He had taken off his boots, so Matt whispered to his brother to turn on his side as he pulled part of the blanket from under him. There was just enough of the blanket to cover him. Leaving his brother asleep and snoring his running motor snore, he turned off the overhead light and left.

Walking down to the bathroom, Matt started the shower, undressed, and stepped into the bathtub as the warm water sprayed on his head. He still had his throbbing headache. The hot air and the warm spray helped ease some of the pain. As the water flowed down his back along his spine, he felt the heat warm his sore muscles. He took a couple of deep breaths, taking in the hot steam into his lungs. Standing there, he took the soap, scrubbed his body, and shampooed his hair. Before stepping out, he turned off the shower and grabbed a towel. In the medicine cabinet, he took another four aspirins and drank a glass of water. He opened the bathroom door. As he walked down the hall to his bedroom, he called out, "Next."

Ready for a shower, Chet had already packed for his trip tomorrow to go to Sophia's graduation. He stepped into the bathroom and took a quick shower, shampooing his hair and scrubbing his dirty, sweaty body. As the warm water eased his sore muscles in his arms, back, and legs, he thought of seeing Sophia. For two weeks, he had counted each day, eager to see her. Finishing his shower, he went to his bedroom, set his alarm, and turned off his light. He crawled into his bed, stretched out his long legs, and flexed his back muscles.

As he relaxed there in his bed, he thought of the long drive, but he wanted to see Sophia. From her last short visit to the ranch, she learned what a future with him would be like. During her phone calls, she still talked about her career plans of teaching. He found that the Hadley's principal mainly wanted her for her minor studies in physical education. He wanted her to teach P.E. classes in junior high, no business classes. She absolutely did not want to teach there, so she refused their job offer. For summer, she would continue her search for a teaching position. For now, he looked forward to bringing her back with him to stay at their ranch. He just didn't know if they had any future together. Knowing he would see her tomorrow, his desires stirred. Closing his eyes, he recalled her sweet kisses and her beautiful body that he wanted to hold. If he were going to get any sleep, he'd better get his mind off of her.

His mind turned to the one mistress that he thought about most nights—their ranch. With his brothers, his dad, Dave, and Hans, the hard work of branding of their young calves felt good. Those calves were their future. He then recalled that his dad told him about Hans' proposal to buy a few of their cows. The money would certainly help with their summer expenses. In the late fall, they'd sell off the steers to get them through the winter. His mind kept jumping from thoughts of Sophia to the ranch until finally he dozed off and fell asleep.

****

Meanwhile, in the kitchen, Clyde and Fred were about to say goodnight, when he turned to his brother and said, "Listen. I had Anna box up all of Beth's clothes and put them in the attic today. I hope that will help you get some more sleep now. She mentioned hirin' a housekeeper. I am goin' to look into it."

"Oh…all right. I'm too tired to think. We'll talk in the mornin'. Good nite," said Clyde. He did want to get some rest tonight.

Fred stepped out of the kitchen through the back porch. "Good nite," he said as he left. He still hadn't moved into the ranch house even though Clyde wanted him to. He liked his privacy. Even though Dave slept in the bunk house, he still had a little more than staying in the main ranch house.

Dave seemed a little strange to him. Maybe, it was his past family experience that left him cold to the world. Fred tried to talk to him about all kinds of subjects—dating, rodeos, horses, cows. He never spoke enthusiastically about anything. Even though he spoke unemotional about everything, Fred felt there were some deep emotions stirring inside of him. He knew that every man had his own private thoughts about life. And some men had demons to battle inside. Dave seemed to have something inside him that held him back from living life with eagerness.

Ever since the funeral, Fred had had his own demons to battle. He had been thinking about settling down with a wife. If he could find a woman this year at the rodeo, he might seriously think about it. If he needed to, he would even leave the ranch, signing over his part of the ranch to his nephews. It would be a hard decision to make, but he wanted more out of his own life than taking care of his brother and his family. He wanted to have his own family. For a moment, he thought of Anna, but she would want someone younger than him. He would have to look around at the rodeo this year.

Fred quietly stepped into the bunk house. The skunk-smelling Bandit had followed him in and laid down on his rug at the end of his bed. Asleep on the other side of the room, Dave snored as he slept. Fred looked down at his dog, and whispered, "Good nite, Bandit. You stink, buddy. Sleep well." He walked over to his bed, pulled off his boots, undressed, and crawled under the covers. Drained of energy and weary of today's work, he fell asleep quickly.

Over at the main ranch house, Clyde had gone around and checked the fireplace, turned off the lights, and headed towards his bedroom. He had cancelled the night watch on the herd after their long day of branding.

Fred had told him that Anna had taken care of Beth's belongings. As he came into his bedroom, he checked the closet. Her shoes and clothes were gone. On top of the dresser, the blue perfume bottle and her other bottles that stood as sentinels were not there anymore. The drawers were empty. Beth's smell and presence had disappeared.

He went to the bed and took off his boots. Before undressing, he went over to the dresser again and looked into the little wooden jewelry box. Their golden wedding rings were still in the box. He picked both of them up; her diamonds sparkled. He didn't remember them sparkling before. Putting them back into the jewelry box, he closed the lid—closing the pain of the years of marriage.

Finally, he felt himself free from her. His mind, his heart, and his soul felt the relief from the years of hurt, rejection, and loss. His brother was right, and Anna had helped. Pity that such a young woman such as Anna was widowed with four children. As he undressed and crawled under his covers, he thought that he too was a widower. At least, his three sons were grown.

His mind wondered over the last conversations of the day--- Tom working for Hans, Matt playing his guitar, Hans story of the dwarves, Hans wanting cows, and a housekeeper. *What was that all about?* Sleep overtook Clyde as he breathed deeply.

Chapter 30

The Predator

As the sun had dipped behind the mountains, the waxing moon could be seen in the western sky. The crescent was bright. The dark forest had grown silent for the rest of the night as birds and small animals sought their resting places. After the rain the night before, the forest had stayed wet with little sunlight reaching the ground. The smell of decay mixed with wet grass and pine filled the air.

High above in the rugged mountains deep within the forest, the big brown grizzly could smell the burned flesh of the young calves that were miles below in the field. His mouth drooled. He had foraged for green grass and had eaten his fill. Some time ago, he had detected a deer rotting in a mountain creek. That had taken away the hunger pains. As he rubbed his back up against a pine tree and marked his territory, he smelled the burned flesh moving through the forest coming up from below.

He quickly moved towards it. The smell became stronger and stronger as he barreled through the forest. The smell provided him with a beacon that lured him on. Soon, he saw the two calves, eating the fresh grass. Slowly, he stalked towards the smell of fresh meat. He growled low, deep within his throat. His tongue licked the drool coming from his mouth. One of the calves raised its head and scurried away bawling. The other raised its head and froze. That's all he needed—just a pause. Running it down quickly the calf was an easy prey. He tumbled and rolled with the calf in his mouth. Clawing and biting, the grizzly mangled the calf as it bawled and struggled with his little body. Finally, the small calf succumbed to the grizzly.

Tearing open the belly, the grizzly devoured the innards and part of the hind quarter. He sat licking, eating as his hunger slackened. The small bones of the calf crunched under his powerful jaws and teeth. Grabbing the left-over meat in his mouth, he moved higher up into the mountains away from the fields below. He lumbered deeper into the forest with his prey. Finding a couple of old crisscrossed dried out logs, he stashed the left-over calf in the center, covering the meat with leaves and dirt. No magpies or ravens would get his cache. He'd be back to eat another day and finish off his kill.

****

The next day, the early morning had turned the dark skies into grey, lighter behind the mountains where the sun would rise. The brilliant sky turned a reddish orange as the sun rose higher. Heavy fog hung over the river and light mist had settled above the forests. The open ground had dried up by late afternoon yesterday. The puddles in the pasture and on the two-track roads were gone and dried up. Left were the cracked dried out mud.

At the ranch house, Clyde rose and headed out to the barn and stable. Upstairs, Chet had set his alarm to go off before sunrise, so he had gotten up and had dressed. Carrying his bag with him, he went downstairs to the kitchen.

Lying in his bed with his clothes on, Tom heard his brother's alarm go off—buzz, buzz, buzz. He sat up, realizing that he had on his dirty, stinky clothes from branding. *Phew, he stunk like cows and sweat.* He quickly went into the bathroom, undressed, and took a needed shower. As he came downstairs to the big kitchen, Chet had started the bacon. He told him that he would be leaving in a few minutes but wanted to have breakfast at least started. The coffee on the stove had been brewed, filling the kitchen with it rich smell.

Chet went to get a thermos from the pantry. Pouring the coffee into the thermos, he told Tom that he had written down Sophia's phone number and it was on the fridge—just in case they needed to call him. He said he'd be back tomorrow. Looking into the fridge, he saw the leftovers. He took a couple pieces of cold fried chicken and a biscuit. He slipped them into a paper sack along with a few cookies left in the cookie jar. Before he picked up his bag, his lunch, the

364

thermos, he put on his coat over his sheep-skin vest. Saying goodbye, he left the ranch house.

Starting the engine took a few tries; Chet worried that he might need a new battery. After the engine started up, he let it warm up as he reached into the paper sack and ate the two cold pieces of chicken followed by a biscuit. That was his breakfast.

Before leaving the ranch, he saw his dad hitching up the draft horse Jack to the hay wagon. As he drove slowly by, he beeped his horn lightly. He waved goodbye to his dad as Clyde raised his hand goodbye. Pulling onto the highway, his mind shifted to the long, lonely drive he had in front of him. But at the end of it would be Sophia—finally he'd see her again.

As Chet left the ranch, Fred and Bandit had joined Clyde getting ready to feed the herd. He had saddled his buckskin Captain today as he would make a wide sweep up into the forest. Tom had come from the kitchen to milk Sunny. Blue followed behind him as the two dogs met. They sniffed each other, wagged their tails, and chased each other. Bandit smelled better than yesterday.

Earlier that morning, Fred had taken the skunk-smelling Bandit out to the creek over by the little bridge. After he had tried to sleep last night with that awful smell, he decided to try the mouthwash treatment. He had taken his bottle from the bunk house. Down by the creek, he had poured the mouthwash all over the dog, had grabbed him by his four legs, and quickly had dunked him in the creek. Surprisingly, the smell had disappeared from his coat. Bandit had shaken himself all over after the dunking but had seemed happy to get rid of the smell.

As Clyde mounted Captain, Fred called Bandit to jump up onto the hay wagon to ride with him. He patted him on the head and roughed up his body. At least, he didn't smell bad anymore. Taking the reins, he drove the hay wagon out toward the herd. Blue stood watching them leave. He headed back into the barn with Tom who was talking to Sunny as he sat and milked her.

365

Coming closer to the pasture with the herd, the cows were waiting for the hay wagon to get there, bellowing and bawling noisily. Clyde noticed that at the far end of the pasture, a single cow stood with her calf on the other side of the barbed wire fence. *What the hell?* He quickly pressed his heels into Captain as he began to trot and rode around towards the calf who bawled at his mother who responded back with a moo.

Reining his horse to a slow walk, Clyde untied his rope from his saddle. When he rode closer, the calf started to run away. But Captain cut him off. Back and forth Captain kept the calf cornered. He let his horse do his work. A good cutting horse didn't need much directions. After a while, the calf, breathing hard, stood for a few minutes. He lassoed it and dallied his rope around his saddle horn. Tugging the little calf around to the gate, he dismounted. Taking the rope from the horn, he led the calf into the pasture. The calf pulled at the rope when he saw his mother, who mooed at him. He took off the loop around the calf's neck as it took off, loudly bawling toward the cow.

Closing the gate, he mounted and rode towards the hay wagon and Fred who had been throwing out the hay. Fred had watched his brother bring in the calf, so he had taken a few minutes to count their calves. He counted only thirty-nine—missing one. As his brother rode up to the wagon, he told him they were missing a calf. The two discussed what they should do.

They both thought of the grizzly, but neither wanted to say it out loud. They hoped that the lost calf would be up in the forest wandering around. Finally, Clyde rode the fence line and found the place where the calves had gotten out. The nails that had held the barbed wire to the fence post had loosened and fallen off, leaving the barbed wire on the ground. They would have to come back and repair it.

After they would have a quick breakfast, they'd ride back. Driving back to the ranch, Fred with Bandit drove the hay wagon. Unhitching Jack and taking him into the stable, he brushed him down quickly and gave him some grain and water. Clyde left Captain saddled but loosened his cinch, tethered near the water trough.

Back at the ranch house, Matt, Tom, and Dave had finished cooking the bacon, mixed a batch of pancakes, and grilled about six pancakes. They had sat down and had eaten. They now were drinking their coffee while they waited for Clyde and Fred to come in from feeding the herd. When the two came into the kitchen, they told them about the missing calf.

"We'll ride up after breakfast and search the forest above the ranch," said Fred. Both of the older brothers sat down at the kitchen table. Matt got up and cooked six pancakes for his dad and uncle. They piled their plates with the warm pancakes, poured maple syrup over them, and took the rest of the bacon. As they ate their breakfast, everyone sat quietly thinking about the missing calf.

"We need to get ready to drive the herd up to our grazing lands. Before we do, the two mules need new shoes on them. Dave, you're goin' to need to get ready to go with the herd. Today, make a list of food you want us to buy. Gather up your gear. Tomorrow, we'll round the herd up and push them up past that national forest trailhead," said Clyde.

"Sure," said Dave. He looked forward to taking the herd up into the rich, grazing lands above the ranch. The winter pasture where the herd had been would need to be dragged, irrigated this summer, and allowed to grow.

"What about Twister and his little harem of heifers?" asked Tom.

"Twister needs another month with the heifers. Then, we can drive the heifers up to the summer camp," said Clyde.

"Should I ride up with Dave to help him set up camp, dad?" Tom asked.

"No, I think you should call Hans and find out exactly when he wants you. Sounded like he needed you right away, Tom," replied Clyde. His youngest son wanted to be in on everything. He liked his enthusiasm. He was always eager to volunteer.

"I could ride up with Dave," spoke up Matt. Clyde nodded. Maybe Matt had started to change his views about the ranch. But Matt wanted to scout out the area for fishing spots and especially, he wanted to see the summer camp with its little cabin. His dad realized that he thought that they would going directly to the summer camp. He didn't know that they would gradually move the herd up.

"Matt, you know that Dave will be gradually movin' the cows up to the summer camp. The forest has many opened valleys all the way up into the mountains." Then, his dad explained that they'd push the herd into a valley above the ranch, set up the salt blocks near to the herd, and make a camp site with a tent for Dave. The salt blocks would be near a source of water-- a spring, a creek, or a pond. After the herd had eaten down the grass, Dave would them push them higher, moving the salt blocks with him. Finally, he would work his way up to the summer cow camp and the little cabin. His dad finished, and said, "Yes, Matt, you can help him. You can ride up with the supplies for him each week." As he went over the details, Matt understood. He definitely didn't know his dad's grazing plans for the herd.

"You should take Bandit with you, Dave. He knows you from sleepin' in the bunk. I'll be goin' on the rodeo circuit in a few days. He's good to have with the herd---both to manage and to guard," added Fred. He would miss taking his dog on the trip, but he thought that Dave would need him more up there than he did. His dog was showing his age. Rodeoing would be too unsettling for Bandit.

"Let's go, Fred. We'll ride out and find out what happened to our calf," said Clyde, standing. Joining his brother, they headed out to the stable. Fred saddled his horse Chief. Both men had their rifles loaded and in the scabbards. Clyde went into the tack shed and picked up some tools and nails to repair the barbed wire fence.

Matt and Dave left the kitchen to work on the mules, putting on new horseshoes. They would need to file down their hooves and put the new shoes on them. Tom stayed and did the dishes since it was his turn. He said that he'd drive into town later and pick up any supplies that Dave needed.

The two older brothers rode out to the pasture. Fixing the dropped barbed wire didn't take long. The two mounted their horses and rode into the forest, making several sweeps of the area above the field. With the dog running ahead of them, Bandit found the blood-soaked ground and a few remains where the calf had been taken down. The magpies had been pecking and fighting over the remains. Bandit chased them away, barking at them. Dismounting, Clyde and Fred walked around the area looking for any tracks. They found the grizzly's huge paw marks not far from the kill. Shaking their heads, they were disheartened at losing a calf. More importantly, they would have to go back to the night watch again. One night away from guarding their herd resulted in losing a calf.

Chapter 31

The Graduation

Driving for about two hours, Chet's strained eyes had been glued to the highway in front of him. The sun had risen higher above the mountains. The warmth had cleared away the low-lying fog along the river. As he drove south along the river, he pulled down his visor to shade his eyes. His white pickup seemed to fly down the road towards Sophia.

Coming into the Blue Ridge Canyon, he noticed the brilliant green hills lining the sides of the canyon. At the turnout with the picnic tables, he stopped to stretch his legs and have a few cookies with coffee from his thermos. He walked down towards the wide river flowing next to the road. As he stood on its bank, he could smell the dark blue-green river—a mossy wet smell. The deep river had huge granite boulders of all shapes and sizes scattered along its banks. They had tumbled down centuries before from the rocky ridges high above. Some were sitting in the slow-moving river with moss clinging to their round surfaces under the water.

Looking high up into the narrow, sharp blue sky above the canyon, he gazed at a bald eagle soaring above the rocky cliffs. With its wide wings turning against the wind, the giant eagle landed on the edge of a big brown nest—the eyrie. He could see the various sticks and branches piled high sitting on top of a steep, rocky ledge. With something in its talons, the eagle looked to be feeding its young. Chet felt its powerful presence high above him as his soul imagined the spiritual soaring at being so high above the earth.

Turning, he sat down thinking how grateful to be living close to nature. The warm coffee from his thermos filled his mouth and the cookies filled his stomach. Finishing, he strolled back to his white pickup. Through the rest of the Blue Ridge Canyon, he drove its narrow-paved road, around its many tight curves, and through the darken rock tunnels. The traffic had been lighter early in the morning but had become heavier as the day went on. He had to slow down as he followed a line of cars through the canyon.

After leaving the canyon, the prairies opened wide and were filled with miles of sagebrush and grass. Around the ranches and farmhouses, rows of big old cottonwood trees stood, bent a little from the wind. Hours later, he finally arrived in the college town of Birch which had the only state university. The crowded town had narrow streets, and as he drove closer to the campus, large trees lined the streets. Looking up, he saw the tall white dormitories rising above the streets.

Sophia told him to call her when he got into town. He pulled into a gas station, filled up his pickup, and paid. Outside, a pay phone booth sat on one side of the station. Walking over to it, he picked up the receiver, dropped in a coin, heard the dial tone, and dialed her number. Waiting, the phone rang and rang. Then, he heard her sweet voice say, "Hello."

"Hi, Sophia. It's Chet."

"Oh. I'm so glad you are here. I've been worried about you. It is such a long drive. When did you leave?" she asked.

"Before dawn. Give me some directions. I am at this gas station near the tall dorms," he said.

"No...no. You stay there. You are close to the gym, so I'll drive over and meet you there. My parents are here staying at my apartment. We'll be there in about ten minutes," she said.

"Okay. I'll pull over to the side of the station. Goodbye," he said.

"Yes, see you soon," she answered. The phone went dead as he hung up the receiver.

He had a few minutes, so he decided to use the station's restroom, to freshen up and change his shirt. He parked his white pickup over by the side of the station. Taking in his bag into the restroom, he first washed his face and hands. Then, he took off his sheep-skinned vest and his blue-plaid

371

western shirt. He reached into his bag and pulled out a
freshly ironed white shirt with a few wrinkles in it after
being in the bag. He slipped the white shirt on and buttoned
it up. Under the collar, he added a bolo tie with clasp of
turquoise stones that Fred had lent him. He slipped on his
sheep-skinned vest again. He didn't want to wear his well-
worn ranch jacket to this fancy affair. His cowboy boots had
been polished the night before. His jeans were clean but
were a little worn. To him, he looked fine.

Looking into the mirror over the little sink, he pulled out
a comb. He ran the comb through his thick dark brown hair,
parting it on the side and sweeping his hair into place.
Finally, he reached and pulled out a small bottle of pine
scented after-shave. He splashed a little on his cheeks and
neck. Folding his blue-plaid shirt, he put it in the bag.
Walking out to his white pickup, he waited for Sophia's red
and white Bel Air. He had never been to a college
graduation, so he didn't know what to expect. He figured
it'd be similar to a high school graduation. He nervously
thought about her parents, meeting them for the first time.
What would they think of him?

Coming into the station, Sophia drove up in her red and
white car and parked next to Chet's pickup. He got out of
his pickup as she too jumped out of her car. They met in
front of their vehicles. He looked at her in her black
graduation gown, her blonde hair cut short again, and her
smiling lips.

He reached out his arms to her as she moved into his
broad chest, hugging each other. They stayed together as
their hearts soared. She could smell a fresh pine smell as she
leaned into him. Pulling back, he breathed and said, "Hi,
Sophia. You look so pretty. I've missed you." His dark
brown eyes roamed over her lovely face as she smiled and
blushed a little.

"Hi, Chet. Yeah. Let's go. Follow me. After we park, I'll
introduce you to my parents," she said as she nodded her
head towards her car.

"Sure. I'll follow you," he said. They got into their
vehicles and he followed her to a huge parking lot near to an

enormous gymnasium. Stepping out of their vehicles, Sophia introduced her parents, Art and Wanda Schmitz, to Chet. The men shook hands. Her dad Art stood under six-feet tall, a thin man with wavy blonde hair and greying sides. Small like Sophia, her mom Wanda, short and plump, had light brown hair. She smiled brightly at this tall, broad-shouldered man. They were friendly in their manners, making Chet feel at ease. Sophia said she had to go get in line, but they should go through the front doors and find a seat in the bleachers.

"We'll meet back here when the ceremony is over. Chet stay with them. I'll see you all later," said Sophia as she started toward another entrance to line up.

"Okay," said Art. "Guess we're on our own. We'll take pictures after she graduates, dear. Leave the camera here." She nodded and slipped the camera into a bag in the back seat of Sophia's car. Locking the doors, Art and Wanda started to walk towards the big doors of the gym. Chet walked beside them. As they walked through the doors with the crowd of people, they were handed a program outlining the ceremony and listing the graduates separated by their degrees and major fields of study. With the crowd, they shuffled slowly into the gym, up the stairs, and into the bleachers.

Finding empty seats about halfway up the bleachers, the three sat down. The seats were filling up fast around them as people moved up into the bleachers. In the gym, the loud voices created a huge sound echoing up through the rafters. Chet didn't like noisy crowds like this; he preferred the quiet solitude of the ranch and the mountains. Eventually, people were sitting beside him, behind and in front of him. He was surrounded. The still air began to get warm and stuffy with all those people crammed into this gym.

Chet kept his eyes on the program, looking through it to find Sophia's name. Her mom sat next to him, trying to engage him in small talk, but the noise level was so loud he could barely hear her soft voice. He just smiled at her and nodded his head, hoping that he hadn't hurt her feelings for not talking. Finally, she gave up and looked through her program. They waited and they waited.

After a while, the band began to play the graduation marching song. Everyone stood up as the long lines of black robed graduates with their square graduating caps filed into their rows and rows of folding chairs on the main ground floor. Once the program began, the distinguished speakers droned on as they delivered their speeches. Afterwards, the graduating students filed up and received their degrees as their names were announced, crossing the stage. Friends and family members called out, excited to see their loved one get his or her degree.

Chet scanned the black robes for Sophia. He didn't see her until she stood and walked slowly in line toward the stage. She looked so small in that sea of black gowns and black caps. Flashes of the camera bulbs captured the students shaking hands with the college dignitaries. Sophia kept her eyes looking forward while other students were trying to find their families in the huge audience stacked up on the bleaches above them.

Chet watched her step up to the stage, receive her degree, shook hands, and walked off the stage. She was all business as her parents and he watched her. Excited, Sophia breathed a big sigh as she filed back to her seat. As she moved slowly back, she thought of him sitting above in the bleachers and her heart skipped a beat. *He had come to her graduation.* She was more excited about seeing him than receiving her degree. Now that she had graduated, her mind filled with thoughts of them being together. She didn't know her future, but she wanted him to be part of it.

Time went on as more students received their various degrees. The bleachers were becoming hard as the time turned into hours. Finally, they were finished. Next, the turning of the tassel came as the students yelled and threw their black caps into the air. Chaos ensued as the graduates hugged each other. Eventually, the band struck up another marching song as everyone stood while the graduates filed out.

Anxious to leave, Chet wanted to get out of there, but Art said to wait until most of the people had left. They sat for a while longer until the bleachers were almost empty. They then left the gym, walked to their car, and waited for Sophia. She came walking with her cap off but her gown still on. Her mom started talking about taking some pictures. Sophia had to put her cap back on. Chet stood back while the three of them took different shots of their daughter. Finally, her mom asked him to take a picture of the three of them. And Sophia wanted one with Chet, so he posed with her while her mom shot the picture. Her mom said she'd get him a picture of the two of them. Even though her mom wanted to take more pictures, Art suggested that they leave—enough pictures. He said he was hungry. Chet heard that the two women had prepared a little lunch for them at Sophia's apartment.

Leaving the parking lot, Sophia drove with her parents while Chet followed her back to her apartment. As they parked in front of the four-plex, he noticed that many of the occupants were packing up. Young people were loading their opened cars doors and trunks with their belongings. Her place was on the bottom left. With keys, she opened the door and they walked into an apartment in disarray. Boxes and a few suitcases were sitting around the small living room with piles of bedding and pillows.

"Sorry for the mess, Chet. But my roommate is leaving today, and I am packing up and leaving tomorrow," explained Sophia. She had taken off her black robe, kicked off her black heels, and grabbed a red sweater that sat on the couch. She had on a beautiful shiny white blouse with a black pencil skirt. To Chet who hadn't seen in her in two weeks, she looked gorgeous. Picking up her heels, her gown, and the red sweater, she said she needed to change. She'd be back in a minute.

"Please, sit down, Chet. We'll get something to eat in a minute. Dad, go ahead and make your call," his daughter said as she headed into her bedroom. Chet sat down on the couch while her dad went over, pulled out a high stool, and picked up the receiver of a phone sitting on a small lunch counter. As he dialed the number, he explained, "I have to check to see if I have any service calls." He sat down on the stool. He then said, "Hello, Ruby, this is Art. Do I have any calls?"

Wanda had gone into the small kitchen and was getting down plates and cups. She looked over at Chet, and quietly said, "Do you drink coffee or tea?"

"Either. Whatever you are fixin' will be fine," he answered.

"Sophia likes coffee in the morning, but tea in the afternoon," she said. She had a tea kettle in her hand as she filled it and put it on the little stove.

Art listened on the phone for a few minutes, and said, "Thanks. We'll be leavin' in an hour and I'll be there by five. Will that work? Bye." He had jotted down some information on a small tablet next to the phone. Tearing off the note, he slipped it into his pocket.

Looking at his wife, he said, "I've got a service call. We'll have to eat and run."

"What, dad? Aren't you staying?" asked Sophia, coming in from her bedroom. Changed, she had on a sweater—a blue turtle-neck—and a pair of black slacks with a pair of brown loafers.

"Sorry, angel… But you know how the plumbin' business is. You go when you get a call," Art said as he gave his daughter a little hug as she stood next to him. "Don't frown. This is your day. We're so proud of you. Let's eat." Art adored and loved his daughter. Graduating from college was her dream. Both parents had supported her. She was their only child.

Wanda had finished setting the plates, silverware, and cups out on the counter. The four could not all sit around the little table, so they split up in twos—mom and dad at the kitchen table with Chet and Sophia on the stools at the counter. Wanda pulled out a hot macaroni and cheese casserole from the oven putting it on a hot pad on the counter. Sophia walked over to the little fridge and pulled out a bowl of green lettuce salad with a bottle of salad dressing. With their plates, they each dished up the casserole and salad. Sophia forgot the bread, so she went to the cupboard and brought the loaf with butter to set on the counter.

"Chet, sorry, but this place is so small," said Sophia, apologizing.

"It's fine. The lunch looks delicious," he said as he dished up his plate and took a piece of bread. He walked around and sat on one of the stools. They were all hungry after the long graduation ceremony. The tea kettle whistled. Wanda rose and turned off the stove, pulling out two tea bags from a small box in the cupboard.

Art looked at Chet and asked, "Would you want a beer with me? There's a six-pack in the fridge." He nodded, "Sure," as Art stood, stepped to the little fridge, and pulled out two bottles of premium beer. With an opener from a drawer, he popped off the caps. Handing him a beer, he stood with his bottle raised, and said, "Cheers." Chet raised his bottle. The cold liquid felt good as they swallowed. He would have had tea, but the beer was better.

Wanda had poured her and her daughter water for a cup of tea. They settled down again and ate their meal. Since they were in such a small space, they talked easily among themselves. Her parents asked Chet questions about his drive here, about his family, and about his ranch. As they talked and ate, he noticed that her dad Art was casual and relaxed while her mom Wanda was more poised and mannerly. He could see that Sophia got her grace and good manners from her mom. But they were both friendly.

Evidently, Sophia had filled them in how they had met, had called each other, and had told them of her visit to his family's ranch. After she returned from her visit, she couldn't stop talking about the beauty of the mountains and of the many horses. Of course, they helped pay their daughters bills, so they knew that her phone bills were higher since she had met this cowboy Chet. They didn't know how this affair would work out. Her dad had his reservations about this young man who lived on a ranch so far away. For Wanda, as long as her daughter was happy, that's what counted to her. As they finished their lunch, Art

377

said they best get on the road and back to Scottsville before five tonight. Wanda started to put everything away, but Sophia told her that she'd take care of cleaning up.

In a few minutes, they had their coats on, said 'goodbye,' 'happy to meet him,' and then they were gone. After they had left, Chet sat back down on his stool and had another helping of the casserole. She took a long breath and sat down on her stool next to him. He noticed that she hadn't eaten much. She was sipping her tea.

"Eat Sophia," said Chet as he ate.

Looking at his empty beer, she asked, "Do you want another beer?"

"Sure. Sit and finish your lunch. I can get it," he said as he stood. He walked behind her on the stool and put his arms on her shoulders. He leaned down and brushed his lips against her cheek. "You look beautiful, Sophie." She looked up at him and smiled. He continued to the little fridge and pulled out a bottle of beer. "Do you want one?" She shook her head, "No, maybe later." He found the opener in the drawer, popped off the lid, and came back to the stool. He took again a long drink of the cold liquid. His plate was nearly empty; she still had nearly a full plate. Turning to her, he scooted his seat closer to her; his legs were stretched out with her sitting on the stool between them.

He took her hand in his, he said, "Talk to me, Sophie. You know I'm a good listener." He stroked her soft hand, looking at her long, pink fingernails. Something was bothering her; he could tell by her voice.

"Oh, I've been a bundle of nerves with graduation, packing, and moving," she said. He waited for her to go on. "I'm sorry, but I can't come back with you tomorrow like we planned. I have to pack and move back home. My roommate will be coming back here soon to load her things today. We're checking out, so there's a long list of things to do. Just a lot of stuff all at once."

"Oh…. Will you come later?" he asked. Bottom line, he wanted to know if she was still coming to stay for a few days. He knew she could handle the rest. "Sophie, I'm glad to be here with you. Graduation was long, but it's great that you have your degree. By the way, I liked your parents. They're nice. I don't know what they think about me, but it doesn't matter. It's you I care about."

His past affairs had changed him. He wanted to establish a solid relationship with Sophia. His desires wanted him to rush ahead and ravish her, but he held back. He'd take this slow and get to know her—really know her. He loved being around her.

As they talked, she relaxed more, picked up her fork, and ate her lunch. He wanted to see her eat, so many times he had watched his mom skip many meals. And then, she would get depressed. She'd lose weight and would look frail. He didn't want Sophia to go down that path.

While she ate, she talked about how her parents had planned to take them out to dinner that night. But her dad's business was vital to him. She went on to tell Chet that she had set up the books for her dad, had helped him with his inventory, and had helped him make business projections.

To him, it sounded interesting, so he asked, "Did your college help?"

"Oh...yes, my business courses gave me the skills to help my dad. He went under when he first started his business years ago. He did odd jobs while we lived on my mom's salary. Then, she put in for a teaching position in Scottsville. When we moved there, he started up another business there. I was older and my schooling helped. We put our heads together. I've helped him bring in a steady income from his plumbing business," she explained. She was proud of her dad.

"That's great. I'm takin' care of the books for our ranch. You could probably give me tips about doin' it. It's a lot of work. I spend most of my nights pourin' over the numbers," he said.

"Oh. It can be complicated, but I enjoy working with numbers," she answered.

Recalling her friends wanted to get together, she asked, "My graduating buddies are meeting at the Wild Goose Bar. Would you want to go? This will be the last time that we'll see each other. Many of them are going on to jobs. Some are going on to begin their masters at other universities."

"Yeah, sure. I'd like to go out with you," he answered. She obviously wanted to go out to celebrate. He would want to go out too if he had just finished a four-year degree. But for Chet, there never had been the money for college. He had never thought much about it until he had met Sophia. Being a wrangler and working with livestock had been his future. He loved and enjoyed that life.

As she finished eating her lunch, she sipped the last of her tea, wiped her lips, and turned her body towards him. Coming off the stool, she stepped into him and put her arms on his shoulders. One hand went up to his dark brown hair as she fingered his hair on the top and down the sides of his head. Both hands went to the bolo tie with the turquoise that he had cinched up to the top button of his white shirt.

"Let me see, how does this tie work... mmmm... this has an unusual setting," she said looking closely at it. She slid the clasp down to the metal tipped ends.

"Yeah. It's a bear's claw. See the five parallel stones, each one longer than the next. They represent the claws," he explained. His heart was pounding in his chest as he thought of her so close to him with her warm body and her short blonde hair framing her lovely face.

She frowned at the thought of a bear. "Why would you wear something like this? Bear claws?"

"It's just a tie and not even mine. It's my uncle's. If you don't like it, I can take it off," he answered. He didn't understand why she didn't like it, but he took it off and set it down on the counter. "There. Is that better?"

"Yes, much. I just don't like the thought of bear claws and your neck. I hear they are dangerous. Are there bears near your ranch?" she asked.

"From time to time, there have been bears above our ranch in the mountains.... But, let's get back to us," he said wanting to avoid talking about the bears, particularly about a certain grizzly.

She first unbuttoned the top button of his shirt, the second button, and finally, the third. There, she could see his neck and the top of his white t-shirt. She leaned in and kissed his neck; she smelled fresh pine. She moved up to his lips, lightly touching his lips with hers. He had his hands on her small waist which naturally sought out her soft skin under her blue sweater. One hand slipped up to her firm round breast and one hand moved along her soft skin to her back. Pulling her into him, he returned her kiss. Her lips opened and he felt her small tongue seek out his. A hint of spice from her tea touched his mouth. They passionately kissed. Goosebumps went all over her. His heart was pounding, and his mind emptied as his desire took him deeper into thoughts of her.

BANG. Her front door flew opened with a loud thud. In a protective move, he jumped up quickly and pushed her behind him. Sophia straightened her blue turtleneck sweater, poked her head around and called out, "Martha? What's wrong?" Her roommate held her mouth with her hand. Behind her, a guy walked in, concerned about her.

"I need the bathroom quick..." she rushed into the bathroom off of the small living room. The door was opened as they watched her retch into the toilet. She went down to her knees and put her head in the toilet again with several dry heaves. Sophia thought *Oh, Martha. I knew that you were pregnant.*

The guy looked at Chet and said, "Hi, I'm Harvey. You must be Chet. I'll take care of her, Sophia." He rushed in to help her. Turning on the water faucet, he filled a glass and held it out to her. She moaned into the toilet. He closed the door to the bathroom. They could hear him consoling her through the closed door.

Looking at him, Sophia said, "Maybe, we should leave them. Harvey's with her. They are getting married. My other friends should be down at the bar by now." He nodded at her. "Let me put the dishes in the sink before we leave." She picked up all of their empty plates and put them in the kitchen sink. Taking the casserole, she covered it and put it in the small fridge. The salad bowl was empty. She took a washcloth and wiped the small table clean. The dirty dishes could wait.

Finally finished, he helped her with her jacket as she picked up a small clutch purse setting on the counter. He slipped on his vest and buttoned up his shirt. Before leaving he picked up the bolo tie and slipped it into his vest's pocket. He wanted to make sure he returned this to his uncle who said this was his best bolo tie. When he went rodeoing, the girls always liked his tie. Chet wouldn't be wearing it again.

They took his white pickup and she gave him directions that took them to the crowded downtown streets. Every parking place along both sides of the street was filled. Seeing the Wild Goose Bar, he pulled up and told her to go on in that he would drive around the block and find a place to park. She jumped out and said she'd wait for him inside. Driving around the block, he found a place to park, not far from the bar on a side street.

Walking towards the bar, he noticed that the temperature had dropped. Leaving his ranch coat in the pickup, he walked quickly toward the bar, chilled by the cold night. He could see his breath as he hurried along. He thought about the ranch and wondered how things were going. He felt lost in this crowded college town with its narrow streets and vehicles everywhere. But he had been happy seeing Sophia and having her in his arms. He couldn't get enough of her. He hoped that they would have some more private time together later tonight. The roommate worried him. *Would the two be there tonight? No, she said that Martha was leaving.*

He stepped into the smoke-filled, loud, crowded Wild Goose Bar. He looked for Sophia; he saw her surrounded by her friends to the left of the door. A guy had his arm around Sophia as he smiled at her. Seeing Chet, she waved for him to come over, slipping out of the guy's arms. Chet got a glimpse of him as he looked back. A flash of jealousy went through Chet at seeing Sophia in the arms of another guy. He worked his way through the crowds until he finally came up to her. Introductions were made but he couldn't hear their names. They seemed to know him, and the guys shook his hand. Looking at the guy who had his arms around

Sophia, Chet seemed to feel a definite dislike emanating from him. Standing a head above all of them, Chet tried to hear the guy's name. But the noisy bar made it impossible to hear. Sophia worked her way over beside him. Putting his arm around her, he gave her a squeeze, and she wrapped her warm arm around his waist.

"Let's get a table and some drinks," said one of her friends. He led them toward the back. Almost in single file, they moved through the crowd. Coming to a round table, a group was just standing up to leave, saying they were going to go to another bar. Sophia's friends took the table and they all sat down. A barmaid came around to clear the empty pitchers and mugs. As she loaded her tray, one guy told her to bring a pitcher of beer. Another guy handed her some money and said, "Bring us your best bottle of tequila with shot glasses." *Tequila?* Chet thought, these college guys have taste for shit. He decided to go easy on the liquor. He had a long drive home tomorrow and he didn't want to start out with a hangover. Besides, the last time he was with Sophia he had been drunk. He wanted a clearer head tonight.

The barmaid came back with a bottle of tequila, shot glasses, cut up lemons and limes, and a couple of saltshakers. The guy who paid for the bottle, opened it, and started filling the shot glasses as the others passed them around. The girls chose not to drink the tequila, so one of the shot glasses ended up in front of Chet. He took it in his fingers and looked at the golden liquor that tasted like piss and bit like a snake. The dish of limes and lemons sat in the middle of the table. The guys raised their shot glasses, waiting for him to join them. He nodded, picked up the nasty shot, and chucked it down as the others did the same. This was smoother than he thought—a different kind of tequila.

The barmaid came with the pitcher of draft beer with mugs. One of guys started pouring beer for the girls. Sophia got a mug as she took a sip. The cold liquid felt good on her dry throat. Glancing at Chet, she was happy that he had come out with her to celebrate with her college friends.

383

They were all different individuals from other states with a variety of backgrounds. They were an interesting group since they had created a study group through their four years here. Chet signaled to the barmaid to bring another pitcher and handed her some money. He wanted to drink a beer instead of the tequila.

Her friends talked among themselves about their future plans and when they were leaving. Chet scooted his chair nearer to Sophia and put his arm behind her on the back of her chair. He wanted to pull her into his lap, but she sat with her back straight, poised in front of her friends. Every once in a while, her hand would go to her lap. Finally, she slid her hand over to his thigh. She rested it there for a few minutes and then she squeezed his thigh with her warm hand. Her touch drove him crazy. He wanted to leave, but just then, the barmaid brought his pitcher of draft beer and a mug. Chet looked up at the smiling barmaid and told her to keep the change. She winked at him to say 'thanks' and pocketed the change as her tip.

Filling his mug and topping off Sophia's mug, he handed the pitcher to the others who wanted more beer. The guys were on their second round of tequila, but he shook his head as they filled their shot glasses. He had flipped his shot glass over; he hoped they wouldn't be offended. They didn't seem to mind as they chucked down another shot. They were celebrating and probably be here for a while—at least until the bottle was empty. Chet and Sophia sat, drinking their beer, and holding hands under the table. He had taken her hand in his and stroked the top of her hand across her small knuckles. She had such soft, small hands. Her sharp, long pink fingernails poked his palm every once in a while. Everyone was talking to each other, but Chet sat silently, looking at Sophia, her short blonde hair bounced as she spoke.

Turning her head to him, her brown eyes showed a question, she whispered, "Do you want to go?"

He just nodded his head slightly. He was ready to leave after the tequila shot an hour ago. She made her excuses to leave, said her goodbyes, and stood up as she slipped on her jacket. He stood up and said, "Thanks for the drinks. It was nice meetin' you. Good luck in your future plans." While they were leaving, he heard them speak about him. He heard 'he's seems nice' and 'where did she meet him?' and 'he's a real cowboy.' The comments didn't bother him since he knew he didn't fit into their college world. He couldn't wait to get out of this crowded bar and town. He had noticed the well-jacketed fraternity guys among her friends, especially the one who had his arm around Sophia. Yes, he'd take the solitude of his ranch any time to this world.

The two finally found the front door. They left as the two stepped out together with their arms wrapped together. In the cold night air, he guided her down the sidewalk and turned down onto the side street where his white pickup sat. Opening the door, she stepped up into the cold pickup. He went around to his side and stepped up and sat behind the steering wheel. Turning the key, the engine again took a few tries before it turned over and started. He revved it a couple of times and then let it idle. He turned the knob on the radio, seeking a station for them to listen to some music.

"What's wrong with your pickup?" she asked. She had to keep her car running for four years so she knew that problems could arise with cars.

"I might need a new battery. But it'll be fine. I should be okay," he answered her. He pulled out of the parking place; she gave him a few directions on the way to her apartment. Stopping in front of her apartment, he parked with the motor running. The radio played a hit song by Elvis Presley, one of her favorites. He waited until the song ended.

Glancing at her, he quietly asked, "Should I get a motel room, Sophia?" He didn't want to force her into a situation she didn't want. In the past, he wouldn't have asked—like with Lois, Anna, and Betsy. He wasn't going to repeat the past. Sophia was not a one-night stand for him. She wasn't a widow with four kids. She wasn't a divorcee with abuse issues. And the murdered Betsy still stung hidden within his soul. All those affairs had put him in a bad situation and affected him deeply. They had changed him. With her college degree alone, she was different—beautiful and ready for life. He wanted her to be with him.

"No...Chet. You couldn't get a motel room, anyway. The motels are filled," she answered as she moved nearer to him. She put her hand on his thigh again. He slipped his arm around her.

"But where would I be sleepin' if your parents hadn't left?" he asked.

"With us, in the apartment. Martha planned on loading up this afternoon. Her bedroom would have been empty for my parents. And, if you wanted, we could have had my bedroom. If not, there would be the couch," she explained.

"But what about your parents? What would they think about us sleepin' together?" he asked.

"Yeah... well.... with my dad, you'd probably be sleepin' on the couch tonight if they hadn't left," she replied as she smiled at him. Even though it was dark, the lights from his dash showed her blush. She moved towards him as he moved towards her. They kissed. He looked into her brown eyes as he wanted to know if she wanted him.

"Should we go in?" he asked. She nodded as he turned off the engine. He came around and helped her out of the pickup. With her keys, she opened the apartment door. Turning on the switch, the place looked empty—the boxes and stuff were gone. As she said, her roommate had moved out. There was a note written on the outside of an envelope with a set of keys setting on the counter. Sophia picked up the keys and the envelope, looking inside.

"Oh...she left me some money to cover cleaning the place. She comes with money, so she has helped pay for groceries and just about everything. I told you that she and Harvey decided to marry. He still has a year left, so I don't know what her plans are. I hate to see her drop out without finishing her degree, but it happens," said Sophia after reading her note and looking at the money. She slipped the envelope with the money into her small clutch purse.

Going into the little kitchen, she asked Chet, "Do you want another beer? Dad, left it for us."

386

"Okay," he said as he waited. She took out two bottles, opened them, and brought them over to him. She switched off the overhead light and turned on a lamp. Sitting together on the couch, she cuddled up, slipping her brown loafers off. He put his arms around her. They sat silently and drank their beer.

She bowed her head and took a deep breath. *How to tell him?* "Chet, I need to tell you something about me. . . ah...I've never been with anyone," she whispered, a little embarrassed but wanted him to know. "I've kept myself buried in my studies. Yes, I've dated and been out...but never ..." She left those final words unsaid.

Looking at her, Chet opened his eyes wide at her. He couldn't believe what she had just told him. But he recalled her shyness when they first met. He had been too drunk to catch it. Now it came down on him like a lightning strike right to his gut. *My god, she had been so open with him, kissing and touching him. He'd never thought that she was so innocent.* Taking their beer bottles, he set them on the coffee table in front of the couch. Moving closer to her, he pulled her tighter into him. He breathed in the sweet smell of her hair.

While she leaned in against his muscled chest, she sought out his warm skin under his white shirt. She pulled it up, slipping her warm hands under his t-shirt. Stroking his chest, her hands moved down to his firm stomach and around to his back. Her touch sent his mind spinning. *How does he tell her that he's been with others? Should he tell her?* He wanted to be open and honest with her—to tell her about Lois, about Elizabeth.

"Sophia is that why you were so nervous earlier. I'll sleep on the couch. We don't have to take this any further. But I want to tell you though that I've been with others," he said quietly.

"Yes, I've been a bundle of nerves. But have you been with anyone since you've met me?" she asked.

"No...no. but I want to tell you," he whispered back.

"Right now, I don't care.... Come on, Chet. We've got this night to ourselves," she said as she continued to move against him. She moved over, straddled him, and settled down into his lap. Her fingernails dug into his back. With her head above him, he looked up at her. One of her hands moved along his waistline to his firm stomach. Her hand started to move lower, but he took her hand and held it in his. He pulled her closer to him. He couldn't resist her much longer. He tried to say something, but she covered his mouth with a kiss. She deep throated him with her tongue. He moaned.

She whispered in his ear, "No more talk….come on."

"Are you sure, Sophia? …. I have protection….slow down, Sophie …. Soph…," as he tried to talk to her. She kept kissing him between his words. She ground her hips against him, stirring both their desires. His mind emptied and his desires took over.

She breathed heavily and whispered back, "yes… yes, I'm sure…" He stood up. With her legs wrapped around his waist, he held her tight against him as he moved toward her bedroom. Stopping in the hall, she indicated her bedroom to the right. He managed to close the door and turned the lock. She pulled back and looked at him with a question in her eyes.

She had a puzzled look on her face. He softly whispered, "I don't want anyone openin' this door while I'm kissin' you again." She sweetly laughed as she recalled that her roommate Martha and Harvey had burst in on them earlier. Walking slowly over to her soft bed, he gently laid her down as he slipped in beside her. The dark room surrounded them. As they kissed, their passions rose into a whirlwind of desires as they made love.

In the living room, the lamp casted a little yellow light into the dark apartment. The two half-filled bottles of premium beer sat on the coffee table. In the small kitchen, the dirty dishes sat in the sink. The little fridge turned off and on throughout the night. Outside of the apartment and down at the local bars, the college crowds continued to party through the wee hours of the night.

388

Chapter 32

Summer Grazing Lands

The early May rose-colored dawn brightened the grey sky with a cool breeze blowing down into the valley where the Battle Axe Ranch sat. The warm spring days brought out the purple buds of the lilac bushes along the north side of the log ranch house. Birds chirped, robins hopped along the ground looking for worms, and the herd bellowed and mooed, waiting for the hay wagon to bring their morning feed. After breakfast that day, the herd would be rounded up and driven out of the pasture into the grazing lands above their ranch.

Waking up rested, Clyde dressed and headed out to the stable to hitch up Jack and the hay wagon. Fred and Bandit came out of the bunk house, bundled up against the cool morning breeze. As he guided Captain out of his stall, Fred noticed that he was limping. When he stopped, he held up his right hoof. He noticed that his horse did not want to put any weight on that right hoof. Wanting to take a look, he moved his hand down his horse's leg and said, "What's goin' on Captain?" He lifted up the hoof and saw a small, rock stuck in the sole of the hoof. Taking out his pocketknife, he quickly flicked it loose. The end of it had a sharp point that had buried itself into the soft flesh. A little blood came pouring out of the wound. "There, that should be better."

He turned Captain around and put him back into his stall. Walking over to get a bucket of water, he came back to his horse and cleaned the wound made by the tiny rock. Walking over to the tack shed, he came back with a bottle of disinfectant that he applied. He cleaned out the stall and threw in some fresh hay. He said, "Rest, today, and let that wound heal. I'll check it again tonight."

He went down the way and stopped in front of the roan stallion Legend's stall. He neighed at him and snorted. Legend was a grey and white roan with a dark mane and tail. He had a lot of spirit in him and Fred liked that. In the last few weeks, he had been training him and wanted to work him more today. He decided to saddle him and ride him.

Slipping on a bridle, he spoke to Legend, "Now, listen up. I want you to behave yourself. Don't make a fool out of yourself. You're goin' to get a chance to show me what you're made of. This is your day." Legend listened to this man who seemed to know him. As he guided him out of the stall, the older horse stamped and pranced around. "Easy, boy. We're not ready to go yet."

As Fred saddled him, Legend stood waiting for his chance to run. Clyde had already left with the hay wagon, so he mounted and turned the stallion toward the pasture and said, "Let's go, Legend."

The horse felt the pressure on both of his sides and the words that told him to go. He trotted for a while and then moved into a full gallop. Fred stood up in his stirrups and let Legend have the reins. This older horse had powerful legs and enough spirit to ride all the way to the edge of the timber. Pulling him gently up with the reins, he slowed him down to a trot and then to a walk. Moving the reins against his roan's neck along with a gentle pressure of his left heel, he guided the horse to the left. Then, he did the same but to the right side, the horse went right. He kept doing that a couple of more times. Easily, Legend responded to the reins and the pressure of Fred's legs.

As Fred noticed that his brother was still feeding the herd, he headed the roan stallion into the forest. He made a wide circle, looking for tracks or signs of their grizzly. The roan moved through the pine trees, around the big rocks and the downed timber. The forest sounded alive with birds chirping and small animals scurrying under the shrubbery. With the warm spring, the insects and flies were buzzing above his head. Legend's black tail swatted flies landing on him. He stopped at a creek, dismounted, and let Legend drink while he crouched down and cupped the icy, cold water into his mouth. He looked along the wet banks for bear claw marks or other tracks. He saw deer and small game tracks.

Mounting Legend, he rode parallel to their pastures. Their ride covered a lot of area, from the flat forested ground to a few gullies, flowing with the melting snowpack. Down one side through the cold water and up the other side, Fred rode. Coming down to the pastures again, he gave the roan stallion the signal to go—trotting into a full gallop. The old horse had a good stride. Riding closer to the ranch, he slowed him to a trot and walked him down the dirt road towards the stable. Snorting, Legend breathed hard after the run. Bandit came running up to Fred and the horse. Clyde watched his brother ride in with the roan stallion. He asked, "Did you find any tracks, Fred?"

"No...but that grizzly could be up there, and I wouldn't have seen him. Maybe he had his fill with our calf and moved on. We can only hope," he answered as he dismounted. "Legend did well. I might take him and Jinx with me on the rodeo circuit. Captain came up lame from a sharp rock."

"Oh? We'll have to watch that he doesn't get infection," said Clyde. He didn't want to call the vet and have another bill to pay, but he didn't want to lose Fred's horse either.

Before going over to the ranch house for breakfast, Fred tied the roan near the water trough, uncinched the strap under the saddle. He walked into the stable and came back out with a bucket of grain for the older horse. "Here, Legend. Eat and fill your belly. I'm ridin' you today." The roan put his head into the bucket and muzzled the grain into his mouth as he chewed. He stroked the roan's neck and mane. After he finished the grain, he moved around and checked each of his hooves, cleaning out the debris from the forest. Finally, he took the bucket back into the stable and headed to the ranch for breakfast.

The big kitchen smelled of fresh coffee. With Chet gone to see Sophia's graduation, no one had fried up any bacon or sausages. Matt put on a big pot of oatmeal this morning. After Tom milked Sunny, he made a stack of toast. From the fridge, the boys put the apple butter and the cream and milk on the table. Dave had come in and had set the table with silverware and set out the cups. The bowls sat on the counter next to the stove with the warm oatmeal. Clyde came in and filled his bowl, poured a cup of coffee, and sat down at the table. Soon, Fred came in and got his breakfast. The others all sat down and ate their oatmeal and toast. Today would be a busy day. The herd would be driven out the pasture and up to grazing lands above the national forest trailhead.

As they sat, Clyde spoke up, "I hope the herd doesn't get all upset about movin' out. They are so used to being down in our pasture."

"Well, Clyde. When they smell and taste that fresh green grass up in that wide valley, they won't even miss that old pasture," said Fred, laughing to himself.

After breakfast, Tom would be driving over to Hans' new ranch, the Norsemen Ranch, to start working for him. Although Matt was planning to work at Hans' ranch, he today wanted to ride his black stallion Diablo up with the herd so he'd know where Dave would be camped. His dad told him that he would be taking supplies up to his camp each week. The men finished their breakfast. They put their bowls, cups, and silverware into the kitchen sink as they filed out of the ranch house and over to the stable.

It was Dave's turn to do the dishes—his last day since he would be gone most of the summer with the herd. He rolled up his sleeves and filled the sink with water and dish soap. As he did, he thought of all that he had done to get ready for today's drive. He had rounded up his gear—his sleeping bag, one of the small pup tents, an iron skillet, a few tin plates with utensils, an old camping coffee pot, his fishing pole with a new package of hooks, and a few of Chet's western paperback novels. He didn't know if he'd read or not, but if he had them, he might. Dave hadn't ever been up watching a herd by himself, but he looked forward to the solitude. Bandit was coming with him.

He knew that Fred would be taking off for the rodeos and that he would miss the early spring and summer rodeos. But in the fall, there were other rodeos around town and county that Dave would go and participate. In the past, he and George would team up and go to them. He had called his friend and told him he'd be gone at their summer cow camp this year. George said when he got back, they'd go out and party all night.

As Dave thought about the girls that he knew, he recalled that a few were seniors and would be graduating high school at the end of the month. He wondered if any of them would stay around here or take off. Some of the young graduates wanted to escape this small mountain town. He never wanted to leave; he looked forward to settling down someday. Maybe, the girls he knew would still be here in the fall—Suzie, Rebecca, Deirdre, and now, Torri. But so far, none had turned his head enough to get serious.

Recently, he had written a letter to his folks who had moved to Montana to let them know he was doing fine in Riverside. His mom had written him back and told him that his dad was foreman at a ranch named the Circle R and that they were doing fine. She wrote that the ranch was as beautiful as the one they had in Hadley. She wanted to hear if he had a girlfriend and that someday she wanted grandkids. He smiled at the thought. She ended her letter with the words *'Dad wants you to know that if you ever want to come to Montana, he'd have a job waiting for you at the Circle R.'* She finished her letter with advice to him, *'Always wear a good pair of socks. Love, Mom. P.S. I bought you a journal to keep a record of your life. You were always smart in school.'*

Making a living on his own was one thing, but to deal with his friend Ronnie's death was another thing. During most of the times, the work at the ranch had kept him busy. But every once in a while, something would trigger a memory of his close friend. His insides would churn around like a deadly whirlpool pulling him down. In the Greek stories that he had read in high school, he recalled a deadly whirlpool named Charybdis. The loss of Ronnie felt like that for him. He couldn't avoid the feeling of himself drowning in those deep, dark waters that turned inside of

393

him. In his mind, this cruel world didn't care who died and didn't. *Why did Ronnie have to die? He was so young.*

After moving in with the McClure's, Ronnie and he had become close as brothers. The whole family had taken him in when he was homeless and looking for work. More recently, when Ronnie's sister Torri had broken down at the party up at Skyline, his heart ached when she lashed out at Matt. He understood her anger—and her sorrow. Taking her home that night, he knew that her dad was there to help her. At least, she had someone to talk to. He didn't.

Life did not hold much joy for him. When his folks lost their ranch, he had run away so they wouldn't have to worry about him. People thought that his folks had shown him the door, but that's not what happened. He couldn't bear the anguish that they were going through. He took it on himself to leave. He ran to ease the worry for his parents and to escape the hurt.

This year, going up to a cow camp was similar. He needed this time to himself, with Bandit, for his heart to heal. From his mom's letter, he now felt the pressure to succeed—to have a steady job, to settle down, and to marry. With his emotions all warped with sorrow, he wouldn't be much of a husband. He had seen some marriages go bad when people married for the wrong reasons. He would wait for the right girl. In the meantime, he looked forward to the solitude and maybe, he'd write in the journal his mom sent with her letter.

This morning, Dave had finished the dishes. He had wiped down the counters, the big table, and the stove. He did enjoy working for the Fletchers, even though, they had to work together to cook their meals and wash the dishes. But the rest of ranch house looked dirty and unkept.

Putting on his jacket, he headed out to the stable where he loaded Tabasco with his gear and the first week supply of food. He packed Baby Doll with two of the salt blocks. The others were saddling their horses: Matt with his black stallion Diablo and Clyde with his buckskin Chief. Fred had the roan Legend already saddled but had to cinch up the strap. Bandit and Blue were excited to see everyone getting the horses ready. They would be expected to work the herd, running behind back and forth. They would nip at the heels of the stray cows, steers, and calves to keep the herd together.

The men mounted up and rode out toward the pasture. First, Matt and Tom rode around and opened up the gate. Then, they started to drive them out of the pasture beyond into the timber. The dogs worked behind the herd and helped drive them out. The time went by slowly as they eased the cows and calves out of the pasture. The herd was loudly complaining, mooing, and bellowing. The young calves were bawling. Some were frisky and wanted to run off, so the dogs had to keep them contained within the herd. Loudly, the bellowing herd moved slowly up into the timber. Clyde told them to drive the herd past the trailhead where their grazing lands began. As the herd moved into the forest, some of the cows wanted to stop and eat the fresh young grass among the pines. The riders had to keep pushing them along.

With the two mules, Dave rode ahead of the herd. He had looked over the national forest map and knew that they were heading north to a wide valley that had a creek running near it. He wanted to look around before he set up the salt blocks; they needed to have a little cover from the rains. After the herd was settled in the valley, they'd set up a camp for a while.

Eventually, the herd managed to make the trek up into the forest, past the trailhead, and into the wide, grass-filled valley. Looking around, everyone thought it was a good spot for the herd. The cows, calves, and the steers were glad to stop and finally eat the lush green grass.

Taking Baby Doll, Clyde rode with Dave and set up the two salt blocks, one at each end of the long valley. Clyde told him to see if that worked out for this big herd. If not, he could change them. Dave said he liked the idea. They rode around and found a place that looked like a good spot for a camp. Matt helped Dave unload Tabasco while Fred and Clyde set up the pup tent.

As Fred looked through the canned goods that Dave requested, he noticed many cans of Spanish rice. "Hey Dave. You like these cans of rice?" he asked.

"Yeah, they do taste good with fried fish. Have you ever tried it?" he asked. He planned on eating a lot of fish this summer.

"No, can't say I have ever tasted Spanish rice with fish. But if you like it, that's what counts. What happens if you don't catch any fish?" he asked.

"I usually catch fish, Fred... But if I don't, a couple of cans of Spanish rice is a good meal," he answered.

"No beans?" asked Matt, looking at Dave.

He shook his head, and said, "Well, you can bring a few cans up next week, but don't forget the Spanish rice."

As the men talked, he and Dave had been finding rocks to make a fire pit for the camp. Breathing hard, Matt carried two medium rocks and put them down.

"I like the spices in the rice," he replied, squatting down as he arranged the last few rocks to complete the circle for his campfire.

"I hope you have enough. It looks mighty short on canned goods," said Clyde, looking over his meager supplies.

"They look fine to me. If you don't mind, I'd like to keep Baby Doll instead of Tabasco. She has a milder temperament," Dave said. Everyone chuckled since that's how Tabasco got his name.

"It seems to me, you would want to keep Tabasco here," said Fred in joking manner. Obviously, he had the hot spice in mind and not the mule.

"Yeah...okay. I get your meanin'. He does have a hot temper," he said, laughing at the thought.

"Yeah, we better head out. Did you bring an axe?" asked Clyde. Dave lifted it out of his gear just as he asked.

"Keep your eye opened for that grizzly. Did you bring enough ammo with you?" asked Fred. Nodding, he indicated that he had plenty ammo.

"I hope I meet up with that old grizzly. I'll show him not to mess with our calves," said Dave.

"Looks like you are goin' to need some wood for tonight. There's a storm brewin' up here," said Matt. They all looked up to the mountains and saw some storm clouds forming in the early afternoon.

Before mounting their horses, they said 'goodbye.' As they rode off, Fred called Blue to come. Reluctant to go, he wanted to stay with Bandit. But he soon was running beside Fred, heading through the forest back to the ranch.

After they had left, Dave went to work rounding up some firewood. He looked forward to a quiet evening by the campfire. If it did rain, he had the pup tent to keep him dry. He and Bandit would be fine this summer. He looked forward to the time alone—time to heal and to think. He'd have to be vigilant for predators, not only grizzlies, but coyotes or mountain lions.

The three Fletchers moved through the timber, spread out looking for any stray cows or calves that had slipped away. They kept a watch out for any tracks of the predators. The dark clouds behind them had a few rumbles of thunder that could be heard in the distant mountains. The rainstorm would most likely stay up in the mountains.

By late afternoon, they were back at the ranch. As they rode up to the stable, they noticed that Chet's white pickup was parked by the ranch house. He had made it back from Sophia's college graduation. The men unsaddled their horses, fed, watered them, and brushed them down.

Fred asked Clyde to take a look at Captain's front right hoof. They went over to his stall and examined his hoof. They talked it over. Clyde wanted to fix up a bandage and cover the hoof so it wouldn't get infected. And that's what the two of them did, going into the tack shed they found some gauze along with a disinfectant in a medicine cabinet kept there for such situations. Fred said he'd check on Captain in the morning.

Walking over to the ranch house, Matt came in to see Chet sitting at the kitchen table drinking coffee. A fresh pot sat on the stove. The kitchen had a warm feeling with the flavor of food in the air.

"Hi, Chet. How was the trip?" he asked his brother. He got a cup and poured himself some coffee. "Do I smell somethin' cookin'?"

"The trip was long. But Sophia was great. Oh… I bought a chicken when I came through town at the Mercantile. I picked up a few groceries—you know we always need somethin'," he said. "I roasted the chicken in the oven. I would love to have had fried chicken, but I'm not a cook."

"That reminds me. I heard Fred talkin' to someone to cook and clean for us," said Matt.

"What? I hope we talk it over before we hire someone. The money is tight," he replied.

"I know. Tom went to work over at Hans' ranch today. I'm goin' to join him startin' tomorrow. Just to let you know, I'll be payin' you back for that ticket," said Matt.

About this time, Clyde and Fred came in from the stable. Seeing his son, he asked, "How was the graduation?" He felt glad that his son had made it back safely after that long drive.

"Great---long, but I met her parents. Her dad is a plumber and her mom is a teacher," replied Chet.

"Do I smell somethin' cookin'?" said Fred, as he opened and peeked into the oven.

"Yeah, I've roasted a chicken. It's ready to eat. How was the drive today? I'm sorry I missed it," said Chet. He stood as Fred grabbed the hot pads and pulled out the roaster. The two proceeded to prepare the chicken with gravy for dinner. Matt set the table. He went into the pantry and brought out two cans of green beans. Opening them, he put them in a medium saucepan to warm up on the stove.

"Dave is camped up north in that first wide valley above the trailhead. The herd did fine. By the way, we lost a calf to a grizzly the other day," Clyde said. He was still upset at losing the calf.

"Where did the grizzly take it down?" asked Chet. He worried that the grizzly had come down to the pasture.

"Above the pasture, in the timber….two calves got out through a weak spot in the fence line. Loose nails on a fence post had dropped the barbed wire enough for them to get out. Fred and I repaired it. Those calves seem to find a way out," replied Clyde.

"I'll make a note in our record book of the loss," said Chet, disappointed to hear about the calf. He poured the coffee. Sitting down, they passed around the chicken, the gravy, and the green beans.

From the back porch, they heard Tom return from working at Hans' ranch, driving his red pickup. He came in after washing up. Everyone said 'hi' and they began to eat. He stopped at the fridge, pulled out the pitcher of milk, and set it on the table.

Blue, who had been under the table, jumped up and padded up to Tom who bent down and gave his dog a rub about his head and ears. Wagging his tail back and forth, Blue was happy to see Tom. He then went back under the table for a well-deserved rest after a long, busy day. After filling their hungry stomachs, Clyde and Fred leaned back in their chairs and sipped their coffee while the young men had seconds.

"Tom how did the work go at Hans' today?" asked Clyde.

"Fine. He has a lot of repairs to do. Today, we worked on putting new posts in their old corral. So many were rotted out. Tomorrow, he wants to put in another corral. Matt, he wants us to build it," replied Tom as he swallowed his last bit of the chicken. Nodding, Matt finished up his plate.

"Clyde, I'm goin' on the rodeo circuit for the next few weeks. My rodeo buddy Jasper Partum is comin' to pick me up. Since Captain's gone lame, I thought I'd take Legend along with Jinx this time," said Fred. He looked around thinking he would miss seeing his nephews, but he felt the excitement of the rodeo calling him this time of the year. This would probably be his last time at the big rodeos. In the mornings, his bones were telling him that they were done with those wild broncs.

"Sure... we'll be fine without the roan. I hope you win some money, Fred," said his brother.

"You know I usually do come away with cash in my back pocket, Clyde. I promise not to buy anythin' we can't use on the ranch, though," said Fred, joking. They knew what he meant—one time he bought the red Corvette which was useless on a ranch.

Chet wished that he could go with his uncle, but he had more responsibilities now doing the books for the ranch. Besides, Sophia was coming to stay a few days. He looked forward to showing her more of their ranch and to take her riding. Noticing that everyone had finished dinner, he said, "I bought ice cream for dessert." He went to the fridge and pulled out the ice cream and a can of chocolate syrup. Quickly, he scooped out the creamy, cold dessert into some bowls and handed them around. Passing around the syrup, they enjoyed their favorite sweet dessert. As they finished, Chet said he'd do the dishes. They would have to start a new cycle for washing dishes since Dave was gone. The men put their plates, bowls, and silverware into the kitchen sink. Clyde took down the whiskey bottle and headed for the living room. They carried their cups for a little taste of the rich amber liquid.

Putting in a fire, Tom squatted in front of the fireplace waiting for the fire to take hold of the wood. Blue came and rested near the fireplace, curling up on the rug. Clyde poured a little whiskey in everyone's cups. The Fletchers held up their cups and said, "Cheers." They sat down for a comfortable evening in front of the fire. After a long day, the warmth of the fire and the amber liquid relaxed them before bedtime.

In the kitchen as Chet was cleaning up after dinner, he recalled his night with Sophia. The two of them had made love several times, each time more satisfying than the last. He wanted to call her tonight and hear her sweet voice. With her moving back home today, he needed to know that she had gotten there safely. They had had a little argument over her roommate Martha leaving her to clean the apartment all by herself. He felt that Sophia was being used. But she said that her roommate had done this every year, leaving her money to cover it. He nearly stayed to help her with the cleanup, but she would not hear of it. However, he did help load her car with her belongings before he left.

Images of her beautiful blonde hair against her black gown and cap came to him. She had a lovely neck that he had kissed easily, not to mention her soft pink lips. They talked through the night. He loved her little pearl earrings. He found out her ears were pierced. She said it was 'all the rage' with the sorority girls who came from the eastern cities. Assuming she had been dating, he asked who she had dated in college; she hedged and said, 'no one of interest.' He asked about her fraternity friends that he had met that night at the Wild Goose Bar. He felt she held back the truth, for he knew that the way one of them was looking at her that he was interested in her. His heart filled with jealousy as he thought of another guy kissing her or touching her. She didn't want to hear about his relationships, so he never told her about Lois or Betsy (his Elizabeth). Even if she did want to hear more, he could never tell her about finding Betsy murdered. He thankfully felt relieved that she wanted to leave those affairs in the past.

They had made no commitments that night or the next day, but he made it clear that he liked her. They both would have to decide if their relationship went any further. His emotions tumbled inside of him as he thought that she lived so far away. Another guy could easily step in and take her from him. *Would she be faithful to him?* He had to trust her as she would have to trust him.

As he finished up in the kitchen, he walked down the hall to their office. He wanted to call her, but he noticed a couple of bills sitting on the top of the desk. More bills to record. Picking up the receiver, he pulled out his wallet. She had written down her home phone for him. He dialed it, waiting as it rang.

Her mother answered, "Hello,"

"Hi, Mrs. Schmitz, this is Chet. Is Sophie there?" he asked.

"Oh, hi, Chet. Just call me Mrs. S. like the kids at school. No, Sophia isn't here," she answered.

"Did she get home from college okay?" he asked.

"Yes, she did. We really enjoyed our short visit with you, Chet," she said.

"When will she be back tonight? I'd like to find out when she's comin' to see me," he said.

"You know, I don't know. She didn't say when she'd be home tonight. And she didn't say when she was coming to see you either. Do you want her to call you tonight? It's so late. Will you be up?" asked Mrs. S. She had thought highly of him, but her husband kept his opinion to himself. Art thought that his daughter could do better than Chet, who was just a cowboy.

"Yes, have her call me when she gets in. I'm workin' on our books, so I'll be up for a while," he answered. *He could be here all night waiting.* But he would wait. He wondered where she had gone tonight.

"Sure. I'll leave her a note. Goodbye, Chet," said Mrs. S.

"Thanks. Goodbye," he replied. As the phone went dead, he sat there at the desk. Putting down the receiver, he started to look closer at several bills. He opened the drawer and took out the ranch's record book. The columns were filled with the names of the stores, the amounts charged, and the subtotals. As he recorded the new charges, his tired eyes blurred. The long drive had made his eyes sting and water up. When he had finished recording, he heard his family talking. With the other phone in the living room, he got up, turned off the light, and left the office.

Walking into the living room, he went over to the coffee table that held the whiskey bottle. His uncle handed him his empty cup. "Here, use my cup. I am headin' to bed," Fred said as he stood up.

Chet poured a little of the whiskey into his uncle's cup, "Thanks. I just brought the records up to date. Does anyone have any other charges?" He lifted the cup and let the strong, rich liquid flow down his throat. He looked around at his brothers, his dad, and his uncle. They all shook their heads. *Did they know that the ranch was 'skating on thin ice' with all the money going out and nothing coming in?* He poured a little more whiskey into his cup, sat down, and sipped the smooth liquid.

"I'll be bringin' in my pay at the end of the week, Chet. Hans is goin' to pay me and Matt weekly, since there may be some weeks, he won't need us," said Tom, thinking of the wages coming from Hans. And Matt indicated that he'd also have wages to hand over.

The road construction company had called and turned him down. They said that they 'couldn't use a reckless driver.' Again, that bad reputation had hung on him like glue. *Would he ever be clear of that ugly rumor?* The anger rose in him, but he felt helpless. Reluctantly, he would go to work with Tom on Hans' ranch. *Ranch work, ranch work, ranch work.* He couldn't get away from it.

Chapter 33

Discontent

When a few nights ago Matt had taken the Blue Demon out for a drive, he had driven into town. He had seen Craig's turquoise Bel-Air parked at Bert's Café. He had pulled in and parked next to his car. Through the window, he had noticed that Craig was alone eating at one of the tables. Wanting to talk to someone, he had stepped into the café. Craig had seen him and had waved him over. He had sat down as Torri came over to their table. Even though she had written that note to him, he had kept his eyes away from looking at her. He hadn't forgotten her harsh words despite her note of apology. He quickly had ordered a cup of coffee and a piece of pie—'any kind' he told her. She hadn't said anything but had taken his order. In a few minutes, she had carried out his coffee and a piece of cherry pie.

Matt had wanted to hear more about Craig's Army experience. He had gladly told him more of his travels and of how much he enjoyed seeing the world. Matt's mind had soaked in all his stories and imagined how great it would be to get away. After they had finished eating, Craig had walked up to the front counter to pay. Matt wanted to pay for his pie and coffee, but Craig said he'd get it. Matt then walked back to leave a tip on their table. Torri had stepped over to clear it. Both stood next to the table.

"Did you get my note?" asked Torri, looking at him.

"Yes," said Matt. He had kept his eyes averted.

"I meant it—you know. Look at me," she had demanded. She had wanted to see his eyes looking at her. She needed to see his eyes to know that he forgave her or not.

This had been an awkward situation for him, but he had looked down into her brown eyes, and quietly had said, "Okay....thanks." He had handed her a few quarters from his pocket and had left the café. Craig had been waiting outside, leaning against his car.

"So, what was that about?" he asked. He had recalled that night up at Skyline with Torri.

404

"Oh... it's nothin'. She just said she was sorry," he answered.

"Good... you didn't deserve that," Craig replied.

They then had driven up to Skyline, had parked their cars above the town below, and had talked some more. Craig had stopped and bought a six-pack of beer. He had given one to Matt as they drank and talked.

Matt had asked him, "How did you hear about joinin' the Army?"

"Oh, that's easy. The recruiters showed up at the high school. They gave us senior guys a little presentation about joining. My two brothers had joined out of high school, so I did too. If you are interested in signing up, call the school. The recruiters will be there this month, talking to the seniors again," Craig explained. They drank another can of beer and talked more about the European cities and more stories of his military days. Finally, Craig said he had to get some sleep before work.

Coming home late that night, Matt had enjoyed driving his Blue Demon with the radio tuned to the Oklahoma station playing the countdowns. He could tell that his car liked getting away from the ranch just like he did. *Who wouldn't after being parked in a shed all day?* After leaving Craig, he had driven the Blue Demon out of town past the Battle Axe Ranch and toward Carter's flats where they had raced. With only his headlights, the dark night had surrounded him as he drove along the yellow striped highway.

With no cars behind or in front of him, he had shifted and pushed the gas pedal to the floor. The car leaped forward, eating up the pavement as it had traveled down the dark road. He heard that special devil engine sound, a sort of a deep, dark rumble, singing out to him that it was still alive and doing well. That sound he had recognized as his old Red Devil's engine—a special thunderous sound only with a deeper echo. The new tailpipes had banged out their loud voices as he drove. The roar of the devil engine and the loud pipes had created a chorus of sounds that was music to his ears. After a few miles, he had taken his foot off the gas pedal as he cruised along. Finally, he had turned around at a turnoff with a row of mailboxes. Returning to the Battle Axe Ranch, he had parked his Blue Demon in the utility shed. *Thanks for a great ride, Blue Demon.* Matt had come into the ranch house, walked upstairs to his bedroom, and sat on his bed, feeling that he was close to making a decision that his dad would certainly not like.

****

After the long day of driving the herd, the Fletchers sat in the living room, as the fire continued to pop and snap. Standing up, Fred said 'goodnight.' He left the living room and walked out to the bunk house. The phone rang and Chet jumped up to answer it. The others stood up, leaving him to talk to his girlfriend Sophia.

Matt and Tom took the stairs two at a time with the dog Blue bounding up the stairs after them. Tom called out that he wanted to shower 'first.' Before going in to take his shower, he called out, "Hans wants you to look over Moonbeam when you come tomorrow."

"What's wrong with her?" Matt called out to his brother.

"Don't know. He thought she might brighten up to see you again," said Tom as he closed the door to the bathroom. He started the shower, took off his clothes, and stepped into the shower to clean up after a long day working over at Hans' ranch. Matt sat on his bed, pulled off his cowboy boots and waited for Tom to finish. The long ride on Diablo had left him with a throbbing headache. He needed a hot shower and some aspirins for his nauseating headache.

Downstairs, Clyde took the whiskey bottle back to the kitchen and set it in the cupboard. Turning, he walked down the hall to his bedroom, closing the door. He'd take a shower after his sons were done upstairs. The shower water might be lukewarm by then, but he'd didn't mind. He pulled off his boots and laid down on the bed to wait. He started making a list in his mind what they needed to work on next—drag the fields, clean out the stable, irrigate the fields, feed the heifers and their bull, plant the vegetable garden.

In the living room, Chet sat down on the chair next to the small table as the phone rang. He picked up the receiver.

"Hello...Sophia?" anticipating her on the other line.

"Hi, Chet. Sorry I wasn't here earlier when you called," she said.

"That's okay. I'm still up. When are you comin'?" he anxiously asked.

"Tomorrow. Will that be all right?" she asked.

"Yeah," he replied. He wouldn't get much sleep tonight thinking about her coming.

"I'm going to leave early. What should I bring? I don't have any cowboy boots if we go riding," she said, worried about what clothes to bring.

"You could just wear my white shirt like you did this morning," he whispered quietly. He recalled her long legs and her warm body against him as he took her in his arms and kissed her.

"I'll need more than that to wear... Get serious, Chet," she replied quietly, smiling to herself.

"I like my shirt on you," he continued to tease her and to think of her with nothing on but his shirt.

"Chet....come on," she said sweetly. This morning, his warm, calloused hands were all over her. He wanted to take it further, but she resisted and said 'no.' She pushed him back with her hands on his chest. They had a lot to do that morning. Halfheartedly, she had to pack, to load her car, to clean, and to check out of her apartment. And he had a long drive ahead of him.

"All right....bring blue jeans and whatever tops—maybe a sweater. Don't worry about boots. My youngest brother has a pair he grew out of. Maybe, they'll fit you. Bring extra pairs of socks and a warm jacket. It is colder up here in the mountains," he answered.

"All right. I'll be there sometime after lunch... I miss you, Chet," she whispered quietly in the phone.

He heard her charming voice and whispered back, "I'll see you tomorrow, love." She hung up as he listened the phone go dead. Putting down the receiver, he stood up. Going over to the fireplace, he poked down the burning wood to hot embers. His insides warmed at the thought of her coming. Like the hot embers, his desire for her burned inside, thinking of his sweet Sophia.

Chapter 34

The Rescue

The next morning dawn showed a brilliant sky turning from grey to a golden orange to yellow behind the tall white peaks of the mountains. For the first time in months, Clyde slept in. They didn't have to feed the herd, only the heifers and the bull Twister. He'd feed them after breakfast. Over at the bunk house, Fred had packed his clothes, so he'd be ready when his friend Jasper showed up. More importantly, he had been cleaning and oiling both of his saddles that he used for roping and riding the broncs.

A few days ago, after Anna had talked to him about getting a housekeeper to clean and cook, he had called this older woman, Violet Olsson. They were to meet in town at Bert's Café. He hoped to talk to her about coming to work at their ranch. If Chet agreed, they could hire her. They needed someone desperately. He wanted to get that settled before he left to go on the rodeo circuit. After last night's discussion about money, Fred decided that he'd wire any of his winnings right away so that the ranch could pay the bills.

As he walked over to the ranch house from the bunk house, he thought of how beautiful the morning looked. The cool May morning would be turning warmer during the day as the mountains and the valleys kept turning greener and greener. He would miss these stunning mountains for a few weeks, but they'd be here when he got back. Walking into the kitchen, he smelled bacon frying and coffee brewing as his stomach growled.

Chet looked at him and said, "Morning, Uncle Fred."

"Mornin'. When is your girl comin' up to see you?" he asked.

"Sophia should be here this afternoon," he said, smiling at his uncle.

"You might sweep and clean that one cabin with the big bed for her. And put a fire in the wood stove before night fall, especially if you're romancin' her. Take her out to dinner and dancin' one night, too. Show her a good time, Chet," suggested Fred. He hoped that Chet had finally found someone to settle down with. His nephew's affairs had ended in bad situations. He hoped this one would not.

"Aren't you the Casanova. I'm goin' to take her ridin'. I wonder if one of Tom's old cowboy boots would fit her?" said Chet as he finished cooking the bacon. He mixed up a batch of pancakes for Matt to grill when he came downstairs. Tom had already been up and was out in the barn, milking Sunny. He'd be in soon.

As Fred poured himself a cup of coffee, he thought for a minute. He recalled that Beth had an old pair of cowboy boots. He would go up to the attic and bring them down. Those boots were just wasting away up in that box. He was sure that Clyde wouldn't mind. He wouldn't even notice.

He said, "Remember your mom had an old pair in the bottom of her closet. Anna boxed 'em up with her belongings that day we branded the calves. After breakfast, I'll go up and get that old pair of boots that your mom wore. Those might fit Sophia better than Tom's pair. You might even have time to polish them up for her."

"You don't think dad would mind?" Chet asked. Fred shook his head 'no.'

Matt walked into the kitchen and poured a cup of coffee. He took out the grill and set it across the two burners on the stove. He turned and said, "Good mornin'." They replied the same.

Finally, Clyde came into the kitchen, smelling the coffee and bacon. His stomach growled. He barked out, "Good mornin'." Just then, Tom came in from the barn, separated the milk, and brought in the milk and cream to put in the fridge. His dog Blue had followed him and sat waiting to be fed this morning.

"I'm lookin' forward to workin' at Hans' again today," said Tom. He looked at Matt who had just finished cooking their pancakes. Setting the food on the table, the men passed around the pancakes, the bacon, and the maple syrup. Silence fell on them as they ate and filled their hungry stomachs.

When they had finished with breakfast, Tom and Matt left to work for Hans at his ranch. For some reason, Matt wanted to drive his Blue Demon. He said he had an errand in town after working today, so Tom drove his old red pickup. Chet said he'd wash the dishes again; Fred poured himself another cup of coffee.

The phone rang out through the silent ranch house. Clyde got up and walked down to the office as the phone rang out a second and then a third time.

Clyde picked up the receiver and said, "Hello."

The voice at the other end said, "Hello, Clyde. This is Brian Echarte." *The superintendent of the coal mine. Why is he calling me?*

"Oh, Brian. How are you?" he said.

"Not well, Clyde. We have a mine fire goin' on up here. Your old crew members Randy Hawthorne, Gavin Wulf, and Levi Moore, a new guy, you never met, are underground. The rescue teams have been in twice and have found no trace of them. We know they are somewhere on the East Side and we hope they have barricaded themselves in a fresh air pocket."

Brian paused and Clyde said, "Go on." *His crew members were missing.*

Brian cleared his throat and continued, "Herman Grittsfeld, the guy that took over for you, has lost it. He was yellin' and screamin' at the rescue teams, cussin' them out. I had to send him home....Clyde, the guys on the rescue teams asked for you and the state mine inspector agreed with them. He and I went to HR and checked your records. Listen, Clyde, your certifications are still current. They have not lapsed. Legally, you are ready to go. I feel bad about askin' you this, given the situation, but can you help?" *That bastard Herman.*

There was a long pause. Taking a deep breath, his mind raced ahead thinking about the critical situation in the mine. Clyde cleared his throat, and said, "Okay, I'll be there. I'll leave in an hour after makin' some arrangements here at my ranch. I can be there in Scottville in about five hours."

411

Brian replied, "Great, but, listen, I can get you here in one hour. I made a few calls. Do you know the small spraying company outside of Riverside? The owner, Jack East, has agreed to fly you up here in his helicopter. Just drive out there and ask for him. He is on standby, waiting for you."

After another long silence, he said, "Okay, I will be at his place in an hour." They both hung up the phone. *A helicopter?*

Clyde slowly walked down the hall. In the kitchen, he told Fred and Chet what was going on. They both were shocked at the news of a coal mine fire. But when he told them about his crew members still underground, they understood why he wanted to go help.

Clyde then headed to the bedroom where he pulled off his cowboy boots and undressed. From the bottom drawer of his dresser, he pulled out a pair of long johns and topped them with a faded red sweatshirt. Underground, a coal mine is cold. In the back of his closet, he found his ragged canvas work bib overalls. He pulled them on and fastened the straps over his shoulders. Next, in the bottom of his closet, he brought out a well-worn pair of leather work boots. After slipping on a thick pair of work socks, he pulled on the boots. The leather still smelled of the mine. Tightening the laces, he wrapped the long ends around the top of the boot before tying them with a double bow tied knot. Standing up, he glanced at himself in the mirror. *Now I'm ready to go underground.*

He walked down the hall to the kitchen. Looking at his brother, he said, "Could you dig out my old miners' lunch pail that's in the pantry. Pack some sandwiches and water for me."

Fred jumped up and said, "Sure, Clyde. Is there anythin' else you need?" Seeing him dressed in his bib overalls, Chet recalled when his dad worked at the coal mine.

As he headed out of the kitchen, he answered, "An apple would sure be nice."

Leaving the ranch house, he walked over to the tack shed where he had stored all his mining gear. There he pulled his old miner's belt off the nail where it hung. It was well-worn leather belt about three inches wide with a pocket for a mine lamp. He affectionately rubbed his fingers over the brass tag riveted to the belt. A grin flashed over his face. He wrapped the belt slightly below his waistline and cinched it up.

He reached for his miner's hard hat that hung on another nail near the belt. The hard hat was covered with stickers. Like many miners, the hard hat represented a history of its owner. It sported several strips of highly reflective tape on the back, front and each side. He settled it on his head. Finally, he reached for the heavy canvas work jacket that also hung there. Like his leather boots, it too smelled heavily of the mine. He settled it comfortably about his shoulders, turned, and headed back to the ranch house.

When he came back into the kitchen, Fred met him with the full lunch pail and a thermos of coffee. Clyde said, "Thanks Fred. I know you and the boys will take care of the ranch. You probably will not hear from me for three or four days. Will you drive me out to the crop sprayin' business?"

He replied, "Yeah, is that's East's place? I will grab my keys and meet you at the pickup."

Chet spoke up, "Be careful, dad. Don't worry about the ranch. We'll take of everythin'."

On the drive to the crop sprayer's place both men were silent. They had been through much together and neither was inclined to express emotion. They drove through town to the other side of the lumber mill. As they turned into the drive to East's place, the pickup's wheels crunched the gravel.

Parking before the office, Fred looked briefly at his brother and said, "Take care of yourself. About that housekeeper, I'll let you know."

Clyde smiled weakly and said, "Do what you have to, Fred... I'll be careful." He laughed to himself. He stepped out the pickup and waved to him over his shoulder as he walked to the office door. He heard his brother's pickup back up and drive away.

He entered the office and asked, "I'm lookin' for Jack East."

413

The guy behind the counter said, "That's me. You must be Clyde Fletcher."

"I am," he replied.

Jack asked, "Have you ever flown in a helicopter?"

He replied, "No... in fact I have never been off the ground in anythin'."

Jack said, "That's okay... I will tell you what to expect."

Clyde looked him over from head to toe. He appeared to be middle age with close cropped hair. Wearing a leather flight jacket and khaki pants, he looked ex-military in every aspect of his appearance.

Jack said, "You may want to use the bathroom. Take a good drink of water before we take off." Clyde said that would be a good idea. He pointed to a door at the end of the hall. "When you're done, come out to the flight line. I'll be doin' flight pre-checks on the bird; see you there." He turned and left.

When he was done, Clyde left the office building. He saw Jack walking around the helicopter touching this and that. It appeared that the touches had a purpose and were part of a routine. He took a good look at the machine. It looked like a dragon fly with a skimpy tail. The cab was a large clear plastic bubble enclosed with two seats—no doors.

Jack waved him over. When he reached the helicopter, Jack said, "Climb into this side and I will fasten your seat belt. Do not take if off until I specifically tell you to. After landin' we will have to wait until I kill the engine and the rotors come to a stop. Only then will I tell you to unbuckle and exit the craft. This is important. Get out with the rotors turnin' and they could take off your head. It has happened, unfortunately. Do not move until I tell you to. Go ahead and get in."

When Clyde had settled in the seat, Jack reached into the cab, fastened the seat belt around him, pulled it snug, and latched it. He wondered what Clyde would be doing.

"Are these teams like firefighters goin' into a burnin' house?" asked Jack.

"Yes," he answered.

He said, "Now, keep your hands and feet inside the chopper cab. We do not want anythin' hangin' out. You will feel some vibrations, but that is normal. Don't be alarmed."

Jack walked to the other side of the craft and climbed in. He tightened his seat belt and pulled on a set of headphones. He looked at Clyde and said, "Are you ready?" He nodded yes. "Good – hang on and remember what I have told you."

Jack fiddled with some switches on the panel in front of him and with a humming sound the rotors began to move, increasing in speed until Clyde heard the engine start. Then the speed of rotation increased. When the sound steadied out, Jack looked at him and flashed a 'thumbs up.' He replied in kind. Jack then pointed to the horizon and grinned. The rotors increased in speed making a repeated loud 'whump' sound.

When the chopper broke free of the ground, it felt like it had pulled itself out of a mud puddle. It hung there a foot or so above the ground. Suddenly the tail pitched up and it started moving across the ground picking up speed and altitude as it moved along. There were some strong vibrations, just like Jack said there would be.

After they were about one hundred feet above the ground, the vibrations ceased and were replaced by the monotonous 'whump' of the blades and the loud high-pitched scream of the engine. The combination of sounds make conversation impossible, but Clyde did not mind. He was not interested in a chat. He noticed they were headed for a notch in the foothills in the distance. That made sense as they would not have to be very high to get through those mountains.

Clyde was soon lost in thought. His mind filled with the questions he would need to have answered: the extent of the fire, the status of mine ventilation, the latest carbon monoxide, and the mine atmosphere oxygen readings. His mind kept working on more questions: What did the combustible gasses look like underground? How many rescue teams were on site and what extra supplies did they have? What arrangements had been made to feed the mine rescue crews and did they have a place to sleep? Did the

415

benchmen have adequate working areas? How much sleep had they had, and which crew was up next to enter the mine?

With his questions and actions determined, Clyde let his mind enter a calm meditative state. His mind wandered. He recalled a poem that he had written as a young man. *What had he called it?* The words tumbled out of his consciousness. He remembered the words, clear and firm.

The Miner

Have you walked through the earth with your brothers?
Have you felt the cool dark on your skin?
We have, my grandfather, my father and me.
If you dare, come walk with me,
But I must warn you, danger lurks there,
Control of nature is won not given.
Prometheus paid his price and so have we.
My grandfather, my father and me.

Clyde took a long pause as he finished the poem in his head. Today, his job was to make damn sure no one paid a price this time around.

Many mines housed mythical beings. They were never clearly seen. They were noticed out of the corner of a miner's eye as he turned his head. These mythical beings would move just outside the circle of the light from a miner's head lamp, never clearly lit but there, moving ahead of him just out of his reach. This mine housed a dragon. That dragon would not win this time. Clyde would see to it.

His attention was drawn to the horizon, He could see the mine site there growing larger by the minute. They had begun a slow descent, drawing ever closer. Soon he made out a man on the ground moving his arms in what appeared to be signals that Jack was responding to. Slowly, they descended, and the helicopter hovered above the ground and the vibrations started again. They eased to the ground. When the skids touched, it felt like a hand had released them. The guy on the ground crossed his arms above his head and the engine began slowing down. He gave Jack 'a thumbs up' and backed away never turning away from the helicopter. The engine came to a stop and the blade rotation began to slow. After a minute or so, they stopped. Jack pulled off his headphones and hung them up.

He turned to Clyde and said, "How was that for a first flight?" Clyde's ears were numb from the sounds that had beat on them for an hour. He really did not hear Jack but flashed him 'a thumbs up' and smiled.

Jack said, "Stay right there. I will come around to your side and take off your seat belt.

He soon appeared at Clyde's open door. Reaching in, he unbuckled his belt.

He said, "Okay now you may get out." He stepped back out of the way.

Clyde stepped out and stood, a little shaky for a minute. Then his legs stabilized. Jack offered his hand, but he waved it off, and said, "I'm okay. Thanks."

He looked over Jack's shoulder and saw Superintendent Brian Echarte and the State Mine Inspector Ron Ackerman. Clyde had known Ron for far more years than he had known Brian. He walked over to them.

They shook his hand and Brian said, "Thanks for comin', Clyde. The guys really need you."

Ron said, "We have a situation map up at that the mine office. It has the fire and ventilation status marked on it as well as the latest gas readin's at various locations. They have not changed much, if at all. The Federal Mine Inspector is up their waitin' for us. He is a new guy, neither Brian nor I know him. He seems steady and calm. You know how it is. If they are not like that, they could hurt more than help an effort. We think he will be okay."

Clyde asked Brian, "How many teams do we have and what are their status?"

Brian answered, "We have two teams -- the ones from the mine. You know the guys. The same ones that were on the teams when you worked here. Team One just came off a rest cycle. They are fed and ready to go. Team Two is chowing down. They will get some sleep while their bench man goes over their equipment."

Ron entered the conversation and said, "P Coal down south is sendin' two of their mine rescue teams. They are on the road and should be here in about an hour. They are bringin' their equipment plus six rescue units and spare cartridges. The mine supply house down there sent them along. The P Coal bench men will have to go over their units to prep them for use. Let's go up and meet the Federal Inspector."

With that, the three men headed to the mine office. When they entered the office, Clyde felt like he had come home. Nothing had changed. The Federal Mine Inspector was indeed young. A fresh-faced kid, lanky but solid like most of them.

He approached with his hand extended, "...names Kelly Jones; I am new to the district. You must be Fletch. The guys speak highly of you."

Clyde grasp the outstretched hand and shook it firmly, and said, "Yeah. I am Clyde Fletcher. Glad to meet you." Kelly noted that the miners didn't use his first name; they called him 'Fletch.'

Kelly Jones, as the Federal Mine Inspector, had issued an order taking over control of the mine. That was standard procedure, but he had just provided the oversight allowing the local mine officials to run everything. Again, that was normal for a mine fire. He was not officious nor overbearing.

He motioned Clyde to approach the map on the wall and said, "Let's get you briefed and up to speed so we can continue with operations." Brian and Ron took turns explaining the items marked on the map and the map itself.

When they were done, Brian asked, "Do you want to hit the head and grab a bite before we go meet with the teams?"

"Yeah," Clyde replied. "but I do not need to eat. I brought a lunch, but it will keep for later." When he was finished, he washed his hands in the sink and splashed warm water on his face. He took a deep breath and pulled in the moisture. Drying his hands and face with a paper towel, he took another deep breath and headed back to the main office.

418

When he saw Brian, he said, "Time to go see the teams now."

The teams were housed in the training center above the change house. Team Two was up there sleeping but a couple of Team Two members were with Team One standing in a group just outside the change house door. They greeted Clyde with handshakes and much shoulder and back slapping.

Clyde looked at Dewitt, the team captain, and said, "Fill me in, Dewitt, on what you know."

Dewitt quickly and efficiently spoke, "When the guys gathered at the rally point before leavin' for the surface, they took a head count. One of the new guys, Levi Moore, was missin'. Randy said he would go look for him, the guys should move on out, and he would follow with Levi in tow. Gavin said he would help Randy. You know how those two are—they stick together. When the guys left, Randy and Gavin were headed up to Number Ten to look for Levi... No one has seen them since, Fletch." The captain paused for a moment. "Team Two had finished goin' through number Ten Panel and found no evidence that Randy and Gavin had ever been there."

Clyde inquired about conditions. Jackson, the Team Two gas man, spoke up and said, "There was bad air everywhere we took a readin'...the ground conditions were iffy in some spots."

Nolan, the Team Two map man, spoke up, he said "I have the ground conditions plotted on the map. We have ventilation at our backs and the fire does not seem to be spreadin'. Of course, we do not know what it looks like in by the fire front." *That was good news about the fire, but the bad air means we may not find the three alive.*

Clyde looked at Dewitt and said, "Captain is your team ready to go in?" He felt they were ready.

He replied, "Sure are. We are rested and fed. Our benchman has our units rebuilt, tested and ready to go. Just say the word and we are ready to go to work." *We need to get down there and find them.*

419

Clyde said, "Stand by. I am goin' to go back to the mine office and get the mission planned out. Take it easy and I will get back to you in about fifteen minutes." He turned and strode toward the mine office. Brian and Ron followed along behind him.

When they got to the office the three of them with the federal inspector Kelly Jones drew up a written mission plan for Team One. Clyde said he would go in with them. Kelly said he would be going in, too.

Brian went to his desk and rummaged around one of the drawers. He came up with a circular piece of brass. He said, "Here Clyde. I still have your old brass. It matches the number on your belt."

Clyde's mind flashed back to when a new miner had asked him why there was a matching number on his belt. He recalled his satirical reply—'it's to identify the bodies.' That would have been thought a smartass comment by a non-miner but unfortunately it was the truth. That was exactly what the number on the belt was for. Many times, the recovered bodies were damaged beyond recognition but the number on the belt certified who they were.

He looked up at Kelly Jones and said, "We leave in five minutes. I will meet you over at the change house."

Along the way, Clyde stopped by the lamp rack and picked up a mine lamp. The mine was pitch black down there. He checked to see if both bulbs lit. They all had two. He slipped the battery into the holder on his belt, ran the cord under his arm and over his shoulder. He hooked the light on the bracket on the front of his helmet and snapped the cord into the tab at the back of his helmet. The old sense of the solid weight on his belt was comforting.

When he reached the change house, he told Dewitt, the captain, "Have your guys gear up and meet me for a briefin' just outside the door. We're goin' in. Kelly Jones and I are goin' in with you. Tell your team to brin' two of their spare units outside for us. We'll see you in a few minutes. I will be waitin' here. Hey, also bring three air bottles equipped with full masks. Dewitt, I have a hunch we will find the guys holed up in Panel Eleven."

The guys returned just as Kelly Jones showed up. Clyde said, "Form a circle around me and I will fill you in on the plan." He waited while they formed a circle. He then explained, "We will work our way up the East Side until we reach Panel Ten. You guys have already been over that ground, but we will take our time usin' standard procedure all the way in. When we move in past Panel Ten, we will slow down. That is new ground so we will have to be damn careful. Next, we'll turn into Panel Eleven. We'll check the low rooms first and work out way up to the higher rooms-- one by one. We must be meticulous. We don't want to get careless and have to go over the ground again. Got it? Are there any questions?" He paused for a moment.

When no one replied, he looked at Dewitt, the captain, and said, "Captain, form up your team. I will rope in behind you." He nodded. "Kelly will rope in between the gas man and map man. Who has the stretchers and air tanks?"

Dewitt, the captain, replied, "The medic will handle the stretchers. The tanks are in a cart at the rear. Charlie will pull the cart."

Clyde said, "Now let's rope in. We'll head off when you say we are ready captain, just give the order. Everyone put on your mask and do a seal check."

After much rustling and shuffling, Dewitt looked down the line and inquired if everyone was ready to go? In a firm commanding voice, he said, "Equipment check—each man check the equipment of the man immediately in front of you. Then raise a closed right fist." All the miners did and raised their closed right fists.

Dewitt then said, "Count off."

Clyde responded to his command to count off, "Lead Miner, ready to go."

One by one, they stated their position in the team and announced they were ready to go.

Clyde said, "Okay, captain ready. Let's move out."

They walked toward the mine portal. Somewhat in step, the rope connecting them never growing taunt but always with a bit of slack. When they reached the mine portal, each man in turn paused at the tag board and took the brass from

421

his pocket. Each hung his brass under the word 'IN' which labeled that portion of the board. Then they walked on.

The group moved along a path as old as mining itself. Not in the middle of the drift where the roof was weakest and not against the rib, what non-miners would call the wall. Each miner knew what happens when a section of the rib kicks out. It would inflict horrible damage to a man's legs.

Each miner's head swiveled, scanning the ground looking for loose rock. Their eyes would scan the far rib, up across the back, and down the other rib. They were looking for loose rock or cracks. Each miner was ready to call a halt if he saw something.

As they moved along, the gas man would call out readings as he made them. Once in a while, the ground man would call a halt while he looked over the conditions. He would then point something out to the captain and the map man would call out that he got it.

Then, the captain would call out, "Everybody ready? Count down again." After the miners counted down, he called out, "Move out." They moved along, repeating the process as they moved until the came to Panel Ten where Dewitt called a halt.

He said, "Gather around me." He looked at Clyde, and said, "Lead miner, how do you wish to proceed?"

Clyde replied, "We are movin' to new ground. We must go slower. Everyone got that?" He looked at Kelly Jones and asked, "Any instructions?"

Kelly replied, "No you guys are doin' well—proceed."

Clyde said, "Okay captain. Let's go."

Dewitt called, "Line up." The miners did.

They moved down the drift and turned into Panel Eleven. Exploring each of the lower rooms, they came up empty handed. As they moved to the upper rooms, the gas man called out the air was improving. That was a good sign, for there could be a good air pocket up ahead.

Then there it was at the edge of the captain's head lamp range. A temporary bulkhead. Clyde's heart skipped a beat. *Damn! Maybe we found them.* They worked their way to the barricade. It was a small lean-to made up of some timbers and plywood covered with a tarp made out of brattice cloth—the material used to rig curtains to direct ventilation. The base of the lean-to was secured with large chunks of coal. It looked intact.

Dewitt struck the plywood with a hammer three times. They listened and heard a three-tap reply. *We found them.* Silently, they all felt relieved.

He shouted, "One tap for 'no,' three taps for 'yes.'"

He hollered again, "Are there three of you?" The taps said 'yes.'

"Are any of you injured?" A one tap replied, 'no.'

"Are you well?" Three taps. Great.

"Do you think you can walk?" Again they heard a positive reply with three taps.

He yelled, "The air out here is better than the rest of the mine but still unacceptable. We are going to open a hole in your barricade and pass through three air bottles. Put them on as soon as you get them. Are you ready to proceed?" The three answering taps were music to the members of the rescue team.

Dewitt stepped forward and said, "Pass the bottles to me." When he had them in hand, he began to pry loose a corner of the barricade. When he opened it, he put a bottle into the hands that had been extended through the barricade. Finally, he passed the last two bottles through the hole.

He waited a minute and called out, "Are you ready?" Three taps—good. He began to tear down the barricade. Soon they could see the three guys, huddled on the floor of the mine. They were all thankful to see the miners alive.

The team medic moved forward. He took the men's pulses and shined a small flashlight into their eyes. He looked closely at the faces behind their air mask faceplates. He turned to the captain and told him they were okay.

Dewitt said, "Stand up and stay there for a minute. If you feel dizzy, wait until you get your balance." They stood up and the medic again made his checks. He told Dewitt they looked okay.

He replied, "Good. Rope them in just ahead of you where you can keep an eye on them."

When everyone was roped back in, he said, "Report." Each man called out his position and number and stated ready. The three rescued miners sounded strong. He called to them to move out and told them to go slowly. Every so often Dewitt would call a halt and ask the medic to check the three rescued miners. They continued toward the outside at what seemed a snail's pace.

Eventually, they actually saw the light at the end of the tunnel. As they moved out of the portal into the daylight, there was no one there to greet them—a safety precaution. If the mine blew, there was no sense taking out some guys on the surface along with those underground.

When they passed the tag board each man in turn removed his brass from the 'IN' board and put it in his pocket. The rescued miners also followed suit. Approaching the change house, they were greeted by cheers and applause from a mob of miners.

Dewitt yelled, "Fletch found them first time in!" Another team member yelled, "We found that dragon and tied a knot in his tail!" All of the men were shaking their hands, patting them on the back and laughing with mile wide grins on their faces.

Brian and Ron ran up to greet them. Dewitt said, "Let's find these guys a place to lie down and get some food and water into them." Brian and Ron cleared the way and found some cots. The three rescued miners took off their gear and sat down on the cots. They were exhausted and thankful to be on the surface and out of danger. Another man brought them mugs of soup and glasses of water.

The medic said, "Sip the soup and water slowly. Do it too fast and you'll get cramps."

With a few words of thanks, Clyde took off his gear, walked over to the mine office, and picked up his lunch pail. He found a place to sit down and ate his sandwiches and the apple. Pouring out a cup of coffee from the thermos, he relaxed for a while. Closing his eyes, he took a couple of deep breaths. Relief flooded his body and mind.

About an hour later, Brian walked into the mine office.

Looking at Clyde, he said, "That pilot Jack is in town sleepin'. Flight rules require him to sleep a set amount of time before flyin' again. When he has his time in, he'll fly you home." Brian paused for a minute, looking at the man he admired. "You did well, Clyde. The three rescued men owe you their lives. They told me to tell you 'thanks.' You are standin' tall with the guys. You're now a legend, my man—doesn't matter if you like it or not." He slowly shook his hand and said, "I am forever in your debt." He felt gratitude to him for saving those men. It could have a been a whole different story without Clyde in charge of the rescue team. He made the right decision to call him.

When Jack finally arrived, it was nearly sundown. He said, "We have just enough light to get us home. We better get a move on. Do you remember the drill?" Clyde replied that he did.

As they were getting ready to leave, Jack said, "The guys told me to take care of you. If even you lose one hair on your head, I am in tall trouble. Come on let's get out to the chopper. Sorry you do not have time for 'goodbyes.' Daylight is wastin' and we need to go." The two hurriedly headed to the chopper and took off for Riverside.

The flight back was enjoyable, and Clyde used the time to look around. He felt glad to be above ground again. And riding in this chopper gave him a beautiful view of the vast prairies below and stunning mountains in the distant horizon. Like a burning red-orange ball, the sun moved toward sundown. As the sun slipped behind the tall peaks of the mountains, they landed. He waited until Jack told him he could exit the chopper.

When he shook Jack's hand, Clyde said, "Thanks for the ride back home. Could I use your phone to call the Battle Axe?"

Jack replied, "Sure. I'll stay here with you until someone picks you up. I'll brew up a pot of coffee for us." The two walked into the office. While Jack made the coffee, Clyde dialed the number, reached Fred, and told him to come get him.

"Man… that was quick. You just left this mornin'. What happened?" he asked.

"We found them, Fred. They are okay. It took a lot less time than I expected. When can you get here and pick me up?" he replied. He eagerly wanted to get home and get a shower.

His brother made a rude comment, and said, " I would have already been on my way if we had not been actin' like two old ladies talkin' over a fence." He hung up. Clyde chuckled at his humor.

Clyde turned and Jack handed him a mug of steaming coffee and said, "Take a seat. You have just enough time to drink that before your brother gets here. I want to hear what you think of flyin' in a helicopter. Sounds like tame stuff compared to what I hear you were doin' down at the mine." They sat and talked about the flight. Clyde wanted to know his Army experience. He told him all about hooking up with Dennis Carter (Dr. Carter now) and the MASH unit in the Korean War.

"Yeah, Carter and I were a team. He flew with me as the paramedic; he took care of the wounded and I flew them out with my chopper. In fact, he's the one who encouraged me to come here and set up my business. I can fly and put that chopper down just about anywhere I want to. Doc left the service before I did because he got wounded on one of our missions." The two sat, drank their coffee, and waited for Fred to come.

After a while, his brother drove up to the office and picked up Clyde. The grey twilight had moved to nightfall. When they pulled into the ranch, it was dark. Clyde was home and in one piece. Stepping out of the pickup, he took a deep breath of the fresh night air. They walked into the ranch house. His three sons were in the big kitchen, putting dinner together. All of them were eager to hear from their dad about the mine fire and the rescue.

Seeing his sons, he said, "I'm goin' to go change and take a quick shower before dinner." As they turned and looked at him with questions in their eyes, he continued, "We found the trapped men and they are all fine." They had a noticeable relief on their faces as they knew how dangerous a mine fire could be. And Fred recalled the time when a miner was killed in that mine years ago.

Clyde left the kitchen and walked down the hall to his bedroom where he undressed, taking off his boots and his old mining clothes. He dropped them on the floor. They would need to be washed and cleaned up before hanging them again in his closet. Going into the bathroom, he turned on the shower. He stepped into the bathtub as the hot water and soap washed off the smell of his sweat—and the smell of the coal mine. With the hot water spraying over his head, down his torso, his legs, and to his toes, he breathed in the warm steam, clearing his mind of the tension and stress that he had down in that mine. He felt the relief of knowing that the three miners were safe and home with their families again—Randy, Gavin, and the new guy Levi. He threw off those thoughts as he finished his shower. *Now, back to the ranch.*

When Clyde walked back into the kitchen, his sons and brother were sitting at the big kitchen table waiting for him. That morning Fred had put on a pot of ham and beans to cook in the oven. Ready to eat, Fred started by dishing up everyone's bowls with ham and beans. Silence fell on them as they ate; there seemed to be tension in the air. Clyde felt it as he ate. Every once in a while, he looked at each of his sons, waiting for them to say something.

Finally, he realized that Sophia should be here eating with them. He turned to Chet, and asked, "Where is Sophia? Wasn't she drivin' here today?"

With a disappointed look, Chet answered, "She called and had to reschedule her visit, maybe next week. I told her not to worry that we had a lot goin' on here at the ranch any way."

"I hope she comes. I know how much you like her," replied Clyde. He openly mentioned Chet's feelings for her, since he wanted his oldest son to settle down with someone. Chet would be having a birthday soon and he'd be twenty-two.

"She's definitely comin' later," he said. He handed his bowl down for seconds as Fred filled it.

"And how did work go at Hans' today?" he asked looking at Tom and then at Matt.

"Hans marked off the new corral. We had to clear out the rabbit brush and the sagebrush. It was a lot of work. We got most of it out—still need to clear some grass and weeds out tomorrow. Oh, Matt checked Moonbeam over," explained Tom. He liked working with Hans.

"Oh, what's wrong with her?" asked Clyde. He looked at his son to tell him about Moonbeam.

"Heidi didn't think she was actin' like herself, so I went down to the pasture where Hans had put the horses. When I whistled twice, she came right to me as she did before. Not seein' her for quite a while, I was surprised when I saw her. She looked bad to me. Her coat didn't look good, and her ribs were showing. She kept bitin' me. So, I spent some time with her, you know, stroking her and lookin' at her hooves….," he broke off his story.

Clyde interrupted Matt, and said, "Son, what's the bottom line? What did you find?" Irritated with his long story about Moonbeam, he wanted to know what happened without all the details.

"Oh… she had an abscessed baby tooth. They had been too busy movin', so Hans hadn't checked her over. He was glad I discovered the abscess. We took her into their old barn, held her down, and pulled the baby tooth. Hans lanced the pocket of pus on the inside of her mouth. Heidi certainly was upset, but after it was over, she settled down. Moonbeam will be fine now," concluded Matt.

"I assume that the bull and heifers got fed this mornin'," said Clyde, going on to his concerns with their ranch.

"Yeah, Clyde. I fed them. I am leavin' for the circuit tomorrow. My friend Jasper called and he's pickin' me and my horses up early in the mornin'," added Fred. He hadn't told his brother about meeting with Violet, the housekeeper, today. He'd tell him later.

They had finished their dinner and Tom passed around the two cans of white pears for dessert. Each scooped out the sweet fruit into their empty bowls as a package of cookies came around. As they ate the fruit and cookies, they sipped the last of their coffee and milk. Taking their dirty bowls and silverware to the sink, the men moved toward the living room where they could relax. It was Tom's turn to do the dishes, so he stayed in the kitchen while the others left.

Chet walked over to the fireplace, slipped in some wood chips, and placed pieces of split wood on the grate. Noticing that their pile of split wood was nearly gone, he'd have to split some more wood tomorrow. He lit the fire. As the wood chips burned, the fire danced up and around the split wood. Finally, the fire popped and snapped, sending sparks up the flue.

Clyde had brought in their whiskey bottle to have a little. After the long day he had at the mine, he wanted a little drink. He filled his cup a little more than usual as he gave each of the others just a little. They raised their cups and in unison, said, "Cheers." Fred added, "We're glad you're back safely." Everyone nodded and extended their cups for a little more of the rich amber liquid. Relaxing, they felt the heat from the fire warm their faces and bodies.

Brooding, Matt sat in one of the chairs by the fireplace. He watched his brother put in the fire as he thought how he was going to break the news to his family. He sipped his second sip of whiskey. Deciding to wait until morning, he got up, and said, "I'm tired. I'm goin' to bed. See you all in the mornin'" He left and went upstairs to his bedroom. Needing a shower after working at Hans, he went into the bathroom and took a quick shower. He then slipped into his covers and fell asleep, dreaming of getting away.

Tom came to the living from the kitchen, and Clyde poured a little whiskey in his cup, and said, "I hope you aren't drinkin' too much at your parties. You know you're still seventeen."

"No, dad. I just have a beer or two. I know enough not to get in trouble with the law," he said. Nodding, his dad approved. The men sat around sipping the whiskey and watching the fire.

After the night drew towards midnight, the two other boys left to go upstairs to bed.

Fred also left the warm living room. After leaving the ranch house, he headed toward the stable to give his horse Jinx and the older horse Legend a little extra feed tonight. He walked over to the tack shed, checked over his rodeo gear—the two saddles, the bridles, and the saddle blankets. Thinking of taking off tomorrow, he walked over to the bunk house where his clothes sat packed ready to go. He undressed and crawled under his blanket on the bunk bed. As his head hit the pillow, his eyes closed, dreaming of roping those calves.

Clyde stayed on the old couch, drinking more whiskey. He had a good buzz going on as he closed his eyes and fell asleep with the warm fire burning down. Later that night, Clyde woke up with a start, still sitting on the old couch. The cold fireplace had nothing left but grey ash. He stood up, took the whiskey bottle into the kitchen, and went down the hall to his bedroom. Undressing, he crawled under the old red quilt and fell back asleep.

Chapter 35

The Unexpected

Early that next May morning at the Circle G Ranch on the other side of town, John Grady was loading up Violet's belongings and her bed set in his horse trailer. Taking the housekeeping job at the Battle Axe Ranch, she had to move there today. After a call from Fred Fletcher and a meeting in town, she had decided to take the position. She had misgivings about working for the Fletchers, but when Fred had told her that Clyde's wife Beth had died and they needed someone, she made up her mind to go. She had no choice, since no one else had responded to her ad posted on the billboard at the Mercantile.

Her life had been a series of disappointments ever since she graduated from high school. She thought that she would marry and raise a family but being so shy in all her years at school, no one was interested in her. She hadn't met anyone she liked either. When Ken Grady had an opening for a cook and a housekeeper years ago, she had applied and worked there until just recently. After Ken's nephew John married Janet Orsay, they moved in and his wife took over the housekeeping and cooking at the Circle G Ranch. Violet had stayed on a while hoping that she wouldn't have to leave, but it became clearer each day that she had nothing to do.

When she met Fred at Bert's Café, she liked him immediately for he was so friendly and genuine. He spoke about the Battle Axe Ranch being so beautiful that she was taken in easily by his descriptions. She asked a lot of questions about the ranch and found out all the details about the log ranch house and the three small cabins. He told her about their horses and the herd. Mentioning that they had their outfitter's license, he told her about their plans to have guests and to take them riding, fishing, and hunting. They would need someone to help with cooking and cleaning. She asked about the family—his brother and nephews. She felt comfortable sitting and chatting with him as they sat at a table.

His first comment came a surprise to her, as he said, "I thought you were old."

"I am," she responded. "I'm in my thirties." She didn't tell him her exact age.

"You look like you're in your twenties. Do you have any family here in Riverside?" he asked.

"No, they moved to Winston after I graduated. My dad works at Bob's Grain and Feed. My mom does odd part-time jobs around town. They are happier living in a larger town," answered Violet.

"Why do you want so little in wages? Your ad says just room and board with an allowance," said Fred. He wondered why she didn't want more—like a monthly wage.

"I don't need money and things. My folks have always sent me money when I needed it," she answered. She didn't tell him that she had a twin sister who had suddenly died. From her sister's life insurance, they had put the funds in a bank account for her. Her parents had access to the money, but they made it clear it was hers. Her sister had been the weak one; she had been the strong one. Her sister had been the popular one in school while she shied away from her classmates and people in general.

When they were born, the twins were named Rose Olivia and Violet Olivia. After graduating from high school, her folks and sister Rose had moved to Winston while she had stayed in Riverside. She found work at the Circle G Ranch for Ken Grady. Then, Rose had died of a brain aneurism a year later. One day she was fine; the next day she was gone. Her parents were devastated. Hearing of her sister's death, she had gone to the funeral in Winston and had felt that half of herself had died. That was nearly fifteen years ago. She had mourned her sister for a while, but she kept herself busy and didn't think about it very often now. She was known as 'Lettie' at the Circle G. With the ad, she had used 'Violet.'

She took the position at the Battle Axe Ranch. She had packed all her belongings along with her special cookbook of recipes. She had her own bed, dressers, and a rocking chair that she was taking with her. She did have an old upright piano she hoped that the Fletchers wouldn't mind. This would be a new adventure for her. Fred mentioned that his brother Clyde ran the ranch and he was sure that once they got to know each other, she would fit right in with his nephews and his brother. He explained that he would be going on the rodeo circuit for two weeks but would be back at the ranch after that. They shook hands before they left the café.

****

Early that same morning at the Battle Axe Ranch, Jasper's pickup pulling a long horse trailer came down the road to the ranch. The grey predawn sky turned a bright clear blue as the eastern sky glowed a pinkish orange. The birds were up chirping, loudly. The morning doves were up cooing with their soft, whispers in the air. The heifers in the pasture were loudly bellowing and Twister was busy humping another young heifer. Jasper drove over near the stable and parked his pickup and horse trailer. Anxious to get on the road, he wanted to get Fred and his horses loaded in short order.

Fred heard the pickup coming and met him as he pulled up. They shook hands as they re-united as old rodeo buddies. The two began loading his two horses, his saddles, the bridles, the blankets, and his bag of clothes. Fred said he needed to go say goodbye to his family, so he walked back to the ranch and into the kitchen.

The boys were fixing breakfast with Chet frying up sausages today. Tom had milked Sunny, and Matt was toasting bread for the fried eggs when everyone came in to eat. Clyde came down the hall, poured himself a cup of coffee, and sat down at the big kitchen table.

Fred came in and stood in the doorway, and said, "Hey, I'm takin' off. We're all loaded and Jasper's waitin' for me. We've got a long drive in front of us, so I'll see you in two weeks."

433

Everyone said parting words to Fred – 'goodbye,' 'be careful,' and 'win some money.'

As he was ready to leave, he turned back and said, "By the way, Clyde. I hired that housekeeper. Her name is Violet. She's movin' in this mornin'. John Grady's comin' with her stuff. Oh, you can thank me when I get back." He laughed to himself as he left the ranch house. He got into Jasper's pickup and the two drove off down the dirt road to the highway and off to the rodeos.

After his brother left, Clyde sat there. *A housekeeper?* Why did his brother hire a housekeeper? They were doing fine. And then, he recalled that Fred had told him about this a few days ago. He hadn't paid much attention to it because he thought he was just talking, not going to do it.

"What's this about a housekeeper?" asked Clyde.

"Hey, dad. It's about time," said Chet. The others felt the same way—they were tired of cooking, doing dishes, washing their clothes, and watching the ranch house get dirtier and dirtier. Finally, they could focus on the ranch and leave this cooking and housekeeping to someone else.

Clyde just shook his head, and asked, "How can we afford to hire someone, Chet?"

"Last night, Fred and I talked about hirin' Violet. She only wants room and board with a monthly allowance which amounts to almost nothin'," answered Chet. His uncle had kept him abreast of the meeting and all the details. He knew his dad would come around after this older woman had taken over the cooking and the cleaning.

After Matt had fried up the eggs, they sat down to eat their breakfast. Matt had been nervous this morning since he planned on telling his dad his decision. As they ate and finished their eggs, toast, and sausages, he said, "I have an announcement to make this mornin'." Everyone waited.

Finally, Matt stood up and said, "I have signed up for the Army."

Looking up at Matt standing there, everyone held their breath for a second while the news sunk in. His brothers knew that he had never been happy working on the ranch but going to the Army really surprised them. *Matt in the*

Army? Tom's eyes popped open wide while Chet put his head down and shook it slightly at the thought of his brother being in the Army. But he was nineteen and old enough to make his own decisions.

Clyde stood up and face his son, "What the hell did you say?" This news surprised him.

"I'm goin' into the Army. I'm leavin', dad," he said, standing his ground.

Chet jumped up as Clyde started to move toward Matt. Taking his arm, Chet said, "Let him be, dad. He's made the decision. We can't do anythin' about it."

"I have plenty to say about this. It's that damn car, the Blue Demon. I know you've been drag racin' that car. I know about your ticket, Matt. Son of a bitch....if you're leavin', then you sell that damn car. I want that car out of my sight... off this ranch... Do you hear me?" shouted Clyde. Those cars had changed his son.

"Dad, the Blue Demon doesn't have anythin' to do with my decision. I want to do somethin' different with my life. Besides, I'm goin' to send you my pay," he responded. His dad was being unreasonable like he always did with him.

Clyde took a couple of deep breaths as he shook his head, "You have no idea what you're gettin' into, son. You follow that dream. Chet, let me go. I'm goin' out to feed the heifers." He stepped away from his son and started to leave the kitchen. *What an ungrateful son he had raised. He's following his dream and it ain't ranching.*

There was a knock at the front door. Clyde turned and headed toward the front door. His sons followed him with Blue anxious to see a new visitor. As he opened the door, a tall woman with a tightly, braided bun in a long coat and a blue cotton dress stood on the porch. Shocked at all of the eyes on her, she quietly said, "Hello, are you the Fletchers?" Around her face, wisps of her light, blonde hair had escaped her hair being pulled back. She wore bangs across her porcelain forehead.

She held out her slim hand to shake Clyde's rough, tanned hand. He automatically extended his hand and shook her hand. He felt a lightning bolt had struck him as his heart skipped at beat. He looked into the eyes of this beauty—this angel. One eye was blue; one eye was grey. She shyly looked down and then up again.

She softly said, "I'm the new housekeeper. My name is Violet but call me 'Lettie.'"

Nervously, she pointed behind her with one of her little fingers, and said, "John Grady's out there with his horse trailer filled with my belongings. Will you help him? I'm moving in this morning."

About the Author

JMC North

Retired Assistant Professor of English with thirty years' experience, BA and MS. Special interests: dramatic literature, mythology, epic poems, gothic genre, and folklore. Member of the Phi Kappa Phi Honorary Society. Traveled America, toured Scandinavian countries, and the Mediterranean islands and countries.

Contact: http://www.Facebook.com

http://twitter.com/jmcnorth

http://www.goodreads.com

On Amazon: https://www.amazon.com/author/jmcnorth

Books by this Author

Battle Axe Ranch Series

Battle Axe Ranch: A Wyoming Novel Book 1

This emotional story is the struggles of two Wyoming ranching families caught up in a cultural clash of the 1960's hot rod culture and set against the rugged Rocky Mtns. The story is a poignant journey of friendship, romance, love, betrayal, grief, and death. Conflicts arise among grandparents, fathers, mothers, sons, and daughters.

Tempered by Fate: Book 2 of Battle Axe Ranch Series

Book 2--A continuation of the *Battle Axe Ranch Series* with individuals struggling to improve their lives amid the backdrop of the wild and rugged Rockies. Set in the 1960's, the characters deal with new twists and turns of fate, new romances and love, friendships, rumors, and betrayal. Complicated conflicts continue and surprising experiences arise. Experiences that give readers insight to areas they may not have traveled themselves.

Frankenstein

A Reader's Theater Script Adapted from the Novel

This gothic story is a psychological journey into a ghoulish world. The reader's theater script is adapted from Mary Shelley's *Frankenstein; or, the Modern Prometheus*. It features the major themes, main characters, settings, and important events of the novel for a mature audience. Written for twelve main characters, the script portrays the infamous story of Victor Frankenstein and his Creature.

Made in the USA
San Bernardino, CA
02 August 2020

75787596R00270